JACK FLINT
AND THE
REDTHORN SWORD

'Donnelly uses Celtic myths with charm and verve'
The Times

'keeps the reader on a knife-edge until the final page'
Scotland on Sunday

'Incredibly good ... fast-paced, action-packed, thrill-seeker ride of a story'   *The Truth about Books*

'A rich cavalcade of influences echo through Donnelly's assured and lively debut novel ... a strong and substantial first offering to the fantasy genre.'   *Books for Keeps*

JACK FLINT
AND THE
REDTHORN SWORD

JOE DONNELLY

Illustrated by Geoff Taylor

Orion
Children's Books

First published in Great Britain in 2007
by Orion Children's Books
Paperback edition first published in 2008
by Orion Children's Books
a division of the Orion Publishing Group Ltd
Orion House
5 Upper St Martin's Lane
London WC2H 9EA
An Hachette Livre UK Company

1 3 5 7 9 10 8 6 4 2

A catalogue record for this book
is available from the British Library

ISBN - 978 1 84255 609 2

Typeset by Input Data Services Ltd, Bridgwater, Somerset

Printed in Great Britain by Clays Ltd, St Ives plc

www.orionbooks.co.uk

In memory of Friday nights of laughter
and tall tales with the Kerrigan Clan

ONE

The high stone wall that circled Cromwath Blackwood had drawn him with a powerful, mysterious gravity, ever since he'd been a small boy.

Now Jack Flint was going to break all the rules, ignore all the warnings and climb the wall to see just what was on the other side.

He and his best friend, Kerry Malone, had planned it for weeks, curiosity and apprehension jangling in them both. The wall around those dark trees was old, forbidding, and everyone had heard the tales. Nobody really knew for sure, because nobody went in there.

'Maybe it's caves,' Jack said as they sauntered down to the bus-stop after school. A cool sea breeze mixed salt with the scent of autumn heather. Far above, a jet contrail split the cold blue sky. 'Or old mine workings that people could fall in. Anyway, we'll find out for ourselves tomorrow.'

'No,' Kerry said, shaking his head. 'I think it's a haunted house. That's why they built the wall.'

'You wouldn't build a wall for that,' Jack said. 'You'd just knock it flat. Caves are the best bet. Remember that boy who went in and got lost for years?'

'That was ages ago,' Kerry countered. 'If it ever *really* happened. I don't believe it.'

They were all set for tomorrow. They had ropes and maglite torches ready in Kerry's backpack, and their fishing rods as a cover story. Nobody would be any the wiser, so long as Clarice didn't keep Jack around for weekend chores, and as long as the Major's gamekeeper didn't see them scaling the ivy that grew on the south wall. There was always the chance that the Major would be up in the turret with his brass telescope trained on them. With luck, Jack thought, they'd be up and over before anybody noticed. The thought of it made him tingle with excitement.

Cromwath Blackwood! Every place has its legends, and here on the peninsula, where the standing stones squatted like ancient beasts along the ridge where the edge of Scotland met the sea, the Blackwood was the focus of many childhood stories.

Jack liked the scary one about Thomas Lynn. Some said it happened sixty years ago, before the war, and some said it was before the Great War; nobody knew for sure if it ever really *did* happen.

Thomas Lynn had climbed the big wall one autumn night and went into the Blackwood.

2

Then he vanished.

And he'd been gone a long time, whenever it was.

Next time anybody saw him was when he was found beside the old stone cairn on the top of Dumbuie Hill, a good ten miles away. And when he did turn up, it looked as if he'd been sucked into some kind of hell and spat out again.

He was in an awful state, an old hand down at the fishing quay had told them one Saturday morning when Kerry was earning some money unloading boxes of fish.

'He was burned bad all down one side of him, skin on his bones melted like tar.

'An' toes an' fingers gone, like they'd frozen off, or maybe *chewed* off. Who can tell? Worst was the stuff growin' on him, a poison fungus rooted right in him, suckin' the life out. A woeful way to die, I can tell ye.'

He took a suck on his pipe, 'The mystery was, he came back ten years *after* he disappeared. Ten whole years. Can you imagine that?'

Jack and Kerry nodded. It was an old story, but it still gripped them.

'And he was not one day older than he was on the day he climbed over that wall.'

'You believe any of that?' Kerry asked. He was almost the same height as Jack, with a smattering of sepia freckles across his nose and an Irish accent to match.

'All those old fishers, they believe in kelpies and little people and the Loch Ness monster.'

'There has to be something in there,' Jack insisted. 'They put a wall round it to keep people out.'

3

Jack had pondered endlessly on the walled coppice since he was just a kid, living in the big house on the Major's estate. Then he'd imagined there were monsters there. Dragons. Caves of treasure.

Now he was almost fourteen, he knew it would be something much more mundane, but still Cromwath Blackwood tugged at him, fired up his curiosity. Always had. It was secret. Forbidden. It was something he and Kerry could share, and in a small town like Ardmore secrets were hard to come by, even harder to keep.

Nobody they knew had ever gone over that wall and gone inside.

School was out and the weekend waited, open for exploring the unknown.

Jack turned to face Kerry. 'Maybe it wasn't built to keep folk out.'

'Why build it then?'

'I can see it from my bedroom. Sometimes I've seen the tops of the trees whipping about when it gets dark, like something's shaking them, even when there's no wind. And when I was a kid I heard things in there.

'Now you're winding me up.'

'No,' Jack said. 'At night. Like screaming. High and shuddery. Real creepy. Like people wailing and crying. I had nightmares for weeks.'

Kerry still looked sceptical, but Jack went on.

'Maybe they put up the wall to keep something *in*.'

He let that idea float. Kerry walked with it until they reached the corner.

'Aye, maybe. But there isn't a wall high enough to stop a Malone.'

'Sure,' Jack said. 'Tell that to your dad.'

Kerry just laughed. Jack was his best friend, so he could make a joke about the luckless Fergal Malone, odd-job-man, drinker, poacher and general rapscallion who was spending a three-month holiday in Drumbain Jail. He'd been sent up for using dynamite from the quarry to blow a few salmon from a pool in Brander Water, and almost blowing himself up in the process.

Jack and Kerry had been friends since they'd been six years old, when Kerry's dyslexia slowed him up in school and Jack used to try to help him with the letters in books. After that, Jack had read to him and then, when the Major let him use the library in the big house, he'd sit with Kerry and read aloud the tales from the myths of ancient times. Tales of Thor and his hammer; wars with ice giants and trolls; the quests of Celtic heroes like Cuchulainn and the battles they fought in Scotland and Ireland long ago.

Kerry loved those stories, but for Jack Flint, they came completely alive when he read them. Sometimes he felt as if they were more real than the world he lived in.

Perhaps that wasn't surprising. Apart from his friendship with Kerry, Jack Flint was a bit of a loner. Oh, he did well enough at school, and seemed to get on with most people, but there was something in him that made him feel he didn't quite *belong*.

With Kerry it was different. He couldn't read very well, and he dodged school now and again, especially when the salmon were running up the river, but he was steady and he was staunch, and that was what mattered.

For an orphan like Jack Flint and the son of a ne'er-do-well like Kerry, it might have been an odd friendship, but you couldn't pick your friends, not your real friends anyway.

TWO

The nightmare jolted him out of sleep and Jack woke, trembling in its aftermath while the images fragmented and faded.

He hadn't had this dream for a long time. When he was small, it sometimes came every night and he would wake, wailing until Clarice came bustling in to smother him in her warm arms while the snarling, howling sounds faded in the glow of the bedside light.

Jack shook his head, dispelling the last of it, shaken but glad he had not cried in his sleep.

Whatever had sparked the dream, maybe talking about the sounds he'd heard long ago coming from behind the Blackwood forest wall, or maybe the tussle with Billy Robbins after school, he didn't know, but just on the point of waking, he'd felt he'd gone back somehow to when he was small and his dreams were fresh and so scary his heart would stop dead in his chest.

It was dark and he was moving through a forest, carried between the trees in strong arms, while behind, orange eyes, big as saucers, reflected moonlight and blinked ghostly in the depths.

Pale things flitted fast, slobbering and snarling as they came and Jack could hear the ragged, exhausted breathing of whoever carried him, sense the desperation to keep moving.

In the dream, Jack didn't know what chased them in the dark. He had no words, no comprehension.

All he knew was that if they caught him it would be terrible. But he was so frightened that he couldn't even cry.

And the arms carried him until they came to the tall, pale shapes . . .

In the aftermath, he could still see those sickly orange eyes and the thin, flitting forms between the trunks, and for the first time in his life he realized that the dream had to have come from somewhere. He couldn't have imagined something like that.

It had to be a memory. What kind of memory, he just didn't know.

Morning came. He was half awake, sore when he moved.

Jack bent towards the mirror, touching the bruise high on his cheek. The strange thing was, it hadn't hurt much at the time. Billy Robbins' punch had made his head spin, but the hurt came later, when the bruise began to swell.

Jack couldn't fight. Never had any reason to until Billy Robbins, the school bully and a boastful bigot, had picked on Kerry, because he was Irish, because he was dyslexic, and because, like Jack, he was near enough an orphan.

On the way down to the bus-stop, Billy Robbins had started again, and Jack had stood up for Kerry and Robbins had swung at him and knocked him down. If you couldn't pick your true friends, you couldn't pick your enemies either. They picked you.

He stepped back from the mirror. His first black eye, so he supposed he could count himself lucky. Some boys would fight over nothing any day of the week but Jack wasn't cut out to be a fighter. Just what he *was* cut out to be was anybody's guess.

Straight black hair fell over his brow and he hoped it was long enough to hide the bruise, but it wasn't and he knew Clarice wouldn't miss it. She had eyes like a falcon and she knew him inside out. She could spot dirty fingernails at a hundred yards and unpolished shoes from a mile.

How *did* you get that, Jack Flint? He could just hear her say. It was always the full whack, the full *Jack Flint* when she noticed something out of line, which was half the time at least.

'You and that Kerrigan Malone!' She'd say. 'Have you two been fighting?'

She'd bring Kerry into it right away, nothing surer.

Then she'd grab him, quick as a snake, and draw his face down to hers, peer over her glasses at the damage and then she'd get that worried, concerned look. She was tough, but she loved him even if she had a funny way of showing it sometimes.

Having somebody to love him was half the battle. That and a friend like Kerry.

He went downstairs for cornflakes, smiling at the picture he'd conjured, prepared to bet that this would be just what happened, and sooner rather than later. You had to get up with the milkman to get one over on old Iron Britches. His smile turned into a grin, as he thought of Kerry's name for Clarice. Those two walked wary around each other like cat and terrier, each expecting the worst, a scratch or a bite.

It wasn't that Kerry was bad. No way. But you give a dog a bad name and it's hard to shake. Despite her wariness, Clarice had insisted on taking Kerry into the lodge house when his father went to jail, rather than see him put into care. She knew he'd be like a caged wolf if he couldn't roam.

The Major wasn't in the library after breakfast, which was where he'd be found when he was home from wherever it was he went from time to time. Nobody knew much about where he went, and he never offered an explanation or gave any warning. One day he'd be gone, and another day he'd be back again. It was a mystery Jack had often wondered about but never asked.

The old man could be distant at times, spending days and nights up in the observatory in the turret of the rambling old house, but when he was home, he'd give Jack the run of his amazing library with its treasure of books, or take him hiking on the crest of Brander Ridge, telling him tales of the old days.

Jack climbed the wide stairway, then the narrow steps to

the turret which had a vantage over the whole peninsula.

The brass telescope stood at the north window today, beside a gleaming sextant and other instruments whose purpose Jack had never quite figured out. The walls between the windows were covered with star charts and ancient weapons, and the desk was piled high with books that breathed the dry and dusty smell of age.

He peered through the scope and Cromwath Blackwood jumped into focus. Dark branches clawed over the high wall, tangled, strangled with ivy thick as ropes. Even with the telescope, he could see nothing inside the dense weave of twigs and thorns.

It was dark in there. It was always dark in there.

Jack turned the telescope to point east over the bay, hoping the Major wouldn't notice. He'd have to warn Kerry they'd need to scale the wall on the far side, just in case the Major was up in the turret tomorrow.

He jammed his hands in his jeans and turned to one of the charts on the wall. It was ragged, stained at the edges, and it looked so old it might crumble to dust. The lettering on it, if it *was* lettering, was in a language Jack couldn't read. He turned, and that's when the bronze casket on the far side of the desk caught his eye.

It sat squat, glowing with smooth patina, carved with imps or pixies or demons; solid, heavy, dark with great age. He had never seen it before.

An inexplicable buzz ran through him, like a surge of electricity.

He felt his heart beating, an odd double-pulse, that seemed to be coming from inside and outside his chest.

He couldn't say why, but the casket demanded his full attention.

Very tentatively, he reached his right hand out towards it, felt the silken smoothness of the metal, the undulations of the carving. His fingers splayed on the top, as if they knew what they were searching for.

There was an odd little *snick*.

Jack almost stepped back, but the compulsion kept his fingers pressed to the surface. The hairs on the back of his neck stood on end. A tiny whirr sound came, almost inaudible. His fingers peeled from the lid. He stood there in silence, waiting.

The lid *moved*.

A dark gap showed, and then slowly the top swung up on its own, making the carvings shimmer and dance.

He held his breath, heart still making that double-thump.

The lid raised itself. He moved closer, peered into it and saw the heart, a black stone heart, small enough to hold in your hand, polished smooth as glass. It seemed to pulse and contract with a life all its own.

Unbidden, his hand reached for it.

And without warning a grey shape loomed at him from the side.

A big hand snaked towards his face as he turned, expecting a heavy blow, but instead it flashed past him and snapped the lid shut just as Jack was about to lift the stone heart from its setting.

'Curiosity, Jack lad.' The Major's eyes crinkled. 'It'll get you into trouble one of these days, that's for sure.'

'It was *alive*,' was all Jack could say.

'Trick of the light, Jack.'

Jack looked at him. He was sure he had seen the heart pulse, in and out, like a living thing. The Major met his gaze and brushed his hand over his short silver hair that matched his close-cropped beard. It was hard to tell how old he was, but he hadn't changed at all for as long as Jack had known him.

I'm sorry,' he said. 'I shouldn't have opened it.'

'I'm surprised you could,' the Major said. He drew himself up, towering over Jack, then eased himself onto the marvellous polished desk beside the telescope. He ruffled Jack's hair, letting him know he wasn't really put out, then turned the boy's face to one side, and bent forward to inspect the bruise around his eye.

'That's some shiner you have there. I hope you've a good story for Clarice. You want to try it on me?'

'It was just a scrap,' Jack said. 'I said something and Billy Robbins shoved me around a bit. He was having a go at Kerry.'

The Major held Jack's chin in one hand, inspecting the bruise.

'So you took a black eye?'

'Kerry's a friend, and he won't fight. I had to stand up for him. He would do it for me if he could.'

'Good lad.' The Major looked at him with a smile, but there was a sadness in it too. 'Just like your father.'

As soon as he'd said it, he closed his mouth in a tight line, and Jack could see he wished he hadn't spoken.

'Let's you and me hike up the ridge and see the lie of the land.'

The crags at the west point of Brander Ridge dropped abruptly to the sea. Beyond them the ocean stretched, grey as lead under piling clouds. Southwards, Ardmore harbour huddled in the bay, and down the slope the slate roof of the Major's rambling stone house could just be seen through the pines. All along the crest of the ridge, a line of standing stones hunched like weary sentinels, as far as Cromwath Blackwood in the distance.

Jack was all questions, but with the Major, you couldn't push far. He just came and went and sometimes walked with Jack on the ridge where he would sit, often silent, for an hour or so, watching the sea, then swinging round to gaze a long time at Cromwath Blackwood.

'I wish I knew more about my father,' Jack finally said.

'I know. I can tell you this. He was the best man to have at your back, and an even better one to have at your side. Best friend I ever had, bravest man I ever knew.'

'I can't remember him at all. What really happened to him?'

The Major bent forward and placed his hands on Jack's shoulders.

'I can't rightly say, and that's the honest truth. I know he went on a . . . a mission and he never came back. Where he went, I don't really know. You were just a baby when you were brought here. All I can say for now is your father was a good man with a good heart.' He touched Jack's chest with a finger, right in the centre. 'Just like his son.'

'Can you tell me about him?'

'I can, and I will,' the Major said softly. 'But you've got a year or so to put on you, and a bit of his height as well.

Maybe scrape a razor once or twice over your chin.' He smiled. 'Then you and me, we'll go walking up here again, and I'll tell you all you want to know. And what you *need* to know. And there are things you do need to know.'

'But . . .'

'No buts, Jack. Curb your curiosity and feed your patience. I know it's not easy, but nothing important ever is. All in good time.'

Jack's shoulders slumped. He sizzled with the need to know more; more about Major MacBeth, more about the strange stone heart that had tugged at him like a tide. Most of all, he needed to know about his father, who and what kind of man he was. Because he needed to know about himself.

'All in good time, Jack. And that's what you should be having while you're young and quick. A good time. It's Friday. What's your plan?'

Reluctantly Jack allowed himself to be drawn into the change of subject. The Major was like a clam when he chose, and already it was clear he'd said more than he'd intended.

'We've got the Halloween party tonight. Tomorrow, Kerry and me are going to explore Brander Water, see if we can find the source. And then we'll fish the tarn.'

It wasn't a complete lie, because after exploring the walled coppice, they did plan to go fishing, but even then Jack felt guilty about not telling the whole truth.

The Major fixed him with a look and Jack felt his face flush. It was as if he could read his mind. 'Well, take care you don't get lost up there. It's wild old country.'

Jack forced a smile. 'I never get lost. I always know the way back.'

The Major looked as if he was going to say something else, but seemed to think better of it.

'Just make sure Kerry leaves me a fish or two. He's a devil of a poacher.'

Jack laughed. 'Just a couple for the pan.' Kerry could catch anything that moved.

'And take my midge spray. It's late in the season, but they'll still eat you alive.' The Major winced as he hauled slowly to his feet.

'What's wrong?' Jack asked.

'A twinge is all.' The Major leaned heavily on the gnarled stick, carved with two snakes that merged into one ferocious head burnished to a shine with years of handling.

'Winter's coming. It's the equinox tomorrow. We're crossing over to the dark nights.' And you've the Samhain party?'

'Yeah. A week early, as usual.'

'Always been that way, ever since those stones have stood on the ridge. Halloween's still new-fangled around here. You've read your books, so you know why. Samhain is a night to watch. The old folk knew a thing or two. Full moon tonight, Jack. Keep a weather eye out.'

Jack stopped. 'For what?'

'Full moon and Samhain. A powerful conjunction. Just take care where you step, and don't be late back. It's not a night to be about.'

'I don't believe in ghosts.'

'Oh, there's worse than ghosts, believe me.'

The Major allowed a smile to crease his face. 'You've used the telescope. All those stars. A clever man said the universe is much stranger than we can imagine. Remember the stories you've read. You always had your nose in them.'

'Sure, but they're just legends.'

'There's a kernel of truth in all the legends. That's why they were passed down. Why they've lasted so long.' He changed his stance, cuffed Jack a light one on the back of his head. 'So what are you happy lads going as?'

'I'm Cuchulainn.' He pronounced it Co-hoolin, the way the Major had told him when he was small. The great Celtic warrior hero had always been Jack's favourite. 'And Kerry's David. You know, the giant-killer. He wanted to go as Samson, but his hair's too short.'

'A warped warrior and a giant-killer,' the Major said. 'Two good men and true. Come by before you go and I'll lend you something to make you look the part.'

He paused, as if trying to think his way inside Jack's head. 'But still, mind what I said now, and get home before full dark. And another thing, you take care up at the tarn, and remember . . .'

'I remember,' Jack said, knowing what was coming. 'Stay away from Cromwath Blackwood.'

'Got it in one, son. No place for anybody.'

But the mystery of the walled Blackwood tugged on Jack like a fishhook. Always had, always would until he found out for himself.

'Have you ever been in there?'

The Major gave him a searching look. 'Like I say, Jack.

It's no place for anybody. What's in there is old. Old and dangerous.'

He had such a stern look that Jack felt as if he'd been peeled open, but then the Major touched him on the shoulder.

'Some things were always meant to stay hidden.'

THREE

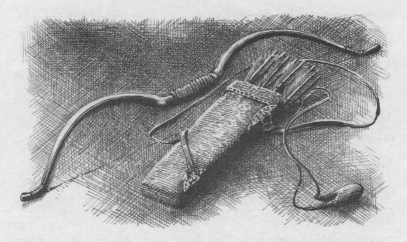

They were running in the dark, and they were running for their lives.

It had happened so fast, so terrifyingly sudden, and now they were in the tunnel with that awful chittering sound behind them, echoing around the hard stone walls.

'Move, lads!' The Major had opened the door in the wall and hustled them through before the next wave came. '*Run like the wind and don't turn back.*'

And they had. Jack and Kerry Malone both, with that shapeless, freezing dark oozing its way after them, too powerful, too cold and relentless to hold back, too utterly evil to face, and yet the Major had turned to face it.

Anger and fear welled up inside Jack.

The Major had shoved them to safety, and they had fled, left him to confront that awful flowing gibbering dark.

Now they were running away with the bag in Jack's hands and the backpack on Kerry's shoulders, scrambling fast, unable to comprehend how a Halloween night could change so quickly and turn the world so inside-out.

The dogs had been bad enough. They had been on the way home from the party, up the steep road, past Dr Balloch's gate when the two Dobermann hounds, black as sin in the shadows, had come racing down from the side of the house, howling like wolves, and launched themselves at the chain-link fence with such force it spanged out like a net and shivered the upright posts.

It had given them such a fright that Kerry had jumped, crashed into Jack, and the two of them ended in a tangle on the road.

Behind the fence the big dogs were baying in sudden fury. Moonlight glinted in their black eyes and caught the curve of bared teeth and the foam that flecked their jaws.

One of the links snapped. The boys found their feet, and fast. They took off up the road, hell for leather, and inside the fence, the dogs came haring after them, gnashing uselessly at the fence.

'Nearly gave me a heart attack,' Kerry said when they finally slowed down. 'What got into them?'

'Full moon,' Jack said. 'Lunatic dogs.'

Moonlight silvered them as they headed back, making shadows reach from the bare birches on the narrow road above Ardmore Harbour. Kerry had scrumped a couple of apples and tried his hand with a sling, lobbing them at the lamp-posts. He looked the part, in his rabbit-skin outfit, but he'd never hit a Goliath, not without a whole lot of practice.

The Major had lent Kerry the sling, marvellously woven of fine leather, from his arms collection in the library. He had handed Jack a recurve bow and a quiver of arrows that Jack had seen on the wall.

'Two heroes, both of you. Don't go spiking folk with those barbs. And watch that amberhorn. It's got a hard draw to it.' Jack had cut the sleeves off an old leather jacket from the attic and swiped a plaid blanket for a cloak and thought he was passable as Cuchulainn.

'They thought I was Robin Hood,' Jack said. It had been a good night, even if they had sneaked out the back door to avoid Billy Robbins, whose gang had been waiting outside the village hall, smoking and taking swigs from a six-pack, just waiting for the younger ones to come out.

Jack hitched the plaid on his shoulder. 'Robin Hood. Can you believe that? They'd never even heard of Cuchulainn. Only the greatest hero ever lived.'

'So you say,' Kerry said. 'But put him up against the Predator, he'd be dead meat.'

'No way,' Jack said. Kerry dug in his pocket and pulled out the little keyring with the tiny laser light on its edge. For the past couple of years they'd signalled each other, Jack in his bedroom and Kerry way down the hill in the sagging cottage where the fields turned to bog. He swung the beam on Jack, centering the red dot on his forehead.

'A bow against a blaster? No chance.'

'Cuchulainn would have eaten him for breakfast and then gone for the Alien.' Jack flashed his own keyring, trying to dazzle Kerry with the light.

'How about Superman?'

'Kryptonite gets him. Nothing could get Cuchulainn.'

Kerry lobbed the last apple, managed to skim the lamp post before they turned the corner.

'One thing I always wondered. With that skin-tight suit, how does Superman go to the bathroom?'

Jack giggled. 'At the speed of light. Maybe in a phone box.'

'That's why they always smell. Imagine if he'd a bit o' wind? It would blow the place to smithereens.' Kerry laughed. 'Hey, maybe that's what happened to Stoneymill Bridge. Maybe I'm Superman's son.'

They were still laughing when they turned the corner by the thick hawthorn and Kerry pulled up dead.

Robbins and the rest of the crew were waiting for them.

The gang came swaggering towards them, Billy Robbins big and menacing in the lead. Jack and Kerry turned and ran back to the gate on the lane, scaled the five bars and into the field, scattering the looming shapes of grazing cattle.

'You know,' Jack said, 'I'm really getting tired of running away. We're going to have to learn to fight, or it's going to get worse.'

'Fight seven of them? You're on your own, Jack man. You've been reading too many books.'

He stopped in his tracks. 'Did you hear something?'

Jack nodded. 'I did.'

He was whispering and he didn't know why. The hairs on his neck started that creepy walk again. A cloud passed in front of the moon, leaving them in darkness. A strange sense of apprehension started to roll in his belly.

Without warning a purple flash sizzled in the sky, so close they could smell the bitterness of ozone, so brief and fierce it burned after-images in their eyes.

A hellish screech ripped out across the night.

'What was that?'

'Somebody let off a rocket,' Kerry said. 'Flash-cash Billy Robbins, I bet.'

Jack found he couldn't move.

Something was wrong and he didn't know what. The wind started as quickly as it had stopped, but it was a cold wind, a winter wind that whirled round the trunks and snatched at their clothes, and Jack shivered.

Overhead, beyond the pine-tops, something huge flew in the night. Jack heard the whoosh of wings and he recalled the flock of rooks that had exploded in panic from Cromwath Blackwood.

'... home before dark ...' the Major had told him. He should have listened.

They moved slowly out of the pines.

'There!' Kerry's voice was hoarse. Jack stood close. 'There. Look.'

Darker than dark, a shadow covered the stand of firs beyond the shrubs.

Two small creatures, martens or stoats, came rippling out, fast. A blackbird squawked, went silent. Two woodpigeons catapulted into the sky. One of them faltered, fluttered madly, and tumbled to the ground.

'What *is* that?' Jack could hear the shiver in Kerry's voice.

'They sneaked up on us,' he whispered back.

Something heavy moved in the shadows. The pair froze,

breath held tight, pulling back into the cover of the trees.

Shrubs whipped back and forth and then a shape came stumbling out. They could hear Billy Robbins' breath. It sounded like somebody choking.

Jack's heart leapt into his throat. Kerry was gripping his arm, fingers dug in hard.

Robbins raised both hands to his head. He stood stock still for a moment and then he turned towards them, even though they hadn't moved a muscle.

He grunted and then came towards them, hands outstretched. His body shook like a tuning fork.

There was a *twist* in the air, an inexplicable shift. Jack felt a wave of nausea loop through him.

Billy Robbins screamed.

Deep shadow flowed out from him as he swayed on the grass and fell onto his back.

Jack and Kerry stood transfixed. The darkness seemed to slither and ripple, a thick stream of night that oozed out of Billy Robbins across the turf towards the Major's house.

When they could finally move, they crept to within two paces of Billy Robbins' sprawled form. Sparkles of silver gleamed like a halo in his frizzy hair and his face was covered in ice crystals. His skin was blue and shiny.

But it was his eyes that rooted them to the spot. He lay there, eyes wide open with shards of moonlight pale as death in them.

And both eyes were filmed with hoar-ice.

Jack grabbed Kerry's arm and pulled him away. He didn't know what had happened to Billy Robbins. Didn't want to know.

He just wanted to be away from here, out of the dark, into the warm.

But when he turned, he saw the rolling darkness was already at the gable wall.

'What on earth is that?' Jack found his voice. It came out in a croak.

'It's impossible,' Kerry whispered. But they were watching it happen. In seconds, the blackness had spread to the window. The light in there began to dim, almost imperceptibly and at first Jack thought he was imagining it, but the dimming seemed to speed up. In less than a minute, it was just a red glow and then it went completely dark. In the turret room above it, the light began to fade.

'I think we should get out of here,' Kerry said. 'This is getting weird.'

'No,' Jack said, squeezing down the fear in his belly. 'We must warn the Major.'

'At this time of night?' Kerry was snatching at excuses. This was more than crazy. 'I'm not sure we should go in there.' The turret light was now almost gone, and the next one along the wing wall was turning red.

'I'm sure we have to.' Scared as he was – *petrified* as he was – Jack knew he had to warn the Major.

He grabbed Kerry and pulled him along, down the path through the evergreen bushes, crunching the gravel of the driveway and round to the far side of the building, only yards from where Clarice would be watching television. The cellar door made no creak as he pushed it open, passed the wheezing old boiler, and up the stairs to the hallway.

Some instinct made him grab their backpacks which

they'd left just inside the cellar door in readiness for their expedition next morning. He passed one to Kerry and they hurried up the stairs to the hallway.

He sensed it again, an absolute, utter wrongness.

The air crackled with an energy all of its own. From upstairs came a low thrumming sound, like a wind in the pylons up on the moor, hardly a sound at all, more a shudder that went through both of them. Yet despite the shivery apprehension, they crept up the stairs, turned at the landing and stood facing the long corridor that spanned the wing.

Darkness was growing there. It crept on the walls like a disease.

The thrumming was stronger here and behind it was a strange snuffling noise that Jack could hear deep inside his head, the way he could sometimes hear the bats hunting moths at night.

They stopped outside the big polished door and Jack willed his breathing to slow. He put an ear to the door panel and listened. All was silent in there. He reached for the brass handle and felt the sharp sting of ice on his skin, but he didn't flinch. Instead he turned the handle, pushed the door open and they walked into the turret.

The Major turned his head, his cropped hair and beard silver against his weatherbeaten skin. His eyes widened when he saw them.

'Lads. *Lads*. What on earth are you doing here?'

'Something's happening,' Jack blurted. 'There's a … a … dark. It got Billy Robbins and now it's in the house.'

'Oh, boys.' The Major wiped a hand across his brow. 'It's the *wrong* time to be here.'

He was at the table, a massive chart spread out beside brass instruments that Jack had never seen before.

'What's happening?'

'You have to go, Jack, you and Kerrigan. Get yourselves out of here. And I mean *now*.'

He reached behind the chair and drew out the big over-and-under shotgun. With ease of practice, he slipped two orange shells into the breech and snapped it shut, and then Jack saw the brace of pistols, big ivory handled guns, in the Major's waistband.

'What is it? What's happening?'

'Thin places,' the Major said, almost to himself. 'And Samhain night.'

He crossed to the door and put a hand on the doorknob. He drew it back, rubbed frost-rime from the tips of his fingers.

'Something bad's going on,' he said. 'Something old and bad's coming this way.'

'Where from?' The question blurted out before Jack could stop it.

'Who knows?' was all the Major said. 'We may be too late. We'll have to buy you some time.'

'But what's going on?' Jack's voice was a whisper and his breath was frosting in the air. Was the light beginning to fade? It was hard to tell.

'Thin places between the worlds,' the Major muttered. 'Thin enough to rip through at times. I'm afraid something's made a breach.' He opened the door, just a crack, and cold, cold air squeezed into the library.

'That'll be the Nightshades, Jack lad. Some would say

the *Banshee*. From a very dark place, and they won't be alone.

'They find the cracks and worm their way in. They couldn't get in here by themselves, so they use another way. Someone flawed and rotten inside.'

'I don't believe this,' Kerry said.

'Believe it. There might be a Shadowmaster guiding them, and they should be sent right back to where they belong. But with you two here, we must try another way.'

He reached into the big poacher's pocket of his tweed jacket and drew out a long, thin thing, broke off the top with his teeth. A white light flared so brightly both boys had to turn away. Crooking the gun in his arm, the Major swung the door open and held the fizzing light high.

In the corridor, darkness expanded.

The Major pushed the fizzing light-stick outwards and the dark fell back, a little.

He turned to them. 'Go on now. Jack, go through that door and wait there.' The Major jammed the stuttering light in the door frame, hefted the gun on his shoulders and stood between the boys and the flowing dark.

Kerry followed Jack through the door into the side-room. Jack held the door, heart beating fast.

'Where is this?' Kerry asked. Old arms and shields festooned the walls. 'It's a dead end. We're stuck.'

The Major stepped back from the door, raised the shotgun and fired. The room shook.

He fired again, right into the mass of black. From way beyond it, in the inky hallway, came a rumbling sound that shivered the stones of the old house.

Shadowmaster, Jack thought. He did not want to see the thing that had made that sound.

'We have to do something,' he told Kerry, hoping his voice wasn't shaking as much as he thought it was. 'We can't leave him there.'

Jack raised the short bow in his hands, but the arrows in his quiver only had wooden tips, and they'd be pretty ineffective against anything. He couldn't think what might work, but his eyes scanned the wall where the Major had chosen the bow only hours before – how long ago *that* seemed now – and fell on the quiver. He crossed and snatched it down.

Jack nocked an arrow. Its point was razor sharp and gave off an acrid smell. He hoped whatever it could do to humans might work on that gibbering dark. He swung the door open just as the black tide poured into the library, night on the move. Whatever the Major had been preparing for, he'd run out of time. Jack drew hard, then loosed an arrow. It flew straight into the centre of the mass, dwindling in the distance as if it had fallen into a bottomless hole. Something moved in there, a poisonous, liquid motion that defied logic.

Jack shook his head. The arrow hadn't hit the wall on the far side. It was as if the wall had disappeared, leaving nothing but a vast space. And how could you fight empty space, even if it *was* moving? How could you fight something you couldn't even *see*?

'Get back, *now*,' The Major roared, almost as loud as the gunshot.

His guns blared again.

'Back! Get back I said.' Moving quickly he swept them before him into the side room.

'There's too many of them,' he said, breathing hard. 'A horde of them. Took me by surprise this time.'

This time?

'You have to get out of here. I've never seen it this strong before. I think there's something they want, but they can't have it.' The Major strode to the desk, past the massive antlers that stretched from side to side, stopped in front of carved bronze box that Jack had opened. Jack heard the snick and when the Major turned, he held the stone heart. It was set in a silver claw on a thick chain. In his other he held a little satchel. He handed it to Jack and then stooped to loop the chain around his neck.

'This is what they want Jack. This heartstone. Take care of it. Don't let them have it.'

A tumble of thoughts ran through Jack's head. Take care of it . . . how . . . where?

'I don't understand,' he began to say.

'I wish there was time to tell you. This is where it starts.' The Major put the gun down and laid his hand on Jack's shoulder, gripping it tight.

'Ah, Jack lad. There's so much to tell you, and I thought I had time. I should have known better.'

'I don't understand,' Jack repeated.

The Major hefted the old gnarled walking stick that he'd always used on their walks up the ridge. He cupped both hands around the polished grip, twisted, and the stick came apart. When he turned back towards them, he had a long straight sword in his right hand, and a short ridged blade in his left. Without pausing, he moved to the corner furthest from the door, touched a stone high on the wall and this time a narrow doorway ground open and another darkness yawned.

'Guard the heartstone, Jack. Guard it well. It's your inheritance. Your father sent it with you for safety. You have to be keeper now. I'd have told you everything, but that's fate.'

'My father?' Jack started. Despite the need to flee, his feet wouldn't move. 'What about him? What *is* this?'

Jack stared at him, willing the Major to say more.

'It's the most important thing in the worlds,' he finally said.

'But what do I do with it?'

'You run, boy.'

He shoved them both and they stumbled through onto a tight stone staircase that spiralled into shadows.

'Trust your instincts. Trust that sense of direction. Trust your heart. You'll know when you get there.'

Jack tried to speak as the door swung shut on them. Before it did, he saw the Major's sword flashing, fast slices of light, and then the door slammed and the Major was gone.

The stairway led them down, well below the level of the foundations. There they ran along a narrow tunnel, and the compass in Jack's head told them they were running north. Behind them, the murmuring was faint, but he knew it would get louder, because with the Major gone, there was nothing to hold it back, whatever it was.

The tunnel curved, damp and dripping with moss, when

they reached the bend at the bottom. It twisted and turned but all the time they were running northwards and the air was getting colder. He could sense the blackness surging after them.

When the ground started to slope up, he could make out the shapes of thick twisted roots poking through the masonry. Feathery tendrils brushed him and he could feel the tug of cobwebs in his hair.

'Move, Kerry! It's behind us.'

Kerry kept going, breathing hard, clambering over the roots which now almost blocked their way, and Jack felt a burgeoning terror that they'd be trapped forever in the dark. It gave his legs new speed and he almost tripped on Kerry's heels.

Suddenly they were out in the air again, racing through trees before they even realized it. Thorns snatched at their clothing and branches smacked them in the face, poking at their eyes. They hared through piles of dead leaves, scattering them in little whirls. Above them the moon was bloated, but not silver as it had been before. It glowed a poisonous orange, sending toxic shadows against the boles of the trees.

'Where are we?' Kerry gasped.

Jack started for a moment, eyes widening, before the full awfulness of their situation hit him.

'We're in Cromwath Blackwood.'

FOUR

The trees became thicker, crowding together to bar their way. Out of the corner of his eye, Jack saw a sinuous shape slither into curling ferns. A flock of something clattered into the air. Mushrooms clung to rotting trunks, almost luminous in the moonlight, dripping with a liquid that Jack instinctively knew was deadly. Under their feet, in the leaves and moss, small things scuttled into root crevices.

'Too far,' Kerry said, gasping. 'Can't be Cromwath.'

'Just move.' Jack could hardly get the words out. He was thinking ahead. Kerry was right, how could this be the walled woodland, it was too big a stretch, but it could be nowhere else.

They had run a mile, maybe more, and the Blackwood was never that big. And what would they do when they came to the far wall? It was twenty feet high, maybe more.

How could they scale that before the flowing darkness swallowed them?

Kerry tripped on a root and Jack fell over him, rolled on the crackling leaves down a small incline and fetched up against stone.

The wall, he thought. *We have to get over.* He got to his feet, helped Kerry up and as they turned to face the wall, he saw that he'd been wrong.

It was a stone, a huge standing stone. Carved creatures cavorted on its surface.

Jack took an involuntary step back and his heart kicked hard against his ribs.

It was not just one stone. It was a ring of stones, massive pillars of carved rock in a wide ring. There were thirteen of them, solid and rooted into the ground. He'd never known they existed. The spaces between them yawned darkly.

An image hovered in his mind, just out of reach, but the sudden appearance of the stones had jarred something deep within him. Somehow, long ago, he had seen them before.

He shook his head. They had no time for anything but flight.

Right in the centre of the ring was a flat slab, like a table top on three basalt legs. The darkness under it was like a cave. Jack took a step forward, suddenly aware of the story about the boy who disappeared here. Kerry was right behind him.

'Where now?'

Jack pointed ahead. There was nowhere else to go. They had to keep moving. He passed into the ring, wishing it was another day, a daylight day with no obscene dark thing on their tail so they could have a real look as they had planned.

'Come on.' He crossed halfway, making for the far side, and then abruptly swerved towards the centre. He hadn't meant to do that at all. His feet took him there of their own accord.

'Where are you going?'

Jack kept walking, unable to stop. The dark under the table stone pulled at him with such sudden force he felt like a moth in lamplight, though there was no light there. His heart thumped in his chest, a great double thump that he felt in his ears and even as he took his next step, he felt that second pulse, and it wasn't coming from under his ribs at all.

It was coming from the heartstone.

One step. Another step. The strange power dragged at him. A third step and he could see shapes swirling there, black on black, hear an odd, far off laughter. He tried to speak but his mouth wouldn't open. A final step and the darkness began to swallow him.

Then suddenly he was on his back and Kerry was dragging him across the rough ground.

'What're you doing, man?'

'Couldn't stop,' Jack gasped, mouth now suddenly working. Kerry turned towards the table slab and the dark underneath.

'It was suckin' you in. I could *feel* it. We've got to get out of here.'

Beyond the ring, in the direction they'd run from, the air was beginning to freeze.

Kerry gave Jack a hand, pulled him up, kept his grip and hauled him past the slab towards the far side, through the space between two massive stones and there was a *twist*, a wrenching shiver that rippled through them both as if they'd been turned inside out and then twisted back again.

Jack saw swirling colours. Kerry shouted, somehow far in the distance. For an instant Jack was spinning in a vortex of light and rushing sound.

And then they were running in a grey mist.

Something reached out from behind them. Jack got a glimpse of it and tried to duck, slipped and went on his back. A long black talon rippled from between the stones as he scrabbled away, heels frantic on the wet grass.

It touched him, just a scrape on his chest near his shoulder and as soon as he felt it a dreadful river of cold splashed into him, burning his skin. His satchel tore away and he yelped in pain, rolling backwards; the contact was lost, leaving only hurt sizzling through skin and bone.

'Run,' he gasped, the short bow gripped in his hand. They raced away, through the drizzle until they ran out of breath and stood, leaning together for support, panting like horses, shivering with fright and the adrenalin rush that fright gives you, and kept holding on until they were able to breath properly again.

Kerry looked at him. 'Got you, didn't it?'

Jack nodded. The pain in his shoulder was like nothing he'd ever experienced. It seared in rivulets of glassy hurt all the way across his chest.

'Let's get out of this fog and have a look at you.' Kerry got an arm round Jack's shoulders and helped him walk, through thick tussock grass, moving laboriously uphill in the gathering light as the mist swirled dense as smoke around their feet. Both of them had noticed that it was daytime here, grey and overcast.

As they walked on, skirting a mound of brittle bare branches, Jack stumbled and fell. He pushed himself up on shaking arms, gagging at the sudden stench. The mist cleared and he found himself up against a gaping, mouldering skull. A big yellow maggot crawled out of the eye socket.

He sucked in a breath, too shocked to make a sound. Behind him Kerry was yelling.

'Get off me. Let go!'

Jack turned from the nightmare skull to see Kerry hopping on one foot, trying to drag the other back. Bony fingers were hooked around his ankle.

They hadn't stumbled through bare branches. They had walked into a battlefield. All around them, all over the dank hillside, lay the bones and broken bodies of dead men.

Kerry was squawking in fright. He lurched away and the thin, white arm popped out of its socket and trailed along with him. Jack snatched at it, gorge rising, fingers clutched on bare bone, and tore it from Kerry's ankle.

'You're okay. It just snagged you.'

'*Jeez*, Jack. Thought it had me. Thought it *grabbed* me.'
He sunk to his knees, gagging in the awesome stench.

Jack winced against the pain in his shoulder, trying to slow his breathing. He eased up, bracing against a broken lance that was stuck in the peaty ground, stuck through the white peeling ribs of something that might have been a man but wasn't quite. It was squat and heavy, with a skull that narrowed above a sharp brow. Yellow spade-like teeth lined a mouth open in a silent scream. A massive spiked club was still gripped in its hand.

'What *is* that?'

'And what the heck is *that*?' Beside them, on its side, an animal sprawled muzzle-down on the turf, its bristling hide spiked with arrows, snout curled in a perpetual snarl. Two wicked tusks curved like scimitars on either side of its maw.

'I don't know what it is.'

'Jack. There's something wrong here.' Kerry wasn't normally given to understatement. 'Where the hell are we?'

Hell could surely describe this place. All around them lay broken bones and shattered bodies; men and things that weren't quite men and strange beasts. Whatever had happened on this moor had been awesome. It had been desperate.

'I don't know that either.' Jack confessed.

'It was night when those things came, and now it's morning.' Kerry asked the questions, but Jack's head was fizzing with them and he had no answers.

When that dark had reached for him, the pain had been so consuming that Jack thought he would die.

Now the possibility struck him that he might well have died, and this was the last sparkings of his cooling brain. He didn't know.

The mist cleared some more, showing the extent of the battlefield. It went on up and over the hill. Rusty armour merged with russet bracken. Above them, threatening clouds raced by and the wind moaned. A flicker caught

Jack's eye, and a harsh sound cut the air. Both boys turned to see a huge crow perched on the breastbone of a half-rotted cadaver.

'Look at the size of that thing,' Kerry said. 'It's a vulture for sure.'

The crow cawed again. From a tussock uphill, another replied. It hopped into view, big as a spaniel, black as soot with a beak like a dagger. The first one flapped over the bones towards them.

'This isn't looking too clever,' Kerry muttered. The crow cocked its head. One eye was missing, leaving an empty crater. Even then, Jack knew that it was looking at him from that cavity, looking right through him.

Kerry stepped back. The bird pecked at his knee. The second one flew across, heavy in the air. It stabbed at Jack as he dodged. Another appeared between the ribs of a big beast. Then another. The first cawed again, and suddenly the sky was full of immense black birds. They came swooping in, so close they could feel the whoosh of wings and smell the carrion breath. A sharp beak caught Kerry behind his ear and drew blood.

'You have to be kidding,' he yelled, whirling away. He grabbed up a sword thrust blade-down into a grey ragged throat, turned fast and hacked at the nearest bird. Feathers flew. He swung again and a crow tumbled to the ground, one wing flailing.

Jack ran to the beast spiked with arrows, snatched the first and despite the pain in his shoulder, drew and let fly into the swarm wheeling around Kerry's head. A huge bird made a surprising thump when it hit the ground, shot right through. Jack nocked another arrow, fired again, surprised to hit a second crow. Kerry slashed at the air. Feathers and what might have been blood followed the swing of the sword.

'We've got to get out of here,' Jack bawled. 'We have to go back.'

'I'm with you there.' Kerry sounded breathless. The crows flapped around, dodging the swinging blade. Jack grabbed Kerry's sleeve and pulled him back the way they had come, running for the ring of stones, down the hill to the pooling mist. The crows followed in a cloud, pecking and cawing. They breasted the slope and Jack almost froze.

The ring of stones had vanished.

All he could see were two big carved pillars standing side by side on the open moor.

'Where the heck are they ... ?

Jack gasped, struggling against the pain, but still running hell for leather, knowing they had to get back between the stones. 'Come on, Kerry.'

They made it ten yards ahead of the birds, and dashed through, expecting that sickening *wrench* again.

Nothing happened. Nothing at all. They ran between the stones, tripping over heather, and the murder of crows flew right after them. Another reached Kerry and he almost split it in half with a manly swipe. A razor beak caught Jack on the back of his head. A bird landed on Kerry's shoulder and went for his eyes. He grabbed at the beak, threw it off him and in ten steps they were crashing into the undergrowth at the edge of the trees. Behind them wings beat at the thick foliage, but the noise of pursuit faded.

Kerry leaned against a tree, catching his breath. Jack slid to the thick carpet of moss.

'We'd better wake up now,' Kerry finally said. 'This is the weirdest dream I ever had in my life, that's for sure.'

Jack felt a hysterical giggle bubble up inside him. The pain in his shoulder was spreading down his ribs in a grinding chill. He felt his vision waver.

'We can't be dreaming. Not both of us.'

'How do you mean?'

'*I'm* dreaming, or *you're* dreaming, but not both of us at once.'

'Oh, don't say that, Jack man.'

'Why not?'

Kerry looked him straight in the eye. 'If this isn't a dream, and we're not dead, that means it's real.'

Jack met his eyes and held them with some difficulty as darkness began to cloud his vision.

'Wherever we are, I don't think it's earth at all.'

FIVE

'I don't think it's earth at all,' Jack said.

Bleak cold was creeping through him, an aching, somehow deadly cold. He knew it was reaching for his heart with icy determination. His eyes closed.

The crows wheeled across a battlefield where beasts grunted and squealed and creatures, grey, warted men, battled with stone clubs against real men, true men in leather armour and bronze helmets. The screams of the dying and the beasts and the harsh hungry cawing of the crows swept like a storm across the dead and the living. Jack backed away, terrified, as the lead crow came winging in and landed on his shoulder, crater eyes festering, wet beak lunging.

He was yelling when Kerry woke him, shaking him by the shoulder. His eyes flicked open and pain surged across his skin.

'Jack, man. Wake up.' Kerry bent over him. 'Come *on* Jack.'

'I was ... I was dreaming.'

'Must have been a real beauty. You slept a long time. Come on,' Kerry said, nodding to where the trees grew thick and the undergrowth even thicker. 'That howling out there, it's getting closer.'

Jack got to his feet, shook his head to clear it.

'You really don't look too good.' Kerry put a hand to his shoulder. Jack could hear the concern in his voice.

He mumbled something, trying to ease the ache away, not wanting to let Kerry know that it hurt so bad he could barely think. They had enough to worry about.

He shouldered the satchel and Kerry hefted his backpack and they began walking slowly and warily between the immense trunks into the heart of the forest, in the opposite direction of the echoing howls that sounded too much like wolves for Jack's liking. They followed an animal trail, dodging thickets of thorny vines as the trees crowded close.

The whole place felt different, strange and so unlike the forests that grew alongside Brander Water. The smell of rot and musky blooms came wafting up as they passed.

They kept going while Jack tried to figure out a direction,

but the compass in his head, the one that always told him where he was and where to go, was failing him, and that was scary too.

Somewhere in the hidden sky the moon rose, but the leaf canopy blotted out much of the light. Fireflies danced sickly green, and the leaves overhead seemed to whisper secrets in the shadows.

Jack felt fingers of anxiety trail up and down his spine. The nausea inside him rolled and looped and every now and then he felt the need to lie down, but he fought against it, and the pain creeping through him. Every now and again he saw, in his mind's eye, the mad face of Billy Robbins as the dark oozed out of him.

He had been touched by that dark.

Eventually after what seemed like miles, they came to a dell where a small clearwater stream tumbled into a pool, lit by a rising moon that now managed to beam through the leaves around the clearing.

'This is far enough,' Jack said. 'We have to rest.'

'Suits me,' Kerry agreed quickly. 'My feet are killing me.'

Together they set up camp in the bole of a forest giant and Jack tested the water. It was cold and pure. Kerry lit a small fire and opened a tin of beans for both of them. In the firelight, in his rabbit-skin Halloween costume, he could have been a stone-age hunter.

'There's fish in the stream,' Kerry ventured, trying to sound positive. 'And I saw rabbit trails. Or some kind of trails. We can put a few snares out and eat.'

'We have to get back home,' Jack said. 'We left the Major. We shouldn't have run.'

'We never had much of a chance, did we? He shut the door on us.'

Jack lay back in the hug of big roots. 'I don't know where this is, but it's not home. The Major must know something. If we get back soon enough, maybe he'll have sorted everything out. He can tell us.'

Guilt overrode the ache in his ribs. He felt a coward.

'What happened at the ringstones?' Kerry asked.

'We just went through and ended up here, wherever this is. How it happened, I haven't got a clue. I felt something. Like I was turning inside out.'

'Felt like the first night on a trawler. Made me want to puke.'

'But now they're gone. The stones.'

He looked steadily at his friend. 'We're lost.'

Kerry opened the backpack and drew out the little telescopic fly rod along with the rope they'd planned to use to scale the wall around Cromwath Blackwood. He had a maglite for exploring whatever it was they had hoped to find, and an old cigar box with thick line, fishing hooks and a lighter for the campfire. And there were a few tins of corned beef and beans, along with some biscuits he'd filched from Clarice's kitchen.

'And I got the Walkman I won at cards and a pack of fifty two, in case we get bored,' he said, trying to make the best of it. He pointed to the satchel the Major had pushed into Jack's hands. 'What's in that?'

The satchel lay between them. It's thick patterned leather was like scuta from something big and armoured, like a crocodile. Jack opened the catch, felt inside and drew out a book. It was small, leather-bound, and even older than the satchel. On the front were some signs he couldn't read. The binding was carved in the same way as the standing stones.

Inside, the pages were blank and felt as if they were made of crackly skin.

'The Major said it was important. But it doesn't look like it's going to be much use.'

Kerry took it from Jack's hand, held it to the light and the embossed lettering stood out in sharp relief.

'*The Book of Ways*,' he read.

'What?'

'That's what it says.'

'Stop kidding around, man. We have to think.' It took Kerry all his time to read a page of a book and even then he struggled.

'*The Book of Ways*,' he said again.

He opened it, stared at the blank pages. 'Bit of a swizz though. Nothing in it.' He slung it back on the satchel. 'It can't be that important.'

The book landed at a slant. The back cover flipped open and the pages riffled all by themselves until they stopped at the beginning.

They both leant forward together.

Slowly, a shape began to appear on that first page, darkening the skin, almost like a photograph developing in the darkroom.

'There must be a computer chip in it,' Kerry said. 'Look at that.'

The image became clearer. As they watched, fascinated, two standing stones carved with shapes and strange lettering, stones exactly like the ones they had seen on the moor, darkened into being. Between the stones was nothing at all.

'Neat.' Kerry lifted the book and held it between them.

Even as he spoke, script appeared, scrolling onto the page as if written by an invisible hand. Jack could make no sense of it.

'The Farward Gate of Temair.' Kerry mouthed the words slowly. 'That's what it says.'

He smiled suddenly. 'Can't believe I can read this!'

Jack's breath came out long and slow. 'No,' he said softly. 'It can't be.'

But Kerry's eyes had dropped back to the page again. New letters, or what seemed to be letters to Kerry, were scrolling, line by line, directly beneath the etching of the two rock pillars. They came to an end eight lines down. Kerry's fingers worked along the line and he read out haltingly:

> From Farward set for set of sun
> First step on travail just begun
> But journey-man be well aware
> A shadow wakes in far Temair.
> Perils from the shadow's wrath
> Lurk to lure from righteous path
> Steel your heart, brave your fate
> Ere you find the Homeward Gate.

'What do you think that means?'

Jack's face had paled to ghostly in the firelight. 'If it means what I think it does, we're in real trouble.'

'As if I never knew that already.' Kerry nudged him on the arm. 'No, but really, what sort of trouble, apart from all this weird stuff?'

'Remember the stories we used to read? The Celtic ones.'

'Aye. Cuchulainn and all them loonies and witches.' Kerry sat, leaning on the sword. It seemed part of him. 'Sure, they were just fairy tales.'

'Temair was from *before* Cuchulainn. It's the oldest name for the Celtic kingdoms in the legends, when the Fomorians were beaten and thrown out.'

He shook his head. 'No. This is impossible. Temair doesn't exist. Temair was the old Celtic kingdom, but long before the Celts ever came. It was Ireland and Scotland before the sea came and split them apart. You must have made a mistake.'

'Maybe,' Kerry agreed. 'You know what I'm like with words.'

'That word. Travail. How's it spelt?'

'I dunno,' Kerry shrugged. 'I can get a sense of it, but don't ask me to spell it. I don't even know what the letters are.' He held the book up and mouthed the word again. 'When I read it, I get the feeling it's trouble, or hardship, something like that. It doesn't sound like a picnic, for sure.'

Jack looked at him, brow furrowed. The fact that Kerry could read the strange script was as puzzling as anything he'd seen so far. He was still not convinced that Kerry wasn't playing a joke on him.

'Are you being serious?'

'Sure. But it's creeping me out. It's like I can *feel* the words inside my head. But I don't know what they mean.'

Jack asked him to repeat the verse, and Kerry did, line by line, exactly as before, and that told Jack enough. Kerry wasn't making it up.

'I don't know what it all means, but if it *is* right, then I don't think we can go back the way we came.'

'How do you mean?'

'The Homeward Gate. The one we came through, it disappeared. Don't you think it means there's another gate somewhere else?'

Kerry shook his head this time. 'You don't really believe any of this, do you?' He stopped short. Those bodies had been real, men and beasts both. 'But I could smell them,' he muttered. 'And this sword.' He grasped it, heavy in his hand. 'It's for real.'

Jack was in turmoil. All of a sudden he remembered the hike with the Major up to Brander Ridge. '*The universe is stranger than we can imagine*,' he'd said. And all this was stranger than anything he had ever imagined.

'So what now?' Kerry asked.

The howling had died away, but it was getting darker in the trees. Moths the size of sparrows fluttered into the light, and whirring insects hummed juicily up against their ears. Now and then a big dragonfly, bigger than anything they'd seen at Stoneymill pool, would zoom in on clattering wings. Eyes seemed to watch them from the darkness.

Jack twisted on to the side that gave less pain, aware of the ache crawling over his ribs as if he'd taken a massive blow, even though it had just been a touch. His mind was buzzing and he lay a long time, thinking, trying to make sense of all the thoughts that crowded in his head, trying to think of a way out of this situation he and Kerry had stumbled into.

Shadows rolled in and small things moved in the undergrowth.

He started when Kerry shook him by the arm. 'I heard something. Out there.'

Jack reached for his bow. 'It's too dark to move,' he said. 'We'll get lost or fall down a hole. We best set up a perimeter.'

'Like in *Predator*?'

Kerry dug in the pack and brought out the rope and thick nylon line he used for rabbit snares and together they set some trip wires, just in case. They worked quickly and surely, as friends do, not needing to speak. Kerry used his weight to bend sturdy saplings and Jack helped him fix them with spring nooses that would snare anything that kicked away the notched stick holding them down.

He had seen Kerry set them up before, back home.

They gathered dry branches to lay all round beyond the fire, so they'd crackle if anything came near. Finally Jack sank onto his haunches, drained of strength.

'I'd better take a look at that,' Kerry said, kneeling beside him. The leather jerkin Jack had made from the old jacket was puckered and twisted close to the neck. It seemed to have shrivelled from heat.

Kerry helped peel it off as Jack winced with the movement.

From his shoulder to just above his heart, what looked like a bruise, not blue, but grey and almost black in the centre, had risen up from the skin in twisting knots. It stretched like a wide hand, dark, too dark against pale skin.

'I don't like the look of that,' Kerry said. 'It's festering. We have to get you some help.'

He wet a handkerchief in the stream. Jack lay back.

'The water looks clean enough,' Kerry assured him.

He dabbed gently and Jack let out a cry, so loud and sudden that Kerry pulled back. Jack slumped against the tree, firelight spangling through his tears. He blinked them back and closed his eyes, waiting for the hurt to die away, trying not to faint. But he failed.

It was pitch black when he came round, gasping for breath and aching all over. Kerry was beside him, dabbing his brow with water from the stream. He made him drink, holding the canteen to his mouth, and the cool sucked away some of the pain.

'You have to stop scaring me like that,' Kerry told him, trying to make light of it, but only sounding miserable and afraid. Jack swallowed some more water. A sick feeling twisted in his belly and he fought it, trying to get his mind into gear. He had to think. The ring of stones was gone, but if the book, however implausible, however *impossible*, was in any way correct, there might be a way home, somewhere in this strange place.

They would have to find it, find it quickly and get home.

Jack didn't know how they could do it, not from those few lines in that strange script, but they'd have to try. He was scared at the prospect. All his life he'd read about his heroes, the great warriors of old.

He might have been dressed like one, but he didn't feel heroic. Not in the least.

He was just a boy, huddled in the bole of a tree, with poison spreading under his skin.

Kerry watched him from the far side of the fire.

'What's wrong?'

'I heard something again,' Kerry whispered. His eyes were fixed on the intense darkness beyond the fire. 'We're being watched. I can feel it. The hairs on the back of my neck are going walkabout.'

A twig snapped. Jack's eyes flicked in that direction and he thought he saw a shape flit from one thick trunk to another. Above them an owl screeched and in the ferns a small animal gave a thin cry. Kerry jerked his head left and right with every sound, hands clasped round the pommel of his sword.

Without warning a loud, piercing screech startled them both. There was a whooshing sound and a wooden snap then branches thrashing violently back and forth.

'We've caught it.' Kerry hoisted the sword and Jack forced himself to his feet. They moved round the far side of the tree, where something was twisting furiously, one limb caught in a noose where the sapling had pulled up to a stretch.

They lunged forward and Kerry raised his blade, ready to strike, when there was a flash in the moonlight and one of the twine cords snapped and sprung the sapling back like a whip. The creature cried out, high and desperate.

Jack made a grab for it and it twisted away. The flash came again and the noose binding its leg came apart like thread. It turned, screeching, came at him and he saw a curved glitter, a flicker of something sharp. He fell back as the shape landed on him and the blade came stabbing down.

It caught the satchel that had swung over his abdomen and the creature grunted as the sharp curve stopped dead.

Kerry dropped his sword for fear of hitting Jack and launched himself at the tumble of bodies. He landed heavily across both of them. The creature kicked and snarled, scratching with a free hand while Kerry held on desperately to the one holding the blade. It fought like a cat. It was thin, wiry and surprisingly strong.

It squirmed, kicked hard and caught Kerry on the thigh, but he rolled with it, spinning away from Jack. They crashed through a patch of ferns, down the steep bank of the stream and landed with a thud on the shingle beside the water.

A paw shot out and raked Kerry's face, going for his eyes. Something clattered on the stones and Kerry saw it was a blade. He made a grab for it, and the thing was on him, scrambling and clawing, and finally Kerry lost patience and threw a punch as hard as he could.

The shape flopped into a bush. Kerry snatched up the knife. He got the creature in a head-lock and dragged it out, ready to slice and finish it off quickly.

The moonlight caught the blade on the way down.

Jack's hand clamped around his wrist and the point stopped just under an exposed throat.

Jack held tight.

'It's a girl,' he finally said.

SIX

Kerry was so surprised he loosened his grip and the girl's hood dropped back. She pulled free and stood gasping on the shingle, hands on splayed knees. Moonlight limned short amber hair.

'I thought it was a cat,' Kerry said. 'Or a wolf.'

The girl wiped water from her face and stood there, chest heaving with effort.

'A wolf?' she said. 'A wolf would have had your throat.'

She had a lilting accent that reminded Jack of the western Irish, or even the Scottish islands, but he was surprised that he could understand her at all.

'And I'll have it, too.' She stuck a hand inside the short cape and another knife flashed, thin and sharp.

Jack put a hand on her shoulder.

'We won't hurt you,' he said. 'Take it easy.'

'You trapped me like a beast. You expect me to believe you?'

'We don't know this place,' Jack said. 'We thought something was following us. You could have been anybody. Anything.'

She considered this for a moment, then nodded and sank to her haunches.

'There's worse than me in these woods, believe me. I've seen them.' She held on to the knife, her eyes shifting from Jack to the blade in Kerry's hand, as if she was gauging the distance, estimating her chances. Jack kept his hand on her shoulder.

'We've got no fight with you,' he said. 'We don't want to fight. But we don't want you to use that on us.' He gestured at the blade.

She held his look for a long moment, then shrugged.

'First, tell me who you are, and what you're doing wandering the darkwood.'

'You came sneaking up on us,' Kerry said. 'First you tell us who *you* are.'

She turned her face up to them and Jack could see how slight she was, hood fallen on her shoulders, breath still coming in shallow gasps.

'I am Corriwen Redthorn,' she said. She might be their captive, but Jack heard pride in her tone.

'Is that supposed to mean something?' Kerry was still on an adrenalin high. He'd never talk to a girl like that in Ardmore.

Jack held out his hand. 'I'm Jack Flint. And this is Kerry Malone.'

She looked warily at the hand, checking him for some sleight, saw none, and slowly reached far enough to touch his fingers. Her hand barely brushed his and drew back fast. Her eyes, even in this light, were luminous green. It was only the briefest touch, but Jack felt a shudder ripple through him, like a jolt of hot electricity that shook him as if he'd touched a live wire.

When he found his voice, all he could say was: 'We're kind of . . . lost.'

Her eyes still locked on his, she said, 'I am the last Redthorn.' She reached again and this time she took his hand in hers and held it tight as if afraid he might disappear. 'And I have been lost for a long time.'

Silence stretched between them. Her statement was so bleak, so empty of hope, that Jack Flint felt his heart flip inside him.

'Well, we're all lost together,' Kerry said.

'Listen, I'm really sorry about your face.' He kicked at the shingle with his toe. 'I thought you were something else.'

She turned towards him as if he'd just appeared, and whatever it was that sparked between Jack and her snapped when she released his hand.

'It was dark, and you had a knife,' Kerry said defensively. 'You could have been anybody.'

'Well, I suppose I could,' she agreed. 'You have to stay in the shadows here. Like an animal. It's the way to stay alive.'

'Can't be that bad,' Kerry said. 'It's not the jungle.'

She glanced at him, as if puzzled by the word, then turned back to Jack. 'And what are you doing here on the far side of Temair?'

'Temair,' Kerry said. 'There's that word again.'

'I was talking to your master,' Corriwen Redthorn said.

'Master? Me?' Jack felt a smile start. 'No. No. We're friends.'

'But he wears skins, and you have the plaid.' She looked Kerry up and down, 'And why is he carrying a man's sword? Is he a squire?'

'It's fancy dress,' Kerry started. 'We were at a party.'

'It's a long story,' Jack butted in. He was relieved they wouldn't have to fight any more tonight, and puzzled by the odd sensation that had jolted him when she'd taken his hand. 'Let's get back to the fire.'

Corriwen ate as if she was starving and did not lift her head until the tin of beans and slices of corned beef were finished. She looked as if she could have licked the last of the tomato sauce from the tin. Jack handed her an enamel mug with dark tea and she sipped at it, hugging the sides to savour the heat.

'Whatever this is,' she said, in that lilt that he still couldn't decide was Irish or Highland, 'it puts heart back into a soul. I never tasted the like. All I've had is a fish and a coney or two. And a bristlehog, though I swear I'll never eat another.'

They watched her sip, a slender figure huddled in her cape and hide boots. Her leggings were thorn-snagged. The two thin-bladed knifes nestled against each other in a twin sheath on her belt. Kerry put another couple of logs on the fire and Jack waited until she had finished the tea before he spoke again.

'So where on earth is this place?' he asked. 'We thought somebody was trying to ambush us so we set some snares.'

'So you're gamepoachers, then?'

'No. We're just lost. We came here through a ... some kind of gateway, and here we are. We want to go home.'

'Aye, and wouldn't we all if we had a home to go to,' she said softly. Jack sensed a sadness in her. 'Here's three of us far from home, and little chance of getting back.'

'So what are you doing here?' Kerry asked. 'Wandering around all by yourself?'

'I'm hunted,' she said. Above them, lightning strobed through the canopy, and she raised her eyes. The light flashed back green.

'I came to find my brother.' It was barely a whisper. 'My brother Cerwin. He stood for Redthorn House and the Dalriada against the mountain people. The Scree. But my uncle Mandrake tricked him. Cerwin did not know Mandrake led the Scree. He fell into a trap.'

She reached a tentative hand and clasped Jack's fingers in her own, holding tight as if she was afraid of falling.

'I found my dear brother and his wasted army on the moor. They had fought hard and sold themselves dear. I never saw such a sight. Mandrake's Scree have been on my heels since.'

'I think we saw the place,' Kerry said. 'On the hill. There're dead bodies all over the place. The smell would have knocked you down.'

Jack punched him on the shoulder and Kerry stopped talking, but Corriwen nodded. 'The best of them lie rotting where they fell. My people and the foul Scree and their beasts, a spread for the roaks and ravens.'

'What caused all this?' Jack asked gently.

'My uncle Cadwill, my father's twin brother, was the cause,' she began. 'Always the jealous one, jealous because he was the younger by mere minutes. The Redthorn sword could have been his but for those few minutes, and a terrible thing that would have been. He has the sword anyway. And the Scree armies. He calls himself Mandrake now, and he has put the Scree over the Dalriada, his own people.'

'Who are these Scree, then?' Kerry couldn't contain his curiosity.

She drew her eyes away from Jack's. 'They are Fomorians. Banished to the north mountains long ago. Savage and soulless ogres they are.'

Jack drew in his breath. He'd read of the Fomorians in the Major's library. They were in the oldest Celtic legends.

'I think we saw some of them on the moor,' Kerry said. 'Looked like they hit every branch falling out of the ugly tree.'

'They fight for Mandrake now. Some say he found riches and pays for his army.'

'I don't get this,' Kerry said. 'You're some sort of princess, right?'

'My father was the Lord Landholder, if that's what you mean.'

'And we've walked right into a war zone? Between you and these Scree things?'

She nodded, her face registering surprise at his ignorance.

'So this bad Uncle Mandrake, he's killed your family and taken over. What's that all about?'

'It's about power and evil,' Corriwen said. 'Mandrake is

evil and he wants power. I'm the last of the Redthorns and until I am dead, he can't be sure of the power. That's why he's hunting me. I'm sick of running and hiding all the time.'

She paused then quickly turned to look past Kerry into the dark forest. Jack saw her body tense, felt it in the tightening grip on his fingers.

'What's wrong?'

'Something's coming.'

'I hear it,' Kerry said.

Jack heard nothing at all. He sat still and listened. Then he heard it, a vibration in the air, so deep it was felt as much as heard.

'Thunder?' Kerry whispered. Corriwen Redthorn shook her head. The lightning had been far away, silent flickers in the night.

It came again and now Jack could hear it clearly. It did sound like distant thunder. Corriwen sat stock still. Her body was as tense as a bowstring.

Jack felt a shiver in the ground.

'Can you climb?'

He turned to her. 'Climb ...'

The rumble was louder, closer. The ground trembled, branches snapped underfoot.

Corriwen was on her feet in one motion, looking right and left. Jack heaved up, gasping against the ache in his chest. The satchel was in his hand. Kerry was beside him. He snatched up the backpack and drew his sword from the ground.

'What's happening?' Kerry asked. 'An earthquake?'

She moved fast, tugging at Jack's sleeve, pulling him

beyond the fire to a tree that might have been a beech.

'Climb,' she said urgently, pushing him towards the lowest branch. 'The beasts are running.'

Jack climbed. Kerry pushed him from underneath until he reached a thick bough then boosted the girl up and followed fast.

'Higher,' Corriwen ordered. '*Climb*. Up and up.'

The branches were so thick that climbing was relatively easy. Jack made it up one, reached another, felt her hands urging him on, until he was twenty feet above the forest floor. He stopped, panting. He could have done this in seconds only the day before. Now it drained him.

The tree began to tremble.

The first big animal thundered through a thicket, sending up a spray of leaves from under its hooves. It came towards the fire then veered away from the light. Jack caught a glimpse of jagged antlers spread so wide they would have spanned a room. One tine caught a reedy trunk and easily lopped it off in passing. They could hear the gasp of breath, see steam rising from its flanks as it ploughed on. Behind it a cluster of smaller deer scampered past and vanished into the shadows.

Another great beast lumbered, bawling, into the clearing. It was black as night with great scythe-shaped horns curving out on either side of its head, heavy enough to completely destroy the thicket as it crashed through. Behind it a whole herd came in a phalanx, smashing the thorns flat. Thick hides and heavy horns shuddered the tree they were in.

Something smaller came whipping out of the undergrowth, snickering in fear, and loped across the clearing straight through the fire. Sparks and embers fountained up. Flames caught dry leaves in seconds. A small bush burst into flames and a runnel of fire climbed a honeysuckle creeper. Smoke billowed towards them.

'Fire,' Jack said. He tugged at Kerry and pointed down. 'We have to get out of here.'

'You'll get squashed flat, man.' The big black bulls, if that's what they were, came on and on, churning up the deadfalls and leaf-litter, snorting in herd-panic, wheeling away when they smelt the smoke.

As soon as they had crashed past, leaving a trail of devastation and splintered trees, Corriwen began to move, hand under hand, back down the tree.

'There might be more,' Kerry said.

'There *are* more,' she said flatly. 'And you don't ever want to meet them.' She used one hand to point in the direction the big animals had fled. 'We follow them.'

'What's coming?' Jack asked. He really didn't want to meet whatever made those slavering, vicious noises out there.

'The Scree,' she said, already three great limbs below him, and moving with ease. 'They're scouring the forest. They want me, but they'll take you both, so climb down, Jack Flint. You're going to have to run.'

His heart sank. He had trouble enough walking.

'Come on, Jack,' Kerry said when they were on the churned ground. Where they had sat, the fire had taken hold of some fallen branches and flames were reaching up towards a thick pine. Already the scent of burning resin filled the air. Kerry snatched at his sleeve. 'I'm not ready to roast.'

They moved, following in the wake of the herd, with the howling too close behind them. The ground was soft, criss-crossed with logs and branches and trunks where they had tumbled. They got to a clearing and Jack had to stop for breath. He felt as if a vice held his ribs. Kerry was fidgeting with the need to keep moving. Corriwen dashed across the clearing, lithe as a cat.

As she ran, Jack saw a huge shape erupt from the bushes. It had a great flat snout and pairs of curving tusks all in a row. Red eyes glinted and hackles bristled, ridged along a humped back, behind a thick spiked collar. On its heels, a grey, manlike figure, squat and muscular, heaved at a length of chain.

The beast came charging at Corriwen, trying to catch her with its tusks. The handler grunted, a sound like stones grinding. Corriwen jinked in mid-step. Jack saw a flash and one of her knives was in her hand, but his mind was telling him it would do no good at all.

Before he knew it, he had the bow off his shoulder and an arrow nocked. The grey handler strode forward, slipped the leash and the tusker came lunging as Corriwen threw herself back, rolling over and over, inches from those wicked scythes. The handler, the Scree, raised a big wooden club edged with stone spikes.

'No!' Jack cried, leaping in as Corriwen tumbled desperately away. The motion caught the great hog's beady eye and it spun like a top, swung its ugly snout and one of its tusks sliced through the side of his jacket as he leapt aside.

The grey Scree raised his club, and brought it down on

Corriwen as she rolled. It missed, and hit the ground with a shattering thump and Kerry dashed in, slashing down with his sword with such force the haft of the club cut cleanly through.

The hog's momentum carried it past Jack into a thicket but it turned fast and came at him again. He raised the bow, drew back and let the arrow fly.

It caught the thing in the eye. It was purely an accident – *surely an accident*, Jack thought – but the shaft buried itself deep in that glittering red bead, right up to the black flight feathers.

The beast grunted, still running, its humped back powering up and down. It came straight towards him and Jack threw himself out of its path. It thundered past, five, six, seven steps then swerved madly and caught the handler with its leading tusk, scoring a gaping slice in his thigh. Then, before it could turn on them again, it flopped snout down into the churned earth and stopped moving.

The Scree roared. Two more appeared beside him, one wielding a long axe. The second held a club. They leapt into the clearing, converging on Jack. He tried to nock another arrow, but they crossed the distance in less than the blink of an eye. Close up he saw their broad warty faces under narrowing skulls, skin the texture of sandstone, and eyes so black they looked like holes into night. One snarled and brought its axe whistling down.

Jack saw it almost in slow motion, the torsion of thick shoulder muscles, the bulge of forearms. There was nothing he could do.

Then Corriwen was beside him, knives out. She was past him, arms a blur and out on the other side, light as a fawn and spinning like a ballerina.

Blood spurted from the Scree's belly. Jack saw two lines, one across the abdomen, another under a thick armpit, that opened like zips, and the creature staggered as the axe swung to the side, missing Jack's head by a scant inch.

It spun on, caught its companion on the knee. Bone crunched. Something flew into the bushes and the third creature looked down at its severed leg with an expression of dumb bewilderment. It tried to take a step forward and toppled sideways. The first one roared and came charging. Kerry caught it with a swipe of his sword and for a second or more it stood, shock plain on its ugly face. Its jaw was trying to work, but no sound came. From under its chin, blood drenched a studded leather jerkin and without a word it fell face-first into the dirt.

Corriwen spun again, stabbed her knife at the crippled creature that thrashed on the ground. It stopped thrashing.

'Move,' she said, 'if you want to live.'

They followed her. Jack glanced back and saw shapes blundering after them. When they reached a rise where rocks poked through, he stopped, gasping.

'Go on,' he urged Kerry and Corriwen. 'I'll never keep up.'

He fitted an arrow and put another two beside him. Even though he had never fired a bow until yesterday, the amberhorn felt right in his hand. He waited on one knee on the rise. Kerry hauled at him but Jack shrugged him off.

Below them, two Scree came running in with a huge dog

on a chain. It snarled and snapped, fangs jagged and white.

Jack took careful aim and planted a barb in the dog's chest. It howled, turned and savaged its handler, going for the throat. Jack let Kerry drag him along the track, manhandling him on behind Corriwen's running shadow.

A deer track made the going easier, but Jack's chest was aching, his ribs constricted so tight that every breath was like fire. He thought he could taste blood, but he forced himself on.

Then they were slip-sliding down a slope. Kerry fell, landed miraculously on his feet, shook his head and grabbed Jack's arm as if nothing had happened. Over the lip the slope steepened and they were not running any more, but sliding through thick, pulpy leaves. Ahead Jack thought he heard water, but his attention was on the sounds behind them.

They hit the flat, the three of them all in a tangle.

'It's the river,' Corriwen cried. 'Into the water. And don't stop.'

The water was cold, shallow but icy and they were out ten feet, fifteen feet before it started to deepen.

'Into the deep,' she cried. 'The Scree sink.'

Kerry jammed the sword through the loop of his belt. He was up to his waist, then up to his chest.

'I hate to say this,' he said. 'But I sink as well.'

SEVEN

Kerry began to thrash and gasp as the water came up to his neck and then he had no footing at all.

'Don't you let me drown!'

Jack, strength-sapped, struggled to hold him up but managed to get the backpack off. The waterproof canvas bobbed in the water and he forced Kerry's hands around it.

Behind them came thudding footsteps and that feral howling.

Corriwen was ahead of them, swimming through lily leaves an arm's-span wide. Underwater roots and stems tangled their feet, but Jack kept going, dragging breath into burning lungs.

A bloated frog noted their passing impassively. Slimy things wriggled around their legs. A dragonfly buzzed iridescent over their heads.

The current carried them downstream as they fought against it, struggling to get distance behind them. Corriwen reached the shingle bank fifty yards out from where they'd floundered into the river and crawled ashore on hands and knees, gasping and shedding water in silvered droplets. She turned as she got to her feet, waded back in and grasped Kerry's arm as he reached the shallows. Together she and Jack helped him to the bank just as the Scree and their beasts came crashing down the slope in a ferocious avalanche.

Without pausing, the first of the Scree lumbered down the bank. Here a slick of duckweed and algae covered the surface and it must have seemed like solid ground, because he didn't stop, but came straight towards them, spiked club raised high.

Then he suddenly disappeared beneath the surface without a sound.

The rest of the harriers skidded to a halt, dogs straining at the end of their leashes. One massive boar swung its head, gouging the ground. The Scree stood in a tight group, black eyes fixed on the water where the first one had gone in. Some bubbles broke through the surface, but there was no other sign of movement.

'They *do* sink,' Corriwen said, breathless. 'The water can't bear them. We're safer here.'

The words were hardly out of her mouth when the first arrow went singing like an angry wasp past Jack's ear. A second one tore at the hem of his jacket.

'We're too close,' Kerry blurted. 'We're sitting ducks.' A third arrow hit the shingle. Jack pulled Corriwen down.

'Over there.'

He pointed upstream where a tumble of boulders and dry logs met the oncoming current. Together they scrambled, keeping low, while a flight of arrows whipped past them into the water, or onto the pebbles. The rocks were only twenty yards away, but it felt like a mile. They threw themselves down in the lee as the arrows thudded into the logs, making them bristle like the hog's back.

'Great idea, Jack,' Kerry said, stifling a laugh. 'Into the river and nearly drown me and now the ugly bugs are trying to make a kebab out of me. If you've any more bright ideas, now's the time.'

'You could have stayed there,' Corriwen said. 'Rather the water than the wolves and bristlebacks.'

Another arrow thunked into the log where Kerry crouched. Its point was thin stone, razor-sharp. Kerry grinned. It was pure bravado. His freckles stood stark on skin gone white.

'Only kidding,' he said. 'I could be heaving greasy fish boxes instead of enjoying myself.'

Jack put a hand over his mouth to prevent a sudden laugh.

The Scree hunters fell silent, though the tethered animals snarled, still on the scent of quarry.

'We must get beyond bowshot,' Corriwen said, just loud enough to hear over the flow. She pointed across the deeper water. 'I think there's an island where we can shelter. The Scree can't follow us there.'

'We'll be trapped,' Kerry shot back. 'Then they'll send those big mongrels. The pug-uglies might sink, but there's no stopping those mutts.'

'They can send them here,' she agreed. 'We can fight the wolfhounds, but not with their arrows keeping us low.'

'We'll be safe enough here,' Kerry said.

'No,' Jack said. 'We have to get to the island.'

There was a pulse in his ears, a slow, muffled thud. Underneath it he could hear something else, a whispering sound that sent a shiver down his spine.

'I don't want to get back in the water,' Kerry muttered.

Jack shook his head, trying to clear it. 'You go out on fishing boats.'

'They've got freakin' great engines,' Kerry said. 'And lifejackets.'

'Just keep close to me,' Jack said. 'Pull one of these logs to the edge and hang on.'

He didn't know if he had the strength to keep himself afloat, but he promised Kerry they'd get to the island. They waded into the water. In three strides they were swimming against the flow, Corriwen and Jack holding Kerry while he clung to the log and floundered.

The crossing was only a hundred yards, but seemed to take hours and by the time they reached the cover of trees on the island, Jack was almost completely spent. He sprawled on the shale bank, and by sheer will-power, kept the darkness from sweeping over and through him. The whispering sound in his ears was louder now, like voices coming closer. There were no words, but he knew he had heard it before, in the freezing darkness that had flowed through Billy Robbins and into the Major's house.

He wondered if that black touch had infected his mind.

On the far bank, the troop of Scree lit a fire, content to

wait for light. The smell of something that could have been meat drifted on the night air. Kerry's mouth began to water.

'One of us will have to stay awake,' Corriwen said.

'They know we're here,' Kerry said, more cheerful now he was back on land. 'If they can have a fire, so can we.'

By the time the moon came out from behind the clouds, he had a good blaze going and had stripped down to his boxer shorts to let his clothes dry in the heat. He set about warming their last tin of beans, then helped Jack out of his jerkin and hung the plaid up on a branch by the fire.

'It'll smell like kippers in the morning,' he said, 'but you need to keep dry.'

He went off into the gloom to collect more firewood.

'Let me see your hurt,' Corriwen whispered after a while. She eased Jack's shirt back and gasped.

Black weals laced across his skin from the dark mass above his heart. In the faint light of the fire, they seemed to pulse and swell. She touched a finger to one of the inky tendrils. Jack moaned and she drew in another breath.

'It's cold, but you're burning up,' she said. 'I think you have a poison. In the blood. What caused this?'

'I don't know what it was,' he confessed. 'It was a dark thing. The Major called it the *banshee*. It ... it ... touched me.'

Corriwen placed a small hand on his brow, felt the clammy heat on it, so hot compared to the icy cold on the skin of his ribs. 'I have heard of this. It's an evil thing.'

'It hurts like all hell,' Jack groaned, as she softly touched the puckered skin.

'Wait,' she said, getting to her feet. She smiled at him, the first time she had smiled since they met, then disappeared into the shadows of the willows. He dozed off, feeling the darkness draw him into its depths, with those voices whispering insistently inside his head. The next he knew she was gently shaking him.

'Our mediciner would help,' she said. 'But he is dead, along with my brother and many good men. But I have watched him tend the wounded and the spellbound.'

The hood of her cloak was bunched full of leaves and roots and when she brought them together he smelt green sap and bitterness mixed with the honey scent of alyssum.

Corriwen began to cut them with one of her long knives. Jack pulled out his keyring and unhitched his little red Swiss Army knife.

'Use this. It's got lots of blades.' He showed her how they opened.

'I never saw the like,' she said, inspecting them all.

'Keep it then,' he said. 'I've got another penknife.'

Corriwen rinsed the empty beans tin at the water's edge, examining it with raised brows, then used two river-smooth stones to mash all the herbs together in a paste. She heated them over the glowing embers then came on all fours to Jack, put her hands to his shoulders and made him lie back.

'The Banshee bane,' she said. 'It has put the cold in you. I can feel it. I don't know of a cure, but this may help you for a while. You need time.'

'What is it, this bane?'

'It's the dark cold. The dark of the dead lands beyond Tir Nan Og. Those the banshee touch take the dark into themselves.'

She began to lay the stuff on his chest and he hissed at the pressure, but in a few minutes the hurt began to recede, enough so he could get a hold of it. He lay back, blinking against the tears that smarted in his eyes.

'You saved my life,' he said when he found his voice.

Corriwen bent in closely, green eyes searching his.

'No,' she said, 'this will not save you. It just eases the pain.' She touched him with gentle fingers. 'I don't know what will save you. Maybe you will fight it off yourself.'

'No,' Jack said. 'Not this.' The lessening of the pain was like a warm balm. It had waned to a size that he could wrestle with and the buzzing whisper in his head diminished to a faint hiss. 'Today in the forest, when those things came. You saved me.'

He closed his eyes and saw the scene again, when the Scree had swung the axe at him.

'It would have killed me, but you risked your life for me.'

She laughed. 'The Redthorns were taught to fight. The Scree are vile, but they are slow thinkers.'

Corriwen paused and held his eyes with hers and his fingers with her own. 'You have a good heart, Jack Flint. A heart worth saving. I saw it the first time I looked in your eyes. You wear your soul on your face.'

He didn't know what to say to that.

Across the water the Scree's campfire flared and they started chanting in low voices. He couldn't make out any words. Corriwen turned to look over the wide river.

'They have hunted me a long time,' she said.

Jack had heard that before, on the night Billy Robbins had come at them in the lane, before the darkness flowed into him. It seemed like a long time ago rather than just a day and a night.

'They seem awfully determined.'

'That's because I am a Redthorn. The people are slaves under Mandrake's Fomorian Scree. He fears that a Redthorn could unite them.' She laughed again, softly, but he heard the bitterness in it. 'I am alone now, with no one to help me.'

'We'll help you,' Jack said. 'If we can.'

She looked him up and down and he was very aware then that he was only thirteen.

'We make a great army, the three of us not full grown.' She paused, her face sad. 'Yet if I can find the Redthorn sword, there would be hope. It has led my people, the Dalriada, ever since we came here. It could free them and lead them again.'

The *Dalriada*. A name from the old legend books, the people of the West who lived before even the ancient Celts.

'And this sword, where is it?'

'My father died of poison. Mandrake stole it when he died. He took it and when he came back, he was rich.' Her mouth turned down. 'But he was mad. He was always a bad man, but when he came back, there was something else in him. I can't say what, it was as if he was possessed.'

'Sounds like a real bundle of laughs,' Jack said. He was holding the pain at bay now.

'He dabbled in old magic. I don't know what, but it's in him now. My father trusted him, but my brother said Mandrake found something in the scripts, something that turned him and infected him. Now he has brought his madness to Temair and I don't think anything can shake his grip.'

'It's very hard for me to take all this in,' Jack said. She sat while he explained how they had got here, through the ring of standing stones and he was surprised when she accepted his story without question. Compared to what she had told him, it didn't seem too fanciful now.

'What I don't understand is that I have heard of the Dalriada before. And Temair. And the Fomorians. But where I come from, they're just legends. Things that happened long ago.'

'What exists *exists*,' Corriwen said, dismissing his doubts with a shrug. 'There's magic in standing stones. Everybody knows that. Maybe you were magicked here.'

'Well, we have to magic ourselves out again,' Jack said. 'Tomorrow we have to get off this island.'

'The far river side is no escape,' she said. 'The whole of Eastern Dalria is Scree country now. And I don't know the lie of the land here in the east.'

Jack looked across the river where the troop was still chanting.

'They can't swim,' he said. 'That's good for us. But there's plenty of wood here. We can build a raft and get downstream if we start before it gets light. What's down from here?'

She shrugged. 'I don't know. I've never been this far on the Marches before. The river goes to the ocean, I'm sure.

75

Between here and the sea, I don't know what waits.'

'But we're stuck here,' Jack said. 'These things can wait us out. Better the devil we don't know.'

She looked at him oddly. 'I never heard that before, but it sounds right. The Scree are devils sure enough. Like Kerry says, they hit every branch on the ugly tree!'

Jack managed a smile. 'We can build a raft and let the current carry us,' he said. 'If we stay in the middle, they can't shoot us. After that, who knows? But we can't stay here.'

Corriwen clasped his fingers tight, then let go. Jack lay back against the bank and closed his eyes, grateful that the pain had ebbed enough to let him doze. When he woke at dawn, Kerry was cooking fish in the smoke from a fresh fire.

Jack started up, winced, groaned, lay down. The sparkle of the rising sun on the rippling water hurt his eyes and he squinted against the glare.

'We're too late—' he began. Kerry eased him down with a hand.

'Take it steady, Jack,' Kerry said. 'They're gone.'

Across the river there was no sign of the Scree or their beasts.

'But they'll be back,' Corriwen said. 'They will get word to Mandrake that they have us trapped.'

'That's what they think,' Jack said.

Kerry came across with big trout steaming on sticks. 'This river's full of them. They're jumping into my hands.'

They ate quickly and Jack managed to stand on shaky legs, shading his eyes against the glare. He wanted to be in shadow, but he fought against it, trying to clear his mind.

'We have to build a raft. We can use the rope.'

They gathered the dry boughs and some logs that had washed onto the island's upstream edge and worked on the shingle. They were lashing the logs when something caught Jack's attention. He turned to look. Smoke was rising high and black in a column way upriver.

'Is that a dam up there?' Kerry and Corriwen stood beside him, following the direction he was looking.

A broad shape, too even to be natural, was almost hidden by mist in the steep valley, ten, maybe fifteen miles upstream.

'Mandrake's Scree have the people working there, men, women and children,' Corriwen said. 'He plans to raise the river. He has them digging a channel from the high mountains of the Marches.'

'What's the point of that?' Kerry asked. 'Maybe it's for a generator or something.'

She looked at him, puzzled. Kerry didn't explain.

'Nobody knows,' she said. 'Mandrake has his own madness. He answers to no one. He has taken everything from us.'

It was almost noon when the raft was big enough to take their weight, lashed together with the rope they would have used to climb the wall into Cromwath Blackwood, and Jack insisted they build a wicket of woven hazel wands on either side. Out on the water, it would give them some protection from bowshots. Kerry cooked the last of the trout in broad river leaves and they sat around the remains of the fire, stoking up for the journey.

Jack opened the satchel and drew out the book. He opened it at the first page and the image of the two upright stones stood out starkly. He showed it to Corriwen.

'I have seen these stones,' she said. 'Not far from where my brother fell.'

'That's the gateway,' Jack said. 'Can you read the words?'

She shook her head. 'I don't know any gateway. Where does it lead?'

'Scotland.'

Corriwen looked blank. 'Is it far away?'

'Further than you'd think,' Kerry said, edging closer, sucking the last from a fishbone. He took an edge of the book, turned the page and as he did so an image began to materialise.

Corriwen watched, nodded in approval. 'You do have magic.'

'A couple of card tricks,' Kerry said. 'But this is the real thing.'

The image became clearer until they could see it was a picture of the river. Below it, letter by letter, the script emerged. This time, Jack could almost get a sense of the meaning, but Kerry drew a finger along them, mouthing the words.

Flee the quake of rainless thunder
Flee a forest torn asunder
Flee the beast and fight the foe
Flee to east and river flow
Storm behind and storm before
Ever harried, hunted sore
Ware the eye of roak and raven
Brave the thunder, find a haven.

'More mystery,' Kerry said.

'Not quite,' Jack said. 'I don't understand it all, but I get some of it. The thunder. We thought it was thunder last night, but it was those animals running. And they trampled half the forest.'

'Okay,' Kerry said. 'What's the good of a book that tells you where you've been? We want something to tell us where we're going.'

'I don't think that's it. I don't know how it works, but I think it *is* a kind of guide book. The Major said it was my father's, and he said it was important. I believe him. It was right about the gateway, and it could be right about the way home. We should pay attention.'

'So how does it work?'

'Magic, of course,' Corriwen said.

'Maybe,' Jack agreed, even though he wasn't sure he believed that. 'But it's odd. I never fired a bow in my life, but I shot a crow ... and then a boar.'

'And I never used a sword before,' Kerry said.

'We'll work it out somehow,' Jack finally said. 'Until then, I say we go with my father's book.'

They loaded the raft and punted into the current which quickly caught them in its flow and began to carry them downstream, far out from the thickly forested banks on either side.

'What's this river?' Kerry asked. 'And where does it go?'

'I think it's the Clydda,' Corriwen said. 'If so, it runs west, to the sea.'

'Good,' Jack said, 'the book says to follow the setting sun, so we head west, so that's where we're going. Have you ever heard of the Homeward Gate?'

She shook her head.

They'd been afloat for less than an hour when they spotted the Scree, grouped on a bank of shingle. Kerry saw them and roused Jack. He sat up slowly and saw them too.

'They must have worked out that we'd float down,' he said wearily. He knelt up, biting against the pain, trying to estimate the distance between the middle current and the end of the bank.

'They can reach us from there.'

'And we can reach them,' Kerry replied. He had piled some round stones, fist-size and smooth, on the front of the raft. He untied the sling from his waist, slid his right hand through the loop and tightened it on his wrist. He fitted a good stone into the woven basket and braced his feet.

The arrows came flying thick before they even reached the shingle and Jack pulled him down behind the wicket. Barbs thunked into the hazel weave and came right through, six inches and more, but the barricade deadened their force. The three of them huddled, letting the current take them past, and Jack prayed that the unguided raft wouldn't spin and expose them. Another volley came, six or seven arrows that hit altogether in a rip of sound and then Kerry was on his feet. He swung the sling twice, like a hammer-thrower, and sent the rock flying.

It caught one of the Scree on the temple and he dropped like an empty sack.

'What a shot!' Kerry bawled, amazed at his own accuracy. 'That's one for the good guys!' He ducked before the next volley came thudding into wood. Over on the bank the Scree roared as the river floated them past, drawing them out of range. Kerry raised his head over the wicket and motioned to Jack to look for himself.

One of the hunters had unleashed a great shaggy animal, more wolf than dog. It leapt straight into the water. A hail of arrows flew over its head, but only one reached the speeding raft. The rest fell yards short. The beast swam into the current and came in a diagonal towards them, gaining speed as the water carried it.

'Look at the teeth on that,' Kerry said. 'Can you shoot it?'

Jack unshipped the bow, but when he tried to draw the string, his arm had no strength. His fingers felt numb. The beast paddled straight towards them, head above the water, teeth like daggers.

81

Kerry slipped a stone into the sling and stood, holding the barrier edge. He let his arm fall back and snapped it forward overhand and the stone went flying. It cracked hard against the dog's muzzle, close to the eye. Blood spurted.

'Bullseye!' Kerry crowed. 'I wish I'd had one of these before.'

The animal took a mouthful of water. Blood blinded its eye and frothed in its nose. Kerry slung another stone that splashed inches in front of it, but didn't deter it in any way. He turned, gripped the handle of the sword he'd stabbed into one of the logs, raised it aloft.

'Come on then,' he yelled. They watched the animal get closer and closer, its one good eye blazing with anger.

Something pale flickered under the surface. Jack caught a glimpse of a shape in the rippling water, and the beast stopped dead. Its paws came up from the surface, pedalled for purchase in the air. The dog howled in sudden panic. It arched its back, tried to snap and its teeth came together like trap-jaws. The shape, two shapes now, rolled under the water and the dog disappeared. A flurry of bubbles pocked the surface.

'Did you see that?' Kerry stood with his sword in both hands, eyes wide and astonished. 'You see those things? They just grabbed it.'

'I saw something,' Jack said.

'It was big enough to take a wolf,' Kerry said. 'And you wanted me to swim in this? You must be freakin' crazy.' He spiked the sword back into the wood while Jack watched the river. Of the pale shapes and the big hound, there was no sign. When he looked back, Kerry had the backpack open and was blowing into one of the polythene bags.

'What are you doing?'

'I'm making water wings,' Kerry told him. 'Nothing's dragging me down into that.'

The shingle bank was well behind them as the river narrowed to fast water. The Scree were too far away to be any danger, for now. Jack leant back against the wicket. He opened his jacket just a little and breathed out slowly. The blackness had spread upwards towards his neck. He could feel it sapping the heat from him, pulsing in the capillaries under his skin. He closed his eyes and when he opened them again, Corriwen was beside him. She had saved the beans tin and again applied some of the paste she had made on the fire, fingers working gently, but no matter how light the touch, it sent daggers of hurt through him. A cold sweat broke out on his brow and the world wavered, like the shapes under water.

He was dreaming again.

Eyes followed him on a lurching flight through darkness. He was carried by something big and strong while behind them, over the broad shoulder, he saw wispy things flitting in the shadows.

He could hear the ragged breathing of whoever carried him, hugging him tight. He felt small and afraid and he could sense the fear in his bearer. The smell of new blood was thick on the air.

Then they were in moonlight and grey shapes towered on either side. Colours whirled and spangled and he cried out at the strange feeling that swept through him and twisted in his belly.

Then the staring eyes were gone, and the colours too, and he was on the ground, in daylight, while all around him stood ...

'The standing stones!'

Jack was suddenly aware that he was not in the dream. But for the first time in his life, he recognised part of it. The massive grey shapes could only have been the standing stones in Cromwath Blackwood. Yet he had never seen them until he and Kerry had fled from the horror in the tunnel.

Or had he?

That recurrent nightmare had been with him as long as he could recall, and now he knew it had to be a memory of *something*.

Had he come through before? Who had carried him?

He had no answer to any of it, but the Major's words echoed in his mind, 'I can't rightly say, and that's the truth. You were just a baby when you were brought here. All I can say for now is your father was a good man with a good heart.'

He'd been a baby when he was brought to the Major's house. And the Major said he didn't know where Jack's father had gone. But he *did* know about the standing stones in the forest, and he had warned Jack to stay away. He must have known where the tunnel led. He had to know more.

And that made it all the more urgent for Jack to get himself and Kerry to the Homeward Gate, wherever that was, and find their way back. He had a lot of questions to ask.

Kerry sat at the back of the raft, eyes fixed on the river. Wherever they were, wherever this Temair was, Jack was glad Kerry was with him, and the red-haired girl with the twin knives. He was glad of their strength, and he knew he had two friends on this raft. With two friends, he'd surely find a way home.

Corriwen put a hand on his forehead, wiped away the beads of perspiration. She spoke softly to him as the miles passed. Dry lightning flickered in the sky and ahead of them clouds piled up as Kerry steered the raft, scanning the water all the time in case any of the things-that-could-drag-a-wolf-under-the-water reappeared.

The roaks came from the towering cloud, black wings spread wide to spiral down from the glowering sky. They heard them first. Kerry pointed.

'We saw them on the hill,' he said. 'They were eating the ...' He stopped abruptly and looked at Corriwen, face reddening.

'Slaughter-pickers,' she said. 'They fed well.'

'Watch them,' Kerry told her. 'They go for your eyes.'

The lead bird swung ahead of them, turned and came in over the water. It darted at Kerry's head. He raised the pole and swatted it, sending a few black feathers tumbling on the air. Another one, much larger, came beating in and Kerry jerked back. It was the same bird with no eyes, just dripping craters where eyes would have been, but it came unerringly, straight for his face. Jack was slumped on the logs, too numb to move now. Corriwen leapt up, hauled the sword and swung it in a tight arc. It missed the bird by a hair.

In mere seconds they were surrounded by the black birds. Kerry swung the pole and caught another in mid-flight and sent it splashing helpless in the water. The others wheeled towards the bank and turned, a flock of monstrous, malevolent proportions. Kerry shoved Corriwen down behind the barrier and got ready to take as many of them as he could.

Something flicked from the water, so fast it was a blur. The lead crow, big as a buzzard, simply disappeared without a sound. Something else stabbed upwards and Kerry couldn't tell whether it was a tentacle or a fish. Another movement flicked in his peripheral vision. Two roaks vanished and a puff of feathers helicoptered into the water.

Kerry stood open-mouthed, unable to comprehend what he'd just seen.

The flock swerved, trying to gain height, and in another blink, three more of them were down. The rest whirled back towards the trees, panicked.

'What was that?' Kerry finally said. Corriwen crouched beside him. 'Did you see it?'

She nodded. 'I don't know, but ...'

'I don't like the look of this,' Kerry said. He hadn't liked the look of anything since they'd stumbled between the standing stones. 'We'd better get to land.'

'We don't know what's in the forest,' she said.

'But there's things in the water,' Kerry protested.

A grumble of thunder rolled around them.

'It's like the book said,' Jack said. 'The Roaks and ravens. It said watch the thunder. We have to get off the river.'

The rumble continued, louder than before.

'It's the lightning that worries me,' Kerry said. 'We shouldn't be out in the middle.'

'Pull in,' Jack told him. 'See if you can steer towards the trees.' He wasn't sure if they'd be safer there than on the water. He tried to remember what was best. At least there would be shelter under the branches.

The rumbling increased as Kerry poled in, fighting the current. The sound snagged Jack's mind. It was getting louder all the time, but he realised he hadn't seen any lightning.

With a huge effort, he forced himself up.

'Move!' he managed to say. 'It's not thunder.'

Kerry turned at the prow. 'What?'

'No lightning. It's not thunder. We have to get off.'

'What is it, then?' He had the pole in the water. The raft lurched and almost threw him out. In a matter of seconds they were carried down to where the river narrowed between high rocky banks and the flow was suddenly much faster as they were whipped round a curve.

Ahead of them the rumbling became a roar. Water-smooth boulders jutted out from the flow.

'Not thunder,' Jack said. 'Rapids!'

'Oh *heck*!'

Kerry dug the pole in, trying to force them towards the bank, but it was too late. White water splashed up from the rocks and the raft spun in a circle. Kerry grabbed the backpack and the water-wings and then cursed very sincerely when he saw the rip in the polythene bag which fluttered uselessly in his hand.

The raft spun dizzyingly. The roaring ahead was now so loud they could hear nothing else. Jack got to his knees. Down there in the dark of the gorge, he could see a mist over the river.

'Oh Kerry,' he gasped. 'It's not rapids at all.'

'Great,' Kerry grinned, relief clear on his face. 'You had me scared for a minute.'

'*It's a waterfall.*'

Jack pointed. The turbulent water rolled past huge boulders and crashed against the banks. But beyond that a misty cloud blocked the entire gorge.

'What is that?' Kerry asked. 'Smoke?'

The raft spun again and they hung on, and with every yard the thunder got louder until it filled the world. The canyon walls shivered and the vibration loosened stones that tumbled and rolled to crash into the river.

Jack grabbed Kerry's shoulder. He had to shout right into his ear to be heard.

'Not smoke. It's spray.'

Kerry looked back at him, not understanding.

'It's not *just* a waterfall . . .'

The river suddenly widened and the great falls came into view. Half a mile downstream, the river simply disappeared into a vast emptiness, and they could see nothing at all.

It was as if the very world ended here.

The blood drained from Kerry's face. He rummaged in the bag for the thick line he used for poaching salmon. A big weight and a treble hook were whipped to one end. Very quickly he unravelled the line, looped one end around a log and used all his strength to cast it at the nearest bank. The hook and weight sailed out towards where the trees dipped their roots into the water.

The weight jerked in mid-air as if it had hit a glass wall. The line was too short.

'I think we're in bad trouble,' was all Kerry said, though his words were lost in the roar. He braced himself on the logs as the raft swung like a pendulum, both hands round the haft of the sword, knuckles white.

'Jack!' Jack could only see his lips move, but he recognised the words. 'Don't you let me drown!'

'I won't let you drown,' he murmured uselessly. They were in the boil now, bouncing up on the flow and over great rocks, twisting and turning helplessly in the river's grip.

The edge came closer and closer. Jack gripped Kerry by the shoulder. The sound was impossible.

Then suddenly they were flying.

Jack saw a flash of sunlight stab the mist and a sparkling rainbow curved in front of him, so bright and clear it shone like jewels. The raft hit a rock. Something splintered and Jack went flying. He saw Corriwen catapult into the air, flex like a gymnast and straighten, soaring like a swallow through that rainbow. Kerry was tumbling head over heels.

Jack flipped behind him and then there was a lurch in his stomach as he began to fall, down through the mist towards the waiting rocks.

EIGHT

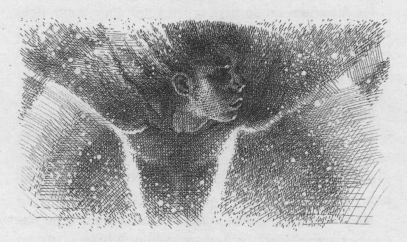

He saw Corriwen arc through the rainbow, body straight as an arrow, arms spread like wings. The colours coruscated around her in dazzling shards and then she was gone. A dim part of Jack's mind was aware that her graceful slow curve through the colours was the most beautiful thing he had ever seen.

Then Jack fell.

He was tumbling inside the deafening roar, pummelled by the falls, gasping for breath when there was no breath to be had. He closed his eyes in sheer fright at the certainty of jagged rocks below, saw himself broken and bloodied in the backwash of the flow. He tried to fight the force of falling water, prepare himself for the end. His eyes opened involuntarily and he saw Kerry plummet past, mouth open in a soundless cry, his sword clenched hard in his hand.

'Drop it—' Jack blurted, but the river foamed into his mouth. Kerry disappeared from view and was gone. Jack fell and it seemed he fell forever.

He hit water, hit so hard it felt solid. Pure white light exploded behind his eyes before everything went dark, and he felt nothing at all. He knew he was dead. There was no sound, no cold, no heat, no light. There was no pain.

For a long time, he floated in that limbo.

Then, as abruptly as if a light had been switched on, he was aware again. He was rolling in the water and the force of it punched him down, down into swirling depths. He gasped for air, coughed the last from his lungs, feeling the huge pressure on his chest and in his ears.

He felt rock and gravel under his feet and knew he was on the riverbed in a world of grey-green. A billion galaxies of bubbles swirled in front of his eyes and pain tore him from shoulder to hip.

The water held him, tumbling him over and over like a cork and then, all of a sudden, he was out of its grip, rolling through the undertow.

He saw Kerry then. He saw the sword first, a glimmering line of brightness in the deep, and then he saw Kerry's trailing legs.

Don't you let me drown.

He had promised Kerry.

Don't you let me drown.

He had promised.

Drop it, he tried to say again, tried to will Kerry to loosen his grip on the sword. Water went into his throat and up his nose and that jerked him out of his paralysis. The sword was dragging Kerry down like an anchor, pinning him to the riverbed. Jack pushed against the rocks, feet sliding on the smooth surface before he got purchase and heaved upwards, lungs bursting, muscles tearing in their own little world of hurt.

For a moment he lost sight of Kerry in the swirling mass of bubbles. A cry of desperation sent the last of his air bubbling up and then he saw him in the water, waving like a rag caught on a nail.

He reached, grabbed, missed, tried again and found a handful of hair. His fingers clenched on it and he pushed up, kicking with both feet.

They rolled out of the undertow and into a deep blue. Far above sunlight heliographed rods of light all around them. Jack kept hauling, gripping Kerry's hair, trying to reach the surface as the world spun from dark blue to deeper dark and just as complete exhaustion and lack of oxygen began to overtake him, he saw something swim towards him.

His heart was pounding so hard in his chest it could have punched through his ribs, but he was too exhausted to feel any more fear. The shape came closer, turning smoothly with the flow and he saw a face, wavering turquoise. Long hair spread like river weed in a halo around it.

It's a body, Jack thought. A dead body.

Then it turned, and green eyes swum close to him as arms reached for him. He held Kerry's hair in a death grip as the eyes fixed on his. The hands that touched his face were as cold as the river. Cold lips touched his and the eyes sucked him into their depths.

The whole strange world, the river, the waterfall, Kerry and everything faded away.

NINE

He sat brooding in Midthorn Keep on the high wooden chair that had long served as the Chief's seat. The Redthorn seat.

The man who was once Cadwill and was now known as Mandrake rested one thin elbow on a carved arm where gargoyles and snakes entwined in a polished embrace. His eyes, black as coal in a greying face, were hooded and his mouth turned down, carving deep lines on either side. He was shaking with a fine rage, trembling like a harp string wound tight. The bearskin robe around his shoulders shivered in a dark-spiked harmony.

The stone walls of Midthorn Keep threw his anger back into the hall as if it had weight of its own, making the air tense and solid. Around the walls, staying close to the shadows, eyes watched, but no one spoke. All heads were down, or turned away.

Mandrake tried to speak, but his throat was locked by his fury and all that came out was a click and a gasp. Finally he managed it.

'You lost them.' His words echoed from the stone. 'You lost *her*!'

Two Scree stood in front of him. One of them shifted his weight from foot to foot. In this light their skin looked like dried fish scales.

'They took down to the river,' the Captain said, his voice like shingle on a tide-washed beach. 'We flushed her out in the forest. Herself and two pups with her. Human boys. They fought.'

Mandrake's brows came down. The furrows deepened on either side of his mouth. Even in the corners those watching could hear his teeth grind.

'Oh, they *fought* you.' Sarcasm oozed like poison. 'See if I have this correct.'

He pointed a bony finger. The nail was long and yellow.

'And correct me if I'm wrong,' he said, in a tone loaded with menace. Everybody there knew he meant *if you dare*.

'So. Brave soldiers. Here was a troop of you, fully armed, and with your hounds and bristlebacks. Am I right?'

The Captain nodded slowly.

'And you heroic warriors meet a girl and two boys in the forest, and they *fought* you.'

Another nod. The Scree scratched his ridged brow with a horny hand.

'That's the way it were, m'Lord.'

96

'And these *children*, tell me, did they fight well? Did they fight like *soldiers*?'

The Scree scratched again, as if he could hook the memory out with his nail.

'They killed a tusker,' he growled. 'Bowed it dead. An' two troopers. It was dark and they had the 'vantage on us.'

'Of course, soldier. I imagine they did,' Mandrake said, very softly. Along the walls, behind the pillars that stretched into the darkness above, figures crowded closer together, each trying to stay out of sight. They had heard Mandrake's voice take on that silky quality before. It was like the stillness in the air before lightning strikes. And Mandrake could strike like a viper. His voice was low, almost kindly now. But they knew it would rise with his anger until the walls started to shiver.

'A girl ...' he said, 'and two boys. That would have been a *big* advantage.'

'We never expected them to fight, m'Lord. Just cubs, they were.'

'Just cubs, lost in the forest and then you lost them. You lost *her*. A full season you've been scouring moor and hill and when you find her,' he raised his hand, waggled his fingers, ' ... you let her slip away.'

'They reached the river, Lord Mandrake,' answered the other Scree. A black sword, jammed in a shoulder scabbard, stuck like a cross above his head. His arms were like beech roots, grey and gnarled. The black eyes under his narrow forehead flickered left and right, wilting under Mandrake's anger. 'They reached the river and one trooper drowned. He went in and never came up again.'

'Good for him,' Mandrake said. 'You should all have drowned if you knew what was right.'

He walked round the back of the high chair. The walls here were festooned with spears and lances and shields and swords, spoils of battle. On the stone behind the chair, the new flag stretched from side to side, red on black, a red dragon with the man's face. The mark of Mandrake.

'So, tallowfingers. You let them *slip*. What happened next? Tell me. *Tell me.*'

'They reached an island in the river. It was too deep to cross.'

Mandrake froze. He took a slow breath. When he spoke his voice was like broken glass. 'Did you *try*? Did you cut a tree and build a *bridge*? A *raft* perhaps?'

The Fomorian gulped. It hadn't crossed his mind. The Scree avoided water, except for the melt that came down from the snows high on the Scree Crags.

'The flow were too strong, Lord Mandrake. We sent a wolfhound after them, but a fish ate it. Up from the water and ate it.'

'So, I understand that despite your orders, you let her go because of a bit of water and a . . . a . . . *fish*?'

The Fomorian hung his head and shrugged his brawny shoulders, making the chain mail rattle on the scabbard. He shuffled on his feet, one foot to another, visibly withering. Beside him, his second in command growled.

'They lashed logs and floated away.'

'Of *course* they lashed logs and floated away.' Mandrake's voice was rising now. The blade was sharpening. 'Of *course* they did. Because they *thought* about it. The idea *occurred* to them. They used their *brains.*

'And you?' He rounded on the second man. 'What have you got inside that ugly Scree skull of yours? Maggots? Faggots? Sawdust and sand?'

'I can't swim,' the Scree grunted.

Mandrake looked as if he would choke. His pale face went beetroot red and all the veins in his temples stood out. He leant against the wall, both hands gripping the stone as if he wanted to tear it down. His finger found the lip of one of the old shields and he snatched it down.

'I would have drowned,' the Scree said.

Everything in the hall went quiet. Mandrake shuddered, like a volcano set to erupt. He spun the shield in both hands. It came down like a hammer on the head of the Scree trooper. The boss caught him square on the forehead.

The Scree blinked, staggered back, raised a hand to his forehead where a gash suddenly appeared and began to fill with blood. Mandrake raised the shield again, jumped both feet off the floor and brought it down with such force the Scree's knees buckled. The black eyes widened so far they looked as if they would pop out. Beside him, the leader's hand darted automatically to the sword on his back.

A groan went up from the observers around the walls.

Mandrake dropped the shield with a clang. The Scree sank to his knees and then, in slow motion, tumbled forward to hit the flagstones head-first with the sound of a hammerblow.

Mandrake turned away, almost casually, reached the wall again, raised one hand and gripped the pommel of a broadsword. The observers shrank deeper into the shadows. Mandrake whirled and caught the Scree Captain between shoulder and chin. His grey head spun off and thumped to the floor.

The Scree lifted his hands to where his head should have been.

Mandrake watched, eyebrows raised, his colour fading after the exertion, but still shaking as if a little earthquake were running through him.

The Scree's fingers dabbed at where his face once was. Blood flowed down his squat chest. Under the table, the mouth on his head opened and closed, eyes fixed on Mandrake, who cocked his head, as if caught now by something of passing interest.

Very slowly, the Scree's knees gave. More blood spilled from the pulsing hole between his shoulders. Under the table his head groaned loudly.

High above, where small windows drew light in across the rafters, there was a scrabbling sound, then a faint swish of wings. A black bird circled down, fluttering in the beam.

'Oh my,' Mandrake finally said. He touched the head with the toe of his shoe. 'As I thought, no brains at all. But they do take a lot of killing, what d'you think?'

No one responded. No one dared.

The roak alighted on the back of the high chair, opened its beak, turned its head from side to side. Its eye sockets gaped. It fixed a sightless gaze on Mandrake.

Mandrake cocked his head, much in the way he'd looked with fascination at the headless Scree, and then he twitched. He turned slowly and the watchers in the shadows saw the colour of his eyes change from black to red. His skin took on a greyer hue, as if shadows were rolling underneath the surface. His eyes seemed to shrink under the eaves of his brows until they could not even be seen.

'*Lost them.*'

The voice that issued from his mouth was not Mandrake's. The watchers edged further back. He was changing again, and when he did that, it was a fearful thing. He twitched spasmodically, as if touched with disease or pain. The blind roak's claws scuttered on the high chair. Light faded and darkness swelled in the air.

'*Lost them.*' Mandrake's voice was a rasping croak. He swung his head, grimacing.

'*Lost them. Lost them.* Fools. *Fools!*' He twitched as if a fly had buzzed near his ear.

'*Lost the girl and lost* him*!*'

The roak hunched silent, black and motionless.

His face contorted, became Mandrake again. 'I've hunted her a whole season.'

'*She has* eluded *us that long,*' the grating scrape of voice came again. His face twisted and ran like wax, mirroring the alteration in timbre and tone. '*Us and those creatures I harnessed.*'

Another ripple moved across his skin. 'We will catch her.'

'*You catch her,*' he scraped. '*You catch* him. *He's the one that we want. He carries a thing I need.* Bring him.'

'He's only a boy. What's his worth to us? Who is he?'

'*An old enemy,*' the voice said. '*Old, but we remember him and his kind. Now is our day for revenge. My roak eyes followed* them down the river, but they fought. Children. Mongrel pups and they fought your Scree and my roaks. Fought and killed. And they had help.'

'Help?' Mandrake asked. 'Who helps them?

'That we cannot see. But they will suffer. Send your Scree. Like locusts. Burn every bush, every tree. Turn every stone. Smell them out, sniff them out. Burn them out. Smoke them out. Spell them out. But take them and bring him!'

Mandrake cocked his head. 'What do we want him for? A boy, my Scree say. Two worthless boys.'

'Two boys and a girl,' the hag voice came back. 'Bound together for what we don't know, but he carries a key and I will have it. I will lay his kind waste and rule all worlds.'

There was a long pause. 'And you will have your spoils.'

'The girl,' Mandrake said. 'I must have the girl.'

'She is nothing to us save that she stands between you and the seat, so long as she walks. But she is bound to them now. I can feel it.'

His shoulders narrowed, hunched. Shadows hollowed his face. 'Trust me, man-draco. I have given you riches. I have given you power. I will give you more, and you will rule this Temair and all its lands. But bring me that pup. I smell fate here. At the crossing of two roads. I feel his touch. I will have him.'

The voice rose, sharp, brittle as ice. 'Muster the Scree. We send the roaks flying tonight. They will show us where.'

Mandrake straightened and the gloom that had filled the room began to lift. His features began to ease and swell back to what they had been before. His hunched form unfolded until he stood beside the high seat, one arm on the backrest. The roak cawed and took off, a whirr of black, up and out of the window and the shadow that had entered the room with the bird evaporated.

Mandrake leant on the chair back, breathing hard.

When he opened his eyes again, the red light was gone.

'Get me the Captain of the Marches,' he screamed. 'Get him to me *now*!'

TEN

J ack was lost in a darkness deeper than night. It swirled around him and through him and he felt his whole being shatter into a million pieces.

Pale faces swam close to him, eyes green as deep sea and hands as cold as death, smooth as marble caressed him and clung to him, taking him down even further.

He saw the ring of standing stones on a bleak and barren moor. A great bird perched on each and the monstrosity had craters where its eyes should be, yet somehow able to see right into his soul and he knew he was watched by something hellish.

Across the moorland ogres marched, bearing clubs, spears, jagged swords, the tramp of their feet so pervasive it was like the booming of a vast heart.

He flew above them, soaring with the huge ravens, as an

awful cold speared him and froze his heart, up in the frigid air above the fields of slaughter.

From this height he could see a wooden dam across a river, where men and women toiled under the lash of the grey ogres. Beyond the dam, the waters were already pooling in a lake that reached the hills. There a chasm was cut into bare rock on the edge of a desert.

He flew forever, surrounded by the carrion birds, until he came to a low black hill in the centre of this salt desert.

He tried to stop, will himself away, but he was carried remorselessly towards the black tor.

From there, dark spread, inexplicably evil, palpable with threat, cracking the salt flats into fissures from which night-things scuttled, grey bats flew in clouds, worms and maggots emerged to trail slime.

A presence called to him, dragging him with the force of its will, and he tried to fight it.

But there was no fighting it.

Come to me.

A crumbling hole appeared in the side of the mound.

He could sense a shadow within a shadow, reaching hungrily for him.

Bring me the key.

He tried to cry out.

Images danced inside his head, unbidden, unwanted.

He saw a golden sword thrust deep into a black stone. On its surface lay the plucked eyes of a bird.

A voice scraped on his brain, and he jerked back.

And another voice called his name.

It came from far away, but he held on to the sound.

Jack ... *Jack* ...

He thought he knew the voice, remembered it from long ago.

Jack!

The call was distant, but clear. It was deep and resonant. Jack felt its pull, turning him away from what waited in the dark.

Ahead of him was bright light, and a tall silhouette framed in its glare. He could see no features, just the shape of a man, one arm raised.

'Come back to the light,' the man called.

The hateful web snaring his mind began to loosen and the hideous touch faded as he felt drawn towards the man. He still couldn't see the face, but he knew who called him. It had to be his father.

Jack ran towards him.

'Jack man! Oh Jack, I thought you were a goner.'

Kerry's voice. Tight and agitated.

His vision cleared and he turned his head. Blue eyes held him and for a moment he was completely confused.

'Ah, so you've decided to join us.'

A warm hand came down on his brow, lightly, like the touch of a feather.

'Lie a while, son,' the stranger said. 'You're out of the water, but you've a way to go before you're out of the woods.'

The hand skimmed his hair back, cupped the back of his head and raised it slowly.

'Not in great shape, are we?' The voice reminded him of the way the Major spoke.

'I lost him,' Jack managed to gasp. There was water still in his lungs; he could feel it crackle deep inside. 'He said *"don't let me drown".* I . . . I promised him.'

He tried to sit up.

'And I lost her,' he muttered. Tears sprang to his eyes and flowed down his cheeks.

'Easy, young fellow. You've been down in the dark a while. And don't you worry.'

He felt another touch, hot and shaky on his shoulder and when the tears blinked away he saw Kerry's face. And beside him Corriwen Redthorn's green eyes, full of concern and misery battling relief and joy.

'Jack man,' Kerry said. 'We really thought you were a goner.'

'You were down in the water,' he started to say. 'How . . .'

'Nearly scalped me,' Kerry said, grinning through his own tears. 'I'm lucky I've any hair left.'

'How did you get out? How did we . . .' Jack coughed and the last of the water came out.

'Ah,' the stranger said. 'That would be my friends, the Undine. You got them in good humour today and I was expecting company. They can lift you up or take you down.'

'Remember the wolf?' Kerry said. 'I thought it was a fish that took it.'

'No trespassers in this water,' the stranger said. 'They don't like those Scree, nor their beasts.'

He began to turn away to where a fire glowed in the corner. 'Let's get some soup in you, take the chill out.'

Jack looked from Kerry to Corriwen.

'He says they're water spirits,' Kerry explained. 'I swallowed half the river and never saw them. When they shoved you out, you still had me by the hair. I had to get a stick to loosen the grip.'

'I saw them,' Corriwen said. 'They were green. And beautiful. And fast. I've heard of Undines, but I never thought they were real.'

'Oh, they're real all right,' the stranger said. 'Them and the kelpies of the seashore, though you want to keep away from them. They're hungry all the time, and they'll take man and horse both, given the chance.'

He brought over a bowl of steaming soup. Jack sipped the broth and tasted some kind of spicy meat. It brought heat back into his bones.

'Just take a sip at a time, 'til you get your breath.' The man sat on the edge of the bench where Jack lay under a coarse blanket. They were in a low-roofed house. The walls were bare stone, with ledges crammed with bottles and bags and pottery jars.

'You did a good job, holding your friend in the water. His head's going to ache a day or two, but it could have been a whole lot worse.'

'He wouldn't let go,' Jack said between mouthfuls. 'His sword. It dragged him down.'

'Yeah,' Kerry said, unable to keep the grin off his face. He had wiped the tears away with his knuckles, but his eyes were still red. 'I never even knew I was still holding on, for all the difference it makes. I swim like a brick.'

Corriwen was still holding Jack's hand, warm and close. Her eyes searched his and he could see she had been crying too.

'I didn't want to lose you,' she whispered.

'Your friends tell me you're hurt,' the man said.

Jack nodded, swallowed drily.

'I can smell it on you, and it's not good. I'd best take a look. Maybe we have something here that can help.'

'Oh, and by the by, you can call me Finbar.' He wore a sheepskin jerkin, with the fleece inside, and a sort of leather cap and a long cloak of small animal pelts stitched together. 'There're a few other names to go alongside it, that were given to me a while back but you'll never get your tongue around them.'

'You live here?'

'Sure I do.' Finbar smiled. 'I'm the Bard of Undine Haven.'

'The Bard?' Corriwen asked, almost reverently.

He nodded. 'That's me. And don't worry about those foul things that were hunting you. This here's a hidden place. There's a *geas* on our haven.'

He smiled again. 'Know what a *geas* is?'

'I've read about it. In tales of Cuchulainn,' Jack said. 'Some sort of spell, isn't it?'

'Right.'

Brave the thunder, find a haven. The book hadn't warned of an impending storm. It had predicted the vast waterfall. And they hadn't so much braved it as just fallen over. It was a miracle they weren't dead.

'Those things and the demon that's unleashed them, can't see here,' the Bard said. 'But I knew they were looking for something, so I presume it must be you.'

'Mandrake wants me,' Corriwen said.

'That I believe, Corriwen Redthorn.'

'You know my name?'

'Of course I know your name. I was there at Redthorn Keep on the night you were born. Can't have a birth without a Bard. Not a Redthorn birth.'

'But how . . .' she began.

'There's a story long in the telling. I know about your uncle and his mad ways, and it's almost time to do something about it. The Bards have been waiting for a sign, and I reckon you and these two lads, you're it.'

She looked at him, puzzled.

'All's not lost. Not when there's a Redthorn left and a sword to be found. We know the old foretellings, we do, and they come true, sooner or later, and better late than never at all, eh? But I tell you, you'll have a fight on your hands, and I hope you're up to it.'

'I have to do something,' she said grimly. 'My brother is dead on the field. Dead by a traitor's hand. Someone will pay. Mandrake will pay.'

He looked her in the eyes. She was such a slight figure. Jack watched the two of them and he saw the resolute set of her jaw. Just what she had been through he couldn't imagine, and his heart swelled with admiration at her courage.

Finbar patted her shoulder lightly. 'Time for plans and explanations later,' he said. 'This here lad's squirming. Let me sort his trouble first, then we'll sit and gnaw the bone.' He was bending over Jack now, pulling back the blanket, easing open the leather jerkin.

'Oh *my*,' Finbar said when he finally pulled the shirt aside. Even the touch of the air felt like acid on Jack's skin.

'Jeez,' Kerry whispered, aghast. Corriwen said nothing. The dark mass on Jack's chest had expanded, reaching up his neck and over his shoulder.

'How on Temair did this happen?' Finbar asked. Jack tried to speak, but exhaustion and cold had worn him down. Kerry had to speak for him. He told their story from beginning to end.

'The Banshee touch,' the Bard said. 'The darkness of the damned and the lost. Grows in you like fungus. Sucks the good out, brings the bad in. You're a tough young man to have come this far – tough and lucky.'

'What's the Banshee touch?' Kerry asked.

'It's the hate from the dark world. Beyond Tir Nan Og, the land of the Fair. It's the terrible place. And that touch, it's been put there for a reason, no doubt. I'll have to give that some thinking time when we're done.'

Finbar turned away and spent some time at the hearth. Kerry tracked him with his eyes, but Jack couldn't move his head. Finbar came back and bent over him. He lifted the heartstone on its chain and examined it carefully before placing it to the side of Jack's neck.

'This won't be easy, young Jack,' he said. 'I'm telling you now. But we must get that dark out of you before it swallows you up and takes you to a place you'll never leave.'

Jack had no idea what he was talking about. He nodded weakly.

'Here,' the Bard beckoned Kerry and Corriwen. 'Be good friends to him now. Each take a wrist in both hands and hold it tight.'

They did as they were told. Kerry felt the cold seep from Jack's skin into his own. Corriwen's face was set. The Bard took a length of hide, wrapped it around Jack's knees and secured it to the boards of the bench. He brought a piece of leather, thick as the heel of a shoe and jammed it between Jack's teeth.

'Is this some kind of trick?' Kerry wanted to know.

'Something like that.' Finbar turned to the fire and when he came back he held a flat slab of obsidian stone between two metal hooks. It was dark, but translucent to a degree, like a black jewel. Heat came off it in waves.

'Fireglass,' he said. 'Made in the heat of the ground below. Now you pair hold tight. Don't let go.'

Without another word, he placed the stone right on the centre of the spreading black pulsation on Jack's chest.

Jack screamed.

As soon as the hot slab touched his skin pain lanced through him, unlike anything he had ever experienced before. His back arched against the thongs and his teeth bit down so hard on the leather that his jaw almost cracked.

'*Jeez* man,' Kerry screamed. 'What are you doing to him?' He could smell burning flesh, hear the sizzle as the hot stone seared Jack's white chest.

'Hold him now,' Finbar's voice was calm but firm. 'Hold him tight.'

Jack screamed again, his whole body quivering like a taut wire. Sweat beaded on his forehead and dripped down past his ears. The sound of that scream made the walls rattle and the jars on the shelf quiver in sympathy.

Kerry burst into tears, but he held on as Jack bucked and writhed on the bench. Corriwen's grip never slackened.

'Fireglass,' the Bard said. 'Faerie tears. It swallows the light, or the dark. Takes the heat, or the cold. Sucks the bad from the good. Let it do its work.'

Jack's friends hung on as if their lives depended on it. They took the Bard's word that Jack's life certainly did.

'He's had enough,' Kerry sobbed. 'You'll kill him.'

'Kill or cure,' the Bard said, under his breath. 'Without a cure that poison will take him to itself.'

They held on and held on and Kerry expected to see the hot black stone burn its way through flesh and bone, but despite that he did not lose his grip. All he could feel was the tremor as if jolts of electricity were surging through his friend.

After a while the Bard took a thick hank of material that might have been linen, soaked it in a bucket of water and used it to lift the stone away. Steam hissed and billowed in clouds around him. He put the slab down on a stool, soaked the cloth again, and put it on Jack's forehead. Where the obsidian block had pressed, the skin was bubbled and blistered. But even as Kerry watched, the swelling began to subside.

'If fate's with us, we've brought him back,' Finbar said. 'How he managed to keep going so long's a mystery to me. He's got a big heart.'

He had hardly finished the sentence when Jack moaned. He pulled on their hands and the Bard motioned them to let him up. He slumped over the edge of the table and retched a stream of black bile.

'He'll clear himself out now,' Finbar said. 'The fireglass has burned the sick out of him.'

He wiped Jack's mouth.

'You have to do this part yourself,' he said. 'You've had the pain, now you have to finish the job.'

'What do I do?' The pain was gone.

'Take the stone and come out to the river.'

Jack staggered to the stool and used the last of his strength to lift the obsidian slab. It felt smooth and somehow alive in his hands. The Bard steadied Jack as he walked through the doorway, and followed Finbar to a shallow shingle bank. Upstream the monumental falls thundered. How he had survived that plunge he could not imagine.

'Walk on,' Finbar said. 'The heat's taken the cold. Now you have to cleanse yourself and the fireglass.'

The water was cool around his legs. Soon it reached his waist. The shingle gave way to fronds of weed and Jack remembered the underwater vision of a pallid face with huge eyes and flowing hair and a touch as cold as death. The water was up past the puckered skin on his chest now, but he kept walking, took a breath and then he was under, in the coolest clear water. He felt the weakness wash out of him, felt the strange vibration of the obsidian stone as it gave up whatever it had taken to the sparkling river.

He knew when it was over. Shapes swam in the water,

caressed his arms and shoulders, silken hair brushed him and he gave thanks to these strange creatures who had saved him from the depths. He turned and walked back until his head broke the surface. He carried the stone up the shingle incline, where the Bard reached and took it from him.

'*Oh* Jack,' Kerry breathed. 'Look at that.'

Jack looked down at himself. His puckered skin was smooth now, washed by whatever magic was in stone and river. Where the vicious black shapes had been, his skin was white and clean again.

Except for the red hand print right over his heart.

And above it, five dots in a semicircle, matching the position where claws might have pierced his skin in that one savage swipe.

'It's the red hand,' Jack said. 'From the Ulster myth.'

'It's much more than that,' the Bard said softly. 'Much more.

'Come in now. We've got some important things to talk about.'

ELEVEN

'There are thirteen standing stones in Old Caledon.'
Finbar had sat them at the low table, fed them grainy bread and wild honey. He had pulled his cloak around Jack's shoulders and brought him to the bench nearest the fire.

Jack saw himself reflected in a burnished pan hanging by the fire, golden in this light, warm and whole again.

And that red handprint stood out like a coat of arms across his heart.

'Thirteen stones where the ley lines meet,' the Bard continued. 'Where the *Way Lines* meet. It's the place where all the worlds touch, where the skin between them is thinnest.'

'I'm not with you,' Jack began to say. 'All the worlds?'

'You're not the first journeymen to step through,' Finbar

said, ignoring the question for the moment. 'And when men come from Old Caledon, it's a sign.'

He held up his hand before Jack could speak. 'Thirteen stones and a capstone in the centre. Thirteen gates between the stones, and an infinity of ways. They built on Old Caledon after the ice, on land that would not shift nor quake, and they did it to bar the ways to worlds.'

'Why did they do that?' Corriwen asked. She seemed to accept the concept of the gates as quite reasonable.

'There's power in *all* worlds. For good and evil, just like there's magic in some worlds, more in some, where magic is young, and less in Old Caledon, which made it the place to join the leys and bar the ways. There's always a power seeking to break through and use the waystones to invade. The keepers and journeymen have always kept them out. So far.

'In Caledon, they set the MacBeatha, the Sons of Life, to guard the ways, all down the generations.'

'The MacBeatha?' Jack interrupted. 'You mean Major MacBeth?'

'From what Kerry told me, that'll be the man. The Keeper of Ways. How you came to be here, I don't know. But there's always a reason.'

'Everybody says he was a major, like in the army,' Kerry said.

'Oh, he'll be a soldier, sure enough.'

Jack sat, listening intently. Maybe this explained the Major's mysterious disappearances – and his equally surprising arrivals. And perhaps his collection of ancient things in the old house. The man who had raised him had kept his secrets to himself, and things had happened too suddenly on Samhain night for him to share any of them with Jack.

Finbar scratched at his beard. 'The last journeyman to come through the Farward Gate was Cullian, when the land was young and all the west was forest. Magic was stronger then in Temair. He brought the sword to face the Morrigan when she was rampaging through the land.

'I've read about her,' Jack finally found his tongue.

'Well then, you'll know she's the Dark Queen. Pure evil. Death and destruction sustains her. And hatred for all that is good. It took a good man, strong enough to fight the hag and bring her down. The sword he brought became the Redthorn Sword, and it has guarded Temair since.'

He paused again, had another scratch. 'We need the sword, and we need another Cullian, because the Morrigan wakes again from the dead slumber. It's a long story, and I don't know where to begin.'

'Might as well start at the beginning, Mr Finbar,' Kerry said lightly. 'For we haven't a clue where we are, or what we're doing.'

'Now there's a thing that's easy said, Kerry.' Finbar flashed him a fast smile and lit an old clay pipe.

'Now, what you have to remember is, the start is a long way back.' He blew out a plume of smoke. 'Longer than you might think. Yet the circle has turned and the past comes round to greet the present. Now we have the last of the Redthorns hunted high and low, and some dark and bad things happening in Temair.'

He turned to Corriwen. 'He'll hunt you down, you know. He can't have you alive while he clings to the high seat. And he's not working alone.'

'I don't understand you,' Corriwen said.

'Your Uncle Mandrake. He's mad, of course. Raving mad, but we always knew he was a bit cracked. Your father should never have let him delve into the old magic. Should have sent him out to the Marches to keep the Scree in their place. Now look what's happened. He's brought them down from the Scree mountains and put the people under a hard hand. Bad times all round.'

'I don't get it,' Kerry said. 'I don't get any of this place at all.'

Jack said nothing. He wanted to savour the comfort of being himself again. And he wanted to hear what the Bard had to say.

'Mandrake's not finished yet,' said Finbar. 'And the shadow that's pulling his strings, the Morrigan, she's not even started, believe me.'

'Now you're talking in riddles,' Kerry said.

'Riddles and conundrums.' Finbar sucked on his pipe for a while. 'They're the secrets that turn the world. There's magic in riddles and conundrums. To every riddle there's a key, and I have a feeling you three are the key to this one.'

'I still don't understand,' Corriwen spoke up again. Jack remained silent, concentrating on Finbar's words.

'You thought your uncle was just jealous, and maybe you can't blame him for that. Mere minutes is all it took for him to be beaten to the high seat and the lordship of Temair.

But Mandrake has always been touched; the dark finds its own cracks to seep into. Like ice. It wedges the cracks apart and makes its own space.

'Mandrake spent too much time studying the old scripts, when there were those that thought it was all myth and riddle. Always remember, there's a key in every riddle and truth in every myth, and what Mandrake wanted was power. Now he has it and he'll do what it takes to keep it. What he doesn't know is that he's just a puppet with a dark hand working his every move.'

'That's the part I don't understand,' Corriwen said.

'Well, little Corrie Redthorn,' Finbar said, 'sit still and I'll tell you. Some of it you'll have heard before.'

She looked up at him, tears springing to her eyes. 'That's what my brother used to call me.'

'He was a fine man, strong and clever, brave as a boarhound. But he had not the slightest clue what he was fighting, that's the truth of it. And that's something you're going to have to learn.'

'Me?' She wiped her eyes with the heel of her hand. 'What can I do? I'm an outlaw in my own land.'

'That's true enough, even if there is no law now. But never say die until they put stones on your eyes. And you're a long way from crossing to Tir Nan Og.'

Finbar turned to the boys, Jack still swathed in the pelt cloak, Kerry in his rabbit-skin tunic. 'And you, you're both a long step from home.'

He moved to the bench by the small shuttered window and busied himself with an array of leather pouches, each tied at the neck with a thong. When he turned back, he held a stone bowl, filled to the brim with what looked like crushed herbs.

'Sometimes you need help to look back,' he said, bending over the glowing hearth. 'Now it's all going to seem a bit strange to the three of you, but remember, I'm the latest in a long line of my people.' He touched his forehead with a finger. 'And what they know and what they were, are all in here. So sit, listen, watch, and we'll see what's to be seen.'

He placed the stone bowl on the embers in the hearth and they watched as it began to glow in the heat. Very soon a pungent aroma of herbs wafted from the fireplace. Finbar sat on a stool, hands flat on the bench. He began to talk, as if to himself, as the roasting herbs sent drifts of white smoke into the room. The scent was both sweet and acrid.

Jack kept his eyes fixed on Finbar as he inhaled the heady fumes.

He stared, nailed to the spot, as Finbar's face changed. His hair colour darkened, then lightened. His beard vanished, became dark and braided, then turned to red, long and bristled.

Finbar the Bard began to speak. Jack could hardly make out the words at first.

'It was when the Fomorians,' Finbar chanted, voice low, 'when the Fomorians were exiled to the Scree mountains. It was in those troubled days *She* ravaged the land.

'The Morrigan was awake and hungry, out of the dead lands beyond Tir Nan Og.'

Jack's eyes closed.

'The witch of the Banshee. The *Morrigan.*'

Jack saw a shadow flow across a fair land. He felt a pain

behind his eyes as the shadow came swooping like nightfall on a sunny day.

'She was the bane of all life,' Finbar said. 'The bane of all men.'

Jack saw ranks of soldiers move out from keeps and stone castles, marching northwards to meet the shadow. And he saw, like pictures flickering in front of his eyes, hordes of the grey creatures, the Scree, cascading like a rockslide from barren mountains to meet the warriors.

He saw them clash. The battleground was awash with blood, filled with the cries of the dying and the awesome, awful laughter of the Morrigan.

The Scree swooped down in their thousands to where the men took their last desperate stand. Among the warriors, he saw swords flash, heard weapons clash. In the midst of it all, a bright shimmering sword was held aloft.

'A Redthorn. *A Redthorn!*' A voice boomed through the cacophony. 'Hold and rally to the Red Hand.'

Inside the flowing darkness *She* shrieked and raved and the earth split and things that should neither breathe air nor be seen by men, crawled and loped and slithered and flew.

Then, at the height of it, in the death of it, when the men were pushed back pace by bloody pace, came another sound.

It was like nothing Jack had ever heard before. The soaring of five voices in the closest harmony, and their music swelled across the slaughterfield ...

He saw five men in white fur cloaks, standing on top of the hills that surrounded the battlefield on the plain, each with arms raised. From their outstretched hands, he saw silvery light, lancing from hill to hill, from Bard to Bard.

Jack heard the power of that song. He could feel it boil in his veins and pulse with the beat of his own heart.

The sound had force. It was a physical thing.

'A Redthorn! *Lift your hearts!*'

The Bards on the hills chanted as one, mingling song with light, and the Morrigan shrieked, blasting men and ogre alike with awesome power.

But the light and the song held it.

The hand in the melee held the sword above the slaughter.

The song swelled triumphant, and the skeins of light snared the shrinking, twisting dark, drawing it to the ground between the five low hills, down to where the glittering sword blade pointed to the now-brightening sky. Light blazed from the blade and the things that had squirmed from the cracks shrivelled and crumbled to dust.

A Redthorn ... A Redthorn ... the light returns to Temair.

Jack saw the stone now, a slab of pure obsidian, polished to liquid ink, as the sword held steady, binding the five ropes of light in a braid of energy.

And then the dark welded with the obsidian rock.

Jack saw the sword, stabbed to its hilt deep in the rock.

The wielder held it there, his free hand raised high, a red gauntlet clear and bright. *A red hand.*

A tall man in plain leather clothes and a wide brimmed hat. There was something oddly familiar about him. About his voice. Jack saw new sunlight glint in blue eyes under the brim.

It was the same man in the vision; the one who had drawn him out of the dark, towards the light.

The sight of him gave Jack a shiver of something. *Recognition?* No, it was more than that. As if, somehow this man and he belonged to each other.

The man drew the sword from the stone and held it up for the living to see.

Sitting there in the diminishing smoke, heart thudding, Jack became aware of Finbar's voice.

'They snared her in a song of power and the light of true day.'

Finbar the Bard was himself again.

'The Morrigan. The sword trapped her spirit in the rock.' He opened his eyes. 'They built a hill around the stone, and put a *geas* on it, a curse and a prophecy, because no deed is forever, no victory complete, no matter how folk might wish it. It was long ago, in the beginning of Men in this place, when the Dalriada fought the Morrigan and her Fomorian hordes and banished them to the barren mountains.' Finbar nodded. 'As ever, it was between dark and light. Between good and evil.'

'The curse!' Jack found his voice. He had *felt* her touch, and now he understood. She was breaking the *geas*.

Of that he was suddenly, completely certain.

'They trapped her in the high salt barrens, heaped earth to form a Barrow on it, and buried twelve heroes who died on that day to guard her spirit.'

'But what exactly was the curse?' Jack insisted.

Finbar closed his eyes, brow furrowed. When he opened them again, they blazed with fierce wisdom and he seemed to grow in Jack's vision, showing some of the power that he really had.

> Until the Cullian sword returns
> 'til heroes fail their lien
> 'til waters drown the binding stone
> This holds the Baneshee Queen.
> A blade to wake from deadly sleep
> A flood to free in fathoms deep
> For in the ebb the foul takes form
> To ride the night, on wings of storm.

'So something's happened,' Jack said.

'Yes.' Finbar said. 'Something *has* happened.'

'The Morrigan,' Jack insisted. 'Whatever she is. She's out.'

'Not yet,' Finbar replied. 'But she's working on it. The Redthorn sword turned the lock on her long sleep. It could wake her again. I fear it already has.'

'And what will she do?'

'She's the Morrigan. She'll lay waste to everything she touches, all she sees. But there's more than that.' Finbar's expression was grave. 'She wants more than Temair.'

TWELVE

High in the turret of the keep, with the shutters closed tight and no tallow torch or even a candle to light the room, Mandrake was awake, and trembling.

He heard the sound of ponderous footfalls on flagstones, slow and deliberate, getting nearer with every heavy tread. They grew louder and louder until the walls began to shake.

He knew what was coming next.

Doom ... Doom ... the thick oak door shivered. Dust puffed out and dry splinters of rust and old wood tumbled from the hinges.

Stay away. Stay away ... he tried to speak.

The door creaked. It had been locked with a massive iron hasp, but still, it opened, shuddering. A grey mist oozed through the portal.

Then came the smell. Fetid, cloy and clogging in the air, dank on his sweating skin.

He knew his older brother came, the reek of death on him. Lugan Redthorn's feet scraped the stone flags. His skin sloughed off a skeletal face and in the pits of his eye sockets, red pinpoints glared.

'A curse on you, brother.' Lugan's voice was the crackle of dead winter leaves underfoot.

'*Forever cursed.*'

Mandrake cringed, trying to back away from the apparition, but there was no escape. Lugan's face was black with the poison of the mandrake root and the wolfbane that had killed him.

Now Lugan stood before him, rotting and rotted, a ghastly spectre. Mandrake cringed again.

Another shape came behind, taller than the first, broader, hair in thick red braids, every inch a man but for the dreadful gash that cut from forehead across his eye and nose, down to his chin.

Young Cerwin Redthorn stood beside his father, dead men both, but alive with an anger that they carried with them from the other side.

Cerwin leant forward. Around his head, a crown of five stars sparkled. Like his father, he raised a hand and pointed it at Mandrake's heart.

'The sword. You stole the sword.'

Mandrake tried to breathe, tried to cry out, but no sound would come, no breath.

Cerwin had blood in his eyes. His hand dripped red down into darkness.

The Red Hand. An omen. The red hand and the circlet of stars.

Drenched in a cold sweat, Mandrake wondered if the Bards had turned the tables and put a curse on him.

But inside him, somewhere deep down where his most bitter thoughts lurked, he knew it was not this. He could feel the corrosion eating him, worse than acid.

There was always a price to pay.

Mandrake had learned the forgotten legends of the Morrigan when men fought the Fomorians and he knew their power had come from her darkness.

He knew all of it, the great *geas* laid on the Morrigan's stone prison whose location had been forgotten down the generations.

And it was in the study of the dark arts that he had, after years of searching, finally come to understand how they had trapped the ancient Morrigan.

But equally important to him was the final knowledge of where it had been done, and even more, how to bring her back to this world.

When the time was ripe, he used his knowledge to gather what he needed, and he had watched Lugan Redthorn slowly die.

Then he had stolen the Redthorn Sword, the sword of Cullian, the fire-blade that had trapped the destroyer in a prison of stone, and as Lugan lay dying, he had taken it with him when he fled the Redthorn Keep and set out on his journey.

Even in her long, long sleep, she called to him. She whispered promises of wealth and power beyond his dreams.

Lordship of Temair and all lands would be his. And more. She promised him the Lordship of worlds.

He had gone on the hard journey, alone, at first on horseback until the horse had died under him, then on foot, with nothing but his hunger and anger and need to keep him going.

He walked through swamp and marsh, climbed treeless slopes where nothing moved under a sun that scorched by day, and a frozen moon by night, until he came to the high Salt Barrens.

Delirious with thirst and blinded by mile after mile of dry salt dunes, he stumbled and staggered on, weighed down by the sword, eating lizards and scorpions that lived under the rime of salt.

The closer he came to the Black Barrow, the more devastated the land became, the more he felt the awesome gravity of her presence. Her voice told him where to dig and after that, when he had almost killed himself in prying a massive stone loose from where it had sat these thousands of years, he was inside, out of the burning light, into the darkness where foul water puddled at his feet.

It seemed he wandered in dark tunnels for days, under the weight of the stones, images in his head, images of her pale face, its lips the colour of new blood. He sensed her, felt her in every pore of his body, his nerves tingling with anticipation.

When he saw the great stone slab, he knew he had found her.

And when he rested the sword upon the stone, he felt her power surge through him as she woke. He prostrated himself on the slab, saw her swim up towards him, her beauty impossible, eyes as black as caves, her arms reaching for him.

Mandrake lay there a long time, bathing in her terrible power, filled with the urgency to break the last *geas* and bring her back into the world.

Together we will rule, she sang in his mind.

Together we will rule worlds.

She promised herself to him, to have forever, her terrible beauty and her might.

He raised the Redthorn Sword and plunged it deep into the stone.

In a shattering instant she came awake and her power as it surged through him was vast. It threw him shivering to the ground where he lay in a stupor, overwhelmed by the force of her will.

He was never sure how long he had been in the darkness, but when he came out again into the Salt Barrens, into the sunlight that hurt his eyes, great flocks of roaks and ravens wheeled about him.

He could see what they saw and he could use their eyes to go where she had shown him the cave halfway to the Scree mountains. Long ago treasures had been hidden there, and with the roaks as companions, he found wealth beyond his wildest dreams, wealth that would enable him to return to the Redthorn Keep with an army.

Now he had wealth and power, the sight of the roaks and knowledge beyond even his own twisted ambition.

The melding with her mind had changed him. He kept to the shadows and wakened in the night when she would come to him, to whisper her plans.

Now the whole of Temair lay under his hand while the people who had looked to Lugan Redthorn for leadership worked under his command, slaving on the great project that would finally free her from the fireglass prison.

Up in the high tower, the visions faded.

He would let neither the ghosts of Redthorns, nor the Bards, stop him now.

In the room where he had raised dark magic, he mixed his own vision, and flying with the roaks in the early morning mist, he saw through their eyes.

He saw a boat emerging from the mist, oarless and rudderless, moving with an uncanny power.

As the roaks spiralled to the water, he saw the three of them, saw her red hair clearly against the grey of the cold water.

Mandrake laughed.

She stepped off as soon as the boat touched the bank, Corriwen Redthorn and the two boys, and the mist closed in over the water as they began to walk down a forest trail.

The roak-eyes followed them into open country where fires had blackened the fields and smoke rose in shrouds.

He summoned his guard. They came warily, for a night summons to Mandrake's tower was always fraught with danger.

'Bring the Scree hunters,' Mandrake croaked. 'We will not miss them this time.

'Go and find her and bring her alive,' he snarled. 'I'll roast her and feed for a week.' Mandrake turned, 'And those boys. They have something I want.'

He reached the window, threw open the shutters, and stared into dismal dawn. As his retainer watched, his expression changed yet again until he was no longer recognisable.

Whatever Mandrake had become raised bony arms to the sky, as if it could pull down the moon and tear it apart.

Then it began to laugh.

THIRTEEN

As soon as they emerged from the mist, eyes high in the sky saw them, and from that moment, they were hunted again.

Finbar the Bard had stood with them, one hand on Corriwen's shoulder as the boat came gliding from below the mighty waterfall. It was long and narrow and slid across the water towards them until it nudged the bank.

'Has he got a remote control?' Kerry asked. Jack shrugged. Kerry was putting on a brave face, but Jack knew he was apprehensive about getting back onto the water again. The boat bobbed and Jack saw its ribs were long bones glued together, or maybe just articulated from some great fish. The hull was thin and scaled, and patterned the way a salmon would be, if a salmon could grow ten feet long. He didn't even ask the Bard.

This world, this Temair, now felt completely alive.

'Where will the river take us?'

'Where you have to go,' Finbar said. 'The Undine will guide you partway there. From then on, it's not clear. But go west. Safe journey to you three.'

Jack was torn between the need to be gone and the desire to stay and talk more to Finbar. Kerry had packed his backpack and stuffed in it the big smoked haunch of meat the Bard had cured over his hearth. Corriwen said nothing for the moment and Jack couldn't tell if she was reluctant to leave the protection of Finbar's haven.

She caught his eye and while he couldn't read her expression, something passed between them, something important. As if there was a whole big plan and the two of them were right at its centre. He had promised to help her, though what he could do, he wasn't sure at all. What he really was sure of was that he would try his best. And he knew, just as surely, that she would try to help Kerry and him find their way home.

'Don't worry,' Finbar said. 'Well, worry as little as possible. We'll be with you. The bards will watch your progress. Whatever She throws at you, we'll try to catch it. But that doesn't mean you don't look out for yourselves. It's a hard road to the Homeward Gate, and a lot of troubles between here and there.'

Jack knew Finbar knew more than he was saying; he could read it in his eyes, but the Bard wouldn't be pushed further.

'You're mended and whole again,' he'd said, and that was true enough. Jack's senses seemed exhilaratingly acute.

Before they got into the boat, the Bard took each of them by the hand. He patted Kerry on the back. 'You're a good friend,' he said. 'And resourceful too. Watch out for both of them. Without you, all fails. They will need your help.'

He took Jack's hand. 'Set yourself to the road, Jack. You've come a distance and you have ways to go. Use your book. It speaks riddles, but it tells truth. That much I know.'

Jack had watched the Bard embrace Corriwen and tuck her cloak around her, as a parent would a child. He couldn't hear what was said.

It had been a strange night. It might be an even stranger day. He was filled with a mix of excitement and foreboding. Underneath it was the new determination to help Corriwen find safety, and then get himself and Kerry to the Homeward Gate, even if Jack was unsure now where his true home really was.

The boat settled under their weight, Kerry sat low in the back, both hands gripping the sides. Jack looked for the oars he assumed would be stacked on the ribs, but without a sound the craft slipped away from the bank and they were off. Under the surface, pale green shapes, glimmers of motion, were making the boat move. In minutes the bank was far behind them, and Finbar just a silhouette on the shore.

They were silent, each lost in thought while the water creatures moved them on, heading away from the faint glow of the rising sun that tried and failed to pierce the mist. Kerry fell asleep, reassured that the boat would not sink, both feet up on the rim, head on his backpack.

Jack and Kerry had sat together outside the small stone house, each on a smooth stone not far from the river, but far enough from the falls to be able to hear each other. Finbar the Bard had drawn Corriwen aside while he cooked over the coals of an open fire. The two of them talked, heads close, the girl's face angled up attentively while Finbar spoke.

'So what do you think of her?'

Jack started out of the memory of the man with the sword and the red gauntlet on the stone.

'Who?'

'Corriwen. I saw you looking at her.'

'Well, she's pretty special.'

'I never met anybody like her. She's ...' Kerry paused. 'She's cool.'

Jack knew that was not the word Kerry had been searching for. Kerry looked suddenly glum.

'I saw the way she looks at you.'

'I never noticed.'

'She thought you were the boss. Right away, that's what she thought.'

'I'm not the boss. You know that.'

'But she thought it,' Kerry insisted.

'Well, she was wrong,' Jack replied. 'Anyway, we've got other things to think about. And we're not going to fall out over a girl. Not you and me, okay?'

Jack didn't want to talk about Corriwen. There was something in the smoke-dream that was important to remember. He didn't know why. He closed his eyes and breathed in the cold, clean air, feeling his strength return with every breath, and pangs of hunger begin to stir.

'I think we're in trouble,' he finally said. He rubbed a hand across his chest underneath the jerkin. It tingled a little, not painfully, but with inner heat. That was so much better than the draining cold.

Jack took a moment getting his thoughts together. 'We're stuck here. I need to get us back home again.'

'Easy said. I thought it was a dream, but listen, Jack, this place is for real.'

'And that's why we have to find the way home. Finbar seems to think I'm supposed to be here for some reason. But I don't want to be here. It's weird and it's dangerous, but that's not it. I have to get back to see if the Major's all right. He said something to me just before we ... before we fell into this place, wherever it is. *When*ever it is.'

'So what did he say?'

Jack fumbled with his jerkin and drew out the heartstone on its chain.

'He told me to keep this safe, because it used to belong to my father. It's my inheritance. He knew my dad. I need to find out what it's all about.'

Kerry's eyes followed damsel-flies dancing over the silvered water.

'Dads aren't all they're cracked up to be. Look at mine.' He turned to his friend. 'And anyway, I thought you were an orphan.'

'Me too,' Jack agreed. 'But now I don't know. My father disappeared. The Major said he was on some kind of mission. Like a soldier.'

He paused, collecting his thoughts. The smooth obsidian stone gleamed.

'Finbar says this is some sort of key. Like for getting through the gateway to get home.'

'So?'

'It belonged to my father. And so did the book. I've been thinking maybe he came through the gateway, just the way we did. Or one of them.'

Kerry shrugged. 'Maybe he did.'

'But there's more. When we came out of the trees into the circle. I recognised the stones, even though I never saw them before. At least so I thought. But when I was a kid I used to have these nightmares. Big shapes all around me. I never knew what they were. But I think they were the standing stones.'

He lowered his voice. 'I think somebody brought me through, when I was a baby.'

'What, like from a different place?' Kerry gave him an odd look. 'Like here?'

'I think so,' Jack said. 'I'm not sure where. But it fits. I never knew it before, but thinking on it, I never felt as if I belonged.'

'You never looked any different to me.' Kerry's eyes dropped. He looked like someone who realised he was losing something special. 'We've always been friends.'

Jack gripped him by the shoulder.

'Always will be. You know that. That won't ever change.'

'So what are you saying?'

'I just feel different, that's all. As if I was ... sort of *waiting* for something to happen. Now I've got this stone, that's supposed to be some kind of key. Only I don't know how to use it.'

'So, what's the next move?'

'If somebody brought me through, then maybe I can go the opposite direction. All my life I've never known who I really am, and the Major can't say. I've never had the chance to find out.'

'You're Jack Flint,' Kerry said. He seemed heartened by what Jack had said. 'What else is there to know? Me? I'm Kerry Malone.' He punched Jack on the shoulder. 'And we're both stuck here in fancy dress. Can it get any better?'

Jack managed a smile. 'I wish it was that simple. But we have to do what the book says. We keep going west until we find the way back. The Major said curiosity would get me in trouble some day, and he was right. But now I know I wasn't curious about the right things, and I'm going to do my best to find out.'

'Okay,' Kerry said. 'I suppose I should come along and keep you out of trouble.'

He forced a grin. 'And make sure you don't get the girl.'

'Look, if you feel that way, why don't you just tell her.'

'I don't know how I feel,' Kerry admitted. 'It's kind of confusing.'

He smiled, a real one this time. 'But you know, if you ignore the big freakin' hounds, and those crazy pigs. And those ugly-bug loonies. And green women under the water. And an old guy who thinks he's a Jedi Knight ...

'If you ignore that lot, this place could be a whole lot worse.'

Now Kerry was asleep and Corriwen sat beside Jack at the prow.

'Finbar spoke with me for a long time,' she said. 'It gives me some hope.'

'Me too,' Jack replied. 'But I don't understand half of it. I don't know what I'm supposed to do.'

Finbar had taken Jack outside when the velvety blue had faded to purple and the stars had come out. Jack did not recognise any of the patterns in the constellations.

He had tapped Jack on his breastbone, where the heartstone swung on its silver chain.

'That's a powerful talisman,' he said. 'Probably what kept you alive. A long time ago, this talisman was here.'

'It was my father's,' Jack told him. 'But I never knew him.'

'Then he was here before. I think you realise that.'

Jack nodded. 'I'm beginning to.'

'You've stepped between worlds, a long way from Old Caledon.'

'But we have to get back.' Jack almost said 'home'. Now that word didn't feel right.

'That's easily said,' Finbar said patiently. 'Mandrake's hordes have taken over Mid-Temair while the folk have been set to work on the dam and digging a tunnel though the mountains. He means to bring water to flood the salt plain.'

'To break the *geas* ?'

Finbar nodded. 'Nothing surer. But there's more to all this now. It's no coincidence that you are here with that heartstone. You've been led here, and that can only mean one thing. She means to have the key which will break open the gateways.'

'A key?'

'Every gate has a key. And this is the master of them all. Nothing passes a gate without the key. That's what she wants, and that's why the road ahead is full of danger for you.'

'Why would this Morrigan want it?'

'To smash the locks between the worlds and let the evil of the underworld loose. The end of Temair will also be the end of Old Caledon. She is plague and famine and death in one. It's a big burden laid on you, Jack, but you are the Keeper of the Key now. The Journeyman. Our future and your world's future is on your shoulders.'

Finbar drew on the pipe. 'Look up,' he said, raising a hand to the jewelled sky. 'That's the direction you have to travel, and it's no coincidence.'

'I'm not with you.'

The Bard opened the leather jerkin. Jack's skin was blue in the light. The air was cool, not cold. He felt more alive than he had ever felt before.

The shape of the hand showed clearly against his skin, almost black in this light. Above it, the five dots that looked like claw marks stood in a semicircle.

'Now look there,' the Bard said. Jack peered up at the sky. Finbar guided his eyes.

He saw it then. Five bright stars in a perfect semicircle. Brighter than any others in the night sky, sparkling like diamonds.

'The Corona,' Finbar said. 'The crown of Temair.'

In a moment of clarity, Jack recognised the similarity. 'It's a match.'

'Yes. And the red hand. Now here's a thing you'll think strange. When the bards put a *geas* on the Morrigan, they foresaw a day when the shadow would come back, even though the binding they put on the black tor was powerful enough to last these numberless generations. But they knew that nothing is forever. As I can look back, so the five bards together can see what may come, and this is what they passed down to us.

Comes Coronal, from west to east
The Red Hand set to slay the beast
Blood to blood, heart to heart
Cullian's sword replays its part

'That's just like the rhymes in the book.'

'Your *Book of Ways*? That's vital. If your father had the book and the heartstone, then he was a traveller. A *journeyman*. And the Major, the MacBeth, he is the Guardian of the Ways. Where is your father now?'

Jack shook his head. 'I really don't know. He disappeared when I was small.'

'Who knows, perhaps he went through a farward gate?

But then how did the heartstone get back to Old Caledon? That's a mystery. But it's here now, and so are you. It's the puzzling out of riddle and rhyme that's the trick. Temair turns and the circle comes back to the start and things that are meant to be, well, we don't have much say in the matter.'

'So what's meant to be?'

'Well, you can work it out for yourself. The red hand wielded the Cullian sword that became the Redthorn sword. And you have the mark of the Corona on you. No matter what brought you here, you were meant to be here.'

'What do I have to do?'

'You and Kerry, well, I think you didn't just chance upon Corriwen Redthorn. She's got a big task, too, and you must help her.'

'She saved my life,' Jack said. 'I'll help her if I can.'

'Nobody said it was going to be easy,' the Bard said. 'But there's good news in with the bad.'

'I hope there is. It doesn't sound good so far.'

'Well, here's part of it. We Bards, we're handy for weddings and birthings and the like. A light touch of magic, you could say. But we stay out of the rest of man's troubles mostly, until we get a sign. Waiting for the sign can be a long task, but here's the sign.'

He touched Jack on the chest again, between the hand and the marks that matched the stars. 'So now I have to call my brothers together and see what we can do to help.'

'Is that the good news?'

'That fireglass heart, *She* means to have it, and she'll send everything she's got at you. But there's more to it than just talisman. This heartstone is the key to worlds. And the key to time itself.'

'I don't understand.'

'You will. Now you get a good night's sleep if you can, so you're fresh for the next step.'

Corriwen Redthorn had listened intently as Jack related the conversation.

'So here we are,' he finished. 'He said I'll figure it all out.' Jack shook his head. 'I'll give it my best.'

'I'll help you if I can. There's always some hope,' she said. 'I had almost given up until I met you. And Mandrake's Scree had hunted me so long I was ready to give up. You helped give me hope again. And so has Finbar.'

The mist cleared, as if they had passed through a gauze curtain into sunlight. Neither Jack nor Corriwen could say how far they had travelled, but now, after hours in the white stillness, a forest loomed.

The boat arrowed across clear water to a space where trees overhung the shore, and finally bumped against a steep earth bank. Kerry woke with a start and looked around, rubbing sleep from his eyes.

'We there yet?'

'Wherever it is, we're here.' Jack turned to Corriwen. 'Recognise this place?'

She shook her head.

They unloaded the things they had brought and stood for a moment on the bank, looking across the water. Without warning, the boat pulled away and as silently as it had come, sped away.

Kerry lifted the backpack. Jack slung the bow across his shoulders.

'This is where we begin, I suppose,' Corriwen said in a small voice. She was thinking of what the Bard had said. *A hard road ahead.* She checked the matching knives in their sheaths, straightened her shoulders and regained that resolute expression. 'Where now?'

Jack pointed to the track that angled away from the water, perhaps tramped by animals coming to drink.

'That way looks the best bet. It goes west.'

They followed the trail for hours, unaware that eyes high in the sky had caught the movement in the narrow belt between fog and tree-line.

Sometime in the afternoon, Kerry made a fire and skewered some of the haunch. It dripped fat tantalisingly into the embers and they ate with their fingers, and drank water from a clear stream. When they had eaten, they walked on, through fern-packed glades and under spreading trees with trunks as wide as houses.

Finally they came to the edge of the forest and found themselves on a wider path that became a hard-pack cobbled road between fields that had been tilled and planted once, but now were overgrown with weeds and nettles.

'The place looks deserted,' Jack said, conscious that despite the solitude, he was whispering. Ahead, the sun slid towards the horizon, red in their eyes, casting shadows behind them. They walked together, with Corriwen between Jack and Kerry, watching for signs of movement or attack, but saw nothing, not even animals in the fields. They did not see the flock of roaks circling high above them, mere pin-points in the sky.

They came to a village, a handful of wooden houses, or what was left of them. The ground was trampled, as if a herd of beasts had rampaged through. Walls leant at crazy angles and most of the woodwork was smashed or charred.

'This is Mandrake's work,' Corriwen said. 'I'm ashamed to have the same blood.'

'You can't pick your family,' Kerry said. 'More's the pity.'

As soon as he spoke thunder rumbled in the north and lightning stabbed down on a coppice of distant trees. Jack licked a finger and held it up to the breeze.

'Looks like a storm. And it's coming our way.'

'We need shelter,' Corriwen said. 'But there's none here. There's not a roof left to hide under.'

They pushed on, past the ruined hamlet, following the road as the gathering clouds darkened to purple. Thunder cracked, much closer now, and for the first time they saw the roaks wheeling and tumbling in the high wind as if they were dragging the storm down on them. The three travellers quickened their pace, over a slope and into a valley where they saw ruins no more than a mile ahead. There were no lights, but they could see the shape of houses and barns in the gloom. The last rays of the sun peered from under the clouds and tinged the slate roofs the colour of blood.

They were halfway down the slope when the storm hit.

The wind whipped around them, shrieking through the gaps in the wall, and over the wind and thunder, Jack thought he heard the howling of wolves. He couldn't tell which direction the sound came from.

The hail started as they ran down the road. At first it was hailstones, driven almost horizontal by the ferocious wind, but in minutes, they were as big as marbles, and bigger still, lashing down as if aimed by a malign hand.

Each time the lightning stabbed, the old houses were outlined against the sky. Kerry put the backpack over his head for protection, grabbed Corriwen and Jack and huddled close under its meagre shelter, and together they raced for the nearest building and threw themselves inside.

A massive roak swooped behind them. Kerry batted it with the bag, so hard it flattened against the stone wall. Corriwen spun and slashed it with her blade. Hailstones battered the roof and shattered slates while lighting struck, so close they could smell the burn in the air. Jack kicked a wicker door closed and jammed a heavy trough against it.

'This is crazy stuff,' Kerry said. 'It's like somebody's aiming the lightning at us. And them hailstones.'

'Mandrake,' she said. 'And the thing that is pulling his strings.'

Feral howling cut through the drumming hail. Too close.

'Wolves or Scree,' Corriwen said. 'We're hunted again.'

'They might not find us,' Kerry said hopefully. 'We should sit tight.'

They huddled in a straw-littered corner, listening to the

hailstorm rage, and the howling came closer still. Abruptly the hail stopped and for a moment an eerie silence stretched out in the barn.

Somewhere in the night they heard muffled voices.

'Scree,' Corriwen whispered. Her hand went to her belt and drew out a knife.

Just as she spoke, something moved in the shadows and she twisted towards it, blade ready.

'It's only a rat,' Jack whispered.

The rat scurried from the corner, rustling through the straw. Little red eyes glittered. Another came out from the bales with yet another on its tail. These two stopped and stared at the three fugitives. Another movement caught Jack's eye and he turned to see a rippling wave of shadows flowing away from the wall and in an instant the whole floor was alive with rats.

'This is really creepy,' Kerry whispered.

Instantly the rats, as if guided by some invisible conductor, began to squeak, hundreds of them, a barnful, all in unison, in a sudden ear-splitting cacophony.

Kerry raised his hands to his ears. 'Can't we shut them up?'

'They're calling to the Scree,' Corriwen said. The rats moved, surging forward in a black mass, and in seconds they were all over them, squealing and nipping and clawing at their clothes.

Corriwen's blades flashed and rats fell off her.

The door thudded and Jack saw the leather hinges begin to stretch.

'*Move*,' he said.

'Move where?'

A pulley rope dangled from a high rafter. Jack grabbed Corriwen's shoulder, ignoring the rats that were hanging on to his leggings, and boosted her up. Without a sound, she started to climb. He followed as the wicker door bulged and cracked down the centre. A grey arm shoved through and fumbled at the latch. Kerry grabbed his pack, dug into a pocket and fished out his matches. Without pausing, he struck one and held the flame against the frayed end of the rope. It caught instantly and then he was clambering up, bracing his feet against the wall, while below the flames licked up.

The door crashed open and Scree came charging in. The burning rope dripped fire on the dry straw. In moments, the first bale caught and the Scree were blundering, some of them ablaze, in frenzied circles.

Jack urged Corriwen on, towards the gap in the gable wall onto the long barn roof. It was slippery with moss and ice where the hail had gathered and they scrambled on all fours across the ridge, down the other side, and used the cover of the farmhouse roofs to get as much distance as possible. On the narrow cobbles below, the wolf-hounds snarled and strained against their leashes and Jack heard the unmistakeable grunt of a great hog. Kerry led the way, unerringly finding a route across the roofs, sliding down the gutters between them, until they came to a rickety outhouse and managed to drop to the ground.

They ran blindly down narrow alleys. Kerry drew his sword from the backpack and Jack unslung the bow.

They raced between two dilapidated shacks and suddenly they were in an open square.

At the same time, a horde of Scree, their huge hounds baying, came thundering round the corner. Kerry skidded to a halt and Jack almost bowled him over. Corriwen stood, catching her breath, knives raised for battle.

'*Uh-oh,*' Kerry gulped. They spun, scooted back down the alley, had almost reached the end when a hand caught Corriwen by the neck.

She yelped as her feet left the ground. She slashed out, razoring a grey forearm from elbow to wrist, fell to the ground and rolled away just as another Scree grabbed her. Her knives clattered to the cobbles.

Kerry dived in, swinging his sword like an axe, but it caught the Scree on a metal shoulder plate and the force of that almost sent the sword spinning out of his hands. Jack turned, nocked an arrow, aware now, despite the surge of fear, that his strength was back. He loosed one barb and caught the lead Scree in the chest. He tumbled and the hound, held by his companion, turned like lightning, snapping at his master's face. The second handler tripped and Jack managed to set a black arrow into the ridged back of a great hog.

For a moment mayhem reigned, and it looked as if the scrum at the end of the alley was such a tangle that they might get away, when the second wave of Scree came charging in. Corriwen was slung across broad shoulders. She screeched and flailed to no avail. Kerry tried to slice with the sword, but the second Scree warded him off with a stone-headed club.

'Get her!' Kerry cried.

Jack saw the Scree approach and in a flash he realised they would be caught in the middle.

He grabbed Kerry, whipped him around and through the window of the nearest shack, then dived through after him.

'*No!*' Kerry shouted, 'They've got her!'

'Too many,' Jack gasped. 'We can't help her.'

'You can't give up on her!'

'They'll kill us.'

'We can fight for her,' Kerry shot back. 'If you care about her!'

Jack dragged Kerry with him. They tumbled outside, rolled together on the ground and then, without any warning, dropped into a deep runnel that was ankle-deep in fast-running water.

Jack held on to Kerry, forced him to run and they splashed down the runnel. Behind them, two Scree leapt into the ditch, chain-mail jangling.

The runnel curved to the left and instantly Jack saw the grating that barred the way.

His heart leapt into his throat.

Trapped! He might have said it aloud. Kerry was yelling in fury, trying to shake free of Jack's grip.

The wooden grating was like a gate over the tunnel ahead where the water disappeared into darkness.

Jack couldn't stop. Momentum carried them down the slope. The big grate loomed and they slammed into it.

The Scree were only fifty yards behind, slow and ponderous, but determined.

Jack gripped the grate. Each cross-hatch was more than a foot wide.

'Can you get through?'

'They've got her,' Kerry cried, anger blazing in his eyes.

'Get through!' Jack ordered. He grabbed Kerry's collar and used all his strength to force his friend through the grid. It was just wide enough. The backpack snagged. One strap broke, and then Kerry was inside the tunnel. Jack didn't hesitate. He wriggled through and into the dark.

They came out perhaps a furlong downstream, slipping and sliding down a steep weir into a lade where the water deepened. Jack made out a wooden millwheel and they hauled up onto the lade-edge.

Above them a roak called out, alerting a troop of Scree who turned at the culvert and came splashing upstream towards them.

'Do they never give up?' Jack asked.

'You do,' Kerry spat. Jack ignored him.

'Wait here,' Jack said. He clambered to the edge of the rill behind the wheel. Here a gate held the water back, balanced by a heavy stone attached to a wheel locked by a spar. Jack put his shoulder to it and strained until the spar began to creak outwards. Kerry saw what he was doing and stepped in to help and both of them wrestled the spar free. They jumped back just as the wheel began to spin as the weight fell. The gate rose and all the lade water gushed out in a torrent and slammed into the Scree.

One second they were there, and the next, they were gone – Scree, beasts and all.

Jack gritted his teeth, raised his fist in gesture of victory.

'Come on,' he said. After a while they came to a coppice of trees and ran for the shadows.

When they stopped, heaving for breath, Kerry turned to Jack.

'You rat,' he snarled. 'You left her.'

And without warning Kerry swung a fist and punched Jack as hard as he could. His best friend went sprawling into the bushes and Kerry held back sudden tears.

FOURTEEN

Every lurch along the rutted road was not quite agony for Corriwen Redthorn, but it came close. It was painful and uncomfortable and every step the great hog took heaved her back and forth on its smelly flank.

They had tied her with hide thongs and slung her across one of the beasts. She just hoped the hog was steady on its feet. If it fell she'd be crushed for sure.

Every now and again, it would swing its snout around, fix her with a beady eye and drool sticky skeins from between its razor tusks. The hog stank, more so than the Scree who lumbered alongside, hobnails grinding on the cobbles.

She bit back futile anger. She had survived these months alone, months on the run with the Scree hunting her, living off the forest with no company but memories of her father and brother and awful memories of their passing.

When she had stumbled across the slaughterfield and found Cerwin, battle-helm split and his red hair plastered to his broken face, she had wept bitterly, but she had also vowed then to repay Mandrake for what he had done.

It had seemed a forlorn hope, when she was all alone, but she held on to it, nursing the anguish and loss and the bright spark of righteous fury. She was the last of the Redthorns and she needed to stay alive, for the sake of her father and brother and for the people of Temair.

Now she was not alone.

Even lashed across the back of the stinking boar, she knew she was not alone. She had felt it the first night she had met Jack and Kerry in the forest. When she had looked into Jack Flint's blue eyes and held his hands, she had sensed deep inside herself that somehow this meeting was meant to be.

She imagined the pair of them coming after her, strangers from a strange land who had become her friends.

She recalled her last conversation with Jack, while Kerry was still asleep on the boat as it sped across the water.

'He talked to you too?' Jack had asked, keeping his voice low.

'When you were sleeping. Finbar says Mandrake took the Redthorn sword to awaken the Morrigan. But if he breaks all parts of the *geas*, then she will be free, and Finbar says that will be a terrible thing for Temair. And your world, too.'

'That's the impression he gave me,' Jack agreed.

'Did he tell you about the sword?'

'Beyond what I saw in the flames, no.' Jack closed his eyes, recalling the image of the tall man and the sword of light.

'It was Cullian's sword,' Corriwen said, 'that caught the Morrigan and allowed the bards to trap her in the black stone. When he drew it from the stone, it locked her in sleep. It was given to my family and it became the Redthorn sword, a symbol of peace in Temair. It unites all the clans.'

'So who was this Cullian guy?'

'He was the hero who brought down the Morrigan and saved Temair. He was like you, Finbar said. He came from the east and then he went west and was never seen again. But he rallied the people of Temair against her and destroyed her power. Finbar said we must make the wheel turn full circle.'

It sounded so much like the stories he'd read in the Major's library. Tales of the great Celtic heroes of myth; Cuchulainn the warrior and his brother Ferdia. Of battles and bards; witches and warlocks, spells and curses. The stories had fascinated him, but he had always believed they were only stories.

Now he was walking in a world of myth.

But he had to believe it was real. And that raised another question in his mind.

What other worlds were beyond the stone gates in the ring of Cromwath Blackwood?

Kerry snored in the boat thwarts. Corriwen Redthorn held Jack's eyes with hers.

'Will you help me get the sword back?'

'If I can. I'll do my best. But there's only three of us, and I've never fought before.'

'The best we can do is the best we can expect,' Corriwen said. 'We have killed Scree and slaughtered their beasts and we are still walking free.'

'We'll both help you,' Jack said.

'I'm the last of the Redthorns,' Corriwen said. 'It's time to turn the tide. I have to find the Redthorn sword. For the sake of all Temair.'

Kerry Malone never cried.

He was crying now, and it tore Jack's heart.

Jack hated this, the anger and despair, the desperation of losing a friend in this frightening place.

Kerry had hit him hard. Hit him in anger, and that had never happened before. Jack had picked himself up and instead of fighting back, he had clamped his arms around Kerry and held him tight. Kerry strained against him, and then the strength went out of his arms and Jack could feel him convulse as sobs racked him. Jack couldn't help it. He began to cry too.

'All those heroes you told me about,' Kerry had said, 'they're just in books. You'll never really be one. She would have fought for you. Now she's gone.'

'So would we be if we'd stayed. There was nothing we could do. There were too many of them.'

'What's that got to do with it?'

'We can't help her if we're dead,' Jack replied. He meant what he said, but the import of his words surprised him. *Dead.* He hadn't considered that possibility before, not really, not while he was still trying to comprehend all this strangeness.

But they could have been killed. In the forest, in the ring of standing stones. In the river, or in the plummet from the waterfall.

'All you want to do is get home,' Kerry said, voice beginning to falter as he too considered what Jack had just said. 'After she saved your life.'

Jack was stunned by Kerry's accusation, but he knew Kerry was only partly right. He *did* want to get back, more than anything.

Corriwen had saved his life when the Scree had come at him. She had pushed herself in front of him, knives fast and deadly. That was a fact.

'You're right,' he said finally. 'She did save my life. And I *do* want to get back again, more than anything. But, honest, Kerry, we couldn't have saved her, not then. We did the right thing, and that gives us another chance.'

'What do you mean?'

'When you were asleep, she told me she had to find this sword. The Redthorn Sword. It's important to her. I said we would help her all the way.'

Kerry wiped a tear-smear on his dirty face.

'Really? You told her that?'

'Sure I did. I thought you'd be okay with that.'

Jack loosened his grip. Kerry backed away. He sniffed, embarrassed by his tears, then turned back and crushed Jack in a hug.

'Sorry, man,' he said. 'I never meant to . . .'

Jack hugged him back. 'I know that. We're not going to fall out over a girl. Not ever. Even one like her!'

'Friends?' Kerry let go, stuck out his hand. Jack took it. They smiled sheepishly.

'Always.'

They started off along the road together.

'They won't harm her,' Jack said. 'Mandrake wants her, so they'll take her to him. We can find her, and this time we'll be more prepared. I promise you.'

'Promise?' Jack remembered what the Major had said about the old heroes and their blood oaths. Now was the time to be a hero.

'Really promise. We're going to find her and help her do what she has to do.'

'You mean that?'

'I swear. Cross my heart and hope to die.'

They moved at first light. Jack had first closed his eyes. Since he had come here, come with the sickening touch on his skin, he had been lost without his sense of direction. Since they stepped off the boat it had come back again. He kept his eyes closed, back to the rising sun, then stuck out his right hand. That's north. So that's south. He pointed ahead.

Jack Flint had his bearings now, the feel of this world.

'The village is that way. We can pick up their trail there. But first, let's try something.'

He opened the satchel and drew out the book, handed it to Kerry and they watched, fascinated and expectant as the words evolved on the blank old page.

Even Jack could understand the script now.

Ever westward, never tarry
Perils wait and hunters harry
Ware the skies and soaring eyes
Find a keep where danger lies.

'Looks like it agrees with us.'

'We keep going west and look for a keep,' Jack said. 'How hard can that be?'

Kerry found the trail beyond the village, and at first it wasn't hard to follow, but a mile or so beyond the last of the scattered houses, the road petered out and then vanished altogether into open country.

They travelled fast, travelled light, keeping to the lee of stone walls and ragged thorn-hedges, huddling in sheep pens at night. Jack was certain of the direction – *ever westwards* – but it was Kerry who kept to the trail, skilfully reading the signs the way he had followed rabbit tracks at home.

He would find a scuff-mark on stone, a boot-print on hard turf and he even got down on his hands and knees a couple of times, sniffing at the ground like a bloodhound. He told Jack the smell of the hogs was hard to miss.

At one point, on the drying clay, he found a hand print. A small human hand print, and they knew for sure they were on the right track.

In three days and three nights, they reached their destination, and Jack knew they had found the right place.

The keep towered high into a sky that shaded to black in the west as darkness fell. Moss grew on its dank north side, and on the east face, ivy clung to the crumbling face. A raised ditch had encircled it, but it was worn down in places, overgrown with thorns, mounds of gorse and bracken.

Jack and Kerry made their way round the keep, keeping close to the scrubby cover, counting the guards. There were two on the battlements, resting against tall pikestaffs, and two on a drawbridge. They were sitting together, playing dice.

'What now?' Kerry wanted to know.

Jack shrugged. 'I'm thinking.'

'Yeah. We need a cunning plan.'

'She's in there,' Jack said.

'I know. But how do we get in?'

'We wait for dark. See if we can sneak past the guards. The place isn't that big, so we've a chance.'

'Could we climb the ivy?'

'It doesn't look strong enough. If one of us fell, we'd be scuppered. And I don't fancy landing in that water. There's things in there, I bet. Eels or something worse. You can never tell in this place.'

'What about the guards?' Kerry asked. 'You reckon you could take them with the bow? I could maybe knock one off with the sling.'

'Maybe we could, but if we miss, they'll come after us.'

'Come on Jack, man. You're the brains here.'

Just as he spoke, he heard a noise from over the lip of the hollow. A harsh voice. It sounded so close that Kerry froze. Another voice replied, guttural and rough. They couldn't hear any words.

Jack put a finger to his lips. Together, very warily, they crawled up the slope of the hollow and belly-walked like poachers through the bushes.

On the drawbridge, one of the guards had crossed the moat and was peering into the gloom.

The two guards went back over the drawbridge and hunkered down, almost the same colour as the old stone, and looking every bit as hard. One of them reached for a cup and rattled it. Small white things rolled out onto the planks.

'Knucklebones,' Jack said. 'They're playing a game.'

There was just enough light to see what they were using for a cup. It was a skull, white in the dark, sawn off at the top. From where Jack crouched, it looked too much like a human skull.

'Let me try something,' he said. He wriggled backwards and Kerry followed him. Under the thick cloud, the world slipped into shades of grey and black. Jack found his pack and rummaged about inside. He drew out the little laser keyring he and Kerry had fooled around with on the way home from the Halloween party, on the night when this had all started.

They wriggled back to their vantage point.

'Let's see how bright they are,' Jack said. Kerry sprawled beside him, using the backpack for cover. Jack flicked the little light on, and a small red spot appeared right in the centre of the skull's eye socket. Kerry aimed, and a second dot winked into being in the other socket. From the distance it seemed red eyes glared from the skull.

The first guard reached for the gruesome dice-cup, and instantly jerked his hand back.

Jack and Kerry switched off the lights.

The guards stared at the skull, their postures showing bafflement and alarm.

Jack flashed both beams onto the wall, just beside their heads.

Then Jack flicked the light off and Kerry followed. One Scree scratched his head with a horny hand.

Jack aimed at the wall and Kerry followed suit, making the red eyes stare out at Scree head height. Both guards hefted their spears as the boys whirled the lights on the wall in dazzling circles.

Jack aimed again and planted the light on the back of the first one's head. The other guard saw it and he went into a crouch, unhitching the big club on his belt.

Without a pause, he swung the club. From forty yards away the blow sounded like a hammer on an old door. The guard straightened up, like a bull that's been poleaxed and isn't quite sure if it's dead yet. His mouth opened, and then, without a sound he toppled into the moat and disappeared with an oily splash.

The first one ran to the edge and peered into the water.

Ripples hit either bank and rebounded to meet in the middle. Down below, under the surface scum, there wasn't any sign of movement.

Jack flicked the light onto the wall and the Scree spun. He trailed the light down the wall and the Scree backed off. The little point came tracing across the planks and the guard shuffled backwards, growling wordlessly. He backed against the low banister and stopped. Jack swung the keyring fast now and the red light zipped forward, like an angry glow-worm, fast enough to take the Scree by surprise. He jerked, raised a foot as if to kick it away, backing further still.

The motion was just enough to make him lose balance and he fell against the flimsy banister which cracked like matchwood. He pinwheeled for balance, grabbing the pike as if it could stop him, and then, with a startled roar, flopped backwards into the water. There was a flurry of slime and foam and then, moments later, nothing at all.

'The Scree sink,' Jack said. 'Corriwen was right.'

They scrambled out of the bushes and darted across the bridge into the shadows of the doorway. A small hatch in the wooden door had a simple latch. Jack lifted it and Kerry followed him into gloom that was hardly relieved by smelly tallow torches. Some yards on, they found themselves in a narrow passage.

They sneaked to the far end, nervous as mice. The passageway took a sharp right turn, when Jack stopped so suddenly that Kerry barged into him. Corriwen's knives were hanging on a big hook. Before he could speak a big Scree trooper came lumbering down the passage.

'Back,' Jack hissed. They turned back the way they had come, reached the fork, took the right side this time, turned a corner.

And barged right into the belly of another guard.

It was like hitting a solid stone wall.

Something came down from the dark and swatted Kerry to the ground. Something else came down and clamped on Jack's head. He felt himself swung off his feet, the pressure of calloused fingers so powerful that he thought his eyes would pop out.

'Been lookin' for you,' the Scree growled. 'Save us plenty time.'

FIFTEEN

Corriwen's heart sank like a stone.

The room was dark but not dank. There was a bench against the wall and a straw mattress on the floor. She had slept in worse places.

But then, she had been free.

Through the bars in the window she had seen the flash of black hair and in the torchlight a glimpse of blue eyes that had met hers for a brief moment, enough to know that Jack and Kerry had been caught.

She knew the Scree had sent word north to the High Keep where Mandrake sat and plotted, but he probably knew already that she had been seized. It was only a matter of time before they came face to face.

Somehow though, a small ember of hope burned. They had given her hope, and she would not lose it, not now.

The Scree were strong, so carting both boys presented no problem to them.

They were thrown bodily into a dingy cell at the bottom of a flight of stairs.

'What about this stuff?' The trooper held up the backpack and satchel in one hand, the bow and Kerry's sword in the other.

The Captain looked at them. 'Bow and blade, no. The rest, no harm. Touch nothing. They go to the Black Keep with all they have.'

They stumped back along the passage.

'Another fine mess you've got me into,' Kerry said, breathing hard.

'I saw her,' Jack said. 'She's a prisoner here.'

'Yeah, and so are we.'

'I know but this place doesn't look too secure.'

'Okay, so let's dig our way out,' Kerry said, heavy with sarcasm. 'Like your Mounty Cristy guy.'

'Monte Cristo,' Jack corrected. 'And it took him years. Anyway, you heard him. We're getting sent to Mandrake. We have to think of something fast.'

There was a three-legged stool in the corner which Jack put against the door. He stood on it and peered through the bars.

Beyond the grate, dim torches glowed, giving off a scent of burnt fat. A Scree guard sat at a bench. Beside him, on a hook on the wall, dangled a bunch of iron keys.

'I've got an idea,' Jack said. He unzipped the backpack and drew out the little poacher's rod they would have used at the tarn once they'd explored Cromwath Blackwood.

'Can you snag the keys with this?'

Kerry nodded. He telescoped the rod to its full length, unwinding the line slowly and quietly. He rummaged in the pack and found a decent-sized caddis-fly lure and hitched it with a blood-knot.

With Jack beside him holding him up so he could use both hands, Kerry eased the slender rod through the barred hatch. The fly danced in the breeze that wafted from some unseen vent. Gently he eased it closer to the wall where the keys hung. The Scree was hunched over a meaty bone in a bowl. Occasionally he would take a bite, teeth crunching on the bone as if it was sugar candy.

The fly snagged on a crack in the wall and Kerry pulled back a little, as if he was teasing a brown trout. It pinged away, swung back and almost caught on the big keyring. They jingled. The Scree turned his head and in that split second, his eye caught the fly. He jerked back and swung his hand at it. Kerry tried to retrieve it before the Scree realised what it was. He pulled back on the line just as the fly whirled round the guard's head and the rod stopped dead.

'What's happened?'

'It's stuck,' Kerry whispered. 'I think I hooked a Scree.'

'Oh, that's just brilliant.' Jack craned to see. Down the corridor the guard lifted a piece of food from the bowl and started crunching again. Kerry pulled on the line and the

Scree stopped chewing. Jack could see it now. The thin nylon line had wrapped itself around the guard's throat and the fly had hooked into a scaly ear. Kerry tugged the line again and the guard coughed as it tightened on his gullet.

'Uh-oh,' they both said at exactly the same time. The Scree bent over, almost dragging the fishing rod out of Kerry's hands and then he started to choke on a piece of food. He coughed, coughed again then grabbed at his own neck, gasping for breath, wheezing like a steam engine. He staggered to his feet, unable to breathe, and the line broke. Kerry pulled the rod back through the hatch before the Scree turned and saw him, but the guard, when he did turn, had his eyes closed tight and his face was an ominous shade of purple. He reared back, slammed against the wall, and whatever had lodged in his throat came bulleting out along the passageway and smacked against the heavy cell door.

The guard whooped in a huge breath and grabbed for a flagon on the bench, upended it to drink, then slammed it back down when he found it was empty. Still coughing, he lurched along the passageway.

'He's gone for a drink,' Jack said. 'Now's your chance.'

Kerry wasted no time in setting another hook to the broken line. The rod was back out and in seconds he snagged the bunch of keys. Which was easier than getting the rusty lock to open, but finally they managed to turn the key. The door creaked open and they were out.

They retrieved their weapons and then searched for the passageway where Jack had seen Corriwen's knives. He closed his eyes and tried to reverse the route they'd taken after the scrum with the guards, but it had been dark. The castle wasn't a complex maze, however, and when he came to the door, he recognised it immediately. Her knives hung in their sheath a few feet away.

Inside, Corriwen was huddled on a straw mattress. Jack tapped gently and she looked up.

As soon as their eyes met, her face came alive with sudden joy. Jack put his finger to his lips, but Corriwen was too sharp to do anything but wait silently until Kerry found the key that fitted, and opened the door.

She came into Jack's arms in a rush and held him so tight he thought a rib might crack.

'I knew you would come,' she said.

'Typical,' Kerry muttered. 'I get the key and you get the girl.'

Corriwen let Jack go and turned to Kerry to embrace him just as tightly.

'You both get the girl,' she whispered. 'Now can you get her out of here?'

The tower was high above the outer battlements. They couldn't risk going down the stairwell. Jack uncoiled the rope they had planned to use to scale the Cromwath wall and fixed a good climber's knot round a stanchion.

In the distance, lightning strode the barren countryside and thunder talked. In the flashes of light he saw guards on the high points of the battlements.

With the rope tied, he went back inside and peered

through a hatch on a cell door. Inside, an elderly man slumped on the floor. Jack dropped the bunch of keys through the hatch and left the man to make his own decisions.

He threaded the rope through Corriwen's belt, but she needed no help to abseil down. Jack made Kerry go next and followed on afterwards, until they were well down in the shadows. Jack tugged the short end of the rope and the knot high above them slipped easily. He wound the braid neatly and stuffed it in the pack.

'Where now?'

'Follow me,' Corriwen said. They stole round the walls of the courtyard, keeping to the shadows. Under an arch and through a wooden portcullis, they came to the stables. This deep inside the Keep, there were no sentries in sight.

Corriwen pushed her way inside, walking stealthily until she came to a stall. Behind the wicker gate, Jack and Kerry heard something move and smelt the warm heat of a big animal. Corriwen opened the stall and they came face to face with the biggest horse either of them had ever seen. It was half as big again as the Clydesdales that thundered about on the Major's estate.

'Would you look at that,' Kerry said. 'Is that an elephant?'

The animal shook its head and snorted, stamping hooves bigger than dinner plates and sending sparks off the cobbled floor.

'It's a greathorse,' she replied. 'It looks fed and rested.'

'You can't ride that thing,' Kerry said.

'Sure I can,' she retorted brightly. 'We all can. The Scree can't ride a greathorse. It won't bear them.'

'So why is it here?'

'The Keeplord must be Mandrake's man.'

She backed the huge animal out, looking tiny against its bulk, but it came willingly and when it was out, she climbed the gate-bars and got herself across its neck, whispering to it all the time.

'Come on!'

Jack went first and clambered astride the horse, unable to get a grip on its flanks with his ankles. It was simply too wide.

'Hold my belt,' she said. Kerry climbed up behind him, his sword jammed in his backpack. Jack felt his hand clench around his belt. Corriwen did something very fast with the tethering rope and in seconds she had made a set of reins that fitted around the horse's nose. Just as she did so, Jack heard a shout from high in the tower.

'Sounds like trouble,' he hissed. 'We'd better split, and fast.'

Corriwen slapped the horse. It reared, hoofing the air, and Jack and Kerry almost tumbled straight over its tail. By sheer luck they held on and then the horse was off at a gallop.

They came clattering into the open as a troop of sentries sprinted round the corner right into the path of the massive hooves.

'Roaks,' Jack cried. Corriwen hugged the great neck, yelling into the horse's ear. Jack tugged at the bow but couldn't free it. Corriwen swung one hand behind her back. The long knife magically appeared in her grip. He took it. Behind him Kerry had freed the sword and whirled it over their heads in tight circles.

The roaks swooped, wings whistling in the night air.

'Stop them,' the Scree leader roared. 'Stop them now!'

They reached the inner courtyard, hooves clattering on stone and the chestnut mane whipping back to almost cover Corriwen. Crates and barrels went flying. A hutch full of chickens splintered and the birds fluttered out in a blitz. The fugitives came round the courtyard until they reached the archway to the outer yard, made it through and scattered the guards.

'Close them in,' the Scree screeched, his voice almost lost in the melée. There was one Scree at the gate and he started to unwind a capstan which bore a thick chain. Immediately a grinding sound split through the tumult and Jack saw the bridge slowly climb upwards.

'Now, Corriwen!' he bawled in her ear. *'Go for it!'*

Jack risked turning to glance over Kerry's shoulder and saw the Scree unhitch their hounds which came bounding in pursuit.

'Hold me,' Jack shouted to Kerry, as he worked his bow free and twisted to face back.

The dogs were grey streaks in the dim light, faster than Jack would have believed possible.

'Down, Kerry. Down!'

Kerry ducked. The lead dog's eyes glittered. It bunched in mid-stride, uncoiled like a spring, jaws wide.

Jack's arrow took it clean in the throat in mid-air and it did an oddly elegant somersault, sending a plume of blood into the air.

In that split second the horse dug its hooves and came to a sudden halt. Corriwen was thrown straight over its head. For an instant Jack thought they were done for. The roaks were all around them and another wolfhound was in mid-leap, fangs white in the dim light.

Kerry shouted something, tried to reach past Jack to grab for Corriwen, knowing he was too late to save her as she tumbled over and off.

But she had the reins in one hand. She flew over the horse's head, and her feet hardly touched the ground at all before she swung back up, onto the horse's arched neck.

The greathorse snorted. They felt its muscles bunch just as the wolfhound leapt. Hooves lashed out, faster than the eye could follow, and took the hound in mid-leap. They heard the crunch of bones as it landed.

Just as the horse began to gallop, Jack heard a whooping sound in the distance.

'What's that?' He looked left and right, alert for anything else coming after them.

It grew louder as they breasted a small rise, heading south. Jack looked east and saw a white cloud rolling across the moors.

'What is it?' Kerry asked. Jack had no idea, and nor did he know what weapons could stop it.

The whooping filled the air. Around them the roaks fluttered in confusion.

Then the cloud was on them, and they saw it was no cloud.

It was a flock of brilliant white swans. Hundreds of them, thousands of them. A wall of swans flying over the moor, snow wings sweeping the air in great steady heartbeats.

The white wall passed them by like a gale, almost

deafening, and continued west, scattering the roaks and sweeping the sky clean as it went.

Corriwen turned, eyes filled with wonder and hope.

'Finbar the Bard said he would help us,' she said.

'This is one really weird place,' Jack observed. 'But good old Finn.'

Corriwen spoke into the greathorse's ear and they were off again with the wind in their faces and the dawn at their backs.

SIXTEEN

'He knows we escaped,' Corriwen said. 'I can *feel* it.'

After the flight from the keep they travelled by day and kept watch at night. On the first night, they had decided to stick to the shadows as they moved and hide during the day, to escape those eyes in the sky, even though they had seen no roaks since the miraculous flight of white swans.

But the night was not safe either. The night belonged to whatever darkness Mandrake, or the Morrigan, had summoned under the barrow in the blasted lands of the salt plains.

They discovered that when they rounded a rocky crag where scrub junipers clung for life to the unyielding stone. Jack made them follow the stream among tumbled stones, where they found a cave, overhung by a brow of black stone.

The sun was well down now, and the shadows gathering from the east while in the north the storm raged.

He made a fire while Corriwen fed and watered the horse and Kerry quickly plucked and cleaned chickens he'd found at a deserted farm. He wrapped them tight in leaves and rolled them into the hot fire stones and let them steam for a while. The birds may have been scrawny, but the smell of roasting fowl had them drooling and they ate like starvelings.

'What's the plan?' Kerry wanted to know.

'Finbar says the only thing we can do is to find the Redthorn sword,' Corriwen said. 'the Cullian sword. That's what Mandrake used to wake the Morrigan, and he plans to break the great holding curse completely. He has men and women digging a channel through the mountains and when his dam is filled up, he will flood the Salt Barrens. The waters are backing up even now, the Bard says, and if he floods the Black Barrow, she will really be free.'

'And what does she want?'

'In the old days,' Corriwen explained, 'she had great power. She ravaged the land and almost defeated men in Temair. Finbar said she would use gates to other worlds. I don't know what he meant.'

'I do,' Jack said. They both turned to look at his face in the light of the flickering fire. He opened his jerkin and unbuttoned his shirt. They saw the red hand against his skin, the five dots in an arc above them. Between the arc and the hand, the black heartstone on its silver chain threw the firelight back at them.

'The Major gave me this,' he said. 'He told me to keep it safe. It was my father's.'

'I know,' Kerry nodded. 'You told me.'

'It has something to do with the gates. He says it's a kind of key. You both have to know, because if anything happens to me, then, no matter what, you have to get it through the Homeward Gate.'

Jack surprised himself by even considering the thought. *If anything should happen to me.*

Everything had changed, so fast.

'Finbar said it's the key to all worlds,' he said. 'This place. Ours. Maybe more. So it's important. And if my father used it, maybe he came somewhere like this. "A journeyman," the Major said. Maybe he even came here. Finbar thought so.'

'That's what Mandrake wants,' Kerry said. 'I heard the Scree talking when they carted us down. Said everything we have is to go to him ... or else.'

'That means *She* wants it,' Corriwen broke in.

'You really think there are other places?' Kerry asked. 'Like this?'

Jack shrugged.

'The Major knows, I'm sure. That's for later. First, we've got a job to do. Find this sword.'

Corriwen shook her head. 'You've done enough. But this is not your quest.'

'It is now,' Kerry said. Jack nodded.

'The Bard said if the Morrigan gets out, it's Temair first and us next. So it's our business too.'

Kerry threw a gnawed bone onto the fire. 'I always wanted to go on a quest. Never been on one before.'

'Let's have a look at the travel log,' Jack said. 'It hasn't been wrong yet.'

He pulled out the *Book of Ways* and they huddled round the fire-glow, watching until the script appeared.

> Rede of Reed, bale morass
> Quaking path, whisper grass
> Find the ways and hark the water
> Ware the eel and trust the otter
> Chase behind, snare before
> Ever westward, find a shore.

'Marshland,' Corriwen said in a small voice. 'The South-edge Marshes. I have heard stories of Kelpie and the Rushen folk. I don't know what they are, but the marshes are cursed. Men don't go there.'

'Good thing we're just boys then,' Jack said, more lightly than he felt. 'And a girl.'

Mandrake's rage was incandescent.

He knew before the messengers arrived that they had escaped. Her eyes in the sky had seen it all.

'Gone!' He felt his face contort as her influence spread through him like a cold, dark disease.

'*Escaped!*'

His vision blurred then cleared again as the images from the crater resolved in front of him.

He saw them in the dark, sliding down the rope and then fleeing on the great horse, beating off the pursuit, galloping for freedom. He saw the bank of white swans come whooping in from the east.

'The Bards! The *Bards*!' Her anger shrieked in his mind. 'They have dared defy me again.'

She was gone, the last of the Redthorns.

'The Bards.' Mandrake's face squeezed in on itself, cheeks hollowing, skin wrinkling, until he was a hunched and withered thing in the centre of the chamber. His arms reached out, fingers clawed, as if to choke the life out of something.

'*He* is gone with it!' he hissed in her voice, eyes like holes to the bottom of the world. Suddenly he shuddered under the violence of her wrath and felt himself flung across the floor.

'No!' he squawked, terrified. He hit the wall with a thud and fell hard, hurting from chin to knee, tumbled back and was snatched from the floor and hurled in a tangle across the wide bed.

'*No!*' Inside, he could feel the Morrigan's anger explode. He hauled himself to his feet, blood trickling from his nose. Something inside him had burst, but all he felt was her wrath.

'We will raise all dark things.' Her voice was now completely dominant. 'We summon the beasts and the shadows. We call from the depths. We will have them. We will destroy them all.'

Her voice shrieked through his ragged throat.

'*We will bring the nightmare!*'

Suddenly she was gone from his mind. Mandrake flopped to the floor, unable to move for a long time.

But he had no regrets. Even while her rage was unbelievable, he welcomed her foul presence.

Some time later, Mandrake opened his eyes, and managed to get to his feet. He stood there breathing deeply, letting his thoughts fester for a little while.

Then he strode to the door, flung it open and started down the spiral stone stairway, ready and determined to kill something.

Jack woke, instantly alert. Corriwen was huddled close to the glowing embers. Kerry snored lightly beside her, both hands clenched on the handle of the fine sword.

The hairs on the back of Jack's neck were bristling. Far to the north, the storm was a glow that was visible beyond the cave-mouth.

The heartstone beat against his chest and a sense of impending danger rippled through him.

He got to his haunches, eyes wide, ears straining. The stone beat steadily. At the cave-mouth, the greathorse whickered.

Jack moved silently to the cave entrance. The horse blocked most of it and he had to squeeze past its tail. In the night, yellow eyes blinked. The horse stamped. Kerry grunted, rolled over.

'What's up?' he asked groggily.

A shape came loping in and the horse reared. It kicked and a shaggy, snarling creature dropped to the ground, ribs caved in.

'Wolves,' Jack said. 'Out there.' He unhitched the greathorse and drew it back inside the cave. Its head scraped the roof, but it backed in far enough. Grey shapes ran across their vision, snarling and yapping, but none dared enter. Jack and Kerry hunkered by the fire.

'Something else,' Jack said. He cocked his head, straining to hear.

'Yeah,' Kerry agreed. 'And not those mutts out there, either.'

Just at that point, they both looked at the embers. They glowed deep red, but every now and again, they would swell to orange then back to red again, as if bellows were softly pumping them.

Jack looked into the darkness at the back of the cave.

'You hear something?'

Kerry held his breath, listened a while, then nodded. 'Like breathing?'

Jack couldn't quite hear it, but he could feel an odd whuffling in the air, like a small guttering flame. He too held his breath and concentrated. The odd sensation was stronger, and there was something else, a tiny squeak, high-pitched and barely audible.

They sat in wary silence, all senses alert as the feeling of threat expanded in the darkness.

'I hear whispers,' Kerry said. 'There's something in here.'

Jack reached for his bow. Kerry raised his sword.

'Should we wake Corriwen . . .' He began to ask, and just

as the words were out of his mouth, the darkness at the back of the cave began to move and the whispering was suddenly a metallic shriek that they could feel between their ears, like fingernails on glass.

'*Bats!*' Jack jumped back.

They came pouring from the recess at the back of the cave, exploding into the firelight. Hundreds of them, so many the beat of their wings fanned the embers into flame. Corriwen startled awake.

There were thousands of them now, filling the air with frantic fluttering, the sound of so many wings a roar in the confines of the cave. Kerry waved his sword as they circled round his head. He felt something sharp and barbed scrape across the back of his hand followed by a trickle of blood.

The greathorse whinnied and flicked its tail and then, in seconds, it was festooned with tiny bats hooked onto its hide and mane, and grabbing at its ears.

Then the horde was on them. One flapped into Jack's face and he felt a scratch on his cheek – teeth or claws, he couldn't tell. Instinctively he snatched it away with his free hand, beating the air with the bow, knowing an arrow would be useless against so many tiny targets.

He crushed the bat in his hand and was about to throw it off when he saw its face and realised it was like no bat he had ever seen before. The face, in contrast to the grey leathery body, was white as a skull, and worse, it looked just like a skull. It had a tiny, wizened human face and jet eyes and a wide mouth with a row of tiny, glassy teeth. The sight of a human-like face on such a creature was such a shock that Jack dropped it as if it burned.

Beside him Kerry spun the sword, scattering them from the air, papery wings torn and flapping, but still they came, from the black hole in the cave wall. Corriwen was up and her knives a-blur. The creatures clawed at her red hair, trying for her eyes. The horse was blanketed in them, dark wings scuttling over its flanks, little pale faces trying to bite through the hide. Corriwen squealed when one of them bit her ear. She whirled, blades flickering this way and that. Jack snatched two bats from the air and crushed their tiny chests with his thumbs, sickened at the thought of killing something that, however obscenely, resembled a human.

'Too many,' he shouted, dragging another from his collar, too close to his neck. They were all over his jerkin, hooking and clawing.

'Outside,' Kerry said, whirling his sword.

But there were wolves outside, howling for blood. The horse panicked, reared, and was gone, thundering down the hill and into the night.

'To hell with this!' Jack snarled. There were too many bats, far too many to fight. He crouched, flicking them away, while he groped for the backpack. Eyes closed against the thorn-sharp claws, he found the midge repellent spray. Too late in the year to use at home, but just right now ... if it worked.

He flicked off the cap and jumped towards the fire. Flames wavered upwards in the rushing air. Without a pause, Jack depressed the aerosol trigger, aiming the nozzle straight at the heat.

The spray hissed out.

A white flare erupted. The dark of the cave turned abruptly to day in a searing flash.

Jack kept his finger tight on the nozzle. The bats shrieked, so high and loud it felt like needles in his ears. A horde of them flickering past the fire were incinerated instantly, wings bursting into puffs of flame. He followed them, burning them out of the air.

The bats wheeled away, fluttering madly, wingbeats stirring the embers to a roar of heat, and almost as one creature, one shuddering grey monstrosity, they swarmed away from the fiery torch and out into the night.

Jack stamped on two of them, yelling with a sudden savage joy when the dark flock blasted out of the cave and left them breathless, scratched and bitten, but not seriously hurt.

'Where did they come from?' Kerry was sweating from the exercise and the sudden heat. His face was smeared with soot.

Jack drew a burning twig from the fire and searched along the narrowing walls at the back of the cave until he found a small hole, right on the ground, like a rabbit burrow. He held the flame over it and peered down into a black emptiness. He kicked a stone and heard it smack against the narrow sides, echoing as it went down and down and down until the sound simply faded to silence. He dropped the burning stick and watched it flare through the air, falling straight down until it was just a tiny dot in the distance.

'Goes down for miles,' he said.

Kerry dabbed some water on the cuts across Corriwen's hand and cheek. Jack drew a large flat boulder across the floor and jammed it over the hole, and then both of them spread out the sheet of polythene they had planned to use as a groundsheet and hung it over the mouth of the cave, pinning it with stones into cracks and crevices.

Corriwen touched the clear surface, eyebrows raised in curiosity. She'd never seen a polythene sheet before. As soon as the barrier was up, the heat began to build in the little cave, but at least now, there was no way back in for the bat horde.

'We can find the horse in the morning,' Corriwen said. 'If it's still alive.'

'Maybe we should travel in daylight,' Jack suggested, 'even if those crows *can* see us.'

Corriwen shrugged. 'Night or day, she'll send things after us. I don't know what these things were, but they come from the deep dark. We are on the edge of Mid-Temair, I think. Few travel here. Who knows what lives here, and what bends to her will? Everything is strange.'

'You're telling me,' Kerry said.

Corriwen looked at him. 'Yes. I am telling you.'

Jack burst into laughter, a sudden release of tension after the battle, and then all three of them were doubled up, laughing uncontrollably, not knowing what they were laughing at, but unable to stop.

They slept fitfully until morning when they shared the last of the meat off the chicken bones, both boys strangely homesick for a cup of hot tea.

As soon as dawn lightened the sky, Jack felt the hairs on his nape prickle again and he stiffened. A high-pitched screaming came from beyond the polythene barrier, while through the transparent screen they could see shapes banging like hailstones against the flimsy sheet. It went on for an ear-splitting half an hour as the day brightened and the first rays of the sun peered over the distant moorland, and then it suddenly stopped.

After a while they risked peering out.

All around the cave-mouth, thousands of the grotesque bat-sprites lay in crumbling mounds. A few that remained in the air fluttered down to the ground, trailing thin smoke. The three of them watched in amazement as the little white faces gaped in agony and tiny eyes melted into black liquid that dripped and sizzled into the earth. In the space of a few moments, the flying things were like heaps of rotted leaves, subsiding under their own weight, until a morning breeze scattered them like dust.

The sun rose and spread a welcome light over the rough country, though the far northern sky still glowered under a vast storm, and they set out again, heading westwards with the dawn at their backs. Three miles from the cave, they found the greathorse in a thicket of thorns where it had obviously sheltered from the flying nightmares. Its ears and nose were bloody, but it was not badly hurt. Corriwen tempted it out and gentled it against a tree-stump which they used to clamber up on its back. Kerry had filled his water-bottle by the stream and they drank briefly before Corriwen heeled the great mount and they were off and flying.

But in less than half an hour, they were fugitives again.

Kerry spotted them first, after they entered hilly country and rode slowly down a twisting ravine and stopped for a break. He had just gathered a load of firewood when he saw the movement on the brow of a hill. At first he thought they were grey stones left by an old glacier.

He carried the firewood to where Jack and Corriwen sat in shadow, deliberately not looking up at the hill.

'Behind me,' he said casually. 'Look slowly.'

Jack peered through the armful of sticks and saw them, a wave of Scree, making their way fast down the slope. They must have muzzled the hounds, because they came silently.

Corriwen unhitched the horse and they clambered on, keeping the rock between themselves and pursuit for as long as possible, before she dug in and they all held tight as the horse found its stride, thundering down the ravine, hoofbeats echoing all round.

The Scree let loose their hounds as the fugitives raced on, rounding a tight bend to face three narrow culverts where the stone had been worn by ancient waters.

'Which way?' Corriwen twisted round to Jack.

He closed his eyes. This deep in the ravine, he couldn't see the sun, but he didn't need the sun.

'Right.' He pointed over her shoulder. 'That way.'

With just a slight pressure on the reins, and without letting the horse lose its pace, she turned its head and they clattered into the narrow entrance. Here the land was broken like sun-baked clay, a labyrinth of passages between sheer cliffs of hard sandstone. The ravines twisted and turned on each other, some of them so narrow and deep they hid the sky.

Buzzards soared overhead on broad wings and Jack could sense things on the rock walls, watching them as they galloped past. He didn't care to wonder what they were. He just wanted to keep going.

Behind them the hounds howled, high and hungry. They sped on, wondering if they could outpace the dogs.

The Scree had split up, and in this confused tangle of fissures, they could run headlong into more at any time. Jack had an arrow nocked to the bow-string and he flicked Corriwen's cape aside to give him easy access to her knives.

They galloped, desperate to put some distance between them and get onto flat land, when a loud growling sound rolled behind them. Jack and Kerry swivelled, expecting some monstrous hound to be snapping at their heels, but for once there was no sign of pursuit.

The growl got louder, became a rumble. Kerry swivelled again.

'Jeez!'

Jack jerked round and saw the monster rushing towards them, all grey and brown and roaring so loud now the canyon walls reverberated and the ground vibrated under the greathorse's hooves.

'Flash flood,' he cried. And it was right behind them.

'We have to get higher!'

'Which way?' asked Corriwen.

He guessed. They had been, even with the pursuit, heading pretty much in a westerly direction. They came to another fork and he told Corriwen to go left. The horse didn't pause. Behind them all they could hear was the roaring of the flood-rolled debris, no sound of Scree or hounds. With luck, Jack thought, they'd have been caught in it.

'We'd better get a move on!' Kerry's voice was high and urgent.

The horse seemed to find fresh stamina under Corriwen's hand. The rock walls blurred past them.

Already they could feel spray on the backs of their necks. Jack closed his eyes, slid his hand inside his shirt to grasp the heartstone. It pulsed under his fingers.

When he opened his eyes again, they were on a slope and the track winding upwards was easily wide enough to take the horse.

Jack pointed, but Corriwen had seen it. She pulled on the reins and the horse swerved, found solid footing and they were rising.

A split second later, the flood swept past them in a tumbling mass of rock and tree-trunks. They kept going until they were high enough to be safe and then they paused to watch. Inside that maelstrom they could see the grey bodies of Scree troopers tumble. A great hound pawed at the water until a knotty pine spiked it under.

But for the horse and its speed, Jack knew that could have been any of them. All of them. They had escaped by inches.

Corriwen turned the horse, continued uphill until they crested the ridge and followed a long slope down. They were still shaking from the excitement. They kept going for miles, letting the mount canter at ease.

After a while the land bottomed out with not a hill in sight as far as the eye could see.

A veil of fog stretched from horizon to horizon, north and south. In the distance it looked solid, but when they got close it was thin and gauzy.

'I think this is it,' Jack said when Corriwen stopped to let the horse drink. Jack plucked some lily leaves from the water and fed it. He sniffed at the air. It was damp and stagnant.

'Smells like we've found the marsh.'

SEVENTEEN

The *Book of Ways* had warned them of a *bale morass*, and this was certainly the place.

Jack looked behind them and realised they were already far from solid ground. The horse had instinctively found a pathway into the reeds and sedge, but now they could hear the sound of mud sucking at its hooves.

Corriwen suggested they dismount and as soon as their feet touched the ground, it sank under them in slow undulations and bubbles burst through the matted reeds in smelly belches.

'This is not a very nice place,' Kerry said flatly. 'And it stinks.'

Now that they were off the horse, the reeds seemed to crowd around them, swaying and rattling like a million grasshoppers.

They moved deeper, with Kerry in the lead and Corriwen holding the reins. Jack kept looking back over his shoulder for signs of pursuit, but the reeds closed like curtains and very soon there was nothing but tall, thin grass and water in stinking pools.

'It's floating,' Kerry said. 'Like Bemersyde Marsh back home.'

'This is deeper,' Jack said. 'And a whole lot bigger.' He turned to Corriwen. 'How far does it stretch?'

She shrugged. 'Nobody comes here. I heard stories long ago that nobody willingly goes into the morass, and if they do, they disappear.'

'There's a cheerful note,' Jack said, trying to make light of it, but even he could feel the oppressive crowding of the reeds.

Kerry led, because he knew marshes, though maybe none as baleful as this. Jack knew the direction they had to travel, but that sense of direction was useless in this place. Kerry instinctively knew the ways.

'It's easy,' he told Corriwen, showing off just a little bit, although he tried not to look her direct in those green eyes, because when he did that, his voice would stammer and he would feel his cheeks redden.

'How can you see the path?'

He shrugged. 'I dunno. I just know.'

'Just as well,' Jack said. 'Must be in the blood.'

The safe pathways took them south now, as hordes of swifts screamed in the air through clouds of flies, and the horse was struggling, shaking its head and snorting as it pulled its hooves from the glutinous mud. A couple of times

Jack missed the narrow track and went up to his thighs in slime. It was hard going.

They had turned west again, on a ridge of tussocks that was almost completely submerged, when a wading bird flew startled into the air just beside them and the horse bucked. Corriwen had the reins looped in her fingers and she was thrown into a wall of reeds. Jack tried to grab the rope, but the horse slipped from the narrow track and was thrashing in the water trying to lunge back to the track.

In seconds it was up to its flanks in mud.

They hauled at the rope, straining every muscle, but the mud was thick and stronger even than the greathorse. Its eyes rolled in fear.

'How deep is this?' Kerry asked.

'Too deep,' Jack replied. 'We'll never get it out of there.'

'We can't leave it here,' Corriwen said.

'We have to,' Jack said. 'We can't help it.'

'We have to do something!'

As she spoke, the horse lunged again, making one huge, useless effort. It managed to get a hoof above the surface, panting desperately.

But the mud kept sucking and the more it struggled the more it sank. In the space of a few breaths it was up to its neck. Then its cheeks. The mud flowed into its ears. Jack saw its mouth open for one last, choking breath.

Then it was gone.

The surface rippled for a moment and then went still. The bog was silent, flat and empty. And it was now even more threatening than ever. It looked to Jack as if it was just waiting to eat again.

'That was awful,' Kerry said, his eyes still fixed on the mud where the horse had disappeared. Corriwen had the same expression.

'Yeah,' Jack agreed. 'We'd better be really careful we don't go the same way.'

After a minute Kerry turned and they followed, saying nothing at all. The tide was coming in fast.

All around them the reeds swayed in synchronous waves, stalks rubbing against each other in a deathly rattle. They could smell salt on the air now and it was clear they were well into the tidal flats.

They stopped at noon, exhausted, beside an old willow tree that had lost its footing in the quagmire and fallen on its side. It was green still and its branches were growing up from the fallen trunk. They sat there, grateful to have something solid between them and the rafts of reeds and the mud that quivered with every step. Kerry climbed a branch, shinning up with ease until he was above the reed-heads. He shaded his eyes against the high sun and looked back in the direction they had come. Great pools formed lagoons over the pathways they had walked. Beyond the marsh, miles away to the east, the land rose slowly.

'Scree,' he called down. 'Dozens of them.'

'How far?'

'On the edge. We've got hours on them.'

'If they follow us.'

'Oh, they'll follow us,' Corriwen said with certainty. She pointed at the sky. Black dots circled slowly. 'The roaks will show them the way.'

Beyond the willow, wide polders of brackwater threw

back oily sunlight and the surrounding reeds rustled as the incoming water rippled at their roots. Now and then, a big frog would leap out of their way to splash under the surface, and bright-red crabs crawled out of holes and held their claws wide, ready to clamp on their feet.

Here it was poisonously lush. Every once in a while, Jack would catch a motion out of the corner of his eye. He saw Kerry do the same.

'You see anything?' His voice came in a whisper.

'I keep thinking I do,' Kerry whispered back. 'But there's no track out there. Maybe it's birds.'

They paused, waiting for Corriwen to catch up. She had been right behind Jack when they took a dog-leg southwards to avoid yet another pool. They turned simultaneously.

She was not behind them. There was no sign of her. Jack's heart lurched.

'Where is she?'

Kerry hurried back. 'She was there. I saw her.'

There had been no sound except for the unceasing scrapy rustling of the grass.

'She can't have fallen in,' Kerry said. Jack nodded. They would have heard her, but even as he nodded, he imagined her slipping from the narrow track and being sucked under without a sound. The mud would leave no trace.

Something moved off to the side, just a flicker, but when they turned again, there was nothing to be seen.

Kerry brushed past him, eyes on the shifting ground, head low, until he came to the corner where her footprints seemed to stop dead. He knelt, soaking his knees, scanning left and right.

'That way,' he said.

Kerry went off the track and in seconds he was up to his thighs in dragging mud, but under his feet he could feel there was enough firm land to take his weight. He pushed through the water using his sword to slash at the reeds, forcing his own path. Every few yards he stopped, scanned the grass and rushes and saw something, when Jack could see nothing at all.

From behind, Kerry looked like a hunting animal, tense, eyes fixed on a broken reed here, a slowly filling depression, a crushed crab shell. He led them away from the track they had been following, although Jack couldn't tell quite where they were, and the tide kept rising.

Kerry led on, fighting through the morass, until he paused, motioned Jack forward, parted the reeds and they both held their breath, peering across a wide black tarn.

Across the water a small, bare island rose above the reeds. It towered above the marshes, like a dome of solid earth and for a moment Jack thought they might have reached the far side of the swamp.

But when he looked more closely, he realised it was not an island at all. It was a huge mound of grass and reed-stalks and willow-branches. It reminded him of the swans' nest on Bemersyde Marsh where the birds had piled dead vegetation over the years.

This island dwarfed any swans' nest. They could see movement on its top. At first they thought it was a wall of rushes waving in the wind, and that's exactly what it looked like, until Jack rubbed his eyes. Kerry nudged him.

'You see her?'

Jack shaded his eyes.

'You see those things?'

Then he saw them, stick-thin shapes, the exact colour of the marsh grasses, moving as if blown by a slow wind. They had legs like the heron that had startled the horse into the swamp and knotty arms like sticks of bamboo, elongated faces, so narrow that their eyes were almost vertical brown slits. They hissed and crackled and their thin legs gave them a strange, double-jointed gait.

They crowded round Corriwen and Jack and Kerry could see her arms were bound by grassy ropes. The thin people clicked and rustled. Jack could see no way over the deep water to the island.

'That'll be the Rushen folk,' he whispered. Beside him, a black snail, big as a fist, crawled in front of a red crab and was instantly snared in a snap of hard claws. Jack crouched and looked back at the mound. The Rushen people, if they were people at all, had three wide-splayed toes on each foot, and he understood now how they could get through the marshes so quickly. They were so light that they could skitter effortlessly across the bog.

They might look strange, but Jack knew that he and Kerry and Corriwen were the strangers in this infested place. And they had to get Corriwen out.

'How do we get there?' Jack asked.

The Rushen began an alien, reedy chant that sounded like a hundred crickets all chirruping at once.

'What are they doing?'

'I don't know,' Jack said, 'but I don't like it.'

Underneath his jerkin, he felt that odd double beat of his

heart. The heartstone was beating in tune with his own, and he was beginning to understand its warning. Suddenly the stick-thin beings did not seem as fragile as they looked.

Something was going to happen. And when Jack looked again at Corriwen's slight form, stretched and vulnerable between the two posts, one word sprang to mind.

Sacrifice.

All of a sudden, the reed-creatures turned on the summit of the island and looked down into the pool of water.

Kerry pointed. A bow wave rippled on the tarn, a hump of black water as something underneath moved it. Something really big and approaching very fast.

The chant rose to a crescendo.

The waters swirled close to the island and a shiny black eel slithered onto the shallows at the island's edge.

It was an eel like Jack and Kerry had never seen in the pools in the marshes at home. It was bigger than the huge congers the trawlers brought in to Ardmore harbour from the deep off the peninsula. It was as big around as the Scree jailer, black as night down its back, and as it slithered and writhed through the marsh marigolds and algae, they got a flash of the sickly yellow of its belly. Its skin shone with a slimy lustre and its eyes were as big and flat as saucers.

And when it opened its mouth, they could see rows of sharp teeth slanting backwards.

Behind it, another huge eel slithered out.

And the tide was rising.

Sacrifice.

A third massive eel, glistening slickly, looped into the shallows. A fourth appeared, black eyes deadly. The reed people were clicking and rustling, chanting encouragement.

'We've got to get her out of there,' Jack said, unable to draw his eyes away from the gaping maws. As soon as the words were out of his mouth, the thin people turned, jabbering away like twigs breaking and vanished beyond the hump of the mound, leaving Corriwen spread-eagled on the framework. Her eyes fixed on the nearest eel.

'What are they waiting for?' Kerry asked.

'The tide's coming in.'

They could see the water inching up the mound.

Corriwen was struggling with the grassy ropes that pinned her wrists. Another huge eel poked its head out, this one truly monstrous, as thick as a man's shoulders. Lazily it oozed its way up the bank in slow coils. Behind it, the water was seething with more of them. Jack could feel their hunger.

He pulled Kerry.

'Which way?'

'I dunno. It looks like an island.'

'Well, those things got across.'

'They're like moorhens,' Kerry said. 'You see those feet. They can skim across.'

'Come on, man,' Jack urged. 'Find a way. And fast.'

'I'm thinking.'

'Well, do it faster.' They could hear Corriwen gasp. The water was no more than three yards from her feet. She squirmed, horrified eyes fixed on the devil eels.

Kerry was on the edge of the tarn. They were maybe fifty feet from the mound. A big eel popped its head out, inches from his face, yawned like a crocodile and snapped. Its teeth closed together with the sound of a steel trap.

He jerked back.

'This way,' he finally said. Jack followed. There was nothing else to do but trust Kerry. His eyes were drawn back to where Corriwen strained and struggled, and he had to force himself to look away and follow Kerry, who cut off a long length of thick dry reed and probed ahead.

'Faster,' Jack thought, then realised he had spoken aloud.

'Doing my best,' Kerry muttered, concentrating. He really was doing his best. There had to be a way. He tried not to look over at the floating island, knowing if he did so, he wouldn't be able to look away, and looking wouldn't help her in the slightest.

It seemed to take forever, up to their thighs in mud, until Kerry noticed a thin line of tussock grass, barely six inches wide.

'Root-bank,' he said.

And there it was. A line of posts driven deep into the vegetation – like a fence, each post a foot or so apart, a narrow causeway that only the sharpest eyes could have seen. Kerry hauled himself up, and his weight caused the first post to bob up and down and he almost pitched headlong. He swung his arms for balance and stepped gingerly to the next.

'Take it easy,' he said, more to himself than to Jack, and began to make his way slowly across the tops of the posts. Jack followed, heart hammering, urging Kerry faster yet knowing they couldn't risk it.

Too late, Jack thought. *Too damn late.*

Kerry was moving faster. He could see the way. One foot, then another, swinging for balance. He was ten feet or so from the far edge of the tarn when the post wobbled under his weight and he was in the water. Instantly the surface thrashed and the eels came for him. Kerry grabbed for the causeway, got his hands to it. An eel clamped on his thigh. The pressure was intense. In one savage tug he was dragged down.

Don't let me drown.

His eyes found Jack's, and held them in the second before he went under. Globules of air frothed and bubbled to the surface. Another eel came twisting in, tried to bite. Jack was paralysed for a split second, then he risked it all. He scuttered across the posts, bent and grabbed for the pommel of the sword that stuck up from the sheath on the backpack. It came out with a *schick* sound, heavy in his hand and he plunged it into the water, inches from where he'd last seen Kerry's shoulder, trusting in luck or fortune, or whatever it was that had watched over them in the worst of times.

He felt the blade bite and something bucked, so strongly it almost wrenched his shoulder out of its socket, and then greenish blood was spouting up his arm and the eel was twisting and turning on the blade. He jerked, cut it clean in half as it twisted to bite at him. Kerry's head broke the surface, dripping stagnant mud. A second eel looped in, mouth gaping. Jack stabbed it between the eyes, saw the blade come through the underside of its jaw. Another monster spun round and bit a chunk out of its side and then all he could see was snapping jaws and poison-green blood spread across the surface.

He pulled Kerry up. Corriwen was silent now, eyes still fixed on the eel that was worming its way up the slope towards her. Then out of the corner of his eye, Jack saw a motion on the far side of the pond and his breath stopped in his throat.

The silver back of a huge eel was snaking across to the island, bigger than any of the eels that were lunging up to get the first snap at Corriwen. It was moving so fast it left a huge wake. He watched aghast, knowing it would get to the island before they did. All he saw were five or six silvery humps coming out of the water, all in a line and he knew they would be too late.

'Kerry . . .' he started. Kerry turned, black from head to foot.

The bow-wave hit the floating island and the first silver back broke the surface and was on land in a ripple of motion. Jack saw jaws open and white teeth grab the head of the biggest eel, and close with a snap that crunched skull and jaw. The eel quivered violently and Jack saw that the silver creature was no eel at all, but a huge otter. Behind, its family swarmed out of the pool and onto the island, crunching, snarling and snapping, tearing the eels to shreds, shaking them in their jaws.

The words of the rhyme in the *Book of Ways* came back to him, even as he hustled ahead on the narrow causeway and made it to the island. The otter closest to Corriwen turned to look at him with pale blue eyes before it plunged into the rippling mass of eels to savage them again.

Now Jack reached Corriwen and used the sword like a saw, cutting the braided grass that bound her wrists.

Whoever had sent the otters had waited until the last moment, but whoever it was, Jack was very, very grateful. He and Kerry held Corriwen tight, feeling her trembling subside.

EIGHTEEN

F ar, far to the north, beyond the forest and the salt-marsh, the craggy ridges to the north of Mid-Temair, she stirred in the well of darkness.

But now she was awake.

She felt her strength return as the old *geas*, the old binding-curses, wore down and broke one by one. And as her vigour came back, so did her everlasting hate and anger, the very essence of her being. And with it, a burning thirst for vengeance.

Thin places. Thin places, those cracks through which the tendrils of her slumbering mind had oozed like fog, searching for the one to free her. After all these eons of slumber, the finding seemed a mere heartbeat away.

He had been formless; clay to be worked slowly into a shape that she could use.

She had found the weakness in an angry, vengeful mind, and she had nurtured it with dark promises.

She had schooled that young mind, leading it to places where old knowledge waited to be found, arcane knowledge of magic once stronger in this world; dark secrets, waiting only for the right mind with a thirst, and a reason to seek it.

This child of hers, this Mandrake-to-be, had found the knowledge and used it, binding himself to her, hungry for the power that she would have, the power she would bestow.

She had tested him until she was sure that he shunned all good, all light, embracing the night and shadows that lurked unseen by human eyes. Then she had drawn him out, with all that was needed to break the ancient curse.

Oh then ... *Oh, then!* There would be a reckoning. The sons of the sons of the sons of men who had dared face her and bind her with songs of magic and blazing light, they would wither in her wrath.

She sensed the day approaching, awake and aware, impatient to feed and destroy.

And yet. The key eluded her.

She had sensed its presence, not here, but across the chasm of time that was bridged by the ancient stones. She had reached and summoned.

Now the key and its bearer was here, in her Temair.

She would have it.

She was the Morrigan.

The second Bard had warned them that the forest was a dangerous place.

He had stepped from the reeds and whistled to the otters who turned as one, leaving the remains of the eels they had slaughtered.

'I'm Connal,' he'd said, a tall thin man in a long cloak that looked as if it had been sewn together from the skins of rainbow trout. It glistened and changed colour when he moved. 'I am the Bard of Kelpie Holt. You've met my brother, I believe.'

'Finbar's your brother?' Corriwen asked.

'In a manner of speaking. Brothership of the Bardic, we say. Near as you can get to the real thing, I imagine, without having to fight for the shoes in the morning.'

He had looked severe, but his smile was warm.

'I heard from the swans that you'd had trouble. And then I watched you blunder through the flats. Not a place for young travellers to be, I can tell you. There are more bones resting down there in the quagmire than I'd want to count. The flats suck the unwary down, and the Rushen and the Kelpie take the rest.'

He put a hand on Corriwen's shoulder. 'Now, Lady Corriwen. You and your journeymen here, you've put up a fair fight so far. I hope the rest is as easy.'

He led them on, with the otters whistling and frolicking around his feet, like huge quicksilver puppies. Eventually they came to a reed hut, thatched with bulrushes where a flock of golden swifts rested from the heat of the day, so many crowded on the roof that the thatch was invisible.

'Now, do you like roast crab?' the tall man said.

They wolfed the food.

'Here is the quagmire,' Connal said, when they had eaten their fill. The Bard had a big pipe that looked as if it had been carved out of a solid bulrush and he puffed it to a fiery glow. The smoke made Jack's eyes water.

Connal unrolled a sheet of what appeared to be papyrus and he used a stick of charcoal to illustrate it.

'Quagmire here,' he repeated, drawing a vaguely triangular shape. 'And the Holt here. It's a point that runs straight south to the seashore and cuts the marsh in two, and it's a good thing you don't have to travel the other side. It goes on forever, and worse things wait.

'On the far side, the Labyrinth Rills, which you've come through, and the flats. You've met the thin folk, and there's not much to them, I know, but there's plenty of them. They eat raw fish and crabs and the odd traveller. Can't use fire, of course.'

'Creepy little people,' Kerry said. 'Marsh-hoppers.'

'From here, north. It's the only way. You follow the spine of the Holt, beyond the high-shore flats. And from there up to Sappeling Wood.'

'I've heard of that place,' Corriwen said. 'They say Leprechauns rule there.'

'What?' Kerry asked. 'The Little People?'

Connal frowned. 'Whatever lives there, it's their

forest. Don't stray from the road. Not an inch.'

And three days later, all of it on foot, here they were.

The Morrigan rolled in her dark centre, reaching out to sense it again.

It had eluded her time and again, as had that girl-child who had disrupted Mandrake's work, because the strength of old kings ran in her blood. Girl child she might be, but the Morrigan feared the light in her, just as she intuitively knew it in the other, the carrier.

She reached into the night, and touched him.

Jack wasn't dreaming now. He had fallen into an exhausted sleep, every muscle aching, but something had woken him with a start.

He shivered, though not from cold.

Jack was afraid, and the heartstone beat steadily, telling him to be *very* afraid.

Something moved. He heard it.

'Corriwen?' He blurted out her name and his voice was swallowed by the thick velvet black.

'Kerry!'

There was no reply, but there was something with him. Not something, he realised, but someone.

He held what breath he had and listened. Someone took hold of his hand. His heart leapt to his throat, but whatever held him gripped, soft and firm.

'You are safe with me,' a voice whispered. A woman's voice.

'Where am I?' He sounded scared, which was just what he was. 'Who are you?'

'Safe,' she whispered again. 'I am here.'

'Who are you?'

'Your heart's desire,' she whispered, in a voice like a song, and he felt the bands holding his ribs tight loosen a little. He breathed in, cold, clear air which bore the scent of lavender and lilac and summer days.

'Rest, friend,' she said, and her voice was a balm. 'I have waited so long.'

'I've lost my friends,' he told her. 'I must find them.'

'And you will,' she said. Her face was now a pale oval in the dark close to him. She bent towards him and he saw dark eyes in that heart-shaped face, and black tresses that curled around slim shoulders and fell to her waist.

'You have been searching for me,' she whispered.

She stroked his face, her touch like silk, and he lay back, feeling the ache and tiredness drain away.

'Where are my friends?' he said.

'I am your friend. Come to me and forget everything.' The hand trailed down his chest.

Jack felt a pounding in his ears and that double pulse in his chest.

'Give me your heart and be free forever.'

The hand stroked his bare skin and he realised his shirt

was open, but there was no hurt now, just the sensation of smooth skin on his own. He closed his eyes, feeling the need to be at peace. The need to find Kerry and Corriwen ebbed away and he bent towards the warmth.

'Give me your heart,' she said, and in that instant the voice changed from summer to winter and when she breathed on him it was cold and foul, like the smell of rot in that faraway battlefield.

His eyes jerked open and he saw the face, and his heart froze.

Her face was a ruin of wrinkled, peeling skin. A cavernous mouth with cracked lips pulled back from rotten, broken teeth. Her hair writhed like snakes and the touch on his chest felt like the blackest sin.

'Away,' he tried to say, tried to take a step back, but she had him.

One hand snatched the heartstone. The other clawed at his skin. He felt her nails stab through flesh and twist between ribs until she had his beating heart in her hands. She ripped it out, smashing his ribs to splinters and cast him aside, screaming and betrayed, down, down, down while her laugh shook the ground.

He lurched up gasping for air, both hands pressed to his empty chest.

Kerry slapped an arm round his shoulders. 'Jack man, you scared the bejasus out of me.'

'Thought I'd lost you,' Jack managed to croak. 'You and Corrie.'

'No chance of that,' Kerry assured him.

'You scared me too,' Corriwen said.

Jack looked at them, bewildered, but the image hung there in his memory, that astonishing beauty which had turned into unspeakable ugliness. Kerry passed him a drink of water and he sipped it.

He had been awake, but somehow caught in a weird sort of spell in which that awful presence had come in the dark and had *touched* him.

And he felt he would rather die than feel that loathsome touch again.

They were three days out of the swamp now, and they had stopped beneath a spreading oak close to the winding road, a mile or so from a vast forest. They had camped here rather than risk whatever might be in the shadows, for the Bard had warned them that Sappeling Wood was a dangerous place.

'I think we should get a move on,' Kerry said. Jack was still numb from the waking nightmare.

'Connal says it's the only way,' Corriwen said. Her hand automatically moved to the hilts of the knives at her belt. 'But we must be careful.'

'I think we should check the book first,' Jack said. 'It might give us a clue.'

He unbound the tooled leather and opened his *Book of Ways*, and they waited expectantly.

> Verdance deep foreverglade
> Shadow dell and leafy shade
> Softly past the binding shoot
> Wary round the gnarling root
> Safe perhaps upon the way
> Peril those who walk astray

The forest closed around them in a dark green embrace.

NINETEEN

The forest was silent. Totally silent.

Kerry had paused on the road, listening. 'No birds,' he said, voice low, as if it might be sacrilege to speak loudly here.

He was right. No birds sang, where one might expect greenfinch and chaffinch and a scolding wren to flit in a blur between the trunks. No woodpigeons murmured in the depths, no blackbirds stirred up the leaves. Nothing.

'It's too quiet,' Jack said, voice even lower. 'Like there's something in there.'

'There is,' Corriwen said. 'And it doesn't welcome strangers.'

The mist was thicker now, turning the luxuriant foliage to fuzzy shapes. The crowded trunks deeper in the wood were like pillars reaching up to a thick canopy. From the damp ground scents of fern and bramble wafted, growth on growth, lush and loamy.

Despite the silence, they sensed life. They walked, one mile, two, and as they trudged, they could feel eyes upon them, but nothing moved save drops of water on the occasional bespattered leaf.

Every few yards they had to step over a stretching thorn-creeper or a bramble runner that looked as if it was lying in wait.

Jack watched a spiral of fern uncoil, faster than any fern had a right to, like a hairy butterfly tongue.

They rounded a bend that took them due north and stopped dead, as a wide clearing appeared before them. It was littered with broken branches, knee deep in wood splinters and spiked by a hundred huge tree-stumps. Some of the trees had been ten feet across or more.

'That's a whole lot of lumber,' Kerry said. 'Wonder what it's for?'

'It's for Mandrake's dam,' Corriwen said. 'Look, all the tracks go north, and that's where he is. I saw their wagons near the battlefield and wondered. Now I know.'

'Must be some big dam,' Kerry observed. 'Some of those trees must have been a couple of hundred years old.'

'Try a couple of thousand,' Jack said. Over by one stump, a big peavey-axe leant against the chipped bark, its head red with rust. A crude two-handed saw was broken under a heavy branch. A cracked cart wheel lay aslant another stump.

Whoever had been felling here, they were gone now.

They began to pick their way carefully across the sawdust

and shavings, skirting round the wide trunks, when Kerry stopped and held up a hand for silence. They froze. Jack strained and then heard a faint scrabbling sound. It was coming from beyond the nearest row of massive stumps. Corriwen peered round, her slight body pressed against the bark. She beckoned to Jack and Kerry.

They edged round the stump and all three stood silent for a moment.

At first it looked like a moving shrub, a small green shape. But as they watched the movement, it became clear it was a child, a tiny thing in green, bent at the waist and working with a spike of deer antler at the soil between two of the felled forest giants.

Jack saw another motion further away and drew their attention. It was another infant, tending a sapling that had been staked with a hazel wand. This child was carefully placing a protective ring of stream-smooth stones around its base.

Suddenly they could see dozens of them, all tiny, hardly more than knee high, working in silence, planting whip-thin saplings and clearing the soil around their roots. Every few minutes, one of them would look up and scan the sky. Jack looked all round the devastated area, searching for any sign of adults who would be watching after children in this place, but saw nothing.

As he turned to Corriwen, a wide shadow swooped across the clearing. He looked up and saw a bird, coming in low over the stumps. In two powerful wingbeats it shot past, twenty feet above their heads. He saw the legs swing down and vicious yellow talons snap open.

The children scattered like rabbits.

The hawk swerved, banked, then dropped fast. Its talons swung down again and there was an audible snap as they snatched at a small shape sprinting for cover. A piercing cry rent the air.

'It's got one of the kids!' Kerry shouted.

As quickly as it had fallen, the great bird soared up. The child in its talons wriggled and squealed. Jack tried to free his bow, but he wasn't fast enough.

Kerry dashed forward, faster than Jack had ever seen him move, straight towards the big raptor.

Without stopping, he scooped a heavy round stone in one hand, while the other slipped the leather sling from his belt. Still running he swung it twice round his head, like an underarm bowler.

The stone flew from the sling like cannon-shot.

It hit the bird where its wing joined its breast and they heard the crack of bone from where they stood.

The predator squawked, stalled and went into a tight circle. Its one good wing beat hard, but it began to lose height. Kerry drew his sword, waiting for it to fall, but the bird jerked its talons free, losing the weight of its prey.

The child dropped straight down towards the spiked stumps, spinning uncontrollably.

Jack was running now, sending up cascades of sawdust and wood chips as his feet fought for purchase.

The child came tumbling down, head over heels. Jack gauged the distance, leapt on to a broad stump, launched himself up and caught the child in his arms before it smashed on to the hard wood. His momentum carried him well past the far side of the stump. Twisting in the air, he landed briefly on his feet and fell on to his back, protecting the child from his own weight.

'Got you,' he gasped.

Kerry and Corriwen sprinted up to them. Jack had the squealing child tight in his arms. He loosened his grip, got to his knees and looked down.

A small, wizened face stared back up at him, and Jack almost dropped the struggling bundle in sheer fright.

The thing he held was no child. It opened its mouth in a gape that was impossibly wide and its face crinkled into a bark-like mass of creases. Small sharp teeth were visible behind stretched lips underneath a long, hooked nose. Its hair was stiff and bristled, the texture of birch twigs. What Jack had taken for a green romper suit was a covering that felt like young leaves and smelt like moss. He couldn't tell if it was clothes or skin.

Its wide eyes were as flat and as brown as polished oak.

'Leprechaun,' Corriwen said. 'The Little People. It's true then.'

Kerry bent down. 'No, it can't be one of them. I've seen pictures. They wear green jackets and red hats and they tell you riddles.'

He looked around. 'And I don't see any rainbow either.' He bent towards the little person. 'All right, we saved you. So you can tell us your name.'

Its eyes blinked with a woody click, it stared at the mark on Jack's chest, then switched its gaze to Kerry. It had stopped struggling. It looked up at them, from one to the other.

'Come on now, wee man,' Kerry persisted. 'We don't mean you any harm.'

The creature opened its mouth and whispered something.

'What's that?' Jack bent to listen.

'Cut our hearts.' The voice was a whisper of dry leaves.

He wasn't sure if he'd heard right and turned.

And just then, a runner of bramble uncoiled and snaked around Jack's leg.

'What the ...'

Kerry twisted off balance as the ground moved under his feet. A thin root wormed out of the earth and snagged his ankle. The bramble runner flexed and squeezed around Jack's leg and he gasped in pain, reaching to pull it free.

He dropped the little creature, and it hit the ground running, shot across the clearing in a blur of green, and vanished in the depths of the forest.

As soon as he was gone, the bramble runner loosened its grip and unwound from Jack's leg. Kerry was hopping on one foot, trying to free the other. Jack saw Corriwen slash at a thin tendril of ivy that had looped itself around both legs up to her waist. The whole forest seemed to take a breath.

'Let's get out of here,' Kerry said. 'I don't like those creepy wee folk. Never even thanked us.'

They pressed on, staying close together and nervously searching the shadows, aware of the watching eyes, but unable to see anything. Now and then a bird circled overhead, checking them out for size, then wheeled away.

'This is a really creepy place,' Kerry whispered, and his voice sounded small and scared. Jack tried to fight his own apprehension, but he knew if Kerry was scared, there must be good reason. He would spend nights in the forest back home, poaching rabbits and pheasants. Trees and darkness held no fears for him, hid no demons. But this place was different.

'We have to keep going,' he said. 'We really don't want to be here by nightfall.'

They were five miles along the narrowing track when Kerry paused and they all stopped with him. He pointed to the overhanging branches. Jack shaded his eyes against sunlight stabbing through the leaves and suddenly a shape came into focus.

A white skull grinned down at them.

'How did that get up there?'

He stood staring. They all did. Even from here, they could see from the shape of the narrowing head and wide cheeks what it was.

'It's a Scree,' Corriwen said.

Kerry pointed. 'There's the rest of him.'

Another tree loomed on the other side of the road. In its branches, a white pelvis and two dangling legs hung like a skinned carcass in a butcher's shop.

'What do you think happened to him?'

Kerry shrugged. 'I don't think I want to know. This place gives me the total heeby-jeebies.'

'People don't come here,' Corriwen said. 'But Mandrake sent his Scree to fell the trees, I think. Maybe the Little People can fight.'

They walked on, craning back until the Scree skeleton was out of sight, now aware of the real threat in the forest, or wheeling high above it. If something could catch a Scree and rip it in half, then it could easily do the same to any of them.

A half-mile on, they found another body, this one jammed in the fork of a tree that had been cut half through by an axe.

Not a hundred yards from it they came across a heavy wagon, axle deep in the rutted track, weighed down by a huge tree-trunk. Skeletons of dead Scree were scattered around it. They looked as if they had lain unburied for a long time.

But still there was nothing to show what had killed them or their oxen. No one had come back for the wagon, or the newly-felled tree. Jack wondered why.

Beyond the bogged down wagon, the road simply petered out and they came to a stop.

'I thought this went all the way north,' Kerry said.

'So did I,' Corriwen agreed. 'Didn't the Bard say so?'

'Those Scree thought so too,' Jack said. 'That's the way the wagon was headed. But they were wrong.'

'Jack,' Kerry whispered. 'I get a really creepy feeling about this. It looks like the forest didn't like them cutting down the trees. It tried to stop them.'

'You really do have the heeby-jeebies.' Jack shook his head. ' No. It's just overgrown. They probably got caught in an ambush.'

He didn't want to think about what Kerry was saying. Corriwen was white-faced.

'Men don't come here,' she finally said. 'The Little People protect their home.'

'So what now?'

'We can't stay here at night,' Jack said. 'We'll never get out if we do. I'm sure of that.'

'Okay,' Kerry said. 'We'll find a way round.'

They pushed on through the thick stand of saplings and in minutes they were deep in the trees.

Jack turned back towards the road, but it was invisible. He closed his eyes and the compass in his head seemed to swing wildly for a moment before he found north. He opened his eyes, and stopped dead in his tracks.

A wide face was only inches from his own.

He jerked back in fright.

'What is it?'

Jack pointed, unable to speak. Corriwen followed his finger.

The Scree's mouth yawned like a cave. A beetle maggot writhed behind its teeth. Sightless sockets seemed to glare.

But it wasn't just the skull that froze them in mid-stride.

It was the fact that it was glaring at them from the trunk of a tree.

For a second Jack thought it had been nailed, right there into the rough bark. But then he saw the tattered, bony arms and clawed hands sticking out at shoulder height on either side of the trunk. It was as if the very tree itself had swallowed the Scree and let him die screaming.

Kerry backed away.

The heartstone on its chain beat in a slow pulse. Jack's

own heart responded by trying to leap right into his throat.

'I really *really* don't like this ...' Kerry said.

'I'm with you,' Jack whispered back.

The trees rustled as if a wind had stirred the thick canopy.

'You see anything?'

'Sounds like a storm,' Corriwen said.

'Kerry ...'

Jack turned, and this time his heart felt as if it *had* leapt into his throat.

Kerry was gone. Jack grasped Corriwen's arm and whirled around, eyes flicking left and right.

'*Kerry!*'

Above them the branches thrashed.

'*Help!*' Kerry's voice sounded very frightened, and very far away.

'Where are you?' Jack was whirling, searching, while the rustling sound above them grew louder. A green blizzard of leaves twirled in the air.

'I can't see him.' Corriwen was scanning from side to side, her face so white her freckles stood out like inkblots.

'Let me go!' A high and panicked shout from somewhere above, almost a shriek. 'Run, Jack. *Run!*'

'He's up there–' Jack started to say, when close by, something came smashing through the undergrowth. The shrubs and ferns whipped from side to side. Jack saw a sinuous shape writhe towards them. His mind shrieked *snake*, and then he was running. He had Corriwen's sleeve in a tight grip and he dragged her with him.

Kerry screeched again. Jack's thudding heart almost stopped, but his feet didn't even slow. He ran on, with

Corriwen behind him, unable to stop despite the dreadful sensation of having abandoned Kerry.

Now it was simply survival. He got a glimpse of the knife in Corriwen's hand, knew she was preparing to turn, but he hauled on her arm, forced her onwards.

This is it, he told himself. *I'm going to die here.*

Something reared in front of him. Something else lashed in from the side and Corriwen was gone. He felt a brief, fierce tug on his arm and then she vanished. He was skidding forwards and a shape snatched him off his feet, threw him into the air. Another caught him such a blow that his breath was punched right out and the world began to fade away.

When his vision began to clear and his ears stopped ringing, he was gagging for breath against a crushing tightness round his chest. He was moving, up in the canopy, carried along like a trussed turkey. Twigs and branches poked at his eyes and he was forced to blink hard every second to protect them. Nearby he heard a moan which sounded like Corriwen, but he couldn't tell from which direction. He felt like an insect in a spider's web, unable to turn, unable to move.

The trees themselves were moving, the branches reaching like gnarled hands, creaking as they flexed to take him, like a bucket in a relay line.

It was impossible. It was preposterous. But it was happening.

And when he pictured the bones of the Scree, torn apart high in the branches, he was suddenly aware of what the forest might do to them.

They travelled a long way, in eerie silence, until finally Jack felt himself being lowered, so fast his stomach lurched. He plummeted, crashing through thorns to land with a thump on the ground. Corriwen lay a few feet away.

Jack took two steps forward and then felt himself tugged back so violently his feet went up in the air and he cracked his head on a hard trunk, his arms and legs pinioned in a grip that felt like stone. Ivy or honeysuckle tightened around his neck like a garrotte.

They were in some sort of dell, deep in the heart of this forest, a forest that breathed as one creature. The hollow was ringed with trees, bearded with moss. Kerry was there struggling against living bonds that pinned him to a trunk on the other side of the hollow. He caught Jack's eye, his own rolling as he fought for breath.

The forest suddenly went completely quiet, a silence so profound that at first Jack thought he'd gone deaf. Then he saw the Leprechaun, halfway up the trunk, but not clinging to the side. He was peering out of the trunk itself, like an owl, polished eyes fathomless.

But he wasn't even in a hole in the bark. He was oozing from the tree and as Jack's eyes watched, the little creature emerged, inch by inch, as if it was a moving part of the great tree itself. Further up, another pair of eyes opened, and a little wrinkled leprechaun emerged from the bark. Then another, and another, until every tree around was alive with small, hoary bodies, their eyes all fixed intently on the three captives.

The only sound now was the strange click of eyelids as the creatures blinked.

Down in the dell, one of the ancient rooted growths began to twist and creak. Its crumbling surface shuddered. Pieces of bark dropped to the ground.

The creature that hauled itself out from this one was another Leprechaun, but it looked as old as the tree itself. It was small and wizened, skin like hoary oak, sprouting burrs and clusters of thick twigs. It peeled itself away from the tree and stepped on the ground.

It came slowly towards them, as if it had not walked in a very long time, limbs creaking like tortured wood.

'I am the Leprechaun.' The words came out like the crackle of twigs underfoot.

'Too many come here, axemen, sawmen. Kill our hearts. Steal our souls.'

Jack tried to speak, tried to protest, but the creeper round his neck tightened and his throat shut with a dry gulp.

'No more trespass the wildwood. The wildwood takes revenge.'

The blind-sight eyes stared right into Jack's own. They blinked slowly, as if this ancient little thing had difficulty keeping them open. As if it had slept a long time.

'The Leprechaun has spoken. The wildwood feeds.'

On the trunks all around, the tiny creatures began to drum their twiggy hands on the resinous bark. Above them, branches swayed in unison. On the ground, roots flexed and curved. Something grew at amazing speed directly in front of Kerry. It sprouted purple leaves between which bloomed tiny flowers in a colour that made Jack think of venom. It swayed back and forth and then it lashed forward.

Underneath the leaves, spiky thorns *snicked* up and stuck Kerry right under the chin.

He grunted and his head snapped back against the tree. Blood bubbled from his mouth and his face went deathly pale.

Jack felt the pinioning bonds loosen. He coughed, fell to his knees, but before he could move, a thick ivy runner grabbed him around the ankles. At the same time, something coiled around his wrists and simultaneously both tightened and pulled.

Jack felt himself being torn apart.

'No!' Corriwen cried.

She saw Kerry's eyes roll upwards and a mottled toxic purple shade creep up from his neck, then Jack was on the ground as two creepers slithered forward, fast as striking adders, and had him racked between them. She heard him grunt in pain as they tightened and began pulling him in opposite directions.

The Leprechaun king watched impassively, as the rest of the little creatures drummed their rhythm on the tree-bark.

Just as the image came to Corriwen, the bonds on her arms and legs suddenly withdrew and she dropped forward, but she had been waiting for just such a motion. She rolled, quick as a stoat, shot to her feet with her knives in each hand, leapt towards Jack and slashed at the nearest ivy runner. It parted with a snap.

Jack screamed in pain. Above her the Leprechauns gasped. Liquid like blood poured from the writhing end of the ivy stump. She whirled again, ready to defend herself, seeking a way to cut the other tendril that was dragging Jack away into the bushes. Then something moved under her feet.

A plant, broad as a plantain, with rubbery leaves stretching way out on either side, like a green star. Before she could move, the leaves closed over her legs, curling up until she was caught at the waist, then at the chest. Then they folded round her like a giant, pliant hand. She struggled but her arms were trapped. It was swallowing her, growing around her, faster than anything could grow. Faster than anything should ever grow.

An orange flower uncurled like another hand and a sweet heady perfume wafted around her. The flower swayed forward and clamped on her face, drenching her in its perfume. The world began to waver and dance and her lungs began to burn.

Then a tiny shape leapt down from the height of the trees and landed right in front of Jack.

The little Leprechaun was jabbering at the old king so fast Jack could make out no words, no language.

It turned and pointed at him then faced the king again. The king held up a twiggy hand, but the Leprechaun stepped towards Jack.

Hands forced him down to his knees and Jack closed his eyes, expecting the end right here and now.

The little creature peeled Jack's tunic and shirt wide open and the king bent forward.

The red hand and the coronet of dots stood out clearly on his skin.

There was a collective gasp all around them and the hands freed him, so suddenly he almost fell forward on his face.

'Coronal,' the king creaked. 'The Red Hand returns.'

He looked up at the wooden eyes that gazed down from the high branches.

'Free them,' the king said.

TWENTY

At first, the words were difficult to understand, but the Leprechaun reached his hand and touched each one of them, and after that, the words became clear. Jack knew he was hearing them in his head, or in his heart. He couldn't tell which.

The others crowded round, appearing from the crevices and hollows, listening to the king as he sat with Jack and Corriwen and Kerry.

'In the beginning, in the very beginning, the night lady dropped a star from her crown that became a seed. And the whole world became Tree.' He paused. 'The Leprechaun have been in this place since forever. Before the Scree-ogres; before men. Even before the Morrigan. 'And we were content even to share with man those lands *She* had touched and no heartwood could root.'

Jack heard 'heartwood', but his mind showed him other words. The old Leprechaun's creaky voice conveyed sisters. It conveyed sweethearts. Jack knew what he meant. The trees themselves.

'We tended our sisters and nurtured them always, as we still do, content with our glades and peace with the men of Temair under the Redthorn chiefs. No sister ever fell by man's hand. They understood our need and we understood theirs and no harm befell us or the sisters until now.

'To the south was ever the marshland, with its Rushen folk and the Kelpie, to the north were men and their farms and beyond that, the barren crags of the exiles, the Fomorian Scree.'

He bent forward and offered them another drink from something that might have been an acorn cup, if acorns ever grew to the size of coconuts. The nectar it contained was sweet and every sip seeped hot in their blood and made them feel stronger.

The polished eyes clicked shut, and for a moment they thought he had fallen asleep, but they opened again and he continued.

'In olden times, when this Leprechaun was a whip-sapling, there was sorcery and there was evil. Long-gone warlocks fought, and kingdoms fell and settled to dust. In these evil times, they summoned the she-demon from the dark place beyond Tir Nan Og, the land of the dead.

'She is hunger and hate. She may have been summoned by them, but the warlocks also fell, for she knows no friendship or treaty; she ravaged the land. Evil times. Sisters shrivelled and died. There was fire and blight, and the Leprechaun were obliged to fight.'

Jack got the impression of vast eons, a history that dwarfed all the histories he had ever learned in school.

'Came a man on the road, bearing a sword, which is anathema to the Leprechaun, as is the axe and the saw and wildfire. But this man braved the glades to sit with us and made a promise he would free Temair of this bane, or die in the quest.

'He put his hand in the flame and held it there, to show he would rather burn than see fire and harm come to the glades. Thus we knew his truth. When we eased his hurt, his right hand stayed red as blood, a mark for all to see.' The king reached again and touched Jack on his forehead. 'I recognise this Cullian's sap-line. You are ever welcome in our glades.'

Jack felt hot emotions rush through him. His mind sparked in all directions.

Cullian's sap line.

'*Your father has been here before,*' Finbar the Bard had told him. Jack had stepped between worlds, and his father had already been in this one. The heart stone was his inheritance, and already Jack had felt some of its power. Somehow he knew there was even more power in it, and his father had used it. He recalled Finbar's exact words, *If your father had the book and the heartstone, then he was a traveller. A journeyman.*

Whatever a journeyman was, Jack was somehow following in the footsteps of a man he had never known.

And the heartstone that forged the link between them,

that was the key to everything. His past; his future. His *life*.

The Leprechaun king pinned him with those eyes and something mysterious passed between them, an understanding; a connection that spanned ages.

'We helped Cullian, the travelling man,' the King continued, 'because he was the only hope, and the bards who travel freely with our blessing within our glades, came to tell us this was foreseen in their runes.

'We fed Cullain's armies against the Scree when the land was devastated, we gave them shelter and hid them from sight. And now you. You and you and you,' he said, nodding once to each of them.

'You, willow seedling, a Redthorn, whom we trust, and a long time has passed since our paths have crossed. No need. Word was given and taken. You are welcome in our glade, Corriwen Redthorn.

He looked at Kerry. 'Just a sapling yourself, but a stout one. Oak-heart. You will bend when you need when the wind is strongest, but you will not break. You have your roots solid in the earth, Kerrigan Malone, and holding strong, but your heart, your heart is rootless, hither and yon, light as the breeze. Ever welcome in our glades, boy-with-a-sling.'

He turned to Jack.

'And you, Crown-bearer. I know you of old. You bear the Red Hand, the mark of Cullian. It is to you the whole of Temair looks now, the Kelpie, the Undine, the Leprechaun and Man.

'Me?'

'You bear the same fireglass stone that he carried when the forest was young. I hear it beat within you, like the heartwood, our sisters. But it is a sore burden on young shoulders. Too young to face this, say I. Yet face it you must.'

'I don't understand,' Jack said. He turned to Kerry, who shrugged, equally baffled. 'I'm still at school. What am I supposed to do?'

'You must do what your heart tells you. No one can do more. Who can foretell in these troubled times? Let your heart lead you.'

Jack wasn't quite sure which heart the old King was referring to.

'We're supposed to go north,' was all he said.

'The road is no road now.

'That creature of hers, the Mandrake-with-no-root, he sent the Scree to our glades. They killed heartwood with axe and saw, and that we would not suffer. Such pain they cause, but now no more. We grew the road away. There is no way through.'

'Then how will we get there?' Corriwen asked. 'Time is pressing.'

The king's features quivered. It was almost a smile. 'The heartwood have ways.'

'Speaking of Ways,' Kerry broke in. 'Show him the book, Jack.'

Jack fetched it from the backpack and passed it across to the Leprechaun. He ran a hand over it, trailing twiggy fingers over the cover and for an instant Jack thought he saw it covered, not in old leather, but rough bark. The pages flicked open and immediately they saw script appearing on each page.

'Come a hard way,' the Leprechaun said. 'But how to travel is still unclear. And who knows what lies at that journey's end?'

'Do you know how we can get there?'

'The Scree guard the road mouth, what there is of it. So you must go a different way, but we will ease your stepping. Now rest, for there shall be little time for rest on the road ahead.'

He held up an acorn cup and passed it to Corriwen. 'Drink now and sleep well for the journey.'

To Jack, he handed a small bark box which rattled as he took it. He opened it and found a cache of smooth, hard seeds.

'Should we eat these too?' Kerry asked.

Jack shook his head. 'I don't think that's what they're for.'

'Maybe it's beanstalks,' Kerry chipped in. 'Nothing would surprise me here.'

The king merely smiled, creaking to his feet. 'I will consult my dear heart. I see the past, but she may sense some future.'

All the Leprechaun watched him move towards the matriarch tree at the edge of the glade, the one whose roots now encased Kerry like the arms of a chair.

The Leprechaun approached the tree and held his hands out towards it. His fingers touched the bark and the tree's mighty branches eased gently towards the little creature. Without a word, he pressed himself up against the bark and then, amazingly, sank into it.

'The mother says sleep now, and feel no fear. You will scatter her seeds.' With that, he was gone.

Jack looked at Kerry and Corriwen, unable to comprehend what he had seen. Then he whirled with a start.

The glade was empty. Totally empty. All the Leprechaun had melted into the night, into the forest, into the bosoms of their own trees.

All that was left was the three of them in the soft, dying light as a cloak of night drew itself across the wonderful forest and left them to sleep.

At night he thought of Cullian of the Red Hand. He clutched the heartstone, the black obsidian around his neck that he now knew was the key, not only to this world, but to himself.

Today he had thought he was going to die, he and his two only friends in this world.

Now they would live to fight another day, and he had the strange certainty that the battles would become even more desperate in the days to come.

He had faced death today, faced it like a man. And for a while, he was not afraid.

But by the morning he was a prisoner again.

TWENTY ONE

In the dark of night they were rocked to sleep. Jack thought he woke, turning over, feeling gentle hands lift and carry him, like the mother he never knew, and the whispering breeze hushed him and told him to sleep. He thought he was passed from hand to hand, gentle as one might pass a baby.

When he awoke, he and Corriwen and Kerry were lying close together on a bed of dry leaves at the edge of the forest and ahead of them, the land rose towards bare hills.

'Thank you,' Jack whispered. As the old Leprechaun had promised, they'd had no need of roads. They had slept and the heartwood had started them on their way.

There was magic in this world, and not all of it was cruel and hungry. It was good to have allies in this strange and fearful place. They would need as many as they could find.

Kerry yawned and stretched. Corriwen woke with a start.

'It's a good day to get going again,' she said. 'And when we prevail, I will ensure their forest is guarded forever. A tree will never be cut there.'

The set off into open country. Behind them the forest was dark but they missed its security and shade. Out here they were exposed again, and high in the morning sky, small black dots wheeling above told them the roaks were abroad and hunting. They followed a line of low scrub bushes, always alert. They had been surprised too often not to have learned a lesson.

They trudged on, heading north, as the Marsh Bard had advised, moving out from the scrub to broken country of tussock grass and mossy rocks that stood out on the moor like broken teeth. Here and there, clumps of hazels and stunted birches provided scant cover, but there was nothing for it but to keep walking.

A few miles along, Kerry raised a warning hand and as soon as they stopped, they heard it too. The drumming of hard hooves on dry ground. They peered between two stones where the track breasted a hill.

The horsemen were coming fast, at a gallop, haring down the track. He counted twenty or more, big men on big horses, sunlight catching shields and polished leather and the edges of swords. Forty yards away was a small coppice of hawthorn and elder, but thick enough.

'*Run!*' Corriwen and Kerry turned tail and ran, with Jack behind them urging them on. It was only forty yards, and they could have made it before the horsemen mounted the rise, but the heather snagged at their feet and Jack was only ten yards from cover when he slipped and fell headlong. Kerry and Corriwen pulled him upright and they were seconds from the shelter of the trees when the cavalcade came over the ridge and without pausing, came hammering over the heather towards them.

Kerry swore with such sincerity that Clarice would have washed his mouth with bleach.

Jack shoved him between the first scraggy hawthorns and they ran into the coppice, thorns ripping at them.

A greathorse, easily as big as the one that had carried them all the way from the keep to the marshes, snapped saplings down with its bulk and drove between them. A broad sword came slashing down and missed Kerry's ear by a whistling whisker. He dodged, rolled across a fallen log while Jack and Corriwen jinked to the right and into dense cover.

Kerry tumbled, got to his feet, barged between the trunks while behind him the greathorse pounded the ground with its hooves.

'Hold still and take it like a man,' a voice bellowed.

'That'll be the day,' Kerry shouted back. He was on his own now, only managing to keep a couple of steps ahead, ducking and weaving and seeking the thickest growth to keep between him and the crazy horseman with the big sword.

Jack and Corriwen had swerved, and she was moving like the wind. He stayed on her heels, while hooves drummed behind them and branches snapped like kindling. It was clear the horsemen would force their way through and round them up. They would have to stop sometime.

Kerry was running, but he had drawn his sword. He dashed between two elder trees, spun himself around it and sliced upwards with his blade. The point caught the rider just under the knee, and he cursed even more vehemently than Kerry had done only moments before. The horse reared, surprised by Kerry's sudden attack, and the rider went backside over neck and landed with a thud.

'I'll have you,' he roared.

'If you catch me,' Kerry shot back.

The man got to his feet and lunged with the blade. It was twice the size of the short sword Kerry had. One sweep cut three saplings. Kerry gulped.

'Your sword, ye devil,' the big man cried. He was head and shoulders taller than Kerry, with long black hair that spilled from a leather helm, and shells of armour over each shoulder.

'You stole yon sword,' the man roared. 'Thief. Scavenger.'

He lunged again. Kerry tried to parry, the way he'd seen in films, but the man flicked his wrist and Kerry almost lost the sword altogether.

'It's mine,' Kerry shouted back. 'Finders keepers.'

'I know the cut of that blade,' the big fellow bawled. 'Stolen from a hero. You'll pay for it. Give it up.'

'No chance,' Kerry said, quaking inside, but his Irish bravado couldn't put a brake on his tongue: 'You'll have to prise it out of my cold, dead hand.'

The man came on again, three or four quick blurring stabs and each time Kerry jumped backwards. The big fellow was an expert and his blade was huge. Kerry had no chance of winning this. He jerked back as the sword came sweeping in again, missing him by an inch, and stuck fast in a tree-trunk. The swordsman cursed and Kerry turned on his heel and ran before his opponent could lever the blade free.

'Turn and fight, scavenger! I'll have your eyes.'

Kerry had no answer to that. He ran on and the big man came after him.

Jack was tiring fast and the horsemen were closing in.

Without warning a greathorse loomed in from the left, caught him with its slab of flank and knocked him forward against Corriwen. She went down. Jack tumbled, got to his knees. A long lance came spearing in and he threw himself to the side before it skewered him to the ground. The razor point ripped his tunic across his chest and the point skipped off the heartstone. He grabbed the lance, threw his weight against it and forced its point into the bole of a tree. The rider grunted, wheeled the horse and slashed down at him. He rolled back, dragging Corriwen by the hood. The horse pawed the air and a hoof caught Corriwen between the shoulderblades.

'Run to earth, little foxes,' a deep voice boomed. 'At bay and backs to the wall.'

The man dismounted. He looked to be six foot tall and more, with yellow hair tied in braids that hung below his shoulders. He had a thick shaggy beard and blazing blue eyes.

'Skulking spies.'

The rest of the cavalry forced their way through, tall in leather armour and shoulder-plates, emblazoned shields and long spears.

The bearded man turned to one of them. 'Finish them here. We've no time to waste.'

Jack had the bow up, an arrow firm on the string. He swung the arrow left and right, covering as many of them as he could. Corriwen was winded and groaning on the ground, raising herself up on all fours. Her hood had fallen over her hair. Jack nudged backwards, protecting her with his body.

'Make a move and I'll get one of you,' he said, trying to keep the shake out of his voice. 'Maybe two.'

The leader threw his head back and laughed. 'A spy whelp with a big bark.'

Jack gritted his teeth, but pulled harder on the string. The amberhorn bow sang under the tension.

'You're the one that gets it,' he said very quietly. 'I'll put this right through you.'

While Jack was standing with the arrow ready to fly, Kerry was bobbing and weaving as the swordsman hacked and slashed after him. He had no chance in a straight fight with this man, but Kerry was faster and nimbler.

He leapt over a fallen trunk, ran round its roots and in one easy motion scooped up a big rock. He braced himself and swung the stone with all of his strength.

It hit his pursuer right in the belly with a thud and knocked the wind out of him in one great wheeze. Kerry didn't pause for a second. He ran straight in, swung his head hard and butted the man square on the nose. Blood spurted and the big sword went clattering away. Kerry snatched up the blade and jammed it in the ground beside him. Now he had two.

'You little cretin,' the man burbled, both hands up against his nose. 'I'll kill you stone dead.'

'With what?' Kerry took his belt off, looped it round the big man's neck, pulled hard.

Jack flicked his eyes to the right and saw Kerry shoving the man through the undergrowth. He had a huge sword in his hand, jabbed against the man's armpit.

Jack kept the bow taut, the deadly barb aimed at the bearded man's neck and he knew he would kill him if he took a step closer to Corriwen.

'How you doing?' Kerry saw the rip across Jack's shirt, and the black heartstone exposed on its chain.

'Getting by,' Jack called back. He didn't want to show any fear at all, no matter how tight his throat felt.

'Drop the bow,' the fair haired man demanded. 'We'll make it quick ... and honourable.'

'Thanks, but no thanks,' Kerry said. 'Make a move and I'll take his head off.'

They wheeled round. There was a very tense moment as nobody moved a muscle.

Then Corriwen managed to get to her feet and pulled the hood away from her head. She turned her face. The big man's expression changed from fury to wonder.

Her face lit up and she gasped a name that Jack didn't quite catch, and before he could move she was between him and the arrow and then she was in the fair man's arms.

'Alevin,' she squealed again, unable to contain her joy. Kerry looked at Jack and he looked back, completely bewildered.

'You know these loonies?'

She turned from the fair man's grasp, looked at Kerry, then beyond him, and despite the bruise that was blossoming between her shoulderblades, she came flitting across the distance, right past Kerry, and threw herself into another set of arms and started kissing the bloodied man.

'Corrie Copperhead,' he managed to gasp. 'After all this time, we thought you dead, little cousin. I can't believe I see you here.'

They had a fort, protected by a palisade of spiked logs and the narrow gulley that led to it was guarded by armed men.

Alevin, the man with the yellow beard and Viking braids, had been Cerwin Redthorn's right-hand man. The one with the bloodied nose was Corriwen's cousin Brodick and together they led the remnants of the regrouped armies defeated on the slaughterfields that Jack and Kerry had stumbled onto when they had come through the Farward Gate.

It was getting late now and the sky was deep red in the

west. Corriwen could not contain her joy at finding Alevin and Brodick and their depleted army. They could see the renewed hope in her eyes.

They ate venison and thick crusty bread, sharing stories about past adventures. Alevin was a huge man, all muscle and anger, and he glared suspiciously at Jack and Kerry, still not convinced that they were not spies in the camp.

Kerry kept a distance from Brodick, who now had his sword back, convinced he couldn't take kindly to being beaten by a boy, but Brodick, despite the purple bruise on his nose, ruffled his hair and grinned.

'A real champion, this one,' he said. 'No swordsman, mind, but he fair took me by surprise. We could use his like to turn the tide.'

He grinned at the rest of the big fighting men. 'It's the stuff of song. *If you'd rather not be bled ... use a rock, and then the head.*'

They all laughed and Kerry went along with it, surprised at Brodick's generosity.

Alevin was much more serious, and he had a lot to be serious about. He questioned the two of them for hours, demanding to know how they met Corriwen and where they had come from and how they had managed to get this far.

'So it's just a coincidence that you met Lady Corriwen in the forest, and another coincidence that you just stumbled on our redoubt here?'

'We never knew you were here,' Jack explained.

'So you say. But Mandrake has spies everywhere. It would be easy to befriend a lost girl and win her confidence.'

'It's not been easy,' Jack said. 'You can believe that.'

'They have my trust,' Corriwen butted in. 'They have fought for me and saved me, and braved dangers to bring me this far. It is not their quest or their battle, but they have promised to help me if they can.'

'Forgive me, Lady Corriwen,' the big fellow said, quite softly, though his tone was serious. 'I've come a hard road myself and there's more travail ahead. I promised your brother I would fight on, and to do that, I have to watch everything. There's danger all around.'

'Not from Jack and Kerry.'

'You know them. I don't. We have found spies before and . . .' he glanced across at the boys. 'We skinned them alive.'

'Out of the frying pan,' Jack whispered. 'I don't think he likes us.'

'We were betrayed,' Alevin said. 'By our own people. We did not know that Mandrake had bought other chiefs with promises of wealth. He stirred them up, saying the Redthorn sword was lost, and set one chief against the other in search of power.

'We met in fair fight, but Mandrake's cunning ruined us on the day. We thought he fought for us, but he was against us, and while we won the battle, he sent the Scree down on us when we were sick and battle-weary. It was slaughter.'

'I know,' Corriwen said. 'I found my brother. Killed by treachery.'

'I never saw him fall.'

'I took the knife from his back,' she said, face set. 'Killed by his own.'

'So we trust no one. Forgive me, but you are still young. What do you know of war and betrayal?'

'Because I have seen it. I have suffered it. But I also know of loyalty and friendship,' she said. 'And these are my loyal friends.'

Brodick nodded. 'They have come a long way, three young people, barely armed, and have fought hard.

'This stone-thrower bested me, when no Scree could. And Jack Flint has saved the Lady Corriwen not just the once, but time over. Spies creep in the darkness and hide from sight. They don't face danger if they can avoid it.'

Brodick managed to divert Alevin's suspicion, at least for now.

'So, how did you come on us?'

'We didn't,' Jack piped up. 'You came on us. We were heading north.'

'That's Mandrake's territory,' Alevin said. 'And the Scree. Why would you want to go there?'

Corriwen stood up, dwarfed by these big fighting men. 'I don't want to go,' she said, in a small voice. 'But I must. I can find the Redthorn sword.'

'What good would that do?' Alevin said. 'The clans are divided now.'

'But it could make them see sense,' Brodick cut in. 'It has always united the chiefs in the past.'

'It's more than that,' Corriwen told them. 'The Bard of Undine Haven says it's the only way to put an end to all this madness.'

Alevin raised his eyebrows in question and Corriwen told him everything the Bard had shown them of Mandrake's pact with the Morrigan under the Black Barrow in the high desert.

'So how will you find this place, far off in the blighted lands?'

'Oh, that's easy,' Kerry broke in. 'We've got a guide-book.'

Jack kicked him under the table. He didn't want to reveal any more than he had to. Any of these strangers could take the book from them and they would never find their way home.

But now that cat was out. Brodick and Alevin wanted to see it, so reluctantly Jack brought out the *Book of Ways*. As before, it opened of its own accord and the pages riffled as if in a breeze and then stopped. The two men bent over it and everybody held their breath as the script began to write itself line by line down the page.

'Sorcery,' Alevin muttered. 'Mandrake sorcery.'

They read:

Friend and foe together find
Foe and friend in treason bind
Ware the sheath that lacks a blade
Traitor's hand a prince has slayed
Gird for battle, gird for fight
Flee the havoc of the night
Flee to friends who gladly aid
Seek the shelter of the glade.

'Not much of a guidance, this,' Alevin said. 'All I see is riddles and rhymes.'

'That's the clever bit,' Kerry said. 'You have to work it out, but it's been right so far.'

And to prove just how right it was, the Scree attacked before dawn.

TWENTY TWO

The shouts of panicked men woke Jack and Kerry in the low bunk they'd been given in a hut near the outer wall. They stumbled out into sheer mayhem.

On the palisade walk, soldiers were firing clusters of arrows into the dark and torches flickered while something battered at the big timber gate with such force splinters flew.

'To the wall! All arms to the wall!' Alevin went striding past. His twin knives dangled from his belt and he gripped a long two-handed sword.

Scree, all fired up with heat and violence, attacked with clubs and curved blades. Jack saw one of them roll over the spiked wall, three arrows dug deep into its warty hide and it still kept coming.

Jack and Kerry ducked back inside the hut. Kerry drew

out the sword and Jack had his bow. Over by the boardwalk, the dead man's quiver was full of arrows. Jack snatched it up and slung it over his shoulder.

Up on the walk, Alevin paced beside the defenders.

'Throw them back,' he roared. A platoon of men were at the gate, firing through slits even while the timbers buckled. They stabbed long spears between the planks, but it was clear they couldn't hold it for long.

'We'd better run,' Kerry said. 'I think we're on the losing team.'

'Where's Corriwen?'

'Dunno. She was with her cousin and the big guy.'

'We must find her.'

'And we should run like hell.'

'That too,' Jack said, pulling back on the bowstring as another huge Scree popped its head over the parapet. It took an arrow in the eye and fell back without a sound.

'You're really getting the hang of that,' Kerry said.

Just then a troop of men came surging from behind them and almost bowled them over. Kerry was knocked to the side and carried along by the press of bodies. Up ahead the door splintered. Flames were reaching up the timbers.

A hand grabbed Jack's shoulder.

'Can you draw the bow?' A tall man demanded. 'And hit anything?'

'I already did,' Jack said.

'They're High Crag Scree,' the man said. 'Thick skinned. Neck and eyes. Let them get close.'

'Corriwen . . .'

'She's protected. The gate is not.' The man hustled him

towards the gate which was on the point of collapse.

One of the defenders turned. 'It won't hold, Declan.'

'So we give them a hot welcome,' he said. He braced his feet and fired two arrows through the splintered wood. Jack stood beside him, letting loose at anything that moved.

Another crash smashed the gate off its hinges. Something truly huge with rugged spiral horns shook a hoary head and ploughed forward, knocking defenders right and left. The Scree were already running up and over the fallen timbers in the time it took for the gate to fall.

Declan fired non-stop. Every arrow skewered a grey throat and stopped a howling cry dead. Bodies were piling up and the smell of blood was rank and metallic in the air. Behind the first front, Jack saw a tidal wave of Scree, and he knew this bottleneck wouldn't hold for long.

'Fall back,' Declan cried. 'All men to me. Fall back!'

One of Jack's arrows was stuck in the snout of the horned monster which smashed Scree and men alike.

More Scree attacked and Jack was cut off in a desperate skirmish. He picked up a fallen dagger and stabbed at anything that moved before something swooped at him and a stunning blow felled him.

He came to, lying athwart a heaving boat and was immediately sick over the side.

'You okay, Jack?'

Kerry's voice seemed to come from far off and the boat

would not stop moving. Jack groaned, managed to open a watery eye, and saw the ground blur past him. It wasn't a boat. He was lying across the back of a greathorse and it was galloping at full tilt over the heath-land.

'Thought you'd had it,' Kerry said, grinning like a lemon wedge.

Behind them, in the distance, the redoubt was burning and the Scree were roaring in triumph. Jack managed to sit up behind Kerry.

'You were down and out,' Kerry said. 'The guy who had this horse got spiked. It was awful.'

'What happened? Where's Corriwen?'

'I don't know. I just got you up on this thing and took off. I can't steer it, but it's following the rest of them. Just hang on.'

Jack hung on and the great horse thundered behind the mass of retreating men all the way back down the road they had followed, not stopping until they came to within a mile of the brooding Sappeling Wood and the beaten army wheeled in a confused circle. The horse slowed and cantered to where Alevin was already arranging a line of defence.

He turned and saw them, wheeled his own mount.

'You!' He rasped. 'Traitors and spies, you dare face me?'

He drew his sword and came racing towards them.

'Hold!' another voice called out and a rider broke away from the milling horsemen.

Alevin had his sword up, ready to slash it down on them. It could have cut them both in half with one easy sweep.

'Don't be hasty, big brother.' Declan was almost as tall

as Alevin, but broader in the shoulder. 'They fought alongside us, not against us.'

'They brought the Scree.' Alevin's face was a mask of fury. 'I knew they were trouble.'

'We did not,' Jack called out. 'Mandrake uses the birds for spies. The Bard told us.'

Declan rode close, putting himself between Alevin and them. 'They risked their lives with me at the gate. Mere boys, but they took many a Scree.'

Kerry stood up in the saddle. 'Jack made a promise to Corriwen. All he's ever done is try to help her.'

'I have heard oaths before, all broken,' Alevin said, raising his sword. Kerry twisted in the saddle, underneath the blade, even though it put him in real danger. He ripped Jack's shirt wide open.

Alevin's sword halted in mid-strike when he saw the red mark on Jack's skin, and the replica of the Corona stars.

'He wears the Red Hand,' Kerry cried. 'And it cost him plenty. So don't you dare call him a traitor.'

'The Red Hand. The Cullian hand.' Alevin froze. His men let out a collective gasp.

'The Coronal,' Declan said. 'The Bards' foretelling.'

'How did you come by this?' Alevin demanded.

Jack didn't answer at first. Kerry looked at him and Jack's face was slack with shock. One hand was clamped high on his chest.

'I asked you . . .' Alevin began again, and Jack seemed to start, as if waking from a dream.

'No time,' he said.

The heartstone was no longer around his neck. The

sudden realisation drained the blood from his head and the world spun dizzily.

The stone was *gone*.

The loss of it was like a physical blow; as if part of him had been cut out. His father's obsidian heart *had* become a part of him, the key to everything.

And Jack knew now it was so much more than that.

'No time,' he said again, forcing the words out. And there truly was no time to spare. The Scree were haring over the heath in pursuit, knowing the men were trapped against the forest wall.

Jack forced the shock of loss down. He would deal with it later. Right now there were more urgent concerns.

Alevin wheeled the horse to face the beleaguered men. 'We stand here, brave men. It may be our last, but we will take many with us.'

'No!' Jack cried. 'Run for the trees. Get into the wood.'

Another gasp went through the ranks.

'Hold!' Alevin ordered. Beside him his brother made a hand sign that Kerry thought looked like the evil eye. 'Sappeling Wood is forbidden. It has evil magic. No one returns.'

'*We* did,' Jack said. 'You will be safe.' He looked over his shoulder at the approaching Scree outrunners. 'But they won't. Trust me now.'

His eyes held Alevin's. 'I swear you will be safe.'

'Aye, don't worry,' Kerry said, with more confidence than he really felt. How would the Leprechaun welcome these strangers? 'We've got some good friends.'

Alevin sat stock still for a moment. He glanced at his

brother, then at the men who awaited his command. Jack knew he was considering which death he preferred. Out here it was certain.

Finally he shrugged. 'Even to Tir Nan Og if we must,' he said. 'Lead then, Coronal.'

Jack and Kerry dismounted the greathorse and led the trapped and bloodied fighters into the depths of the wood.

Corriwen held tight to her cousin Brodick as his horse pounded northwards, smelling his sweat and the blood from the cuts where splinters had peppered his face. Her cloak was torn in several places and a clawed Scree hand had ripped skin from her back.

When the attack erupted in the darkness, she had woken, her knives already drawn.

She rounded the barracks hut, scanning the jumble of struggling bodies for Jack and Kerry, and thought she saw Kerry up on the palisade hacking at fingers, but she couldn't be sure. As she turned a corner she barged into a Scree who raised its axe and struck at her.

Another sword flashed in from the side and the Scree's arm went tumbling away, still grasping the sword. A second blow cleaved the ugly thing from brow to chin and Brodick leant down from the greathorse, and swung her up behind him.

'Hold tight,' Brodick shouted.

They rode all night, only slowing when the smoke and fire

was a glimmer in the distance. Corriwen knew that he'd had no option but to smash a way through, and told him so.

'I should have stayed,' he said. 'They will think I fled.'

'I saw you fight. And you saved me, too. There was nothing else to do.'

'We've lost the redoubt. And many have died.'

'And many Scree, too,' she replied. 'Did you see my friends?'

'One was on the wall. The stone-thrower. The other . . .' He turned his head away.

'What?' Corriwen demanded.

'I saw him fall,' Brodick said, almost a whisper. 'He was struck down.'

Corriwen's mouth opened, but no sound came out. It was as if a hand had clenched her throat and squeezed. The shock was so great that she felt the blood drain from her head and the world started to waver into foggy grey. Brodick twisted in the saddle and held her tight before she fell to the ground.

The woods enfolded them in inky shadow and the men were afraid, men who had fought a savage battle against Scree. Dawn was breaking, but here it was all gloom. Jack led the way, with Alevin and Declan close, scanning around.

He had promised they would be safe, and that had been a gamble. The Leprechaun had told him he was welcome. But he had said nothing about other people.

The upside was that the Leprechaun folk had nothing against men. But they hated the Scree. That had to stand in their favour.

They walked on. Behind them on the heath, the approaching Scree beat war clubs against shields. Jack could tell some of the men wanted to turn back and face them and die like heroes. Jack did not want to die, like a hero or anything else. He wanted to stay alive and find Corriwen Redthorn.

The loss of the stone was devastating enough. To think Corriwen was lost to them after all they had been through, that didn't bear thinking about. If they got out of this predicament, he would find her, no matter what it took.

They topped a rise and Jack stopped. They were not alone. The forest had been empty and now they were surrounded. He could feel their eyes.

'Hello,' Jack called out. 'If you can hear me, we need shelter again.'

'I hear you, Journeyman,' the crackly voice whispered out. Jack strained his eyes.

A shape emerged in front of him and the old Leprechaun king held up his knotty fingers.

'Welcome again to our glades.'

'Thank you,' Jack replied. Alevin walked forward, with his brother by his side.

'What is this . . .' Alevin began. He was staring at the old creature as if he had seen a devil. 'And how did he come from that tree?'

'It's a long story,' Jack said. 'Let him talk. It's his forest.'

'Battle weary and bloodied,' the king said. 'But not beaten.'

'Well beaten,' Alevin said. 'Too many of them.'

'We see them come. They are not welcome in our glades. They have not learned that lesson.' He held up his hand to the brothers. 'Friends of Redthorn, shelter here in the heartwood. The Scree beasts come at their peril.'

'But they'll come anyway,' Declan said.

'The heartwood knows,' the king said. 'The heartwood remembers.'

'What's he talking about?'

The Scree entered the forest, still clattering shields and swords.

The old Leprechaun led the bloodied warriors along the pathways and into the deep wood where he finally stopped them at the dell.

'Rest and root,' he said. The glade's trees were filled with the little creatures, great polished eyes unblinking in the lightening gloom. 'Be at ease.' He merged into the shadows between two tall buttressed roots.

'Where did he go?' Declan demanded. He whirled round, scanning the trees. All the Leprechaun were gone.

'It's a neat trick,' Kerry agreed.

The Scree captain held a hand up. He was head and shoulders taller than the rest and built like a wall. His teeth were filed to points.

'Finish them,' he said. 'Stamp them down.'

The forest was silent now as they waited for him to speak. They had come deep into the woods, following the trail of broken twigs and the smell of blood and sweat, but it was silent here.

'Find them,' the Scree growled. 'Kill them all.' He raised his curved blade. 'Crush their bones and eat their brains.' He slashed at a branch close to his head. The ground shivered under his feet.

A shadow snaked up from the ground, so quickly that none of them saw it clearly. The captain disappeared in a scatter of dead leaves.

The Scree scratched their heads, baffled. A couple went forward. The captain was on the ground. His eyes rolled and his mouth opened and shut. The first trooper stepped back. The leader was not on the ground. He was in it. Only his head showed above the leaf litter.

One Scree bent to help him up.

Just as he moved forward, something lashed out and caught him by the ankles. It whipped him off his feet. He grabbed at the ground to save himself and his hands found the captain's head. Whatever pulled at his feet yanked hard. The captain's head came with him, dripping blood, glaring at him with ferocious dying eyes. The second Scree looked in amazement as the captain's head scattered droplets and in a flick of green, the other soldier simply disappeared into the canopy. There was no sign of the captain's body, but the head came tumbling down from above.

The Scree crowded together. Something came fluttering from on high and one of them snatched at it. It was just a seed, whirling down on a brown papery vane. Another one fell. It disappeared down the Scree's tunic. More followed it until the air was thick with a snowstorm of seedfall.

'Just seeds,' the second-in-command growled. 'Come on. Let's kill.' He scratched at his neck. A seed landed on his head and stuck to his warty skin. Beside him, another trooper tried to brush something from his eye and then let out a curse.

'Burns, this,' he gasped. He tried to pluck the seed from his eyelid and when he did, the skin puckered outwards. He pulled harder and the skin ripped away. Little bloody roots dangled from the seed. Blood filled his eye. Beside him, another Scree soldier was scrabbling at his cheek where three seeds had stuck fast.

He spun, wheeling, and barged in between the roots of a tall tree. His face hit the rough bark and quicker than the eye could follow, the roots closed around him with a meaty snap.

Way in the depths of the forest Jack and Kerry heard the commotion. Alevin and Declan had arranged the men on the ridge of the dell, armed and ready.

They watched with Jack and Kerry as the Scree milled about, barging into trunks and crashing through bushes, all of them now bawling in terror.

One lurched against a trunk and as soon as he fell against it, the bark oozed a golden resin that poured from the wood and covered the Scree like toffee. In seconds, he was stuck like a fly in amber. The club slowly dripped to the ground, trailing a sticky mass.

The trees suddenly came alive. Branches reached wooden fingers and snatched Scree from the ground. Roots exploded up and dragged them into the earth.

Ivy tendrils struck and garroted; thorns raked eyes and faces. The forest fed.

Jack and Kerry and Alevin's fighters watched in horrified fascination as the trees took their revenge.

After a while, the forest became quiet and still.

'What devilry is this?' Alevin asked Jack.

'It's good magic,' Jack replied. 'The Leprechaun just saved your lives.'

He turned to Kerry. 'We have to find Corriwen. And there's another problem. A real one.'

'What's that?'

Jack pulled his shirt open. The red hand and the crown of stars stood out clearly on his bare skin.

'The stone's gone. And so has the book.' His face was grim. 'Somebody stole them.'

'No!'

Jack's fingers opened and closed, as if he could touch the stone. The loss scared him more than the Scree.

'I have to find it,' he said. 'No matter what. We're stuck without it. I mean really stuck.'

He didn't tell Kerry the other thoughts – the sensation of loss; the connection with his father; the awesome power of the stone that he was just beginning to suspect.

'What about Corriwen?' Kerry asked.

'I don't believe she's dead.'

'How do you know?'

'I don't know. I just feel it.' He tapped his chest. 'In here.'

Kerry frowned and stayed silent for a while.

Then he touched his own chest.

'You know something? You're right. I can feel her here, too.'

TWENTY THREE

They had travelled a difficult road since the battle of the forest. They were hungry and saddlesore, but Jack knew he had to keep going, even when he was half asleep behind Kerry on the greathorse as it trudged up into the dry mountains beyond the plain.

Declan followed close behind, guarding the rear, while Kerry found the trail and Jack used the compass in his head to keep them heading northwards when mist covered the high land at night and blocked out the stars. The little Leprechaun they had saved from the bird clung precariously to the horse's neck, eyes tight shut. He didn't like wide open spaces.

The nights were cold and the days scorched and none of them knew how far they would have to travel.

Without the *Book of Ways* they were lost, and without the

heartstone, they might never find a way back, but Jack was determined to keep them moving.

The old Leprechaun had taken Jack and Kerry aside. 'My brothers, and the heartwood, thank you for saving this sapling from the catcher-bird. You have a long and hard road to travel, and how it will go is hidden in shade. But there are ways and there are ways. And if the forest can help, our sapling will do what he can.'

At that, the little creature, hardly more than knee-high, clambered up the stirrups and clung to the mane. When they left the shelter of the trees, it clamped its eyes shut tight and rode on the horse's neck, while Kerry sought the route ahead.

Jack was convinced that Corriwen had either escaped from the burning redoubt, or that she had been captured. They had searched the smouldering ruins, ignoring the smell and the clouds of flies that covered the bodies of the dead Scree, but found no sign at all, and no sign was a good sign, Jack thought. It confirmed she was still alive.

He had already sensed that. There was no empty hollow in his heart that would have told him otherwise.

Jack had no idea who had felled him; didn't know who had stolen the stone and the book, but he knew that first they had to find Corriwen.

He had made a promise.

It was Kerry who found the first signs. He had scouted along the trail north on foot, after someone said he remembered Corriwen had been with her cousin Brodick when the main gate had been smashed open.

'He was horsed, is what I recall,' the scarred fellow had

said as he sharpened his sword on a whetstone.

Five miles up the track, Kerry found a piece of cloth snagged on a hawthorn bush and thought it might be from the hood of Corriwen's cloak. Further on, he found a strand of red hair caught in an overhead branch, about the same height as a rider might have been. It was the colour of spun copper.

Alevin called a meeting of the troop leaders.

'This young Coronal deserves our thanks, and my apologies,' Alevin started. Declan stood beside him, silent and broad, solid as rock. 'I called him traitor, but he repaid us by saving us.' Alevin put his hand on Jack's shoulder. Kerry beamed with pride. 'He bears the Red Hand of Cullain, and the sign of the Corona. Just as the Bards tell us it would be. His coming here is surely a sign.'

Jack didn't know what to say to that. He felt a blush creep from under his collar and kept his eyes firmly on the ground.

'The Lady Corriwen is gone, but we believe Brodick may have saved her from the Scree. It may be that Mandrake's forces have taken her, but I think she is alive. We have battles ahead, but we are not dead until they put pebbles on our eyes, so hope lives on.'

The men nodded agreement.

'So, will you fight with me to break this curse of Mandrake?'

Every man raised a right hand and made a fist. They swore to fight on.

'And now,' Alevin said, 'we must listen to what this young Coronal has to say. Because it seems Mandrake is not our true enemy. Behind him is something much worse.'

He motioned Jack forward. 'Jack Flint and Stone-thrower. We owe you a debt. It will be some time before we can repay you, so we will borrow more. Tell the captains what they need to know.'

Jack shuffled his feet, aware of all those eyes on him, and even more aware of how big and strong and old they seemed. It made him feel his lack of experience and lack of years.

'All I can say is what the Bard told me,' Jack began. 'The Bard of Undine Water. Finbar.'

He raised his head, focussed on Declan. 'Mandrake, he's trying to raise something. 'Something called the Morrigan.'

A murmur rippled round the men. Some made signs in the air with their hands.

'Long ago, your people buried her somewhere in the desert,' Jack continued, still nervous. 'Or the High Barrens, whatever you call them, but Mandrake found where they put her. He's learned how to get her out. By breaking a spell. You call it a *geas*.'

'Old stories tell of the Bane-Shee curse,' Declan said. 'That's why he's building the dam, and cutting a channel through the hills. He thinks if he floods the desert, then she'll get loose.'

'And if she does,' Alevin said quietly, 'then the battle and all else is lost.'

'That's what the Bard says,' Jack agreed. 'We said we'd help Corriwen find the place, so whether she's been captured or gone on ahead, we still have to get there. That's where your sword is. The Redthorn sword.'

One of the Captains stepped forward.

'No one knows where the Black Barrow lies. The salt desert is blasted lands. Nothing grows there and if you travel there, you're walking dead.'

'I promised to help Corriwen find her father's sword,' Jack said. 'We know we have to go north, and Kerry here's a good tracker. If anybody can find her, he can.'

He raised his eyes again. 'But you have to destroy the dam before the water gets too high. And you have to stop them cutting through the mountains. If you can do that, then everything might be all right. At least we might have a chance.'

'A chance is more than we've had for a while,' Declan said.

'So it seems,' Alevin said, 'we have three ways to go. To find the Redthorn sword. To find the Lady Corriwen. And to prevent Mandrake breaking the *geas*.'

Jack held a hand up. 'I want to find Corriwen.'

'As do we all,' Alevin said. 'This is what we will do.'

Very quickly he laid out a plan for Jack and Kerry to follow her trail, while he would ride hard to the dam and do his best to destroy it.

Declan agreed with most of it, but he stood for a while and scratched at his yellow beard.

'I'm thinking,' he said, 'that two boys alone won't get far.'

'We've done okay up until now,' Kerry said.

'Aye, maybe, but you never walked those blasted lands before. Me neither. But if you've no objections, you'll need a strong arm at your back. I say I take the road with you.'

Jack looked at Kerry. He had seen Declan slaughter those big Scree when the gate fell. Strong arm was one way to describe him. Jack smiled.

'I think that would be a really good idea,' he said.

A week later, they were getting close to the mountain plain and Jack knew they were on the right track. Corriwen had left a trail for them to follow.

But none of them knew Mandrake was travelling westwards, at the head of a huge army, determined to find Corriwen Redthorn and her two companions and to finish Alevin and his fighters once and for all.

He sat inside a black covered-wagon, drawn by half a dozen greathorses. His retinue of renegade chiefs and their men were outnumbered by the horde of Scree who marched alongside, keeping clear of the horses. The hauling beasts whinnied and stamped and it needed riders on the outrunners to keep them moving. They could sense Mandrake's evil and would have bolted if they hadn't been strapped in harness.

Mandrake was alone in the wagon, covered with hides to keep the daylight out. He was talking again, talking to himself, so the renegade chiefs tried to make themselves believe, but they had heard the strange two-way conversation coming from his mouth in harsh scrapy voices. Despite their betrayal of the Redthorn chief, they would have killed Mandrake if his power hadn't been so great.

But his power was indeed great. The heads of the Scree who had limped home, wounded and bleeding after the battle outside Sappeling Wood, were spiked on banner-poles, eyeless, noseless and earless. Mandrake might have been incandescent with rage at the time, but cutting up Scree cowards had calmed him a little.

Behind him, the great storm he and the Morrigan had conjured swirled in a black maelstrom. Under the ferocious clouds rain poured incessantly, filling the lake that was building behind his dam.

The news had come in the night when Mandrake had been walking on the rim of the coffer dam spanning the river gorge. Behind the massive wooden barrier the waters were high, and tossed by violent winds, swamping the valley behind it as the river backed up. Already the pressure was making the dam creak alarmingly, but Mandrake knew it would hold for long enough.

Two miles up from the dam, the people who had farmed the Redthorn lands now slaved, men, women and children, young and old, chipping and cutting at the stone of the thin ridge, driving a chasm towards the flooded valley. Already water was seeping through cracks in rainbow sprays, making the work even more treacherous, but Mandrake had no concerns for the diggers.

There were more of them now, and work was faster, after the rest of the Scree failures from Sappeling Wood had been sent there as their punishment.

'They'll all come out in the wash,' he had cackled, and his retainers had laughed along with him, afraid not to join in.

The time was almost at hand. The waters would soon be through.

Visions came to him, along with the hunger that was always with him. Her hunger.

The visions were of death, blood and bones; of savagery and destruction. He gave himself to the hunger. He saw cracks razor across stony ground and brimstone erupt from fissures and hellish things crawl from the deep dark. He saw flying beasts with skeletal faces filling the air, drawn from a foul underworld where *her* word was law.

He saw Temair ravaged but raised again under his rule. Under *their* rule. He saw infinite power in his hands.

But ... and there was always a but.

The girl had slipped through his fingers again; the boy had escaped, with the key that would open worlds to their oppression.

'Break the *geas*,' his voice cackled. They heard it from outside the wagon, high and shrill; the voice of a hag. 'Dismantle the curse that has bound us.'

'So nearly there,' his other voice responded. 'The water is high and the dam holds. The cleft is almost cut through. The flood is imminent.'

'*We find* him *or else all is lost. World upon world.*'

'Nowhere else to hide. The fools destroyed the fort. They are all on the run.'

'*He escapes us again and again. Everything conspires against us.*'

'Luck, only luck. He is a pup. A piglet. He cannot escape us now.'

'*We must have it. We must have it. The journeyman's key.*

Find him. Find the heartstone.' The cackling voice grew to a screech. '*Find him. Kill him. Break his bones; eat his brains.*

'*But give me my KEY!*'

The black wagon rolled on at a gallop, and the voices inside it continued to screech, while the Scree ran alongside, ready for battle.

The land was hot and parched; water was hard to find. Brodick had rested the horse in the shadow of a stunted tree while Corriwen slept fitfully.

They had come so far together, Corriwen, Jack and Kerry Malone. Now it was just her and her cousin Brodick, and despite the anguish she felt, the empty space in her heart where she had held her two friends close, she knew she had to live with the ache of loss and keep travelling.

She had questioned Brodick about the night of the battle, but all he could tell her was that he had seen Jack fall in the melée, felled by a Scree club.

'Could he have lived?'

Brodick shrugged and put an arm around her shoulder.

'It was a heavy blow,' he said gently, 'and he wore no armour.'

They had ridden for seven days now, ever northwards through stony country and then up to this dry place where the rocks were ground by wind into dry sand. She kept looking back the way they had come, in case Kerry might have found their trail. Corriwen had cut pieces of her cloak and tied them to branches. Twice she had used her knife to cut locks of her own hair and leave them as markers, just in case. The Salt Barrens were to the north. How far, neither of them knew. No one in living memory had ever travelled there. No one, except mad Mandrake.

She had sat behind Brodick, holding on to his belt, glad of the closeness and fellowship of her cousin who had stood over her and fought Scree before they could catch her. She owed him a debt she could never repay. Now he was her protector for the final part of this awful journey. He would keep her safe if he could.

'We must go north,' she had insisted, when he had veered the greathorse east.

'There's nothing there but mountains and blasted lands,' he said. 'It's been cursed since the old days.'

'That's why we have to go there,' she said. 'That's where the Redthorn sword is. Without it, Temair will never be whole again.'

'It's only a sword,' he said.

'It's Cullian's sword,' she answered quickly. 'It has been handed down the generations and kept Temair united against all evil. Mandrake has used it to wake her, so the Bard says. The burden is on my shoulders, and I have to carry it for the sake of my brother and father and for Temair.'

He shrugged. 'It's not where I would choose to travel, but if your mind is made up.'

'I haven't the pleasure of choice. I wish there was another way, but there isn't.'

'Well,' he smiled and ruffled her hair, the way cousins

can, even with a Redthorn. 'If that's the way it is, there's no point arguing, once the dice are thrown.'

'They rolled out long ago.'

'So it's up to the blasted lands, then,' he said.

When she woke, Brodick was just a dark shape. She rubbed her eyes, tried to ignore the fierce ache in her heart, and when she opened them again, she saw the cloud in the western sky. It glowed a fiery red, lit by the embers of the sun. And it hung in the sky, in the shape of a handprint against the cobalt blue.

The red hand of Cullian.

Corriwen's heart did a slow, lazy flip. She blinked against the glare of the fiery cloud, leant back against the saddle. Directly overhead, she saw the Corona blaze, five points of light like jewels on dark velvet. The stars held her eyes and as she watched, out of the evening sky flew five swans, flying high enough to catch the dying rays of the sun.

They flew, not in the chevron formation she had watched every spring when the water-birds came back home, but in a semicircle.

They soared overhead and the last light caught their beating wings until each bird covered each star in a shimmer of light.

At that moment Corriwen Redthorn knew, deep inside herself, heart and soul, that Jack Flint was still alive.

The Bards had sent her a sign.

TWENTY FOUR

Kerry picked up the trail just as Jack was losing hope. Seven days north, they were thirsty and tired and swaying from lack of sleep. Big Declan didn't look any different. He rode his horse as if glued to the saddle and kept a weather eye for signs of pursuit.

The little Leprechaun clinging to the horse's neck made very little conversation. When he did, his voice sounded like twigs in a winter wind.

'He's scared witless,' Kerry said.

'He's not the only one,' Jack replied. 'This is a scary place.'

All around them the land was rising and the scrub bushes had given way to boulder-strewn tracks that seemed to lead nowhere. It was sere and windswept and it was days since they had passed the last, empty hamlet where the people had left in a hurry.

'Taken from their homes,' Declan said, eyebrows drawn together in anger. 'Taken to dig for Mandrake. Free men now slaves.'

Seven days out and Kerry had found the half circle of white stones, close to the ashes of a cold campfire, and Jack instantly knew she had left them another message besides the fiery locks of hair. He fingered the marks on his chest.

'The Corona,' he said. 'It has to be her.'

Declan hunkered down, stabbing his sword into the dry ashes. They could see the muscles stand out under his shirt. His twin sheathes hung almost to the ground.

As he bent to finger the ashes to determine how fresh they were, Kerry nudged Jack in the ribs.

'He's lost a knife.'

Jack looked down and saw the hilt at Declan's waist. Its twin was missing. The boys exchanged a glance, but said nothing. They were both thinking the same thing.

Ware the sheath that lacks a blade
Traitor's hand a prince has slayed

The *Book of Ways* might be cryptic and hard to puzzle out, but not this time. And it hadn't been wrong yet. Its warning was clear.

Jack looked at Kerry and Kerry looked back.

'What do you think?'

Jack shook his head. 'I don't know.'

Declan stood and his plaid cloak swung round to hide the sheaths.

'Only a day ahead,' he said. 'The ashes are dry. We'll find her soon.'

'Great,' Jack forced himself to say.

Kerry lit a fire and they ate a thin broth before Declan rolled himself up in his plaid and went instantly to sleep close to the fire, one hand on his sword. From where they sat, Jack and Kerry could see the twin sheaths, one empty.

'I think we're in a bit of trouble,' Kerry whispered, when Declan's slow breathing told him the big man was asleep.

'We should go by the book,' Jack agreed. 'Alevin says there was a traitor. And the book hasn't been wrong so far. And something's been bothering me. I don't think it was a Scree who stole it.'

'Why not?'

'They're not bright. And how would they know what I had? But others knew I had the book and the stone.'

'You think it was him.' Kerry asked, nodding towards Declan.

'We'll soon find out.'

'So what do we do?'

'A man's gotta do ...'

'Like what?'

'We've got to get away from him. I trust what the book tells us. And I don't believe in coincidences. Not any more.'

'Me neither. But he'll come after us.'

'Not if we do it right.'

'You going to kill him?'

They stared at each other for a long moment.

'Maybe it won't come to that. But if he tries to stop us, then ...' He left the rest unsaid.

'Don't worry. We'll find her, whatever it takes.'

'I know. We find her and help her get this sword and then we get out of here if we can.'

'Can we find the gate?'

'We have to find it,' Jack said earnestly. 'Or we'll be stuck here for good. But I've been thinking about what the Bard said, and what the old Leprechaun told me. They've seen the stone before. And the Leprechaun told me I had Cullain's sap in me. I think he came through the Farward Gate a long time ago. Maybe he was an ancestor of mine or something.'

'Yeah, right. I knew you read too many fairy stories.'

'Like I said, none of this is coincidence,' Jack replied. 'Maybe it's a test. And I think my father did use these gates. That's what a journeyman does. That's why we have to get back, because the Major knows it all. I never knew what happened to my father when I was a baby. But maybe, just *maybe*, he went through one of those other gates and never came back.'

'What difference would that make?'

'Maybe if he did, he's still out there somewhere. Some other world. Maybe he needs the heartstone to get back. I could have a chance of finding him.'

'I'll say this for you, Jack,' Kerry said, turning over to get comfortable. 'You've got a hell of an imagination. But what I don't get is, what am I supposed to do?'

'You're part of it as much as me. Over here, you can read. You can use the sling. That's got to be for something. And we need each other. You're the best friend I ever had.'

'More like the only one.' Kerry managed a grin. 'Okay, we find Corrie, then we look for the gate. Then what?'

'We get you home. And then I have to work out the next move.'

'Home? That's okay for you to say. I don't care if I never see the place again. What have I got? My old man doesn't care. Everybody calls me a thick bogtrotter. I even get my shoes in Oxfam. I'm nobody. Over here, I might be scared to death half the time. But I'm somebody.'

'You want to stay here?'

Kerry shrugged. 'I want to stick with you.'

Kerry was long asleep and clouds covered the moon, but Jack couldn't settle. All sorts of thoughts were buzzing around his mind. Thoughts of Cullian. Thoughts of his father. Of Corriwen Redthorn somewhere ahead of them. But mostly he thought about the words in the *Book of Ways*, and the more he thought about them, the more concerned he became. Finally, unable to leave it alone, he had to move.

He eased himself up and crept silently towards where Declan's horse grazed. It shied and Jack tried to calm it as he reached high to the saddle-bags. As quietly as he could, he opened the nearest and rummaged inside. There was no book, no stone.

In the dim glow of the embers, he crawled under the horse and loosened the thong on the other bag. He reached inside and felt something small and rectangular, wrapped in rough cloth. And there was a small leather pouch which jangled at his touch. Jack stood on tiptoe, trying to get them out of the saddle-bag when a hand snapped around his wrist. A cold point touched his neck.

'All you have to do is ask,' Declan said from the shadows. For such a big man he had moved so silently that Jack had heard nothing.

'I have nothing worth stealing,' Declan said. 'But if you tell me what you want, you're welcome.'

Jack tried to think of something to say, but before he could open his mouth, the little Leprechaun spoke urgently from the shadow of the rock. He was kneeling on the ground, his fingers dug deep into the earth. His eyes were closed.

'Bad comes,' he whispered. 'Grey axe-cutters. Many in the dark.'

In an instant Declan kicked earth over the coals until there was no light. He braced himself, knife in one hand, sword in the other, standing between two stones.

'Let's have them then,' he growled.

Kerry grunted, opened his eyes and yawned. 'What's up?'

Behind him, the little Leprechaun spoke. 'Too many. Biters and tusk-diggers too.'

He bent down to the ground again and this time Jack saw him open a tiny basket that the king had given them. He drew something out and dug his fingers into the soil again, whispering quietly as he did so, then covered up the hole he had dug. He took an acorn cup, loosened the top, and poured liquid onto the spot.

'No time for gardening,' Declan said grimly. 'Time for killing.'

But as soon as the Leprechaun stood up, two leaves appeared from the ground, opening like wings. A thin sprout wavered upwards.

'Jack and the freakin' beanstalk,' Kerry said.

More leaves appeared. The shoot branched. Leaves budded and unfurled. In minutes it was head-height and spreading out to cover the rock.

'Horses in here,' the little creature said. 'We hide tight.'

Jack got the picture and took the reins. The horse whickered, but came along.

'More devilry,' Declan said.

'It worked for us before,' Jack said. 'We can't fight them all.'

'We can take some with us.'

'But that won't help Corriwen. We have to stay alive for her.'

Declan glared at him. 'Never turned from a battle yet.'

'First time for everything,' Kerry retorted.

'Fine. We'll cower like rabbits.'

He took the reins of his horse and led it under the leaves that now covered the entire rock face and overhung the hollow. As soon as they were inside, the vines wove themselves together into a thick mat and then buds began to form and crimson flowers unfolded in wide cups that oozed nectar and gave off a sweet scent.

'Hides smell,' the Leprechaun said. Jack understood right away.

Declan stood with a hand over each of the horse's noses,

whispering calmly to them. His sword was dug into the ground, ready for action.

The Scree hunters poured into the campsite. The hounds bayed, excited. Jack held his breath, parted the foliage and peered out.

'Been here,' one of them grated.

'Which way?'

'Dogs'll sniff 'em.'

One of the hounds strained at the leash and dragged its handler across to the hollow. It whined and pawed and as it did, more scarlet flowers opened and the thick scent wafted out in a cloud.

'Stinks, this does,' the Scree said, screwing up his ugly face. He jabbed a spear into the vines. The tip stabbed between Jack and Kerry and almost nicked the horse on its flank. Nobody moved a muscle.

'Not here,' another Scree bawled. 'But not far. We'll hunt 'em down.'

And with that, they turned quickly and left.

Jack let out a sight of relief.

Declan said nothing at all.

Alevin and his men had raced towards the dam, covering the ground fast. Every mile took them ever closer to the storm that wheeled in the distance.

They were completely unaware that Mandrake and his hordes had headed towards the high country, and that the two opposing armies had passed within twenty miles of each other.

Mandrake had ordered his captains to hurry the Scree on while he rode in the black wagon. Their boots clattered on the stony ground and the big iron-bound wheels crunched rock under their weight.

Outrunner scouts came back, breathless and exhausted.

'No one at the redoubt,' one of them wheezed. 'All burned down.'

Mandrake's eyes blazed from under the shadows of the cowl that hid his peeling, sickly skin.

'The renegade Alevin,' he grated, voice hoarse and crackly. 'What sign of him?'

'All the tracks go east, Lord,' the Scree runner said. 'Lot of horses. Lot of men. And fast.'

'The dam!' Mandrake spat. 'They plan to undo our work.'

One of the turncoat chiefs approached. 'They are too late, surely.'

Mandrake turned on him, and his eyes burned red in the shadows. '*Who is thissss?*' His voice had changed. The chief flinched back.

'*We took the guards away.*' Mandrake cackled to himself. 'There will be enough. It will take days to break that water-wall.'

'*Not enough. Not enough. I planned too long.*' The voice rose high. The chief turned away, frightened of the sudden change in his master, frightened of the consequences of this awful fury.

Mandrake's face bulged as if something else was swelling

under his skin. His eyes blazed and his mouth pulled back to show rotten teeth in weeping gums.

'*Turn!*' he screeched. '*Stop them. Kill them. Break them. Smash them.*'

'But the girl ... the girl ...'

'*We will have her. We will consume her. But first I need the water.*'

The great army wheeled, sending up grit and dry rock dust, and began to move fast back towards the east.

Alevin's men reached the crevice in the ridge where thousands of the people of Mid-Temair had been enslaved. Since the great battle they had been forced to dig a narrow channel from west to east, and they were still toiling like ants when the riders came thundering up the cleft, hooves splashing in water that was already seeping through the solid rock from the vast dammed lake on the other side of the ridge.

Only a handful of Scree guards were on duty, and the sudden attack took them by surprise. Alevin was in the lead, with his men bunched close behind him.

The carnage was as swift as it was awful.

TWENTY FIVE

The ache had faded from Corriwen's heart when she woke before dawn after seeing the red hand in the sky and the flight of swans over the Corona. She rose with the uncanny certainty that Jack Flint and Kerry would come looking for her.

But her heart was not at peace, for when she awoke, Brodick was gone from the spot beside the fire where he had slept.

She shook sleep away and moved to the edge of the hollow where they had sheltered and found hoofprints.

Now she was curious as she followed the trail away from the campsite, for perhaps a mile from where they had slept, and heard the sound of voices.

Her heart leapt. Brodick had found them. A smile dimpled her cheeks and she ran forward to greet Jack and Kerry.

And then she stopped dead when she saw the Scree, and the joy in her heart turned instantly to fear.

The Scree was leaning against the rock, a club over his shoulder. There were others there around a small fire, their hounds muzzled and the hogs pegged beyond the fire. As she drew back out of sight, aware that she had almost run into their arms, she saw Brodick.

His back was towards her. The horse was hobbled some distance away, uneasy at being so near the Scree and their hounds. Her hand went to her knives, wishing she had a sword, or Jack's amberhorn bow, steeling herself for a fight and knowing she would have to rescue her cousin.

Then Brodick stood up. He was not bound and shackled as she thought.

Over the distance she heard his voice, though not the words, and then he laughed. He clapped one of the hunched Scree on the shoulder and Corriwen's heart sank. The troop were just like the ones who had hunted them all over Temair.

And Brodick was laughing with them.

Slowly, quietly, she pulled back, kept low until she was well out of sight, then ran back to the camp, making sure she stayed on rocky ground to leave no prints of her own. Her mind was in turmoil as she wrapped herself in her cloak, lay down again and closed her eyes, trying to think.

She was lying still when Brodick came back, leading the horse by the reins.

'Time to rise, cousin. We have a way to go.'

But where have you gone, in your heart, she asked herself, unable to look him in the eye, lest she betray her thoughts.

Far in the east, the maelstrom was an inkblot low in the sky. Brodick shaded his eyes.

'We should start before that overtakes us,' he said. 'It doesn't look natural to me.'

The forces of evil were gathering to destroy Temair. That much she knew.

'It's Mandrake,' she said, keeping her voice steady, testing his response. 'And that monster he is trying to raise. They have this power now. What will it be like when she is free?'

'What can the Redthorn sword do to stop it?' Brodick asked.

'It will unite the people again,' she said, 'and break Mandrake's power.'

'They are scattered or slaves,' Brodick said flatly.

'For now. But there is hope. If the beast gets free, there will be *no* life. Mandrake knows the sword is important, that's why he has been hunting me. But he has hunted Jack and Kerry too. The Bard says he wants the key.'

'The key?' Brodick lifted his eyes. She saw his interest quicken.

'The heartstone he wore on his neck,' Corriwen said. 'It's the key to everything, so Finbar said. He made me promise not to tell Jack. The stone belonged to his father. He was a great man.'

She was watching his eyes. He had said nothing about his encounter with the Scree hunters and that meant he had much to hide. Corriwen wished she could look into his heart and discover why.

That night, on the same night that Jack Flint groped in

the dark with the saddle-bags on Declan's horse, Corriwen Redthorn did exactly the same with Brodick's.

They were beyond the boulder ground now, and close to the edge of the High Salt Plain. Few plants grew and they stopped for the night beside an outcrop which sheltered them from the wind.

She couldn't sleep and even the Corona high above offered her no comfort as she waited in the cold until Brodick was asleep.

The horse whinnied when she approached and she wondered whether she should just climb on the saddle and leave him.

But she had to know.

Very quietly she opened the saddle-bag and with stealthy fingers, she reached inside.

Far in the depths of the Black Barrow, the Morrigan, trapped since since the days of Cullian the Traveller, sensed the coming together of all the pieces she had laid out.

She reached out, across the flat of the plain. She touched the small, black mind of a coiled adder and it writhed and sank its fangs into its own flesh and died in an instant.

Her strength was increasing.

She reached further and higher and from the crater-eyes of the great roak that circled above the ridge; she saw Mandrake's army turn back towards the dam. She saw Alevin's men ride through the cleft in the ridge and slaughter every Scree, but she knew now their fight was in vain. They would become her unwitting tools.

Too late. Too late.

She saw the small group on two horses, trudging north, heading directly towards where she waited for them, her hunger like a cold fire.

She saw a girl and a man, on the edge of the salt plain, even closer, almost close enough to taste.

And the heartstone. The heartstone was almost in her grasp.

She laughed, in foul glee.

The time was almost here.

Brodick woke when he felt the cold point of her blade against his throat. His hand instinctively moved for his knife.

'Don't move,' she said. 'Traitor.'

'I don't understand . . .' he began to say.

Her other hand held the *Book of Ways*. She raised it and his eyes flicked towards it.

'You stole this.'

Brodick shook his head. 'No. I found it. When the boy fell.'

'Boy?' Her voice was harsh and tight. 'Jack Flint is more a man than you will ever be. He would never betray me.'

'And nor did I, cousin. Nor did I. The book was on the ground. I knew it was important to you.'

'And you never mentioned it? Just kept it hidden.'

'I ... I ...' for a second he was lost for words. 'I saved your life. I fought for you.'

'Just who were you fighting for, Brodick?'

'How can you not trust me?' he asked. The knife was still at his throat. 'I am your cousin.'

'I saw you with the Scree,' she said coldly. 'I thought you were a prisoner. I was prepared to fight for you. But you were no prisoner. You were with the Scree.'

Brodick's eyes flicked to the side, over her shoulder.

'What, those Scree?'

Her head turned before she could stop herself and his hand lashed out, grabbed her wrist and twisted. The knife fell to the ground. She tried to get it back, but Brodick drew his own knife from its sheath before she could reach it and held the edge against her throat. She dropped the book and clawed at his eyes, but her fingers only caught the fine linen of his tunic. It ripped as he pulled away and there, under his chin, she saw the heartstone on its silver chain.

'Corriwen,' Brodick said, his voice now light. 'Cousin Corriwen. I did save your life. And now this!' He shook his head in mock weariness.

'Traitor,' she hissed. She looked at the knife, saw the golden hilt, and in an instant, she was back on the battlefield, cradling her dead brother's head as his eyes blindly sought the far distance and the same golden knife-hilt stuck in his side, glinting with morning dew.

She had known then that Cerwin had been killed by a traitor's hand. No Scree owned a knife like this one. She had taken it, wet with her brother's blood and wrapped it in cloth. It had been in her knapsack ever since. Now that knife's twin was against her neck, its blade pressing tight.

'Not a traitor,' Brodick said. 'Just a realist.'

He smiled patronisingly at her. 'I was on the winning side.'

'You betrayed your people,' she gasped.

'My people? I *have* no people. The third son of a chief on the far borders? By accident of birth, Mandrake was denied the Redthorn seat. By accident of birth, I had nothing. But Mandrake promised me more power than I dreamt of.'

She dropped her eyes, letting him think she was beaten.

'And now I will have even more,' he gloated. 'Face it, Cousin. The war was lost long ago. A new order begins. You could be at my side. Mandrake is sick. I have seen him. Ravaged by his alchemy; riddled with poison. I could have it all. And the Redthorn sword would rule again.'

She raised her face to him, green eyes glittering with anger and betrayal.

'I would rather die,' she said, softly. But now she knew he would not kill her. Not yet.

'Oh, I don't think so,' he said. 'When the war is lost, peace follows. And it will be a different Temair. So, up with you. We have things to do and places to go. I know something Mandrake doesn't.'

Brodick bound her hands with a leather thong and put her knives in the saddle-bag. He picked up the *Book of Ways*, and sat beside her. He opened the book and waited patiently until the old script began to form on the next empty page.

Read on, should heart be strong and true
False heart finds the road to rue
A treasure trail bold feet to follow
A hoard of gold, though wealth be hollow
Left hand finds a heart's desire
Right hand, pain and fear and fire.

He turned to her.

'I knew it,' he said. 'Mandrake found his wealth in the barren lands. There were cities here of old, filled with gold. Before the war with the Fomorian Scree. I read the books. It was before the Salt Barrens were wasteland. People lived here, and they were very rich.'

She turned away.

'You don't realise. I could have turned you over to Mandrake. That's what he wanted. But that's not going to happen. We don't need him when we can find our own wealth. Buy our own armies.' He laughed. 'We could take Temair from him.'

Corriwen said nothing. Brodick had betrayed her brother, and he had betrayed her. Now he was to betray his real master. She felt sick at the thought that he was her cousin.

Brodick ignored her silence as he unrolled his bedding blanket and hitched her thongs to a stake driven into the ground. As the night wore on, he fell asleep, still smiling. She knew he would dream of wealth and power. She waited, quiet as a mouse, until he was sound asleep and then carefully drew out the little red knife that Jack had given to her. It had fascinated her how it could unfold into many blades. Quickly she cut through the knot on the thongs and wriggled her hands free. Brodick had put her twin knives in the saddle-bag and she thought she should just get them and cut his throat while he slept.

But something made her pause. The *Book of Ways* was lying on a flat stone where Brodick had left it. She looked up at the Corona and wondered what Jack and Kerry would do under the circumstances.

The book flicked open, all by itself.

Corriwen started back in surprise.

Immediately the pages riffled in a whisper that sounded like a far-off voice and then it lay still. Her hand reached and lifted the book, drew it on to her knee. Under the starlight, the words appeared on the page and she focused on them. The first time Jack had shown her the old script, she could not understand the words, but as she concentrated on the page, something clicked in her mind and the meaning became clear.

She read them slowly:

> Lead on, brave heart, be true and strong
> Keep a promise, right a wrong
> Left-hand path for greed and gain
> To lose the way, to search in vain.
> Pause for breath, ere journey's end.
> Rest a while, re-find a friend.

Hope flared in her heart again.

The verse was similar to the one Brodick had read gloatingly. But it was different. That message had been for him. This was for her alone. She would be mad to ignore what it said.

It was giving her directions that were different from Brodick's.

The *Book of Ways* was on *her* side. She knew it as surely as she knew that Jack was still alive.

Very quickly she turned the thongs around her wrists again and lay down on her side. Sleep came slowly, but it came.

In her dreams she saw Jack and Kerry on the back of a greathorse. They were galloping north.

And someone was following them.

It was almost completely dark and Jack and Kerry had some broth boiling on the flames when suddenly Jack started.

'What's up?' Kerry asked. Jack glanced beyond the fire to where Declan was hobbling the horses.

'I remembered what it was,' Jack whispered. 'What I saw before I was clonked on the head.'

Kerry raised his eyebrows quizzically and Jack went on: 'It was him. I remember seeing the empty sheath and then something hit me. It must have been him.'

'That's why he was so keen to come with us.'

'And he has the book. I felt it in his saddlebag.'

'So what do we do?' Kerry demanded. 'We can't fight him.'

'We wait,' Jack said.

And an hour later, Declan was fast asleep. They waited another hour before Kerry made two loops of strong nylon line and then, moving silently Jack slipped one round Declan's throat and pulled tight. He woke instantly, but Kerry was ready and caught his wrist with the other line before he could reach his sword.

Choking, Declan tried to pull the nylon away from his throat and as he did so, Kerry looped more line round his feet. In minutes they had him bound like a hog, struggling helplessly.

Jack snatched the saddle-bag and slung it over their mount.

Then they were gone.

Corriwen was in front of Brodick on the horse. He had placed her there, not noticing the loosened thongs, but she could reach neither her own knives in the saddle-bag, nor his in its sheath. But she could wait.

The horse plodded on, following rocky gullies where water might once have flowed, long ago. Corriwen listened for signs of pursuit, hoping and praying that Jack and Kerry would find her soon, wishing she hadn't confronted Brodick until the odds were more even.

Many miles down the trail, they were in a ravine where

powdery sand trickled from bare rock walls. She kept her eyes ahead, alert for movement, but when it came, it surprised her.

Behind her, Brodick was half asleep.

Ahead, the left side of the canyon wall began to shimmer, as if sunlight were catching tiny crystals on the stone. Corriwen bent to shade her eyes, not sure of what she had seen, and as she did, the strange shimmering stopped.

But where she was sure there had been bare rock, another ravine opened on the left side, a fork in the path where there had been one trail seconds before.

The message in the *Book of Ways* suddenly became clear, and using her knees, she edged the horse to the left and into the narrow gully.

'For better or worse,' she told herself.

Five hours later, Jack and Kerry would have missed the fork entirely, but for Kerry's skill. He was leading the horse while Jack sat in the saddle and the little Leprechaun clutched the mane tight.

Kerry paused, crouching over close to the ground, following the tracks that were already silting up as the fine sand drizzled down the valley sides.

'What's up?' Jack asked. He eased himself from the saddle and kneaded his stiff backside.

'They stop here,' Kerry said, looking left and right. 'And

that's wrong, surely. Unless that big horse can fly.'

'I wish ours could,' Jack replied. 'I'm sore all over.'

'So are my feet,' Kerry countered. 'My trainers are just about done in. And I bet you can't get Nikes here for love nor money.'

He was about to say more when the cleft on the left path appeared, a few feet ahead of them. The pattern of stones on either side had made it look like solid rock, but as soon as Jack stepped forward, the gap was clear to see.

'Mystery solved,' Kerry said.

'Maybe,' Jack agreed. 'But why would they take a side road? That doesn't look as if it goes anywhere.'

They followed the fork anyway, leading the horse through a space that was hardly wide enough to let it scrape past.

Soon they came to an arch that at first looked carved by water, but as they approached it became clear that it had been built from solid blocks of stone, weathered and patched with dry lichen. Some sort of script had been carved on it, but it was too worn to decipher.

Beyond the narrow entrance, the old city was a labyrinth of ruins and crumbling walls. At the far end, an ancient castle on higher ground overlooked the ruins.

'This is the place,' Brodick said. 'I knew it. The book was right.'

Yes, Corriwen thought, *but which verse?*

Brodick bundled her down from the saddle.

'You stay here,' Brodick said. 'I'm going to make us rich.'

'There will be no *us*,' she replied, but Brodick had the same strange light in his eye that he'd had when he snatched the knife from her. He wasn't even listening.

She watched him work his way through the labyrinth towards the old castle, while above her, black birds wheeled on thermals. They might have been roaks, but they were too far away for her to be sure.

As soon as Brodick was out of sight, Corriwen loosened the cut thong and then crossed to where the horse was hobbled. In the saddle-bag, she found her own knives in their sheaths and buckled them to her belt. She turned, staying low, about to follow Brodick when she stopped, went back to the horse and unslung her own satchel.

She drew out the gold-hilted knife that she had pulled from her brother's body. The blood on the blade was brown and dry, but the point was as sharp as ever. She nodded to herself, biting on the grief that suddenly gripped her, clenched her fingers round the dagger's hilt and then silently set off into the labyrinth.

Deep in the bowels of the castle it was cold and dank. Darkness shrouded Brodick as soon as he stepped through the gate. Above him an ancient portcullis hung from rusting chains.

He ignored the skeletons that lay crumpled on the castle

steps, and the ones that lay inside the great hall, sprawled on a worm-eaten table.

A battle had been fought and lost here. The bones were old and white but he had no interest in the dead, only what they had left behind. He stepped over bony hands that still held ancient swords, ribs pierced with rusted knives, not giving these old warriors any reverence at all. His mind was fixed on what lay ahead.

The footprints in the dust, old though they were, could still be seen. Somebody had been here before him, and he knew that it was Mandrake.

As he moved in the gloom, he was thinking that he might not be following in Mandrake's footprints for long.

Behind him, Corriwen Redthorn followed the maze of tunnels beneath the great hall, eyes wide as they accustomed themselves to the dark, listening intently for the slow footfall ahead of her and the slight sound of Brodick's breathing.

And behind Corriwen Redthorn, moving just as silently, Jack and Kerry followed.

TWENTY SIX

B rodick finally found the strongroom, deep beneath the castle. He had wrapped an oilskin strip round a long legbone and it served as a flickering torch that sent shadows dancing on cobwebbed walls.

Inside, the scattered treasure glinted; gold plates and brooches, stone-studded daggers and chain-weights of dusty gold.

This was how Mandrake got his wealth. When he came back for the rest of it, Mandrake would get a surprise. If he ever came back.

Brodick filled his saddle-bags until they could take no more. He gathered enough wealth to make him rich far beyond any wild dreams he'd harboured.

And he had Corriwen Redthorn. Together they could

start a dynasty that would rule Temair forever. She would have no choice.

He started back, following his own footprints, bent over with the weight of his treasures.

Corriwen could smell the fatty oil from Brodick's torch and she followed the fumes when it got too dark to see. After a short while, she was feeling her way. She heard the clank of metal, drew her knife, and edged along the narrow passageway.

Jack and Kerry came across the ruined city and hobbled their own horse beside the one Brodick had ridden. There was no sign of either Brodick or Corriwen.

Inside the castle they moved tentatively, stepping carefully over the bones. Kerry used the guttering flame of his lighter to lead them down the narrow corridor, following the footsteps as Corriwen had done until he came to a branch where two passages intersected.

One set of prints went in one direction. But the others went the opposite way.

'Which way now?' Jack asked.

'I can't tell. The prints are all smudged.'

'I can smell burning.'

'Me too,' Kerry said. 'Left or right. You choose.'

Jack chose left. In five minutes the lighter ran out of fuel and they were groping in the dark. Finally Jack told Kerry they should turn back.

'They could be anywhere,' he said.

He heard the clank of metal, but there was no way to gauge how far away or in which direction.

'We could get lost down here,' he said. 'We'll have to wait outside.'

'Good idea,' Kerry agreed. 'Dead bodies give me the heeby-jeebies.' Jack fumbled for his shoulder and they turned, feeling their way along the narrow tunnel towards the light.

Jack stopped, causing Kerry to pull up sharply. The metallic sound came again, but closer.

They eased forward, past one of the branching passageways, and a big shape loomed in from the side and a hand gripped Jack by the throat.

'Got you now,' a man's voice snarled.

Jack gasped, backed into Kerry, who slipped on the dust and went down. All he saw was a pale face in the wan light.

'Brodick,' he cried out. 'It's us. Jack and Kerry!'

The hand gripped tighter, for just a second, then loosened. Brodick's face bent towards them.

'Startled me, you did,' he finally said. Jack spluttered, gasping for breath.

'Startled *you*?' Kerry demanded.

'I thought it might be Scree,' Brodick said. 'I've seen patrols and we had to avoid them.'

'So what's this place?' Jack asked. 'And where's Corriwen? We saw your horse.'

Brodick picked up the heavy saddle-bags. They heard the tinny sound again, but it didn't really register.

'Is she not with the horse?' Brodick sounded surprised. They couldn't see his expression. 'I told her to stay with it.'

'We didn't see her,' Kerry said. 'We thought she'd be in here.'

Brodick grunted, angry in the dark. 'Then she could easily get lost.'

He turned and strode along the passageway towards the light, with Jack and Kerry on his heels.

They blinked in the daylight as Brodick led them out to the portcullis. Its chain wound round a windlass with a big handle that was almost rusted through.

'This place isn't safe,' Brodick said. He dumped his heavy bags just outside the gate and came back to them. 'You'd best wait here and I'll find Corriwen.'

'We could help,' Jack said.

Brodick shook his head. 'No. The tunnels are confusing, and ready to fall at any time. That's why I asked her to stay away.' He grinned. 'But you try telling a Redthorn what to do!'

'Sure, she's a feisty one,' Kerry agreed.

Brodick turned back, stepping quickly over the dry bones into the great hall.

'A really creepy place,' Jack said.

'They like killing each other.'

'Like the old Celts. All their fights were happy, and all their songs were sad.'

'At least we caught up with her,' Kerry said.

'But why did they stop here?' Jack asked.

Kerry shrugged. 'Maybe just to explore. People like old places. I saw Blarney Castle once.'

'She's in a hurry. I don't think she'd stop to explore.'

Before he could say anything else, Brodick and Corriwen came out together. Brodick had his arm protectively around her shoulder.

Kerry whooped when he saw her.

'Told you we'd find her.'

'You sure did,' Jack agreed. His face was split by a huge smile. 'If it wasn't for you being a poacher, we never would have.'

Corriwen came out and down the steps with Brodick's arm still around her. Her hair caught a stray shaft of sunlight through an arrow-slit and made it gleam copper. She walked slowly and didn't wave back.

'Something's wrong,' Jack said.

'What could be wrong?'

Corriwen looked straight ahead. She had seen both of them, but her expression hadn't changed, and Jack knew *that* was wrong. What was in Corriwen's heart was always clear on her face. Something was not right. Brodick and Corriwen approached, and while he was smiling easily, Corriwen's expression was blank.

'Yeah,' Kerry said. He slid his pack off his shoulder and turned away to ease his sword out. Jack felt for the knife that Alevin had given him.

'I wouldn't do that, Stonethrower,' Brodick said. He was only ten yards away. Corriwen made a small gesture with her head and Jack saw Brodick's other hand, and the knife that was in it, close against her neck.

'What's going on?'

'Betrayal,' Corriwen said. Her voice was like ice. 'He has been against us all along.'

'But he's your cousin,' Kerry blurted. 'He can't ...'

'Can. Did. Will.' Brodick showed the knife so they both could see it. 'Now put the sword back, unless you want to see more bones here.'

Kerry slid the blade into the pack. He was grinding his teeth in frustration. They had come a long way. They were tired and sore and any joy at seeing Corriwen again had turned to fear.

'Good men died guarding this city,' Brodick said. 'Such a shame you will too.'

'What do you mean?'

Brodick dragged Corriwen past them, keeping his face to them all the time. He crossed under the portcullis that hung in the archway.

'It means well met, and farewell,' he said. 'For a while.'

With a quick motion, he shoved Corriwen through the arch, swung his sword and slashed at the handle of the windlass. It took two hard blows and the lock-handle splintered. Brodick was already moving when the portcullis gave an almighty groan and the windlass turned under the weight.

Jack started forward, but Brodick leapt nimbly through the archway, just as the gate-spikes came crashing down. Brodick grabbed Corriwen by her hair.

'Let's not say farewell,' he said, grinning. 'Because you won't fare well.' He stood by his two sacks of loot and waved at Jack and Kerry.

'You'll be here when I get back,' he said lightly. 'But a little thinner, I warrant.' With that he turned, yanked Corriwen's hair, and dragged her away.

There was no sign of the horse Jack and Kerry had ridden into the ruined city.

Brodick cursed under his breath. 'We could have used another horse,' he said, 'but this one will have to do.'

'The book was right,' Corriwen hissed. 'It knew you were a traitor.' She turned her head, unwilling to look him in the face.

'Do you intend to take me to Mandrake?'

'Oh no!' Brodick laughed at the thought. 'That would be lunacy. It had crossed my mind, because he set up a fine reward for you, and those two boys. But we don't need them now.'

'You'd leave them to die?'

'We can't take them with us,' Brodick said with a shrug. 'Would you rather I killed them now? Break your heart, would it? Your precious outlander.'

'Both of them have honour, and you have sold yours.'

Brodick laughed. 'Don't lose your heart over two boys, and strangers at that. You're a Redthorn. You know what counts. Money and power.'

'Because I am a Redthorn, I know they mean nothing without honour.'

'Everybody has a price. What could those children offer you?'

He tugged the chain over his head and dangled the heartstone close to her eyes.

'Here, if you want to remember your beloved Jack, you can carry it. It's supposed to be the key to all things. But it locks you to me, I promise you.'

She saw gloating laughter in his eyes. But she took the heartstone and looped it around her neck. 'So where are you going?'

'*We*, Cousin, are continuing your quest.' He touched the heartstone at her breast. 'Mandrake was going demented over this bauble. Well, more demented than ever. What he doesn't know is that I'm something of a scholar myself.'

'It hasn't done you any good.'

'Think what you like. He's not the only one who can read the old scripts. Mandrake doesn't know that *I* know his real purpose up on the salt barrens. He intends to break the curse and free the demon.'

'So you know he has to be stopped.' Corriwen said.

'Really? The Morrigan gave Mandrake wealth and power and control over the Scree. She wants Mandrake to bring this trinket to her. He has failed, but *I* will succeed. And I'll take whatever reward she promised him.'

'So I'll have the Redthorn sword. I have you. And I'll have her blessing. All's well.'

'Now what do we do?'

'We get out of here,' Jack said. 'If we can. These places were built to keep people out. That gate is probably the only way.'

'We'll never lift it,' Kerry said. 'Not in a million years.'

'So we'll climb.'

'The rope's on the horse.'

Jack grimaced. 'That's a great help. Let's think. We have to come up with an idea.'

He had barely spoken when something moved beyond the gate. They shrank back out of sight.

'It's a horse,' Kerry said. 'Definitely.'

'You think he's come back?'

Kerry nodded. He unhitched his sling and found a good stone to fill the cup. He eased back, keeping his arm ready.

Beyond the closed portcullis, a horse snickered. A heavy hoof clipped a stone with a metallic ring.

'I swear I'll drop him,' Kerry said. He turned to Jack and saw he had his bow at the ready, a black arrow on the string.

'Not if I get him first.'

They held their collective breath until the horse approached beyond the portcullis. Jack let his breath out.

'It's *our* horse,' he said.

Kerry looked over Jack's shoulder, sling still ready to swing, and laughed.

'Now would you believe that?'

Corriwen stayed silent, waiting for her chance. Confident now, Brodick hadn't bound her wrists. He moved through the ruined city leaving the house along winding ways littered with fallen masonry.

Further on, part of the hillside had fallen away, taking walls and foundations with it. Brodick pushed against the flank, feet skirting the edge of the drop to the rocks below. He had his eyes fixed to the left, manoeuvring carefully when Corriwen moved.

She felt in her roll for the knife, drew it out and cut the strap holding the saddle-bags.

Brodick looked up and she lashed a heel at his face, taking him on the chin. His foot slid over the edge of the drop, his arms pinwheeled. With another swipe, she slashed the reins as he tried to drag himself back to solid ground and then she cut the strap again. It parted with a twang and the whole bag, filled with the gold Brodick had collected in the castle, rolled off and caught him square on the chest. Corriwen dug her heels in and the horse stepped forward.

Brodick made a grab for the stirrups, missed. The crumbling edge under his foot began to fall apart. 'Damn you! *Damn you!*'

She saw the blood drain from his face, and his mouth open wide, though no sound came out.

'*Witch!*'

She bent over the flank, swinging the knife down, the one she had found in her brother's back. It caught Brodick in the eye and he screamed. The edge gave under his weight and he toppled over the drop. She edged the horse past the drop, then dismounted and ran to look.

Brodick's body was splayed, half covered with rocks and gold coins and jewellery that had burst from the bag. A pool of blood formed a dark halo around his head.

She looked at the knife she had pulled from her dead

brother's body. She had sworn to use this knife on his killer.

Now it was done.

'Trust us to end up with two stinkin' backstabbers.'

Kerry was seething. They had tried the windlass at the gate, but it needed much more than their strength to turn it.

Outside, the little Leprechaun jittered with anxiety. 'I brought horse,' it said in its woody voice. 'Must go fast. Quick. Bad things come.' It squeezed quickly through the bars of the portcullis and looked up at them.

'*Come quick.*'

'We can't get out,' Jack said. 'We'll have to find a way.'

'Climb,' it suggested.

'The stone's too dangerous. It's all crumbling.'

'Must hurry.' It was bobbing up and down, snatching at Jack's jacket. 'Axecutters. I smell them.'

Jack looked at Kerry. They knew what axecutters meant. 'I think we should try the climb.'

It was easier said than done. Ivy clung to the flaking walls, but when they tried it, the creeper was dry as dust and broke free as soon as they put weight on it. A stunted oak tree had rooted through cracks in the paving stones, but it hadn't grown tall enough for them to climb.

'We're stuck unless we can open the gate.'

'Maybe we can get the Leprechaun to hitch the horse to

the winder,' Kerry said. He turned around. 'Where did he go?'

A small noise came from close by. The little Leprechaun was up against the rough bark of the oak, face pressed tight against it, both spindly arms embracing it like a friend.

It whispered reedily, 'Wake up, old brother.'

Jack looked at Kerry, then back to the little creature. Up above, the sparse branches shivered, though there was no wind here.

In a second the little creature's mossy skin changed colour from green to grey and the texture seemed to roughen and harden. They could hardly make out where tree ended and Leprechaun began.

'Forest magic again,' Jack said. He watched, fascinated, as the creature disappeared completely from view.

As soon as it did, the ground shivered beneath their feet.

Kerry took a step back. 'Did you feel that?'

The earth trembled again.

Then, under the portcullis, the ground heaved, sending stones and mortar rolling away as earth and flagstones pushed into a hump. There was a scrape of stone on metal as it ground against the teeth of the gate.

The tree shuddered, as if gathering strength. A crack zigzagged between their feet and the portcullis began to lift, an inch at a time. A root flexed and the gate lifted two feet into the air.

'Now!' Jack hissed. He grabbed Kerry, shoved him forward and down, and the pair crawled under the metal teeth before they could fall again and spiked them dead. As soon as they were through, the big root buckled. Jack got to his feet. Kerry dusted himself down and the gate sank back into its housing with a jolt.

The Leprechaun oozed from the bark and turned green again as it peeled itself away from the tree. As they watched, the few leaves on the twisted branches began to wither. They crumpled and faded, turning from green to red, then yellow. One fell off and fluttered to the ground, and then the rest floated down after it.

'It's dying,' Jack said.

'My brother was old and tired and alone,' the little fellow said. 'He wanted to go.' He held up a small, thin hand. In the palm nested a single dry acorn. 'But the mothers will succour his sap again, in the heart of the heartwood.'

Kerry blinked and wiped an eye with his knuckle. Jack bent to thank the Leprechaun when a scream behind him caused him to wheel round in alarm.

'Jack!' Corriwen came bounding round the corner of the castle gate and straight into his arms. Jack almost fell on his backside.

'What . . . ? Where . . .'

She was hugging him so tightly he couldn't get a sentence out.

'Hey!' Kerry cried. 'What about me?'

She turned, grabbed him by the neck and kissed him all over his face until his ears went red.

The little Leprechaun looked at all this in woody bewilderment. The horse Corriwen had led nuzzled the other roak.

'Brodick,' Jack said. 'What happened to him?'

'He's gone. His greed took its revenge.' She smiled grimly. 'And so did I. For my brother.'

TWENTY SEVEN

Alevin thought that this place of misery was just how it would be in the dead lands beyond Tir Nan Og. And he would revenge the people who had suffered here if it took a lifetime, or his life.

While Jack, Kerry and Corriwen were reunited and making plans, Alevin had led the slaughter of the Scree who worked the Temair people as slaves.

He sat on a stone, bloodied and tired, at the chasm dug into the ridge, now close enough to the lake behind for its water to force through in fine sprays.

'We must get all of them out of here, men, women and children. Every one of these souls who've been stolen. Get them from this foul place to higher ground.'

He looked at the wall. 'When that gives, it will flood like never before. Likely flood the whole of Temair.'

He cursed himself again when he realised he should have gone for the dam first.

Mandrake marched the Scree and traitor chiefs back towards the ridge.

The circling roaks had seen the carnage as Alevin's men swept into the cut.

Kill them. Kill them all. Wipe them out. The followers heard the mantra as the roaks relayed the events on the cleft.

Don't fail me now. His head was bursting with the pressure of her fury. His eyes rolled in their sockets and his face contorted in a dreadful grimace.

But he kept the army moving, as fast as the Scree could march.

When he arrived at the far ridge, Alevin's men had gone, and so had all the slaves.

He slouched in the wagon, while the Morrigan still hissed and spat in his mind.

Brodick was dead, stone dead.

But Declan was alive, which was just as well for them all.

Only a few miles after Jack had led the way out of the ruined city, the Scree troop which had missed them before ambushed them on the narrow trail. As they tried to flee, a lone horseman appeared behind hunters and took them by surprise, one by one, until the last was riven by a broadsword only yards behind Corriwen's horse.

Declan dismounted and cleaned his sword with a hank of leather, then slowly began to whet the blade until it gleamed.

'You thought I betrayed you,' he said to Jack, without raising his eyes from his work.

'I felt the book in your bag,' Jack said. 'Our *Book of Ways*. And it warned us that the traitor would have an empty sheath. Just like you.'

'So you tied me up?' Declan allowed a half smile. His face was still bloody. 'Me? I would have cut your throat if I thought you were a traitor.'

'We don't do that,' Kerry piped up. 'Things are bad enough.'

'It wasn't Declan,' Corriwen broke in. 'Brodick had the book.'

'Then what was in his bag?'

Declan got to his feet and lifted his saddle-bag. He drew out a leather binding, unwrapped the drawstring and showed them. It was a book, but it wasn't the *Book of Ways*.

'My wife. Eileanne. She liked to write verse. And between the pages she pressed flowers. To remember good days.' Declan's voice was soft, and sad. 'I broke my knife in the head of a Scree when I returned and found her dead. And I will take a Scree head for every hair of hers that was harmed.'

He looked at Jack, then swept his gaze across all three. 'And when I give my word, I don't break it.'

Jack felt a rush of shame. He had misjudged Declan.

'But you did the right thing,' Declan said. 'I might really have been the traitor. And it is more important you finish the job you started. One life is nothing compared with fair Temair.'

He wrapped his little book again. 'Next time, just cut the traitor's throat and don't leave him tied with mere threads.'

'That was twenty-pound nylon line,' Kerry said. 'You must be stronger than you look.' Kerry was joking. They had seen Declan fight when the Scree troop attacked.

'The real traitor is dead,' Corriwen said. 'Killed by his own greed.' She pulled close to Jack. 'But before he died, he gave me this.'

She drew out the heartstone and looped it around his neck. 'Where it belongs,' she said.

Mandrake reached the top of the ridge and looked down at the black waters below. It was as if he stood between two wells of hell.

The pictures she allowed into his mind showed him Alevin's men, far at the end of the lake where the great dam groaned under the force of the water.

Mandrake spoke, and jagged forks sparked from his fingers, blue as glacier ice, stabbed at the centre of the storm and were swallowed in the maelstrom.

The ground rumbled. The Scree felt it through their feet.

Way down at the dam, Alevin saw a strange ripple bearing

down like a tidal bore to smash into the bulwarks.

Mandrake laughed. 'Breach it, fools. Breach my dam now!'

Thunder spoke so loud that rocks trembled and cracked. The whole swirling storm seemed to suck into itself and then explode in a vast burst of power. Stone fountained up. A deafening crack split the air. It sounded as if the world had split in two. The end face of the cleft shattered. Broken stones flew like slingshot, as big as greathorses. Boulders the size of houses tumbled in their wake.

And then the water came – such an immense flood that it scoured and gouged, cascading in a white roar down the cut and into the salt barrens.

A hundred Scree stragglers were caught on the edge of it and were carried to their deaths like leaves in a spate-river.

Mandrake watched and inside his head, the Morrigan cackled in triumph.

TWENTY EIGHT

In the Black Barrow the darkness swallowed them; a darkness so deep and complete it felt like a physical substance.

They had seen it in the distance across the dry white land. The Barrow squatted like a malevolent toad.

They stared silently, each of them unwilling to take the first step. Pure evil radiated from the dark bulk. But they knew they had to go there.

Declan led the way into the wide basin, horse-hooves kicking up dust that clogged their throats. Nothing lived here; nothing they could see, nothing normal.

The Black Barrow loomed ever larger. They felt the baleful pull of its power, and still they trudged on, hot, weary, thirsty and, as far as Jack and Kerry and the little Leprechaun were concerned, afraid.

Declan pulled up his horse. It pawed the ground. The animals too sensed the absolute wrongness of the Black Barrow.

'It's old,' Declan said. He shivered.

On its east side they found the broken masonry that had been chipped away by manic hands, and beyond the pile of rubble, a thin, man-sized hole.

The heartstone began to beat slowly against Jack's breastbone.

'This was how he got in,' Corriwen said. 'The Redthorn sword is here. I can sense it.'

Her face was pale under her copper hair, but her eyes were steady. Jack thought she was probably the bravest person he had ever met.

'Rest and take a drink,' Declan said.

They huddled together and drank from water-skins. The water was warm and tasted bitter, but it cleared the dust from their throats. Jack felt the slow pulse of the stone on its chain, as if that heart was afraid too. He drew out the *Book of Ways* and they clustered round.

'Maybe it'll give us a clue,' he said. He laid it flat and they waited. The book shivered, as if it too felt danger. The pages riffled with a slight sigh and they all held their breath in anticipation.

At first nothing happened. Kerry looked at Jack. Corriwen kept her eyes fixed on the blank open page.

Then the page began to darken. But instead of the old script that had resolved itself onto the leaf before, it darkened like a cloud, swirling in slow spirals that deepened from a haze to grey. In mere moments, the page was completely and utterly black.

'Definitely not a good sign,' Kerry muttered.

The page turned itself and the next one was also black; dead black. Then the next and the next. It whirred faster and faster, showing them page after page, each one totally dark, devoid of any script. Just black. It reached the end and closed with a snap.

'I think it's telling us it's going to be dark in there,' Kerry finally said. 'That's a fat lot of use.'

Beside them, the little Leprechaun made a sound. They turned and saw it crouched on the ground, with its twiggy fingers stuck deep in the dry earth.

'Have to hurry,' it croaked. 'Bad ground here. All dead. And the world shakes far away.'

'Someone will have to guard the horses,' Declan said. 'But not me.' He looked at the narrow entrance. 'I must enter with the Lady Corriwen.'

'I stay with the big hoofs,' the Leprechaun said. 'Dead for me in this place.'

Jack stood, tucked the book into the satchel. He touched the heartstone with his hand. 'He's right,' he said. 'The sooner we're out of here the better.' Declan nodded agreement.

'Or we could just turn back and forget all this,' Kerry said. He caught Jack's eye. 'Only kidding. I wouldn't miss all this fun for anything.'

Jack heard the slight quaver in his voice. Kerry winked. 'Come on then. All for one and each for everybody else, right?'

Jack led the way forward, scraped through the Mandrake-sized opening and the cold dark wrapped itself around him with clammy hands. The hairs on the back of his neck hackled as skeletal fingers seemed to trail up and down his spine.

'At least the book got it right,' Kerry whispered. His voice was oddly distorted. 'It's black as a yard up a chimney.'

Jack touched the stone wall beside him. It was damp, not wet, but cold as ice. He snatched his fingers back. There was a scent on the thick air, as if some animal had crawled in and died, and apart from their muted footfalls, it was deathly silent.

They moved down a passage, almost blind in this awful darkness. It reminded Jack of the liquid night that had invaded the Major's house. Kerry kept a hand on Jack's shoulder and Corriwen held Kerry's belt. Behind them Declan was quiet. They moved forward slowly. Jack counted the steps, twenty, thirty, sixty, a hundred.

Three hundred steps on, they came out of the passage and into a wider space. Jack's eyes were wide open, but there was no adjusting to this dark.

'Where now?' Kerry asked.

Shivers were running up and down Jack's spine and he was glad none of them could see his face. Something waited ahead of them. He could feel its presence like an ache. And the heart felt it too. It was beating faster, stuttering against him.

Kerry reached a hand to feel for the wall. He gave a cry of horrified surprise and drew his fingers back quickly.

'Jack,' he whispered. He gripped Jack's arm tight. 'There's a dead body here. I felt it.'

Declan pushed forward and held a guttering torch up to the wall. Its feeble light showed a skull set in a niche on the damp wall. It wore ancient armour covered in mould, but still intact so that the skeleton stood upright. Its bony arm rocked from Kerry's touch.

'The Guardians,' Corriwen whispered. 'The Bards set them here long ago. As part of their binding curse.'

Jack took a step forward, sensing something ahead. He had to force his feet to move, for what he felt ahead of them was worse, infinitely worse, than the touch he had felt when they fell into this world. Madness reigned here.

He could picture the dead heroes, strapped against the walls, swords gripped in hands of bone, standing guard for generations.

'Which way?' Kerry asked. His voice sounded small and distant.

Jack cocked his head. 'This way, I think.'

'Jack? Jack?' Kerry sounded anxious. Jack heard the urgency in his voice and turned. Declan's torch was just a pin-point in the profound black. It was further away than it should have been.

'You okay, Kerry?' The black swallowed his words. Kerry called again, and it sounded as if he was far away. It was as if the very space had expanded between them.

'I can't hear you,' Corriwen called faintly. 'Are you there?' Her voice was barely a whisper, a cry in the distance. Jack turned, trying to get his bearings. Kerry's call faded to silence. Jack called back and his own words were smothered and sucked into the dark. He closed his eyes, trying to project his thoughts and senses.

He called again, once, twice. There was no reply. He turned back, but the wall was not where he expected it to be. He felt as if he was in a vast chamber where there was no sound at all, save the beat of his own heart and the slow intake of his breath.

The heartstone beat in silence.

Jack realised, with awful certainty, that he was alone.

Kerry called his name, but his cry was swallowed up. One minute Jack was beside him, close enough to hear his ragged breath. The next, he was gone. He turned to Corriwen, reached for her elbow, and found empty space. He made a circle with his fingers, called her name, called for Declan.

There was no response.

He drew his sword, feeling puny, straining to hear anything.

He called again for Jack and his words faded as soon as they were spoken. He held his breath, listened. And then he heard it.

The sound of running water.

There was no reply when Corriwen called out, no light of any kind. She felt her way forward, blade out, shuffling in case there were any pitfalls or crevasses that might pitch her to who knows where.

Something stirred ahead of her and she paused.

Corriwen.

A whisper, barely audible. She listened and after a few moments it came again. Her name whispered, no echoes, like a tickle in her mind.

She opened her eyes and for an instant thought she could see something, and took three steps forward, blade in hand.

'Jack?'

The whisper came again and a faint glow brightened as she moved towards it.

'You came back,' the whisper told her and her heart gave a sudden jolt.

'Dear Corrie,' her brother's voice spoke from the waxing glow. A shape moved within it, and despite herself, she stepped towards it.

Cerwin's face resolved in the glow.

'Sister,' he said softly. 'I knew you would come.'

'But how ...' Her voice faltered. His face came clear, shining in the surrounding dark, just as she remembered it. Not the face of a dead man slaughtered on a battlefield. Her brother's red hair gleamed. His eyes were bright with life. There was no mark on his skin.

'I knew you would find a way,' he said. 'To free me from this place.'

'I don't understand,' she finally said, voice cracking.

'He killed me, but I still live. She brought me here, but

you can save me, make me whole again. I know where the sword is. Come with me.'

He reached a hand towards her. Corriwen felt his warmth on her skin and tears cascaded down her cheeks. Her brother was here. By whatever magic he was speaking to her, as alive as when she had seen him last, heading to do battle with Mandrake.

Her heart jolted again. It wanted her to believe that Cerwin was alive.

Her heart wanted this, wanted it so badly it felt it would break. But something in her mind told her: No.

'Follow me,' he said softly. 'The sword will make me whole again.'

A wave of dizziness swept through her, and his face wavered in front of her. For a moment it was as if the past had never happened, the great battle, the bloodied body, the traitor's knife. They all drained out of her mind as she felt cocooned in the warmth of his love.

An image of Jack Flint came to her, calling her name from a distance.

'Corriwen. *Corriwen Redthorn!*'

Jack Flint? Jack who? Did she know someone ... ? She could not remember. Her brother's love enveloped her and she leant into him as he bent to kiss her cheek, the way he had done when she had fallen as a child and he would pick her up and dust her down.

'Corriwen Firebird,' he whispered. The name he had called her as a child. His voice was soft, gentle, the way it had always been.

'Corrie, come with me.' He spoke urgently now.

She shuddered. Something was badly wrong with this.

'Don't wait,' he whispered. 'Come to me.'

Underneath the soft words, she heard the scrape of something dry and old. Her brother reached for her, opened his arms to welcome her.

'Little Corrie, come now!'

She took a step forward, and the smell of putrefaction came thick on the damp air.

A voice called her from far away.

'*Corriwen!*'

Jack who?

Cerwin reached for her then, and as he reached, his hands changed. They twisted and lengthened. His eyes shrank back into sockets deep as pits. He smiled a nightmare smile.

'Corrie,' he croaked, and as he reached, she knew this was not her brother, for Cerwin was long dead.

She felt a scream swell inside her, but her throat locked and nothing, not a sound, would come out.

Far away, Kerry heard the sound of running water, rushing water, but he couldn't tell which direction it came from.

Now he too heard voices whispering. They held no warmth, no life.

He strained to see, hairs crawling on his neck, as little by little the voices became louder. An eerie glow spread around him and he turned, heart hammering.

Dead men were all around him. He could hear the twist and grind as their bones moved, the squeal of rusting armour.

'Outworlder,' a Guardian grated. 'No business here.'

Kerry raised his sword. It felt small and useless in his hands. The corpses were all staring, all starting to move. Skeletal hands gripped sword-hilts.

'We have waited long for you, tasty boy. We hunger here in the dark. We hunger for flesh. We thirst for blood.'

They began to push themselves from the walls towards him.

Declan's torch had died. He stood still, trying to find his bearings.

Then, suddenly, he smelt flowers, sweet honeysuckle and wild lily. He closed his eyes and breathed, drawing in the perfume. It was warm and musky; the scent of summer. He felt himself drift on it. He had travelled long and far in these terrible times and now he felt the ache and exhaustion overtake him. He breathed in again and, suffused with the heady scent, felt himself drift away . . .

. . . and wake beside a clear stream.

It was dusk here and she was beside him. He remembered how they had stolen down to the sparkling water. His wife's hair was long and wild and her face turned towards him.

'You slept long,' she sighed. 'I watched you sleep.'

She had always watched him sleep. The way he had watched her. His heart leapt with sheer love for her.

'You dreamed,' she soothed.

'I dreamed ...' he began. 'Yes. Yes. I dreamed you were ... you were gone.'

'Not gone,' she said, voice like a song. 'Yours forever more.'

'But you died,' he began to say. 'The Scree ...' He paused, dizzy with confusion and longing. His heart ached real pain. Had he dreamt? Had it all been an awful vision?

She drew a cool, smooth hand across his brow. 'Gone? What nonsense you speak. I would never leave you, dear heart.'

She held a posy of blossom. 'See. I gathered more flowers while you slept. Smell them.'

She smiled and her eyes glittered. Declan leant to take her in his arms and her arms went around him. He pressed her close and suddenly her body was bony and brittle, and the scent of the summer flowers turned to something sick and vile.

But by then it was too late.

The mouldering warrior lifted up a blood-scabbed sword. Kerry ducked under the swipe of the blade. It sang close enough to *snick* his hair. He stabbed up with his own blade and the point plunged between dry ribs and rattled uselessly against a dusty spine.

'Tasty boy,' it whispered. 'Feed our starving bones.'

Another lurched forward, its jaw hanging loose.

'Okay, come on then, bag-of-bones,' Kerry snarled, heart pounding. He'd seen many things in his short time in this world, and this was the creepiest of all, but they were still skeletons, he told himself. They were bones, and they were slow.

He swung his sword and clipped the second warrior's arm. It came away at the shoulder. Behind him bony fingers scratched at his throat and squeezed. Instinctively he twisted, and pieces of fingers fell to the floor.

Something else caught at his leg and he saw, with great disgust, that it was the hand of the arm he had cut off.

'Oh, screw this for fun and games,' he spat. He spun, slashed and hacked his way through the ring of impossibly mobile dead men. Pieces flew. Armour cracked. But despite that, they still came on, groping at him, the stuff of pure nightmare.

Over in the corner of the chamber he saw a space that looked like a passageway and shoved his way past the clawing hands into the space and started running.

He was going downhill all the way, gathering speed when he heard the echoing roar of water, but he kept on round the bend in the passageway.

And a wall of water hit him and tumbled him backwards and under.

Jack was lost. In his head – he was sure it was in his mind – he could hear whispering voices, but he could see no movement of any kind.

There was no light here and the heartstone was pounding in tandem with his own.

Sheer willpower kept him going, feeling forward, all senses so acute his nerves felt taut as bowstrings.

Something moved at his side. Jack's heart kicked hard.

It came again. He groped behind him, but there was nothing to feel. Another touch and he swung the satchel round, touched the thick canvas and felt the thing move inside the bag. He was tempted to ignore it, but the twist came again, like a small beast was in there, and he wondered how it had managed to squeeze under the buckles.

Warily he slipped them loose and with careful fingers, expecting all the time something slimy or scaly to strike and bite, but his fingers only encountered the straight edge of the old book. He touched the cover and felt it move, like breathing, once, twice. He could still see nothing, but he drew out the book, and as he did, it pulsed again, in and out, and as soon as it was flat in his hand, it opened and the pages whirred.

The book whispered to him in the riffle of pages.

Follow the heart, follow the beat
Sense in the dark for She-Bane seat

Speed to the heart, speed to the stone
Speed to the sword to find the way home.

His mind understood the words. On his chest the heartstone stuttered faster still and he tucked the book away. He gripped the heartstone, felt it pound in his palm, and as the pounding increased, he walked on, following its direction.

The rushing water slammed Kerry down, rolled him against the walls and swept him back up the passageway. He was upside down, scraping against masonry. His foot found the floor and he pushed hard, terror expanding in his chest as the lack of air making his mind spin.

He managed to claw his way to the surface, kicking his legs madly against the flow. He raised his hands and found the roof, only inches above his head.

The water tried to drag him away, but he held on with fingernails in the cracks.

'Jack,' he bawled. 'Jack man! Don't you let me *drown*.'

The words were hardly out of his mouth when a hand clasped his ankle and began to drag him under.

Jack seemed to walk a long time. 'Hello?' he called out. 'Kerry? Corriwen?'

There was no reply, but the sensation of a heavy heartbeat was strong here. He fumbled on, realised he was in yet another passageway, narrow and sloping down. He had no choice but to follow it.

He walked on, and soon he began to believe he really could hear the steady beat, so deep it vibrated inside him, and the further down the passage he groped, the more powerful it became. In his hand, the heartstone pulsed of its own accord, but to a different beat.

Something waited ahead of him. He knew that now. He felt it. Something malevolent, so evil its badness seeped from the stones. It took all his courage to keep walking. He forced himself on until the tunnel veered and he came out into another chamber.

Instantly the stone in his hand began to glow.

From somewhere ahead came a shuddering sigh, a sound of pleasure, of relief, he couldn't tell. It didn't sound human, not in the least.

'Spawn,' a voice spoke in his mind. It was like the scrape of bone on stone, colder than ice. 'You come at last.'

The glow faltered, dimmed. Jack clutched the heartstone tight and held it to his chest, squashing down his fear. The glow brightened again, stronger than before, as if he had recharged it with his own courage. This chamber was domed, circular, and in its centre squatted a massive black shape. He was drawn towards it and as he came closer he knew he was in the core of the Black Barrow.

The obsidian block faced him, as high as a man, polished smooth.

'You bring the key,' the voice said. 'My key to worlds.'

This was where they put her, he thought. Finbar the Bard had been right. Finally Jack was here, and he was here alone to face the *Morrigan*.

But he now knew the power of the key, his heartstone. His fingers tightened.

'You will never leave this place,' the voice said. It came from all around, and within him. He shuddered, trying to make his lungs work despite the raw fear that jolted through him.

'Bring it to me, Spawn.'

Jack shook his head. Words failed.

Inside the stone block, deep beyond the polished surface, a shadow within a shadow moved. Jack couldn't draw his eyes away.

A shape resolved, and as he watched, defined itself into a face which swam up from its depths towards the surface.

He saw a woman.

She was pale and perfect. Her hair was black as a roak's wing, her eyes even darker. Her lips were blood red. When she smiled her teeth were fine and even.

'Come to me, journeyman's child.'

Jack could not draw his eyes away from the perfect beauty that floated before him. His hand wanted to reach and touch the obsidian block, just to be close to her. He took a step forward and the heartstone shivered and blue light pulsed. He drew his foot back again.

'I know who you are,' his throat finally unclogged and he managed to speak.

'And I know *you*,' she said, fixing those black eyes on him.

'How do you know me?' Jack asked.

'Child. Child. I travel worlds. I can give you everything.'

'Like you promised Mandrake?'

'Like I promised your *father*.'

Jack's heart lurched, as though he'd been punched in his chest.

She smiled. It was the most beautiful smile he had ever seen.

'I know what you do not,' she said. A delicate hand, white as milk, drifted towards him. The nails were black as tar. 'Come closer and see what I know.'

Unable to help himself, Jack stepped closer. Her face slowly dissolved into swirling smoke and he felt a sudden ache as the perfection fragmented, but as he watched, the swirling focussed again, became shapes and he saw ...

Five men on a hill, dressed in white and singing in close harmony, while beyond them, a tall man lifted a great sword to the storm-swirl in the dark sky.

On his chest a white heart beat slow and steady and the man raised his face upwards as a shape spiralled down, screeching in anger, great wings tearing the air while on the ground bodies of Scree soldiers lay bleeding.

It hurtled towards him, but the man stood his ground, sword raised, and the fire from the stone ran up the great blade while the Bards sang. A skein of silver and gold light wrapped around the screeching thing and snared it tight, dragged it into the great stone.

The man did not flinch, he held his sword in both hands now and plunged the blade into the stone until the lightning subsided and the screaming died as if it came from something that fell forever into the dark. The man's shoulders slumped. He sagged to his knees, then raised a face that was scarred and haunted.

Jack recognised him immediately. The dark hair, the set of the jaw. It was what he might look like when he was a man. Older, stronger. Braver. But the resemblance was clear.

'My father,' he whispered.

The scene faded and her face resolved once more behind the polished surface.

'I promised him everything,' she said. 'Together we could have ruled worlds. He denied me, but you will not.'

She stared into his eyes and he felt as if he was falling into the deepest well.

But in his hand, the heartstone suddenly pulsed and a powerful pure light shone out, white as the sun, searing his palm. He held it high, the way the warrior had done. The way his *father* had done with the sword.

And then he saw the sword itself, sunk to its hilt on the top of the obsidian block. Her face shrank from the light, and he knew what he had to do.

He braced himself, grasped the top of the stone, hauled himself up, feet sliding and slipping on the smooth surface. It vibrated under him as if it might explode.

'The key, Cullian Spawn!' she raged. 'I will have my *key!*'

'Not today, lady,' he heard himself say through the terror that gripped him. He managed to get a knee to the top, hauled himself over the edge, forced himself to his feet. The stone shuddered and rippled under him. He looked down and saw her there, whirling around deep inside. She turned her true face up and his heart almost stopped dead.

It was the face of a monster. Her eyes were red, the teeth

sharp in a mouth that gaped like a beast's. Hands like claws seemed to grow towards him, nails dripping with blood.

'Give me the *key*!' she shrieked.

Pieces of masonry exploded from the roof. Stones shifted and ground together.

'Give me the key and I will lead you to him.'

Jack didn't trust his own voice. He dragged his eyes away from the monstrosity, kept them fixed on the hilt of the sword.

He reached for it, grasped it, and a pain hit him, a pain that shrieked through every nerve in his body. His back arched and his legs buckled, but he held on to the sword.

'Too late, Cullian Spawn,' she roared. The whole barrow felt as if it shifted on its foundations. 'He is damned forever beyond the lands of the dead,' she screeched. The voice tore at his mind. 'And so is *she*. You die fatherless, and you die *motherless*.'

Jack jerked back in shock. But his hand still gripped the hilt of the sword.

The terrible voice raged and roared, shattering stone all around, but he kept his mind fixed on the sword. He knelt, gripped tight, then pushed up with his legs with every ounce of his strength.

The blade drew out of the stone with no sound at all.

Jack Flint held it in both hands while around his neck, the heartstone blazed pure white fire.

TWENTY NINE

Inside the Black Barrow, the demon raged. The child had defied her. He had been so close, bearing the key to worlds, but she could not reach to take it.

She was not defeated yet.

Using all her power, she sent her black and poisonous thoughts out and east, to the great storm, until her presence reached the ridge under the swirling maelstrom.

Mandrake stood on the ridge, feet straddling the knife-edge. The words of power, words he had learned in the scrolls and ancient tomes in the Redthorn Keep, had served their purpose. The skies had unleashed the fury of the storm he had conjured.

Below him the flood-water crashed against the weakened ridge and made the earth tremble.

To the south, men were frantically working to break down the barrier.

Mandrake turned his head to the storm where lightning stabbed across the sky and thunder roared like a beast and he laughed like the madman he was.

'Fools. *Fools!*' He screeched in his hag-voice.

'Break it now and weep forever,' Mandrake croaked. 'All is lost for you now!'

He turned from the ridge and began the descent to where the massed Scree troops and the turncoat chiefs waited for his horrific arrival.

On the dam across the narrow ravine, Alevin was frantically spurring his men.

He looked down from the top of the barrier to where his men toiled far below, hacking and sawing at the timbers that buttressed the dam and held the waters back. Already the pressure was so great that even these great trunks were beginning to bend like greenwood twigs. It twisted and groaned and splinters exploded, but the dam still held.

'If the storm comes this way, we're all done,' said a voice behind him.

Alevin turned. One of the soldiers had brought him some bread and water. It was all they had.

'If we don't break this barrier, we're all done. We'll do what men can do.'

'There's something wrong with the lake,' the man said.

'Aye. It's there.' Alevin crouched on the rim, looking down to show the men working like ants. 'There where it shouldn't be.'

'No,' the soldier said. 'I thought I saw something different since the last time I was here.' He rubbed his eyes after the next bolt of lightning almost blinded him, waited until the after-images faded.

'Look there, Alevin. The water is lower. Two feet or more.'

Alevin spun from the drop and joined the man on the north edge. As he turned, he saw a wall of black water racing down the narrow lake in a curling wave.

The water against the lip was definitely lower. A bank of weeds that had been covered before was now glistening on the wooden wall.

And the wave-surge was bearing down on them faster than a galloping horse.

'More sorcery,' Alevin said. 'Mandrake tries to stop us.'

But Alevin was wrong. He was playing right into Mandrake's hands.

Jack was moving in the dark. Only the strange, clean light from the heartstone allowed him to make out anything here, but he was running, fleeing the horror within the obsidian block, running from the awful voice that still seethed like venom in his head.

He made it across the chamber, bearing the great sword as he ran, and dashed into the narrow passageway.

'Corriwen,' he called. 'Kerry!' He had no sense of direction here. But he had to keep moving. She pulled and tugged at him, trying to turn him, force him back, and it took all his effort, all his will to pull away.

The tunnels seemed to go on forever, and the sword was becoming heavy in his hands. His breath came in short, laboured gasps, but he could not stop. She would do anything to get the heartstone, her key.

Corriwen was running too. She could hear the sounds of pursuit. The thing that had looked like her brother, but had warped and melted and changed into something so vile it almost made her heart stop dead, that thing was hunting her.

She had pulled away, slashed with her blade, heart breaking from the loss of her brother once more. The knife bit into something more solid than air, and she felt wetness spurt.

But she had snapped out of the mesmerising hold the creature had on her.

The passageway opened into another chamber and Corriwen stopped, heart hammering, lungs aching.

'Corriwen!'

Something called her name and she jerked around. She turned and ran, feet pattering on the dank slabs. Somewhere, ahead or behind, or in one of the side passages, she could not tell where, other footfalls came louder. A soft glow appeared in front of her. She tried to stop, but her momentum carried her forwards and she slammed against the dark shape.

Instinctively Corriwen slashed at it and heard a cry of pain. She raised her knife again and a hand caught her wrist before she could deliver a killing blow.

'Corriwen,' Jack Flint panted. 'Don't kill me now.' He grabbed her tight. There was blood on his arm, soaking into his sleeve. In the light of the heartstone her eyes were blind with terror. She looked half mad. 'Corrie!' he yelled. 'It's me. Jack.'

She blinked, squirmed to get away, to get the knife free, and then her eyes suddenly fixed on him.

'I've got you the sword,' Jack said quickly. 'Now let's get the hell out of here.'

For a second the strength went out of her legs and her whole body sagged. Jack held her up, tight against him. 'We're nearly there,' he said. He sincerely hoped they were nearly there. 'We've just got to find Kerry. We can't go without him.'

The waters closed over his head and bony hands tightened on his ankles. They dragged him under. Kerry panicked. He tried to kick free. He gained the surface for just a second, gasped for breath, and oily water went up his nose.

His sword was still in his hand, and he stabbed it down, but the water slowed him. It was like moving through treacle. The blade hit nothing at all and then he was under, struggling to get to the surface again while a roaring noise in his ears rose to a crescendo and when he could hold his breath no longer, all his air came out in a rush and a freezing gush of water filled his lungs. He felt his body go numb.

Jack called his name.

'Kerry!'

A noise like a growl came from somewhere ahead, and Corriwen gripped Jack's arm. 'Did you hear that?'

'I heard something,' he said, clutching the sword tight.

The sound came again. More a rasp than a growl. It sounded like an animal. Jack powered on, keeping the blade ahead of him. If it was an animal, no matter how big, how fierce, he would face it.

A shape wavered in front of them and Jack raised the weapon, ready to strike first. The thing spun slowly, as if suspended from the ceiling, and a face turned towards him, and he started to swing the sword in the split second before recognition dawned.

'Kerry!'

He was on his tiptoes, hands dangling, face blank. Bones were strewn all round his feet. A skeleton hand clasped Kerry's ankle, arm-bone trailing on the stone floor.

Jack reached for him. Kerry's body was slack and cold. For a second, when he had seen the shape in the gloom, he had thought it was floating in mid-air. Even now, Kerry seemed to be wavering, as if seen through liquid. His eyes were open and vacant.

Jack reached for him, got an arm round his shoulders, pulled him in tight.

For a second Kerry's form was slack and then he let out a huge gasp. He vomited a stream of black water and his arms flailed madly. His blade missed Jack's eye by a whisker. Corriwen grabbed his arm. It was trembling with energy. Kerry gasped again, retched, and then doubled over in a paroxysm of coughing.

'Don't . . . Don't let me drown, Jack.'

'You're not drowning!'

Jack hauled him up, while Corriwen started clapping him hard between his shoulderblades.

For another instant, Kerry's eyes were sightless and then he blinked, once, twice, and then focussed on the glow from the stone.

'What? . . . Where?'

'It's us. You're okay.'

'Jack man,' Kerry gasped. He coughed again, spat and then shivered all over. 'I was drowning, Jack. They pulled me down. The place was flooded.'

Corriwen looked at Jack.

'Just a trick,' Jack said. 'It gets into your head.'

Kerry shook his head. 'It was up to the ceiling. And the dead men pulled me under.' He looked down at his feet, recoiled when he saw the bony hand clasped to his ankle, and kicked it away.

'Tell me later,' Jack said. 'We have to get out.'

Kerry shuddered. 'Thought I was a goner for sure.'

'Don't think about it,' Corriwen said. 'This place is just madness. It puts lies in your head.'

She reached for Kerry and hugged him tight. 'We are real,' she said. 'We have life.'

'And let's try to keep it that way,' Jack said. 'Come on.'

The hurried out of the chamber, back into another series of passageways, but now they were ascending, and Jack knew they were going the right way. They walked, it seemed for hours, always with that baleful presence probing at his mind. Jack held the heartstone ahead of them and led the way until finally a shard of daylight appeared and they stumbled into the dry barrens and the glare of the blazing sun caught the polished blade of Cullian's sword.

The three of them stood, holding on to each other for strength and comfort.

'Where's Declan?' Kerry finally asked, coughing the last of the filth from his sore lungs.

'Still in there,' Jack said.

'So, do we go get him? Or just wait.'

To the east, the storm was getting stronger. They could see the jagged edge of the ridge cutting south to where Mandrake's dam was. Lightning arced along its sawtoothed peaks.

'Something bad has happened there,' Corriwen said.

'Worse here,' Kerry ventured. 'You think Alevin got to the dam?'

'I hope so,' Jack said. He turned the sword, then passed it, hilt first, to Corriwen. She took it in both slender hands. She seemed so slight she would barely be able to lift it, but she swung it up with surprising ease.

'I never lifted this before,' she said. 'But it feels right in my hand.'

Jack nodded. He had felt exactly the same way when he had drawn the blade from the Morrigan's stone.

'We should wait a while,' he said. 'But we don't go back in whether Declan's there or not. That thing gets in your head and if she did it again, I don't think we would ever get out again.'

He was about to say more when there was a movement at the entrance. Corriwen brought the sword up in both hands, blade foremost. Kerry had his blade up in a flash.

Declan came out of the dark, staggered and fell to his knees. For a horrified second, Jack thought he had lost his eyes, for instead of the bright blue that had flashed as he fought the Scree, all he could see were two black holes.

He was gasping for air, his face drained of blood. He clamped both hands over his eyes and knelt on the hard ground, rocking back and forth, moaning in agony.

'Declan,' Corriwen said. She put the sword through her belt and touched him on the shoulder. He was trembling like a bird, all his muscles bunched tight. 'Declan! We are here.' She drew his hands down from his eyes and Declan blinked hard, as though the light hurt his eyes. 'What happened?'

He shook his head, bewildered. 'I ... I ... I thought ...' his words trailed away. He drew in a deep breath, shuddered, and seemed to collect himself. 'I don't know,' he finally said.

'But you're out now, aren't you?' Kerry said. 'We all made it.'

He pointed to a small hill some distance away. The three horses stood together. The little Leprechaun sat at their feet. Kerry was about to say something when the ground trembled under them and he turned to face Jack.

Jack saw Kerry's eyes widen. He pointed over Jack's shoulder, unable to speak a word. Corriwen caught the motion and looked in that direction. Jack shrugged, turned and froze.

A wave of water, a *wall* of water, taller than a house, taller than the Black Barrow itself, was thundering across the flat, coming straight at them.

As one, they turned and fled for the high ground, not pausing to look back, knowing the wave would surely overtake them before they reached the hill.

And the wave slammed into their backs and tumbled them over and over and over until everything went black.

THIRTY

The backwash of that huge wave sucked them back,
floundering and gasping. Jack felt his muscles weaken.
Kerry thrashed and splashed, hampering all efforts to save
him.

Then the horses were in the water, forcing their way
though the surge, with the little leprechaun clamped around
the lead mount's neck. Without reins or stirrups, it
somehow managed to get the greathorses between them
and the force of the flood. Jack reached a desperate hand,
grabbed the saddle and pulled himself up, forcing Kerry in
front of him. Kerry sprawled across the saddle, coughing
mud and looking very sorry for himself.

Still, he managed to squeeze the little leprechaun's arm.
'You're a good wee man to have around, so you are.'

Jack didn't even have the strength the climb on. He

simply held the girth as Corriwen did on the other side, and let the horse plod through the tumbling water onto the brow of the hill, before he fell down, barely able to move a muscle. It took ten minutes, maybe more, before he could sit up and look to the east, where, far in the distance, water was still spewing out of the cleft that had been cut in solid rock. As they watched, the waters rose quickly in the basin of the high salt flats to form a new lake.

The Black Barrow was just a bleak island in the middle of the floodwater, and then it too disappeared from view.

'We've lost,' Jack finally said, staring bleakly at the water where the Black Barrow had been. Tears of frustration and rage were coursing down his cheeks.

'There's still Alevin,' Kerry said.

'That's the problem,' Jack said. 'I remember what the Bard told me. The dam had to go first.'

'Why's that?'

'It was the curse. It couldn't be forever, 'cos nothing ever is. They had a rhyme for it.'

Jack thought carefully, then he repeated it just as Finbar had told them after they had been saved from the waterfall by the Undine women.

> A blade to wake from deadly sleep
> A flood to free in fathoms deep
> For in the ebb the foul takes form
> To ride the night, on wings of storm.

He shook his head. 'If only he'd smashed the dam on time. We came all this way and I . . . I thought we'd made it.'

'So now what?' Kerry asked.

'I think we should get ourselves out of here.'

Mandrake had watched gleefully as the water roared through the cleft cut in the ridge.

'I did this,' he crowed. 'Ha. Ha ha. And they called me *mad*!'

He raised his face to the storm.

'Nothing can stand before me! *Nothing on this world!*'

The dam bulged further and the edges of the sluice-gate began to give.

'We have to open them,' one of the captains said.

Alevin was watching closely. 'Just a minute more. We're almost there.'

The structure groaned again, pulled from below, pushed from above. Trunks as wide as ten men began to bend slowly, like saplings in the wind. Pieces of stone, where the buttresses had been laid into the solid rock, began to crumble.

'All right,' Alevin said. 'Get the beasts out and on to high ground.'

The captain shouted orders down the slope and immediately the exhausted men slung the long hawsers round the buttresses, then allowed the horses to power their way up and out of immediate danger. Hundreds of men who had worked on the cleft were hauling now, all in unison, pulling as hard as they could.

'Haul it!' Alevin roared. 'Haul for Temair.'

Then a voice shouted from high up on the lip of the dam. 'Alevin! The lake!' The man waved frantic arms. 'The water!'

'What's happening now?'

'Come up and see. The water – it's dropping.'

Alevin cursed through gritted teeth. He wheeled his horse and forced it up the narrow track and finally got to the rim.

'What did you say?'

'The water,' the man said. 'I don't know what to make of it.'

Alevin dismounted and strode to the lip, hardly able to believe his eyes.

The water level had dropped by ten feet, and it was still dropping fast.

'Too late,' Alevin groaned. 'Too late.'

The future of Temair rested on his shoulders and he had failed.

Suddenly, the dam shook with a powerful tremor and the water began to flow away from its upstream face.

'Get out. Get the beasts away!'

Then the dam fell. Alevin ran for his life along the rim. He leapt across the widening gap, managed to get his fingers onto the rock, and then the man who had called the warning reached and grabbed him by the wrist.

The dam collapsed with a colossal crash into the space where the lake had been.

From the comparative safety of the hillock, they had watched the waters rise ever upwards until the Black Barrow was completely submerged. Then everything went silent and still for a long time.

'The storm's coming this way,' Corriwen finally said. Her voice was flat with despair.

Jack nodded. 'I know. But there's nowhere to go.' All around them, the floodwaters stretched over the flats.

The little Leprechaun was down on the ground, hands dug into the thin soil, eyes closed. 'They come again,' he finally said. 'Bad things come.'

Jack had no doubt in his mind that something awfully bad was coming.

Far in the east they heard a low roaring sound.

'I think that's the dam,' Kerry said.

'Too late,' Corriwen muttered. 'Too late for us all.'

An hour later, the water began to fall again, as the floodwater drained back through the crevasse and down through the gorge. Now there was nothing to impede the flow and the new lake simply began to drain away.

And as the storm's fury approached them, the tip of the Black Barrow slowly emerged from the subsiding water.

Jack Flint felt a sense of dread shiver through him.

THIRTY ONE

They watched as the water level dropped. Declan stood on the top of the hillock, leaning against his horse. He had been silent since he had emerged from the Black Barrow. Neither Jack nor Kerry wanted to ask him what terrifying visions he had seen in the darkness there.

Blood soaked into Jack's sleeve from the cut of Corriwen's blade. He was not in real pain, but his arm felt weak and shaky.

Corriwen sat close, with the Redthorn sword on her lap, slowly stropping its gleaming blade with her sleeve. It glowed with a light of its own. The hilt was carved from the same black, translucent stone as the heartstone. The pommel was silver too, with a smoky cairngorm stone at the end, etched with interlocking letters.

Jack could read them from where he sat, and though he

said nothing, his heart quickened. The lettering was exactly the same as the ones carved on the bone handle of the penknife in his pocket, the one the Major had given him, without explanation, when he was ten years old.

They read: J.C.F.

He stared at it for a long time, thinking hard, recollecting the snippets of information he had gleaned all along the way since even before they had tumbled through the stone gate into this strange world.

And the words of the Morrigan came back to him too, though he wondered if she had planted dreams in his head, or whether she had spoken the truth, or if he would die here without finding out any of what was important to him.

Corriwen Redthorn looked up at him. 'I didn't thank you,' she said.

'For what?'

'For this. For saving this for Temair.'

'I don't know if it's made a difference. We were too late.'

'Maybe. Maybe not. Who knows the future?' She touched his hand, letting the sword rest on her lap. She clasped Kerry's hand too.

'And I haven't thanked you for all of it. For coming on this journey with me.' She gave them a small, almost shy smile. 'And for being my true friends.'

'Aw, shucks,' Kerry said, trying to hide his embarrassment. 'Buy me a beer and we'll call it quits.'

They both looked at him.

'I heard that in an old movie.'

By morning, the storm was directly overhead and Mandrake's hordes, thousands of Scree, traitorous chiefs and their horsemen, faced Alevin and his fighters and a raggle-taggle band of weary men and boys armed only with hammers and pick-axes.

Kerry huddled against the other two, with the little Leprechaun snuggled under his arm. He looked up at the maelstrom above. 'Looks like heavy weather,' he said, to no one in particular.

Corriwen was so pale she looked ill. 'They cannot fight. There's too many of them.'

'Oh, they will fight,' a voice came from behind them. They turned as one and saw Finbar standing on top of the hillock. Beside him were four others. Jack recognised the Bard of Otter Holt and three more tall old men with long, braided beards, staves in their hands. They were dressed all in white.

'Comes the day, comes the hour,' Finbar said.

'See the front of battle glower,' Jack said. 'Robert the Bruce said that.'

'Comes the hour comes the hero,' the second Bard said, almost a chant.

'Comes the hero,' said the third, 'comes the heart.'

'Comes the heart and good prevails.'

'Good prevails and evil fails.'

Corriwen listened, but she was not convinced. 'Fine words. But they are outnumbered ten to one.'

Just as she spoke, the Scree began to roar their battle cries. They battered their clubs against broad shields and the hounds set up a howling that was as eerie as it was frightening. On the opposite side of the basin, Alevin's small army stayed silent.

The Scree marched forward. Corriwen could see the black form of Mandrake astride his wagon, urging them on. As the Scree began marching down from the high ground, there was a strange sound, so deep Jack could feel it vibrate in his bones.

'It begins again,' Finbar said. '*She* stirs.'

Without warning, the Black Barrow heaved. Jack thought it looked exactly like a waking beast. Cracks split the ground with a sound like gunshot and stuttered across the basin in hard, jagged lines.

The wind dropped. Corriwen gripped the Redthorn sword in both hands. Jack slipped a black arrow to his bowstring. They waited, breath held.

Kerry heard it first, a sound like a low groan from deep in the earth. 'Is that her?'

Jack couldn't reply. His lungs had locked tight. One of the Bards raised his staff up to the sky and began to chant.

Then there was movement. It came from the cracks where the water had flowed, and at first it seemed as if the sand was shifting. Jack managed to get his breath.

'Look there,' Finbar said. He pointed to the slope behind Alevin's force. They all looked and saw the hill slowly change colour, as if splashed with sage green paint. The desert slope was turning green in a slow wave.

'More magic?' Corriwen asked.

'Not yet,' Finbar managed to chuckle. 'The Leprechaun have come from their glades. For the good of all Temair.'

Jack strained to see. What looked like a carpet of moss growing across the hillside resolved itself into a horde of the Little People, moving fast as rabbits, quiet as mice, flowing down the slope towards Alevin's band.

'They're just little guys,' Kerry said. 'They'll get slaughtered for sure without those trees to help.'

The ground shuddered again.

A shadow wavered up from the nearest crack in the earth. For a second Jack thought it was her, the thing in the Barrow, and then he saw a cloud of black flies, hatching from the earth, hundreds of them, thousands, a huge swarm, buzzing in unison.

The Bard of Otter Holt had closed his eyes and was chanting into the wind.

The flies spun in their own insectile whirlwind and the stench of rot from their number was awesome. Beyond the Barrow, they heard Mandrake's voice, not his words, just the high pitched clamour. And as one, the flies arrowed towards Alevin's line.

'Blood suckers and carrion eaters,' Finbar said. 'Summoned from the depths.'

Beside him the tall Bard still chanted, hands high, holding his stave.

And from the far south from where they had travelled, something glittered in the sky. He sang on as the cloud of biting insects spun round, humming their own death song, towards the pitiful force.

Then the flock of silver swifts, thousands strong, came on singing wings, sweeping over Alevin's head in such numbers they hid the entire force from view and swooped straight for the cloud of flies.

The second bard was beside the first, chanting his own song, facing the west and the far sea. He held his stave up in two hands and closed his eyes. His deep baritone voice spoke to the western sky. Finbar spoke to the east. They chanted, different words, but in rhyme and counterpoint.

The Scree began to charge across the plain.

Corriwen grabbed Jack's hand and dragged him to the top of the hillock. Without a word she stripped off his jacket and tore his shirt open. The red hand stood out clearly under the five points of the corona. 'Take the sword,' she ordered, her face grim.

'No,' Jack said. 'It's yours. You need it.'

'Do it, for me. For Temair.' She pushed it at him. 'And for us all.'

Jack took it. It sang in his hands, suddenly riven with huge power. Instinctively he raised it above his head in one hand. He raised his left, caked with his own blood. Corriwen held on to him as the wind buffeted them. She stood on her tiptoes, cupped a hand to her mouth and called across the distance to Alevin.

'A Redthorn!' she called, clear and high, loud enough to pierce the wind and the screams of the feeding birds. 'A Redthorn! Rally to the Red Hand.'

Alevin's head turned. He raised his sword and a cheer went up from the men around him.

'The Redthorn!' the soldiers roared. To a man, they raised their weapons high and clattered their shields. In front of their horses, something small moved out. Jack recognised the ancient Leprechaun from the forest. He reached the flat and slowly sank to his knees.

'He sacrifices for the poisoned land,' Finbar said. 'In a war that is not of his making.'

As they watched, the old king dug his feet deep into the soil, even as the Scree came charging across the plain, and then his arms began to twist. His fingers lengthened, split into woody twigs, elongated further and became branches. Small leaves sprouted around his gnarled face and shoulders and long, knobbly arms. His body stretched, creaking, and as quickly as they had formed, the leaves shrivelled and died. Bark-like skin simply peeled away.

'He's drawing the poison,' Finbar said.

'What for?' Kerry asked.

'To make it fertile.'

The old king was completely still now. His knobby shoulders looked like dead wood. One of the branches that had grown from his fingers cracked and fell to the ground. The wind blew off another one. The horde of Leprechaun watched in complete and reverent silence.

Then, as the old creature withered and died, a tide of the Leprechaun came swarming from behind Alevin's horses and swept out onto the plain in a green flood.

Alevin's captain blew his horn and the greathorses stepped forward to meet the Scree hordes.

The Scree charged on, their hounds snarling and

slavering in anticipation. The green host of Leprechaun flowed out to meet them and Jack thought their advance was nothing short of suicide. The ground shook as the grey tide charged to meet the green. Then, in the centre of the plain, the Leprechaun stopped all in a line, looking for all this world like a sward of moss. None of the watchers could make out what was happening.

The Scree raised their clubs and spears and raced towards them, set for slaughter.

Without a sound, the Leprechaun pulled back, drawing the Scree towards Alevin's men in a ferocious rush. In the lead was a grey giant, wide as two men, a war club in each hand. He charged ahead, took a swipe at a Leprechaun who ducked and scampered out of reach.

The giant fell. No stumble, no pause. He just fell flat. Beside him another Scree tumbled and rolled, kicking his hobnailed feet against something green that entangled his feet.

'Small, but clever,' Finbar said.

Another Scree stopped dead and started to drag his foot, which seemed to be nailed to the ground. Another clutched at something on his leg.

One of them screamed like a hog and sank to his knees as a thick, thorny tendril reared like a snake and curled around his throat. It tightened like a snare and blood spurted. In an instant the plain was writhing with spiked runners that swelled from the soil and snagged and snatched, tripping, noosing; spiking Scree with jagged thorns.

The old king's sacrifice had not been in vain.

The Scree's bellows of triumph turned to screams of fear.

Alevin's men spurred their horses onto the plain and charged at the entangled front line. The Scree were too busy with their own predicament, trying to free themselves from the garrotes that held them fast. Some of them were blinded by stabbing thorns, some choked where they stood.

And the rest of the front line were cut down by Alevin's fighters in a swathe of blades and clouds of arrows.

But there were thousands more Scree behind the entangled front. Mandrake was on his wagon, waving his arms, giving orders to traitor chiefs. Horns blew and the Scree army swerved around their fallen comrades to attack Alevin's flank.

Mandrake was in an agony of indecision. His Scree were dying in hundreds, but worse, the Redthorn sword had been taken, and the heartstone was still not in his grasp.

He had planned and worked for this, and now, on the point of victory, he had failed her.

Her wrath, he knew, would be devastating. And he would suffer the consequences.

He could see the girl, out beyond the fighting – the *slaughter* – and the boy with the heartstone. And the Bards were there, calling their familiars and the forest people against her. They would fail in that endeavour, he was sure.

But he could not face her, not without the prize she had demanded. The price of his future.

He knew just where he had to go.

Jack and the others stood mesmerised, close enough to the carnage to smell the blood and sweat.

Finbar laid a heavy hand on his shoulder. 'They will come for you now, Journeyman,' he said. 'And what you carry. And for the Redthorn sword. It's time for you to leave the field.'

Jack had been so riveted by the battle that he hadn't even thought to flee. But as Finbar spoke, a phalanx of Scree started to beat its way past the thrashing and dying front line, moving to cut them off.

'We will hold them,' Finbar said.

'How?'

Finbar pointed to the sky in the west. 'You go that way.'

Jack looked in that direction and saw a glitter in the sky.

'My brother has called and been answered,' Finbar said.

And as Jack looked, he saw the shimmering cloud resolve itself into yet another flock of birds, so many they blocked the darkening sky. He heard a faint, high cry in the distance.

'Run, boy,' Finbar said. 'You have braved enough. Time to find your way. Go with our blessing and our thanks.'

Corriwen had her hand on Jack's shoulder. 'I must stay,' she said.

Finbar touched her on the head, as if to give her a special blessing.

'Corriwen Redthorn,' he said. 'You have done your duty. Now pick up your feet, and run. Run like the wind. What Jack Flint carries is far too important to be lost again. He needs you still. We feel her stir. The sands are running fast.'

'I'm with Finbar,' Kerry said. 'This place is getting too rough for my liking.'

Finbar turned to Declan who still leant against his horse, holding the pommel to stay upright.

'You watch their backs,' the Bard said. Declan nodded. He climbed into the saddle, pulled the other horses round and they all mounted quickly. Finbar slapped a horse's rump. 'Now get out of here. We'll hold them.'

Jack turned the horse, with the Leprechaun on its neck, and they left the five Bards together on the hillock. As they spurred the mounts down the slope, the white cloud of birds flew over their heads. Jack saw the wide, white wings of seabirds and recognised them from his walks on the cliffs with the Major. That seemed like a hundred years ago now, but he could tell gannets when he saw them.

But he had never seen so many of them all together.

The tall bard kept up his low chant, staff outstretched, and the gannets came slashing down from the black sky, spear beaks outthrust, wings pulled back, and launched themselves like living arrows into the heart of the Scree hordes.

All Jack could hear, as the horses galloped west, were the screams of the grey swarm as they died under that murderous attack.

THIRTY TWO

O n Jack's chest, the heartstone began to beat again. He could sense the presence, awake and now rousing. Kerry pointed to the sky and Jack raised his eyes.

'It's happening,' Corriwen said, her knuckles white on the Redthorn hilt.

As they watched the storm sank lower and lower, speeding up as it descended on the Black Barrow.

Jack tried to turn, but the scene held his eyes in awful fascination.

As soon as the storm's base touched the black stones, the earth jolted. Even from this distance they could see a shockwave judder across the plain.

A deadly silence descended.

'Jack,' Kerry said urgently, plucking at his sleeve. 'I really think we should—' He didn't even get to finish the sentence.

The black mound exploded. The ground ruptured all around and molten rock spewed up. And in the centre of it all, something began to emerge.

Jack felt her searching mind before he saw the shape. It was like the touch of death.

She rose, like a smoke haze, coiling, weaving, thickening all the time. Bolts of power arced up to a sky that had turned from the black of the storm to a sickly purple. No sun or stars shone.

The Morrigan turned her ghastly head towards them. A flock of roaks circled over her head. Her arms stretched wide, as if to embrace the whole world, became great black bat-wings that spread out on either side.

'Look away, Jack!' Kerry shouted. He yanked the reins and hauled at Jack's horse. 'Come on!'

Corriwen pulled him, forcing him to turn. As he did, Jack felt the awful connection between him and the monstrous thing part with a mental *snap*.

Corriwen kicked her horse and they were off, the howl of mad laughter ringing in their ears.

On the hillock, the bards joined their five staves together in an interlocking pattern, holding them up to the sky. From that pentagram, a spear of white light met the darkness head-on.

Jack risked a look over his shoulder. The Morrigan was powering across the distance towards them.

'Faster!' Jack yelled. The horses were at full tilt, leaping over the smoking crevasses that laced the plain.

An awesome power came twisting out from the demon like a tornado. Jack caught the motion and instinctively wheeled his mount. The others turned with him, and a force shuddered past him, so close he felt the wave of black energy ripple through him. His vision wavered and a deathly cold ripped to his core, and then it was gone.

Jack's horse lost its footing and tumbled, slammed into Corriwen's mount. The other two steeds collided with the first and all the riders went down.

Jack rolled, grabbed Kerry's arm and dragged him to his feet. Corriwen was beside him, Declan had his sword drawn, but Jack knew no sword could have any effect on the raging thing that plummeted towards them. 'Run,' he gasped. Boiling stone erupted from a churning crevasse. Jack leapt onto one of the heaving slabs, with Kerry and Corriwen beside him.

The Morrigan soared above them. Jack leapt from one tilting rock to another. The Leprechaun scampered across the big rocks to the far side.

The slab Jack reached spun under his weight. He felt his skin bake. The stone cracked like thin ice and one part pulled away. Jack slipped to one knee. Corriwen gave a cry as the slab they were on spun off. Declan stood up. He held the Redthorn sword in his hands.

Jack got to his feet again. On his neck, the heartstone was pulsing as fast as his own heart. Above him, above the smoke and heat, the Morrigan wheeled and cackled. Jack turned to Declan and his heart almost stopped.

Declan dropped his saddle-bag. He turned his eyes on Jack and they were as dead and as empty as a corpse's.

'Freedom in all worlds.'

Jack heard the words, but the voice that spoke was not Declan's. It was the same voice that had invaded his mind in the depths of the Black Barrow.

Corriwen screamed a warning and tried to leap from her stone across a gap six feet wide. Kerry held her back.

'You lose, journeyman. Like your father.'

In desperation, Jack fumbled at Declan's belt and managed to grab the knife. Declan raised the Redthorn sword high, and began to swing it down.

Jack thrust with the knife and took Declan under the swinging arm. The knife drove straight in. Declan faltered, just enough to let Jack dodge the blade edge. Jack twisted, grabbed Declan's saddle-bag, the little book fell out and in the heat the edges of its pages began to turn brown.

'Give it up,' the Morrigan's voice spoke from Declan's mouth. 'Fight me and you will suffer forever.'

Declan grabbed for the heartstone on its chain. Jack flinched.

On the far side, the little leprechaun fixed its eyes on the book that had fallen open.

Jack rolled and almost tumbled into the searing flow. Declan caught his ankle and drew him back. He twisted, knocked the little book to the side and the pages fluttered open. Declan suddenly stopped pulling.

A scarlet rose was pressed to the page, still bright.

As Declan's empty eyes caught the image, the rose bloomed from the page. On the far side of the gash in the earth, the Leprechaun hunched, polished eyes fixed on the flower, muttering. The rose petals opened. Declan's death grip loosened abruptly. He dropped the Redthorn sword and Jack scrambled back to the edge of the slab.

He grabbed the sword in both hands.

Declan turned to him.

'Do it now,' he hissed. 'Finish me now before ...'

Jack raised the sword.

Above them, in the smoke and fumes, the Morrigan screamed. A withering bolt of pure evil came blasting down and smashed into Declan whose fingers spasmed around the rose flower and crushed it to nothing. He looked up, lurched forwards.

'Now, boy. End it lest she—'

His mouth clamped shut and his face twisted in agony. The slab rocked alarmingly as Declan's hand found Jack's neck again.

The stone lurched and spilled Declan backwards towards the cauldron of melted rock.

His fingers found the chain around Jack's neck as he fell, dragging him to the edge and then without warning, the slab tilted. Declan's foot hit the molten rock and sizzled in a burst of steam. He screamed once and then the rock simply flicked over and smashed them both into the incandescent heat.

THIRTY THREE

Corriwen and Kerry watched, helpless to intervene as the slab flipped over and Jack and Declan vanished.

Corriwen's knees gave under her and she would have fallen if Kerry's arm had not been locked around her.

Jack had made no sound at all. One moment he was there and the next he was gone, the Redthorn sword in his hand.

Kerry made a sound, as if he had been hit hard in the belly.

In the boiling air, the Morrigan screamed, beating those wings with enough force to buffet them where they stood. Energy shot off her in waves that sent rocks flying into the air. Lightning stabbed up from the ground and the flock of roaks wheeling above her burst into flames and came spinning dead to earth.

Jack was gone.

All they could see was the glow of rock flowing in a river of fire. Of Declan and Jack there was no sign. Way beyond the split and broken land, thousands of Scree knelt in homage.

Corriwen and Kerry turned away in horror and shame. At the far side of the hillock, they came to another crack in the earth where another river of molten stone rushed in a torrent. It was too wide for them to cross, even by jumping from slab to slab.

'We're stuck,' Kerry said. He sounded drained and completely devoid of any hope.

'We must . . . flee,' Corriwen said, hating herself for even thinking it. She had not come here to flee, but defeat had been forced on them just when she thought they had won. Now they were trapped between the Morrigan and the fires that bubbled up from hell.

Behind them, over the roar of cascading brimstone, she felt the dead-touch in her mind and spun quickly.

The Morrigan came swooping towards them, claws outstretched, her face worse than any nightmare vision. She radiated foulness as evil as mortal sin. Kerry felt himself sway, unable to run. He closed his eyes against the vision. He had no energy left even for fear.

Then, without warning, the rocks shook under their feet and the bank they stood on slipped down towards the river of lava.

Kerry fell to his knees, dragging Corriwen with him. The rock tilted further and they slid towards the flow. Then Kerry saw the hand clutching the edge of the slab.

He jerked back as the fingers clawed for purchase and something began to climb out of the brimstone towards them. He backed away, unable to imagine what could possibly defend them against something that could live in a river of fire.

Inch by inch it breached the surface, burning like the sun and inch by inch, made its way onto the slab. Heat came off it in roasting waves.

In its hand was a glowing wand.

Slowly, very slowly, it began to rise to its feet, a glowing man-shape.

'Jack?'

Kerry only heard Corriwen's whisper. 'Stay back,' he said. 'Jump if you can.'

'Jack!' Louder this time. Kerry shot her a glance and saw her eyes were fixed on the incandescent figure that stood before them. It was a human form blazing in light, almost transparent. It turned towards them and raised the brilliant wand and for a second, Kerry thought he recognised the face in the swirling heat.

It raised the wand and he saw it was no wand. It was a sword of fire. It turned away. The Morrigan swooped. A bolt of blinding white light shot from the figure on the rock. It sizzled up the length of the blade and leapt out.

The light pulsed from the stone around its neck, flowing into the sword and as it blasted up, Kerry recognised Jack's face inside a caul of heat.

The light slammed into the Morrigan with such force she was thrown backwards.

As Jack stood there – stood there, however impossibly –

the light lanced out in blinding skeins. The Morrigan shrieked as she tumbled.

As Kerry and Corriwen watched, open-mouthed, the heat drained from Jack's body, turning his shimmering form solid again. The glow faded, dwindling to the centre of his chest, flowing back into the heartstone.

High in the air, the Morrigan began to writhe and change, began to fade back into the smoke from which she had come.

Jack swung the sword down, and shards of its light seared the kneeling Scree, blinding them as they worshipped. They clapped warty hands over their melting eyes.

Behind them, a horn sounded in the distance and Alevin's men and his raggedy helpers came storming across the plain.

The wind caught the fading smoke that had been the Morrigan and wafted it away to the east until there was nothing to see but a smudge in the sky.

Then there was nothing at all.

Jack paused and lowered the sword, shoulders slumped as if he was totally drained, then, slowly, like an old man, he turned towards them. For a moment his eyes were glazed and empty, still hot, and then they focussed on his friends.

Corriwen gasped. As he stood there, they could both see that the red hand mark on his chest, and the five points of the Corona, were gone, seared clear in the heat of the brimstone flow.

Finally the heartstone drained the last of the heat from him and faded to black.

Jack walked towards them and held the sword up to

Corriwen. She put her hand around his on the hilt and together they raised it aloft, the Sword of Cullian.

Kerry gawped at them, still unable to speak. But his heart was bursting with happiness.

THIRTY FOUR

The Bards reached them. Finbar put his arm around Jack.

'Is it over?'

Finbar shook his head.

'Only until she recovers,' he said. 'She can be fought and she can be held, but she cannot be killed.'

'You mean, it's not over?'

'Nothing ever is,' Finbar said. 'The battle between the dark and the light has gone on since the beginning. And it always will.'

He laid a hand on Jack's shoulder. 'I know you have been through more than anybody has a right to ask, but you must protect the worlds. She must not get the key or your Caledon will be next to suffer, and worlds beyond that. We will do our best to bind her again, while she is weak. We have you to thank for that, Journeyman.' He looked out over the battlefield where the Scree hordes had fallen. 'Your part here is done,' Finbar said. 'And you have Temair's gratitude. Now, mount up and ride west.' He raised his staff and pointed towards a path that led to a cleft in the high ground. 'Follow that pass and the trail that leads from it. Stay on the track and you'll find the way home.'

Corriwen held up the Redthorn sword. 'I think you should have this.'

'What would I do with that meat cleaver?' the Bard laughed.

'I promised I would find the homeward gate for my friends. Who knows what will happen when we reach it. Temair needs the sword more than I.'

Finbar shrugged. He was jollier by far than the other Bards.

'Who knows what will happen? The circle turns on. But I believe you will have one more use for this fine blade. When you do, then I will find it and I will keep it safe for Temair. I have my Undines who will guard it well. Nothing gets past them, and my haven is hidden from the eyes of men.'

He helped Corriwen into the saddle, slapped the greathorse on its high rump. 'Now take the heartstone, and take heart. Ride like the wind and don't look back.'

Corriwen spurred her horse up the track. Jack and Kerry followed. They reached the pass in less than an hour and didn't look back as they descended the far side down a rocky slope. By the time they hit the flat, the greathorses were moving at a gallop.

The horses kept the pace up all day, never tiring, only stopping to drink at clear streams in land that became greener and more fertile as they headed west and away from the salt barrens.

They passed through green valleys that were empty, waiting for the return of people to farm them, and rode on as the land rose again, stopping only to eat whatever Kerry could catch, before they were up and riding again.

There was no sign of pursuit as they travelled rocky ravines festooned with trees, through tall timbered forests and then into hill country again.

It took them three days of hard riding before, on a bright morning, they rode out of a steep cleft and saw the standing stones ahead of them.

Kerry punched the air with a fist. 'Yes!'

He banged Jack on the shoulder. 'Go for it, man. We're almost there.'

The two pillars stood in a wide, circular basin surrounded by dry rocks. The faces were intricately carved with the strange lettering they had seen before

'The Homeward Gate,' Jack said. The *Book of Ways* had not let them down.

As they raced for the stones, Jack leant over in the saddle and grasped Corriwen's belt. 'Will you come with us?' he asked as the stones loomed closer.

Before she could reply, a black figure came darting out from between two huge boulders and slashed at Corriwen's horse.

Mandrake barred the way to the Homeward Gate.

His face was wizened and horribly aged. But his axe

whistled through the air and the horse reared in fright, throwing Jack and Kerry to the ground. He swung again, and almost decapitated Kerry, who rolled under the swipe.

'I'll have it!' he hissed. 'By all that's black I'll have it. You cannot deny me this.'

'Screw this for a game of soldiers,' Kerry snarled. He fitted a sharp stone in his sling and swung hard. It caught Mandrake right between the eyes and he tumbled back against a rock, the stone lodged deep in his forehead.

Mandrake raised both hands and chanted in a guttural tongue, ignoring the awful wound that split his face into a spiderweb of black lines.

As he raised his hands, Jack felt himself caught. He couldn't say how, but his motion suddenly slowed, as if he was running through treacle.

Mandrake reached again, screamed, and Jack felt the whoop of some invisible force rush past him, aimed high. It struck the high slope behind them and immediately Jack heard the sound of stones churning and sliding. He tried to turn, but his muscles had frozen. Beside him, Corriwen jerked as if she'd been electrocuted, and Kerry was sinking to the ground, falling so slowly it seemed he would never get there.

The Redthorn sword kicked out of Corriwen's hand and stuck in the ground.

Mandrake's raddled face lit up in a grotesque expression of glee.

Jack heard his voice, slowed down so much it sounded as deep as the roar of tumbling rocks.

'Come now, mistress,' he boomed. 'I have not failed you.'

The heartstone around Jack's neck fluttered.

He forced his hand towards his chest, fighting the paralysis all the way. It seemed to take an age as it floated before him, numb and senseless, but with a supreme effort, he dragged it back, back and back, until it touched the heartstone.

As soon as his fingers found the polished surface, he felt a jolt of heat shimmer through him and the paralysis broke instantly.

Without thinking, he grabbed for the sword just as Mandrake's fingers closed on the hilt. Jack was a split second faster. He snatched the hilt, pushed Corriwen aside just in time. A withering bolt hissed through the air and hit the rock ahead of them.

Jack was now moving faster than he could think. All his senses were now razor sharp, and everything else seemed to happen in slow motion. He had the sword, whirled to the left under Mandrake's swing, twisted round as the axe came again in an arc towards Kerry's lowered neck.

Jack didn't pause. Behind him he could sense the Morrigan's evil presence, drawing up from the hole in the slope where the rocks had slid away. He braced his body, put all his strength into it.

Mandrake's axe was only inches from Kerry's neck. Corriwen was tumbling away from the Morrigan's blast.

Jack threw the Redthorn sword. It whipped through the air. The axe-edge missed Kerry's neck by a fraction and smashed against a rock.

The sword caught Mandrake in the chest. It went right through him and pinned him to a boulder. He groaned and his eyes bulged. Instantly Kerry and Corriwen were unbound from whatever spell he had cast on them. Kerry was on his feet in the blink of an eye. Corriwen caught her balance as Jack half-turned.

Behind them, up on the slope, a gash had appeared in the ground. The rocks on the slope avalanched towards them and a black shape clawed its way into the light.

Jack turned, reaching for Kerry. Then he saw Mandrake. His eyes were rolled up in his haggard, torn skull. No blood came out of the awful wound in his chest. His arms were spread-eagled against the stone with the sword jammed into his dark heart. And as they watched, his jaw opened, but no sound came out except the grind of dry stone, and Mandrake, who had wanted to rule Temair, began to turn to stone as the rock claimed him for its own.

On the slope the Morrigan screamed and more rocks came tumbling. Jack had the heartstone in one hand, his bow in the other. The heartstone beat again, hard and powerful. He snatched at Corriwen's belt.

'Come on!' he cried.

Ahead of them the tall stones stood waiting. The sun had swung down behind them and beamed through the space. The light caught the polished heartstone and reflected into Jack's eyes. Between the stones, the air sparkled like frost.

Corriwen reached for the sword that pinned Mandrake's grey shape to the rock, but Jack dragged her away. They had seconds to spare, no more than that. He pushed Kerry in front of him and they ran for the stones.

'Please!' Jack said aloud. 'Please be *open*!'

They went through and something squeezed at them,

something soft and yielding. Jack felt that same inside-out sensation he had experienced before. Everything went black as all light vanished. A deep throbbing swelled in their ears. Colours exploded in concentric rings. Time stretched and shrank and they fell and fell.

They hit the ground running, feet pounding soft earth. A low mist pooled about their feet. Jack opened his eyes and saw the ring of standing stones around them. Beyond them tall trees dripped dew. The backpack that had been snatched from him on the night they had fled was still lying on the ground.

'We're back!' he cried. 'We made it.'

There was a ringing in their ears and the heartstone pulsed slowly. Above them the moon was silver and bright.

'Close it!' Kerry cried. He had turned to face the gateway they had tumbled through. The air still shimmered like a silvery veil, but beyond that, they could see the rocky basin and the stony shape of Mandrake spiked on the rock.

And beyond that, the Morrigan swept down the slope towards them, faster than an express train, roaring like an avalanche.

'Close the gate!'

'How?' Jack yelled. He looked left and right on the two stones. They were thick with intricate carvings, but there was nothing that looked like a lock. He held the heartstone up to each, but still nothing happened.

And that black demonic form was screeching towards them.

'*The hub of all ways,*' Jack remembered the Bard's words. 'She'll break through.'

For a second he was frozen, scared to move. Behind them, at the three pillars that held the weight of the flat table-stone, came a sound of rock on rock. Jack turned and saw the darkness there that he had seen on the night they had fled, a darkness that sucked the moonlight into itself and smothered it.

'She's coming,' Corriwen cried. 'I can *feel* her.'

'Do something, man,' Kerry shouted, feet still sliding on the wet earth as the awful suction gained power.

Jack kept hold of Corriwen's hand, reached and clasped Kerry's fingers. Instantly something riddled through him, as if he had made a powerful connection.

'Which way?' Corriwen cried, just loud enough to be heard over the roar of wind that sucked everything down into a dark vortex.

Jack tried to remember which way they had come into the ring on Halloween. It had been dark, almost too dark to see. It seemed so long ago.

His sense of direction clicked inside his head and suddenly he knew. They were still holding hands, the three of them, when he pulled them away from the Homeward Gate and ran across the ring. The black hole under the capstone snared them in its awesome gravity. Jack pushed Kerry and Corriwen with all his strength, resisting the drag with all his determination.

Behind him he felt the approach of the demon queen.

They staggered on, gasping for breath while twigs and leaves and earth whirled around like a tornado. Jack took the heartstone in his hand, desperately scanning the stones for a lock.

'I can't find—' he began to say.

And then the Morrigan erupted from between the pillars and smashed Kerry into the air. A clawed hand lashed out, impossibly fast, smacked Corriwen right off her feet and flipped her away.

Jack leapt back as the Morrigan struck. The talons found the heartstone and snatched it, jerking Jack back into the ring with such force he almost blacked out. The chain round his neck snapped and the Morrigan howled in triumph.

Her shape changed and warped, elongated until features became visible.

Eyes as black as sin gleamed in the moonlight as she changed into the woman he had seen in the Barrow. Evil radiated in waves that froze his heart almost to a standstill.

The Morrigan raised her hands high and the moon turned to dripping blood. Her mouth opened in a smile that would have been beautiful, had her features not begun to writhe and change again. The perfect teeth narrowed to glassy shards and the nose became a snout that snorted and twisted on a raddled face, and the eyes turned red.

Jack lay against the stone, stunned. He was helpless. She had the heartstone key and he could do nothing but wait for the end.

She laughed, and stooped to lay the heartstone at the very centre of the slab. Jack saw it settle into a heart-shaped declivity carved into the rock.

The key to all worlds. Jack recalled Finbar's words, though his mind was reeling and every muscle hurt.

As soon as the heartstone touched the centre of the slab,

the spaces between the thirteen stones suddenly blazed with magical light. Jack got to his knees, gasping, as he saw the light of Temair shining through on the far side. In another gap he saw a blue ocean, dotted with fabulous islands. In yet another, a world where ice sparkled like diamonds.

The gates were open. The gates to all worlds.

She stretched a claw towards him.

Then something silver flashed in front of his eyes. Quick as a blink, a silver fish arced from behind where he lay.

It landed dead centre on the capstone and when he heard the metallic tingle, Jack knew immediately what it was.

A slender, almost invisible line stretched from the slab back towards the open gate and Jack saw it tighten. The treble hook snagged itself on the heartstone's silver chain and suddenly it flew backwards through the gate.

The Morrigan's claw stopped inches from Jack's head. She turned her monstrous eyes and saw the heartstone fly past her into the darkness of Cromwath Blackwood.

'Told you I never miss,' Kerry shouted from the darkness.

Jack found his voice.

'Run, Kerry ... she's coming!'

He turned and saw Kerry leap to catch the stone as it flew towards him, snatching it from the air in one easy move. He landed like a cat, on his feet, and then he was off and running through the forest.

'Get ready, Jack,' Kerry shouted. 'Wait for it. You've got to be Goliath.'

Frozen, it took Jack a second to understand.

Kerry jinked left then right, fast as a weasel between the

festering trunks, and the Morrigan came after him in a blur.

Kerry was fast, but she was faster. Much faster.

Jack saw Kerry find a clear space and then the sling swung round his head, once, twice. The heartstone's polished face caught the blood red of the moonlight and Jack ran for it, hands outstretched. It came spinning towards him and he leapt, as Kerry had done, as high as he could.

The Morrigan reached for Kerry and slammed him against a tree with a sickening, pulpy sound.

Jack was in the air, stretched to his fullest and the heartstone thudded into his palm. His fingers closed around it.

The Morrigan swooped at him and he twisted away as she lunged.

She missed him and fell past him straight towards the darkness under the capstone.

There was a sudden *twist* in the fabric of the world and the Morrigan vanished into the sucking dark. Claws scrabbled at the upright stones, snaked out and snagged Jack's leg. A scream of pain tore through him and then he felt himself dragged down. He dug his nails into the earth, trying to haul himself back into the world, but she was too strong. Jack felt the last of his strength ebb away and darkness begin to engulf him.

Through the gateway to Cromwath Blackwood, he vaguely saw Kerry get to his knees and he shuddered as his nails began to draw scores along the ground.

Then Corriwen came dashing in and snatched Jack's hands in her own, bracing both heels in the soft earth.

Jack felt every joint creak as Corriwen desperately pulled at him, while the Morrigan tugged at his leg. He groaned. Corriwen's feet slipped. Her grip broke. Jack felt himself slide backwards into the intense black cold, his vision began to fade.

Corriwen was in front of him again, knives out. She dived headlong and slashed at the claw gripping Jack's leg. The second knife flickered past him and pierced a bulging red eye. The Morrigan's sudden agony blasted out and the standing stones trembled in their foundations.

Her grip broke and Jack catapulted forward. The claw lashed out again, caught Corriwen and batted her away.

Jack scrambled to his feet as the Morrigan began to crawl out of the pit. Without hesitation, he vaulted onto the high capstone. The heartstone glowed in his hand. He bent to the slab, placed the key exactly on the carved heart.

There was a small *snick*.

The key to where and when. Finbar's words flashed in his mind, and he knew now what to do.

The world spun and for an instant every gateway blazed light. Jack pressed the heartstone down then turned it, just like a key in a lock.

The howling wind stopped and he heard the Morrigan's scream fading as she fell down, down, down into the dark. The gateway abruptly shrank to a dot and disappeared. Jack's hand was still turning as he clambered onto the slab, and the heartstone turned with it.

All thirteen gateways slammed shut. Above him, the moon sped backwards across the sky. Daylight flickered, then moonlight, faster and faster as sun and moon wheeled one after the other in flashes of light and dark. He kept his hand on the stone, kept twisting and the flickering light became a blur until, without warning, there was a sudden purple flash in the sky.

His hand jerked from the heartstone, and he was back in the cold October night.

Jack Flint fell back on the capstone, arms spread, chest heaving, utterly exhausted.

He was back.

THIRTY FIVE

'Jack!'

Kerry's voice was faint and distant.

Something shook him. He was too tired and hurt to rouse himself. His ears were ringing and the freezing cold still had him in an icy grip. Every inch of his body felt twisted and torn.

He took a breath. It hurt his throat and his lungs, but the air was cool.

'Come on, man. Wake yourself.' Kerry's face was just a blur. He shook Jack again. 'Rise and shine, man,' Kerry said.

Jack groaned, rolled on the stone, got halfway up. The world tilted and the great standing stones seemed to shift with it.

Kerry's face was a mass of bruises.

Slowly Jack sat up. He closed his eyes, took another breath.

'Is she gone?'

'You bet she is,' Kerry said. 'You did it. But I thought you were a goner this time for sure.'

'That's the way I feel. Did I close it? Did I close the gate?'

'You did something. I don't know what, but there's nothing there any more. She went down there screaming.'

'We're home then,' Jack managed to say. 'We're back. Back to Halloween.'

Kerry groaned this time. Jack flinched at the bruise across his cheek. He had taken a hard blow, but his eyes were still bright and somehow fierce.

'We beat her Kerry, so we did,' he said.

'We did. And I think I got us back to *before*. I mean, before it all went crazy. Now I can ask the Major—' He paused in mid sentence. 'Where is she?'

'I told you. She's gone.'

'No,' Jack said. 'Where's Corriwen?'

They both turned round.

'She was . . .' Kerry started, then stopped. 'I think she was here. I was running with that thing coming on like a train. Then I threw the heartstone to you and she hit me such a wallop I went ass for elbow.'

'She was hit too,' Jack said. His heart lurched. 'She was hit. I saw it.' He started to get up, ignoring the pain as Kerry helped him to his feet.

'She was hit really hard and she went flying.' He took a slow step and then another in the direction Corriwen had

389

tumbled, all the time expecting to find her broken body against one of the standing stones. The final blow from the Morrigan must have been devastating.

He searched around, moving from one stone to another before he saw it. There on the soft earth was a small depression where she had landed, scuff marks in the thin grass. They continued, towards the space between two standing stones. Then they vanished.

Jack looked at Kerry.

'She must have been thrown through,' Kerry said. Regret and relief were struggling in his expression. 'Back home to Temair.'

Jack reached for his friend's arm. It was all coming back to him through a haze of hurt and numbness.

He shook his head. 'No,' he said. 'That's not the gate to Temair. The Farward Gate. She was thrown through the *wrong* one. They were all open at the same time. I saw different places out there.'

They locked eyes. 'Kerry, I don't know where she's gone.'

'Oh Jack,' Kerry whispered.

Jack picked up the amberhorn bow and his backpack. His shirt was in rags. One shoe was torn from sole to heel. The standing stones towered above them.

Beyond them, Cromwath Blackwood's trees crowded close. Beyond the trees, some distance away, was the tall wall that was built to keep people out. Now he and Kerry knew the astonishing secret.

Beyond the wall was a world back to normal, he knew for sure. No creeping darkness, no whispering shade. No madness in the night.

Beyond the wall the Major's telescope would still be focussed on the woods.

Jack had so much to tell him, so much to ask him. All the answers about who he was, all the things he needed to know, lay beyond the wall.

He paused, heart aching with the hunger for that knowledge, to discover the whole truth about his father. He walked across the ring, to the space between the stones through which they had run, panicked, on that first night.

Jack leaned against the stone, utterly worn.

He *had* to get back.

He took one step beyond the ring, aching with the need to find the whole truth about his father.

But Corriwen Redthorn had saved his life. She had helped both of them survive against all the odds and she had helped them get here after all they had been through.

The memory of their travels, their battles; her bravery came back in a rush, and with them the knowledge that he would have to act like the old heroes he had always admired. They made sacrifices. Their word was more than their bond. It was their life.

And Jack Flint owed a debt of life to Corriwen Redthorn. A debt he would repay come what may, no matter the cost; no matter the sacrifice.

He turned back and looked across the capstone to the gateway through which Corriwen had disappeared.

Kerry's eyes followed his.

'What do you want to do?'

'Oh Kerry,' Jack breathed.

Unsteadily but very deliberately he limped across the

ring of stones to the far side. He hurt all over and he felt he could sleep for a week.

'She's lost somewhere. Lost and alone. I don't know where, but I've got the key to open the gate.'

He turned to face Kerry, looked him straight in the eye.

'I'm going to find her,' he said.

Kerry nodded. Understanding was clear on his face. He clapped Jack on the back. They both winced.

'Not on your own, you're not.'

'I can't ask you . . .' Jack began.

Kerry held up a hand.

'You're not. And you don't have to. We're not going to let a girl come between us, are we?'

'Cross my heart,' Jack said.

And together they walked forward into the unknown.

With sincere thanks to my editor Fiona Kennedy who wields a fine blade and pares my excesses. To my agent Peter Cox who arranged the swordplay.

And to my friends and readers in Dumbarton and other parts who demanded yet another tale.

DISCARDED **Date Due**
